# CLAIMING OURS

A MFM SMALL TOWN ROMANTIC SUSPENSE NOVEL

ANCHOR BAY
BOOK 2

KENNEDY L. MITCHELL

Cover Design: Bookin It Designs

First round editing: Kristin Scearce

Second round editing: The Picky Bitch

Proofreading: All Encompassing Books

 Formatted with Vellum

*Don't settle for anyone who makes you feel grateful for their bare minimum effort. You deserve someone who will give it all for you —now and forever.*

# PROLOGUE

"I won't be gone long, promise," I stated, shooting Hank a wide smile as the door snicked shut. After locking the adorable cabin up tight, I tucked the old-school metal key into the pocket of my lightweight jacket. Jogging down the few steps that led from the small porch, I started toward The Nest's main building, desperate for anything with alcohol to help calm me down enough to sleep tonight.

The narrow trail weaved through towering trees, their leaves filtering the late-evening sun's rays, making it dance along the worn path. Above me, birds flew from branch to branch, chirping and singing, no doubt grateful for the warmish weather after the brutal Alaskan winter. Thankfully, it was still light despite the late hour after my errands in Anchor Bay took longer than expected, allowing me to see without needing the flashlight on my phone.

Hands tucked into my jacket pockets, I paused, allowing myself a second to soak up the peaceful moment in the most serene setting I'd ever experienced firsthand. Exhaling slowly, I looked up toward the partly cloudy sky. A wide smile split my face as pure joy and excitement flooded my veins.

This was real. I was *finally* here, about to embark on the adventure of a lifetime. For years, I dreamed of taking two weeks off from work to hike the advanced trail that cut through the rugged Alaskan terrain from Anchor Bay to the Kenai Fjords National Park. After saving all my PTO, and training for the last year to ensure we, Hank and I, were both ready for the challenges the difficult trail had in store for us, my lifelong dream was coming true.

Thin twigs and long-dead leaves crunched beneath the soles of my broken-in hiking boots as I continued along the winding path, the main building of the resort now visible through the trees up ahead. The distinct noise of heavy footsteps close by had me pausing, my relaxed grin fading as I scanned the shadows for the source. Despite being on the resort's property, I was well aware of the dangers that lurked everywhere in the wild state. I hovered a hand over the knife secured to my belt just in case a bear or moose tromped out from the trees.

After a minute of nothing but the birds singing around me, I released the breath I'd been holding and worked to calm my racing heart. Shaking out both hands, I silently chastised myself for being so paranoid. I couldn't get startled at every sound or the next two weeks would be miserable.

Steps a little quicker this time, I headed down the path, though the sense of being watched wouldn't fade despite telling myself I was being ridiculous. Practically jogging, I focused on the automatic glass double doors, desperate for the safety the building promised. Without breaking stride, I stumbled into the main lobby, a hand pressed to my racing heart as if that would stop it from attempting to beat out of my chest.

A young woman standing behind the reception desk startled, eyes wide at my frazzled entrance. Her shocked gaze slid over my shoulder to the doors at my back. Whirling around, totally expecting someone or something to be there, I scanned the empty pull-through drive and parking lot while struggling to catch my breath.

"Everything okay, miss?" she asked. I nodded in response, not trusting my voice not to shake. "Is there something I can help you with?"

I blew out a slow exhale through pursed lips, calming the blood pounding in my ears. With a forced smile that didn't reach my eyes, I spun around. "I leave tomorrow to tackle the Soul Trail and would love a drink before I'm without that kind of luxury for a couple of weeks."

Nodding with a knowing smirk, she pointed down the hall to her right and relayed simple directions to the resort's only bar on the property.

With a wave and a quick thank-you, I made my way toward the small dining room, using the short walk to finish calming down from the off-putting feeling from earlier.

No one was there watching or following me, right? It was probably just a curious animal. Yeah, that had to be it. My nerves were just heightened from the thrill of tomorrow and not having Hank at my side, which made my imagination run wild.

The bar and dining area was a little outdated but fit with the rest of the resort's mountain-style decor. Being the only guest in the room, I picked a stool in the middle of the long wooden bar.

Noticing my arrival, the lone bartender glanced up from

his phone and smiled, tucking the device into the back pocket of his dark jeans. A breath caught in my throat as he sauntered my way. Holy hell, he was hot. His smirk was kind yet promised to fulfill all the dirty thoughts running through my mind. Raking a hand through his wavy hair, he paused directly in front of where I sat and leaned against the polished wood.

Desperate for a distraction to stop staring, I slid a drink menu closer and pretended to focus on the specials listed.

"Welcome to The Nest." I refused to look up from the blurry words, afraid he would notice the flush I felt warming my cheeks. "Just arriving?"

Daring a glance, I tucked a rogue lock of strawberry blonde hair behind my ear and shook my head. "Not exactly, but this is my first time in here at the bar." I broke off his intense stare to scan the liquor bottles behind him just for a reprieve from being sucked into his orbit. "I'd love a drink. What's good?"

His tempting smirk pulled into a wide smile. "Well, I make a tasty martini if that's what you're feeling, or a glass of wine is always good. We also have some of the local beers on tap—"

"A martini," I cut in. That sounded perfect. "Dirty with blue cheese olives if you have them. Thank you—" I flicked my gaze to the name tag pinned to his forest green uniform polo. "—Kale."

"You got it. One martini coming up."

I relaxed against the stool back when he turned to make the drink, not realizing I had been sitting ramrod straight until now. Grabbing the flimsy laminated menu, I used it to fan my hot face. You'd think I'd never talked to an attractive man before by the way I was reacting. Granted, it had been a while since I'd been on a date, but surely I had more game than this.

While I worked to come up with something to talk to Kale about, a door at the opposite end of the bar swung open, a man carrying a plastic crate full of clean glasses stepping through. He paused mid-stride, attention locked on me for long enough that I fidgeted on the hard seat, uncomfortable with the prolonged stare.

"You staying around Anchor Bay long?" Kale asked over his shoulder, breaking the other man's intense focus. After dropping off the crate, he pushed back through the swinging door, though I caught him snagging a last look back my way before he disappeared from view.

I released the held breath burning in my lungs. "No, I actually leave tomorrow."

He twisted around to face me, shaker in hand as he mixed the cocktail. "Well, that's a shame. We have a lot to offer around here."

My lower belly flipped, his husky tone making me forget all about the strange barback's attention. "I've actually been here a few days preparing for the Soul Trail hike. I head out tomorrow morning. Today was spent picking up last-minute supplies, checking in with the doctor here for an emergency antibiotic prescription, and I even made Hank get a full physical to make sure he's healthy for the long trek."

I started to tell him about the doctor's odd behavior but sealed my lips shut to keep the negative comment to myself. This guy didn't want to hear how uncomfortable their small-town doctor made me feel during that brief visit. There was something off about him I couldn't put my finger on, yet I knew it was best to keep my distance from the man. Then again, that's what I thought about the weird guy who hit on me at that Dave's place too. And the barback just now. Maybe knowing I was about to be all alone on the trail, except for Hank, was making me more paranoid about odd looks and too-cozy strangers than normal.

That had to be it, because I wasn't normally this suspicious of everyone who glanced my way.

"Sounds like you've made your way through our town," Kale said as he poured the cloudy mixture from the shaker into the chilled martini glass. Three blue cheese-stuffed olives were added before he placed the very full cocktail on a napkin in front of me on the bar. "What did you think of Anchor Bay?"

"You said 'our town.' Does that mean you're a local?" I questioned, surprised by his claim on the town.

Leaning a hip against the bar, he dipped his chin in acknowledgment. "Born and raised."

Careful to keep the liquid inside the glass and not slosh any over the rim, I lifted it and took a tiny sip. A hum of approval escaped as the cold, perfectly mixed drink slid down my throat. It was exactly what I needed after the busy day and would help settle my overly anxious mind that seemed to think everyone was a threat.

"It's the cutest town I've ever been to for sure. The colorful shops, the people, everything. It's exactly as I imagined it when planning this trip. Even better, actually."

"I hear that a lot from those visiting. What's been your favorite place so far?"

I couldn't help but admire the way the sleeves of his polo strained when he crossed both muscular arms over his chest.

Averting my ogling stare, I sipped the yummy drink, debating my answer. "Well, that coffee shop, Sips, had the best coffee and pastries, but the general store was all kinds of adorable, and then there was the food at Dave's. I almost made myself sick eating so much. Those nachos could win TV cooking competitions."

Kale's grin widened as he nodded. "Sounds like you hit up all the best places. Good. Would hate for you to leave without experiencing all that we offer visitors."

"Kale."

At his name, we both turned our attention to a man hurrying across the room toward us. His slicked-back dark hair and ill-fitting suit had me studying him with a mix of suspicion and curiosity. My apprehension swelled, a slither of unease moving down my spine the closer he came. I took a large gulp of the martini to ease the nerves that had finally settled during the simple conversation with Kale but were now back in force.

The new man's brows flicked up his forehead when his dark gaze landed on me. "Oh, I didn't realize you were with a guest." He studied me for a moment before a slimy grin spread across his too-thin face. "Sorry for interrupting. Allow me to introduce myself. I'm Charles Parks, the general manager here at The Nest."

As I shook his outstretched hand, I dared a quick glance across the bar, finding Kale's earlier smile gone, his lips now pulled down in an almost frown as he glared at Charles.

"So tell me, how has your stay been with us so far? I hope everything here has exceeded your expectations." Hands shoved into the side pockets of his dark gray slacks, he tucked himself between me and the stool beside me, propping an elbow up on the bar. "If not, please let me know how I can meet your needs." Dark beady eyes slid down my frame, making me feel all kinds of gross. My fingers tightened around the delicate stem of the martini glass in my attempt to hold back from tossing what was left of the drink in the disgusting man's face. "In whatever way you need me."

Before I could tell him to fuck off—or that if I was to ask anyone to meet my needs, it would be the hottie across the bar, not some middle-aged creeper who probably just moved out of his mom's basement—Kale spoke up, pulling Charles's attention his way.

"She's heading out on the trail tomorrow." I flicked my attention between the two men as I swallowed a mouthful of martini. "Did you need something from me?"

Charles turned his unsettling focus back my way, that wide, overcompensating smile still plastered on his face. "Yes, yes, but that can wait, Kale. Tell me...."

He paused, clearly waiting for me to offer my name, but I just held his gaze and took another drink to keep from answering. Without Hank by my side, I felt intimidated by his unnerving focus.

My nonresponse clearly didn't sit well with him. His eyes narrowed, and the smile dropped as his lips pressed into a tight line.

"So, Charles—"

"Mr. Parks," Charles snapped and cut a glare at Kale, who, not surprisingly, didn't appear fazed.

"Right. Anyway." I barely restrained the giggle that wanted to escape at Kale's patronizing tone and instead snorted into my almost empty glass. "I heard the guys at Uplift are demanding cameras be installed along the walking path from the cottages to the main building." He grabbed a rag and began wiping down the already pristine bar. "After what happened when their girl Aspen's cabin was broken into last month, I'm shocked they didn't install some themselves."

A corner of Charles's lip curled in a snarl when Kale

mentioned the name Uplift. It sounded familiar, but I couldn't place it. Practically chugging the martini on an empty stomach had my head feeling a little fuzzy.

"Those fu—" He shot a side-eye glance my way before turning back to Kale. "I'm working on it with a company out of Anchorage to get something that meets their 'standards.' I don't know why the owner here won't push back or just drop the company altogether."

"Because they're the only dependable adventure company based here in Anchor Bay for our guests to book through," Kale shot back with a humorless laugh. "And have saved many lives over the years." He shifted his attention to me as he tossed the rag over his shoulder. "Visitors come out here underestimating how difficult the terrain and climate can be in Alaska no matter the time of year. Our weather can change on a dime and catch people off guard throughout the year. The company we're talking about, Uplift Adventure and Rescue, not only runs extreme adventures and other outdoor excursions but also works as a rescue and recovery company too."

I nodded while tipping the glass back, finishing the drink. The martini was amazing and exactly what I needed. One more would be great, but not with Charles sticking around. Instead of staying for another drink now, all I wanted to do was get back to the cabin and snuggle with Hank.

"Well, their community," Charles snapped, tone coated with disdain, "is an abomination, a dark mark in our town. They shouldn't be allowed to live that... lifestyle out in the open like they do. Gives our town a bad name and makes people feel uncomfortable."

"Like you," I muttered under my breath. "Okay," I drawled, and both men looked at me. "That was fantastic," I said to Kale, pointing to the empty glass. "Thank you. It was exactly what I needed before tomorrow and going without alcohol for a while. Can you put it on my room, or do I need to pay here?"

Kale's full lips parted to respond, but Charles beat him to it.

"It's on the house." Charles straightened and smoothed a hand down his tie. "As a thank-you for staying here at The Nest and hopefully an incentive to come back very, very soon."

Hard pass.

"Right. Well, thank you." Sliding off the stool, I put some distance between Charles and me before waving to Kale. Hopefully, he knew I was bolting because Charles creeped me out and not him. "Thank you again, and I hope you have a great night."

"Good luck on the trail," Kale called out as I turned for the exit. "And don't forget your bear spray."

My lips curled upward at the thoughtful concern for my safety. "Already packed and ready to go."

"Satellite phone?" he asked before I take another step, worry etched on his tight features.

"I—"

"Let her leave," Charles commented with a forced chuckle. "A beautiful woman like yourself shouldn't be walking around alone. How about I walk you back to your cabin?" He took a step toward me before I could respond, but I held up a hand, stopping him in his tracks.

Hell to the fucking no. My gut told me I'd either end up a skin suit or as his caged pet if I let him.

"No, thank you. Hank is waiting for me back at the cabin." I arched a brow, not understanding the flicker of anger that flashed over Charles's now-pinched features at the mention of Hank. "Good night."

Turning, I hurried out of the room, feeling eyes following me until I turned the corner. Once outside the glass doors, I inhaled a deep breath of the crisp air through my nose and slowly released it, hoping it would make my frustration fade. Shaking out both trembling hands, I tucked them into my jacket pockets and started toward the cabin. Even though it was darker than it was on my walk to the bar, I didn't feel anxious, my thoughts on the conversation with Kale before Charles ruined the moment.

Now if *he* had offered to escort me back to my cabin, I would've jumped at the chance. Then jumped *him* the second the door closed behind us.

Hank wouldn't have minded me inviting the stranger inside, though he was normally suspicious of outsiders. As my fierce protector and best friend, the purebred husky was a little possessive and aggressive if he felt I was in danger or threatened. Exactly what I needed as a single woman living in Portland and going out on the trail solo.

Pouting at the missed opportunity for a last-minute hookup, I ran a hand through my loose hair. Whatever; it was fine. I needed a good night's sleep before heading out in the morning anyway. No time for an all-night sexfest with the hottie bartender. This would be my last night in an actual bed for almost two weeks, and I needed to soak up the luxury while I had it.

Tomorrow, the epic adventure I'd planned and saved for years for would begin.

Hopefully, it would be everything I'd dreamed about. But how could it not? I'd be out in nature, exploring all this beautiful state offered, with my best friend at my side.

What was the worst that could happen?

<h1 style="text-align:center">1</h1>

BAYLEE

The soles of my trail runners pounded against the hard earth, bits of moss and dust flinging up in my wake. Knowing the turnaround point was just up ahead, I gritted my teeth, pushing my legs to move faster. The ground shifted to sand, then smooth pebbles as I neared the lake's edge, skidding to a stop right before my next step would've been in the clear water.

Breaths sawing in and out, I pitched forward, slapping both hands on top of my knees while fighting against the tremble in my thighs that threatened to send me crumpling to the ground. Though my body was beyond the point of exhaustion, my nagging thoughts and memories made me want to keep pushing. I'd do anything in my never-ending attempts to stay one step ahead of the memories that chased me day and night, eager to hold me captive until I was a sobbing mess, unable to see the beauty around me or the point of living when the person I'd planned my entire future around was gone.

All too familiar grief wrapped its icy, unforgiving tendrils around my lungs and squeezed, making it almost impossible to take a full breath. Shaking my head to keep those happy and horrible memories at bay, I bent forward, the tip of my ponytail tickling along my jaw, to grab a smooth stone. Brushing my thumb over the speckled surface, I curled my fingers around it before launching it as hard as I could into the lake, releasing an anguished scream that echoed through the surrounding trees.

Gasping, I observed the ripples, transfixed that the effects of something so small radiated through the large body of water. It reminded me of the impact of Dean's death, insignificant to many but life-altering to those who knew and loved him.

And fuck if I didn't love him.

Tears welled in my lower lids, making my vision watery.

From the moment I saw him in geometry, surrounded by his friends, laughing so loud and free, I knew he was the one for me. And he was, until that future we planned was ripped away from me, and his life from him.

"I miss you, Dean," I whispered to the cloudy sky. "Fuck, I miss you so damn much. Sometimes it's like I can't breathe." Tears leaked from the corners of my eyes, dripping down my round cheeks. "I'm trying to keep going, but it's just not what we planned. You're supposed to be here with me, making me smile and laugh like only you could." Swiping away the evidence of my soul-destroying grief, I blew out a shaky breath. "Tell me, give me a sign that you're still out there somewhere looking out for me. And are okay with me moving on." I chewed on my lower lip. "Because sometimes I think I'm ready, but then it feels like I'm cheating on you, on us, and on what we had."

That was the unforgiving internal battle I fought daily—being okay with the feelings and desires growing for a certain cowboy in our small community. The guilt that ate me alive after a great date or alone time with Liam made me wonder if attempting to move on from Dean was really worth it.

My mind knew it was. I couldn't stay alone and sad forever. If I were honest with myself, I knew Dean would want me to move on. He'd want me to live a full life. But try telling my heart that. The heart that was so deeply in love with the man who was there one day and gone the next.

His pictures and a folded flag were the only physical things I had left of him.

A slight vibration on my wrist had me glancing down and grimacing at both the time and Liam's name flashing on the screen. Once again, I let the morning get away from me, losing all sense of time, lost in my thoughts and memories. Doing that out here was a danger, not including the hell I'd no doubt get from Liam for going out on my own. With the disappearances and murders happening along the Soul Trail, I technically wasn't supposed to come out here on my own. But I needed these moments of silence, the time utterly alone with my grief. It was my therapy in a way, though maybe the fact that I still struggled daily meant it wasn't working as well as I wanted to believe.

After stretching out the ache in my hamstrings and calves, I turned, putting the pristine water behind me, and started down the trail. In and out, each deep, even breath brushed past my slightly parted lips as I made my way along the winding path back toward Anchor Bay. Frustration at the leash our deputy sheriff put on the women of our town to keep them safe built within me, making me grind my back teeth.

I understood why, but damn, did it suck. Sure, I didn't want to end up like those unfortunate hikers. Most still hadn't been found, their pictures hanging in Uplift's meeting room a haunting reminder of the unknown danger lurking in the shadows.

Where had they gone?

What happened to them?

Who was behind their disappearances and the murders of a few of the missing women's male companions?

I grimaced when the soft dirt shifted to hard, unforgiving pavement as I jogged through the trailhead's small parking lot heading toward downtown Anchor Bay. A small smile pulled at my lips as the weathered, painted buildings came into view. The caw of a bird sounded above me as the scent of salt water and dead fish filled my nose. Soon the pavement shifted to worn wooden boards beneath my feet as I jogged through the heart of town.

Passing Sips, our local and tasty coffee shop, I waved through the glass windows to the owner, Paul McGravey, who was too busy pulling chairs off the few tables to notice. Instead of stopping to grab a cup of coffee, I kept going, smirking to myself as I passed the best bar in town. I slammed a loose fist against the closed wooden door of Dave's in our usual morning hello when I passed on my way home from a run. A group of men outfitted in fishing gear chatting near the entrance of the docks nodded in greeting as I passed, making a genuine grin spread across my face despite my heavy breathing and exhausted legs.

Barely over a year in the quaint town of Anchor Bay, and I already knew every local. Though that had less to do with my morning runs and more about me being the only vet in a two-hundred-mile radius. It was the perfect place to put the past behind me and move on from the soul-eating grief that threatened to kill me daily.

And fuck did I try to move forward. I wanted to live in the moment and cherish every second I had with the amazing people in my small community and in Anchor Bay. Two years after Dean's death, it was getting easier, though there were still bad days where it felt like too much, like today. Which was why as soon as I woke up and felt that weight on my chest and the tears in my eyes, I knew a long run was the only thing that would ease that pain.

I couldn't just stay in bed all day, lost in my grief, when I was needed. Knowing the community depended on me and loving every single one of the sweet animals I treated made every day I pushed myself to keep going worth it. There had always been a bond with animals that comforted me. Their unconditional love drew me in as a child and made me want to grow up to be a veterinarian. And now my career was the one aspect of my life I didn't question or doubt these days.

Feeling another text come through, the vibrations tickling my sweat-slick skin along my wrist, I pushed myself to quicken my strides as I exited Anchor Bay and turned toward the small community where I lived. It wasn't much, but it had everything our group needed and had truly become home to me and so many others.

The self-sustaining, unique setup was started by Brandon Taylor, founder and owner of Uplift Adventure and Rescue, and constructed just outside Anchor Bay, which gave us privacy but was close enough that downtown trails and The Nest, where most of the company's excursion bookings came through, were quick and easy to get to. Privacy was a big one since everyone who worked for Brandon was former military or connected in some way, like me, and dealt with trauma and scars from their past. I never served but was no different in that sense.

Brandon also wanted space and privacy so he and his wife and romantic partner could live in peace. Thankfully, most of the locals didn't care that Brandon and most of his team favored less monogamous relationships, preferring multiple partners. No matter the reason, I was thankful that Brandon, Carl, and Amy built their home here and put a lot of planning and effort into making the community somewhere that fostered a found-family type of atmosphere that most of us here desperately needed.

Once inside our little compound, one main street split two rows of small one- or two-bedroom cabins that then led to a general store at one end, where Brandon's wife, Amy, and their third, Carl, sold farm-fresh produce and ready-made meals. Being a small Alaskan village, we depended on what we could grow and raise to ensure we had enough fresh food to support those in our group.

Every single man and woman here was kind, supportive, and protective—everything that I desperately needed while I healed from my tragic loss.

Sprinting the last bit, I rounded the corner of my one-bedroom cabin, not surprised to find Liam leaning against a solid wooden post waiting for my return.

I forced myself not to grimace, knowing he wasn't happy that I'd gone off running on my own. Not that he'd ever show or voice his frustration at my so-called lack of self-preservation. He wasn't really angry at me or the situation, more worried about my safety. Even before we started dating, or whatever we were doing now, Liam was overly attentive and protective of me. At first, I thought it had to do with our size difference, him being around six foot three and me being about a foot under that, or the fact that these days it was possible that a strong breeze could blow me over. Whatever the reason, he fixated on me initially and still waited patiently for me to figure things out at my slow pace. I loved it—it made me feel wanted and special, precious even.

Approaching the porch steps, fingers interlaced behind my head, I worked to slow my rapid breaths while walking out my jelly-like legs. Liam's observant gaze never deviated as I paced, attempting to cool down from the punishing run, so I did the same to him. The soft red plaid material of his open button-up shirt stretched around his massive biceps that flexed as he crossed both arms over his chest. The tight white undershirt hugged his defined pecs and displayed the ripples of abs that came from all the hard labor he put in with the horses and farm side of our community.

"Baylee."

I jerked my gaze up from the exposed tattoos decorating his lower arms to his gray eyes, finding a spark of humor there at my obvious ogling. How could I not, though, with a man like him standing right in front of me? I was still grieving, not blind.

"Hey, Liam," I panted, though it wasn't all from the run. Heat that had nothing to do with the workout warmed my cheeks. Fingers wrapped around the wooden railing that lined the porch, I steadied myself and lifted a heel to my ass. A pitiful groan escaped at the glorious pain that radiated from my tired muscles. "What's up?" I asked in my lame attempt to play it off like I had no idea why he was here looking all grouchy-hot like an overprotective brown bear.

"What's up?" He shifted to lean a shoulder against a thick post and glared down at me, though there was absolutely zero heat to it. "Woman," he groaned, like I tried what little patience he had left. "Where have you been?"

I released my hold around my foot and gestured to my running gear with a raised brow. A minuscule twitch curved the corners of his lips before he schooled his features back to the stern *"You're in deep trouble, Baylee"* expression.

"You know what I meant. Where did you run, Baylee?"

I sealed my lips shut and avoided his probing gaze.

He grumbled a string of curses under his breath. "You ran the trail, didn't you?"

Not wanting to lie, I nodded as I adjusted my stance to stretch the other leg.

"Little Bit," he growled in that way that made my heart flutter and breath catch. "What if something had happened to you?"

"I was fine. See, here in one piece," I offered, my light tone meant to ease his worry even though I knew it wouldn't work. His perfectly plump lips parted, but I cut him off by gesturing to the sharp-as-hell knife strapped around my calf. "I ran with a weapon and"—I raised my wrist and inclined my head to the smart watch—"a way to contact you if something happened, plus a GPS. You worry too much. I needed to run, so I went on a run."

His frustrated groan vibrated through the covered porch. Liam ran a wide palm down his face in sheer exasperation, grumbling under his breath about frustrating women.

My lips curled in a small smile, loving this side of the normally stoic man. Sure, his body was a lethal weapon, but he was all bark and no bite with me. He loved control—that was obvious—but he also loved my independence and pushback, even if he hadn't realized yet.

"I swear, woman, you're trying to make me consider my last-resort option to keep you safe from yourself and others."

Hands on my hips, I smiled up at his handsome face. Broad forehead, thick dark brows, almond-shaped gray eyes, and a square jaw. He looked like a superhero and was built like one too. His muscles were practically chiseled from stone, and his diverse yet violent background produced a dangerous aura that radiated off him, making everyone terrified of him.

Well, everyone but me. With me, Liam was romantic, sweet, and cuddly. No one would expect that softer side from the former MMA fighter and retired Army Ranger. I treasured that little secret. We were opposites in almost every way except when it came to our shared grief from tragic loss. Though his made him bitter for years after his wife's accident, while Dean's death left me hollow and sad.

At fifteen years older than me and many years since the accident, Liam has had time to process his pain and anger, whereas mine was still fresh, my wounds barely healed. Watching as he ran a hand over his short dark hair, transfixed at the way his defined muscles flexed, a dreamy sigh escaped my parted lips, only for them to snap shut when his comment finally registered.

"Wait, what?" I moved up the steps, his gray stare following me to where I stopped beside him. "What's this so-called last option to keep me safe from myself and others?"

My heart rate jumped at the heat that filled his gaze as a slow, cocky smirk overtook his face. Damnit, why did he have to be so good-looking that I was constantly distracted?

"Tying you to my bed." He shoved off the post and turned, erasing the small distance between us. I took a hesitant step back, my ass pressing against the railing, keeping me from tumbling over as he leaned in close, hands wrapped around the solid wood on either side of my hips, caging me in. "Where I can know exactly where you are at all times and know you're safe."

Throat dry, I swallowed hard before responding. "That seems a tad extreme for one tiny run." He arched a brow. "Fine, a few runs."

With an exaggerated exhale, he pitched forward to seal our foreheads together. "Don't do something careless with your safety on the line, please." His closed lids flickered open. My heart hammered in my chest at the devastation in his sad eyes. "I've already lost so much. We both have. Don't make me live through that hell again."

"Liam," I whispered. Reaching up, I cupped his scruff-covered jaw. "I need it. You know I do. I need that space and freedom to work through my messy thoughts during the bad days, and today was one of them. Tell me you understand, that you won't ask me to give up the one thing that holds me together when I feel like I'm breaking."

I didn't deserve his patience or understanding, but I was thankful for it every damn day. He knew I needed the solo runs, that time away, to process my trauma. Knowing I was still grieving and healing was why he understood that if we attempted a romantic relationship, he needed to move slowly.

And I mean glacier slowly.

Though he didn't know the full extent of why. When was there the right time to tell someone like Liam Wilson, badass veteran and MMA title champion, that you were, despite being in a relationship with your high school sweetheart for almost a decade, a virgin?

I was 100 percent certain he was not.

Very not, if that was a term to describe his sexual history. Not that he bragged about it, but of course I googled him after meeting him that first time, and it was all there. Pictures, articles, posts. So. Many. Posts. With many different women. All beautiful and badass like him.

And then there was me.

If he was the overprotective brown bear in our relationship, I was a tiny gray rabbit.

Lips pursed, clearly not loving my needs but respecting them just the same, he nodded. "I know, and I won't ask you to stop. Just let me know next time so I can secretly follow you."

I bit the corner of my lip to stop my growing smile. "It won't be a secret if I know you're there."

"Maybe that's the point too. I want you to know I'm there for you." My brows pulled in tight. "That way you know you're not alone in your fight, Baylee. I'm here, right here, always. You've done this long enough by yourself. Lean on me, let me help you heal. You deserve to be happy, Little Bit."

Conflicting emotions swirled in my chest as he leaned in, his lips hovering right over mine, allowing me the choice to close the distance or not. What sucked was that I wanted him, craved his lips on mine, longed to be wrapped up in his strong hold and let go of everything that constantly weighed on me. But then *his* face would appear, followed by a trailer of memories starring Dean and me, of his secure embrace and the thousands of kisses we shared, resulting in a tidal wave of guilt that made me nauseous.

Sensing my indecision, Liam tilted up a fraction to instead brush a barely-there kiss on the tip of my button nose.

"You better get ready for work or you'll be late for your first appointment."

The mention of work snapped me out of the shame-filled thoughts I was quickly succumbing to. Muttering a curse, I dipped under his arm and hurried for the front door. It opened with zero resistance, but before I could step over the threshold, Liam's deep voice called my name, stopping me in my tracks with a grimace.

Oh shit, now I'd really done it.

"Yes?" I looked over my shoulder with a wide smile,

hoping he didn't notice that I accidentally left my cabin unlocked in my rush earlier, though I knew he did.

He jutted a single thick finger at the door. "Was that really unlocked this whole time?"

Lips forced down in a false frown, I studied him with fake confusion. "What? No, of course not. We've had too many talks about me locking it despite me feeling incredibly safe here." I snapped my fingers like a brilliant thought just hit me. "You know what? You must have missed me unlocking it. I've gotten superfast at it since I always lock it like you've instructed." I batted my light lashes as I retreated inside the cabin. Easing the door closed, I stifled a giggle at his grumbled response.

"Tying her to the bed seems like a rational option every fucking day."

Locking the deadbolt, I leaned against the solid wood and grinned like a crazy person up at the ceiling. If I were honest with myself, I wasn't opposed to being tied to his bed, but I would want him there too.

Just as I thought that, like so many times before, guilt at fantasizing about another man who wasn't my fiancé, of balancing that edge, of moving on or staying stuck in my sorrow, swelled in my gut, making it twist painfully.

Unshed, frustrated tears burned down my throat as I fought the urge to cry. It was a shock that I wasn't constantly dehydrated from how much I'd cried over the last two years. I slowly realized my grief had become a crutch, and if I wasn't careful, I'd get so used to falling back into using it that I'd never heal properly and move on.

This toxic swell of guilt and anguish had to end. It was time for me to move on with a life worth living, not just surviving.

"Please, Dean," I choked out into the quiet cabin,

begging him or anyone to hear my plea. "Send a sign. Anything to make this"—I pressed the heel of my hand to my sternum to ease the mounting ache in my chest—"fade. I can't move on from you, from missing you every damn day, until I know. Show me something, anything. Please."

Shaking my head, I shoved off the door and started for the single bathroom to shower and get ready for work. No matter the emotional devastation I was working through, there were patients who depended on me, and I wouldn't let them down.

One day at a time. That was the best I could do.

For now.

## 2

### LIAM

Coarse bristles rasped over the horse's shiny coat as I dragged the brush along his spine. I repeated the motion, quieting my mind with the cathartic movement as I worked my way down to his belly and legs. I hadn't always found peace in the day-to-day tasks of caring for the massive animals, but after a year of equine therapy for my anger management issues, I learned the therapeutic benefits of the mundane, repetitive tasks. Now I could immediately slide into the quiet mind space the moment the familiar scents of the barn enveloped me.

Most of those in the community didn't like coming in here, complained that the barn reeked of piss-soaked sawdust and animal shit with a hint of mold, but it didn't faze me. In fact, I'd rather be here with the animals than out there with annoying clients and nosy townies. I had nothing against being around people—I just preferred the animals.

Well, I preferred them over everyone except for Baylee.

Just her name flicking through my thoughts had my gaze sliding over the horse's back to where she stood several feet away outside the goat pen, talking to them like they understood her.

Miles, Langston, and I helped build the massive metal barn a couple of years back. Originally it only housed several wide stalls for the horses I used for the guided horseback trail rides booked through Uplift, plus a large area for the few cows we owned for when it was too cold or bad weather, but after Baylee joined our community, we added a chicken coop with a bit of room for them to wander around, a sheep pen, and now an area for her goats.

Why goats, who I believed were spawned by the devil?

Fuck if I knew, but they made Baylee happy, so I fenced off some available space in the barn for when it was too cold out and sectioned off a new segment of the pasture every month since the little shits ate everything, even stripping bark and leaves off the trees. It was extra work for me, but watching her smile and chat with the living garbage disposals every morning made it worth it.

Some people were said to be born with a green thumb, but Baylee was blessed with unending compassion and patience for all animals, which made her a fan-fucking-tastic veterinarian.

And I would gladly break multiple bones of anyone who said differently.

As if sensing my unapologetic stare, crystal blue eyes flicked my way, followed by a wide, genuine smile. Baylee scrunched up her face and stuck out her tongue before turning back to the newest addition of our goat family. My heart clenched at the happiness radiating off her. I wanted to believe that joy was because we'd made progress in pushing past the friend zone in our relationship, helping her slowly move on from Dean's death, but deep down I knew it was because of the goats.

What a fucking blow to a guy's ego.

After she first moved into our community, it took me months to work up the balls to ask her out on a date. Her hesitant yes had made my damn year. I knew the hesitation and slow pace of the physical side of our new relationship wasn't from her lack of attraction to me, and that wasn't me being cocky. The way that woman eye-fucked me any time we were together spoke to her attraction, and believe me, the feeling was absolutely mutual. Baylee's hesitation then, and still, stemmed from a recent tragedy. That kind of trauma, of having your planned future suddenly ripped away, wasn't easy to move past.

I would know.

I had mostly healed. Several years had passed since my late wife's accident, plus the kick-to-the-balls details I'd uncovered helped me move from grief-stricken widower to constantly pissed off at the world. Baylee's pain and loss were fresh. Her fiancé's death while deployed happened only two years ago, so of course she still struggled. I had no intention of pressuring her into a romantic relationship, to make her move faster than she was ready physically, but I was ready when she was.

Each time I was with her, my chest would tighten uncomfortably, and my heart hammered against my ribs. It felt like a fucking heart attack. She was so damn gorgeous, even when her grief and sadness were clear as day. Her white-blonde hair was as soft as it looked and framed her heart-shaped face. Fair, smooth skin made her almost clear blue eyes stand out, and fuck if they didn't sparkle when she laughed. Full lips that begged to be kissed and a tiny button nose, plus the scattering of faint freckles along her cheeks made her look younger than she actually was. It made our age difference seem that much more drastic, considering I wore my hard life like a badge of honor on my face and body.

But it wasn't just her physical appearance that drew me in like a moth to a flame. Baylee was my opposite. She was full of passion for animals and people alike, whereas I radiated anger and violence, a "fight first and ask questions second" type of person. The woman's heart was too big for her own good. I swore she wouldn't think twice about picking up a hitchhiker carrying a battle-ax in an orange jumpsuit if she thought she could help. Not that she was naïve or lacked a sense of self-preservation—though her solo runs in the morning made me question that recently. She was just kindness personified and saw the good in everyone.

I was the perfect example of her seeing past the bad to the core of who a person was, finding the good in them. There was no reason she should've given me a chance. At twice her size plus my anger management issues, she should've run for the mountains when we first met. But not Baylee Smith. Instead, she stared deep into my dark and damaged soul, stuck out her hand to introduce herself, and explained how we would be great friends.

I didn't know how to respond to her, too confused to refute her claim, not that I wanted to. Other than my Army Ranger brothers, I never had genuine friends—none like her anyway. It was no wonder that initial bewilderment shifted into something deeper than I had ever felt for a woman in my whole damn life.

And I was fucking married once before.

*Obsession* was a close word to describe how my feelings shifted toward Baylee as I got to know her. I craved all of her, wanted to make her mine. Her kind heart, brilliant mind, awkward jokes, her perfect tiny body. I sank my teeth into my lower lip to silence the guttural groan that wanted to escape when she bent over to pet the kid, her perky ass conveniently pointed in my direction. Damn, all the dirty things I wanted to do to her. But that would have to wait.

Based on what I'd picked up on over the past few months, I assumed she was inexperienced compared to me, but I wasn't sure to what extent. If she knew how fucking bad I wanted to teach her everything I knew—and that list was plenty long and disturbing—she'd run away screaming in fear. Not that I'd let her get away.

Fuck, I was demented and 100 percent obsessed with her.

"You ready?" I cut my heated gaze from the woman who had me wrapped around her little finger to Langston, Uplift's go-to guy for all things water related, who rivaled both my size and anger issues. "I don't want to be fucking late for the meeting."

A chuffed laugh brushed past my lips when he turned without waiting for a response and stormed out of the barn, only to freeze when Baylee's voice called out his name. Shoulders practically at his ears, the grumpy bastard twisted, responding to the greeting with a grunt and a return of the wave she sent him, though his was more of a raised hand than Baylee's exaggerated back-and-forth motion.

"Hold up," I called out before he could leave. I secured the metal latch on the stall and double-checked it was locked. "Give me a second and I'll walk with you. Just need to give her this."

Reaching down, I wrapped my fingers around the small cooler that I'd brought from home, sitting just outside the stall. Langston grumbled something about me being pussy-whipped as he leaned against the frame of the barn's tall rolling door, his permanent scowl secured on his face. Flipping him the bird, I strode toward Baylee, where she was measuring out the chicken feed for their breakfast.

"Hey," she said, blowing a rogue lock of hair out of her eyes when she looked up with a smile. "Heading to the Monday meeting?"

I ran my fingers through the longer section of my jet-black hair and nodded. "Yeah, you coming?" The weekly meeting was mandatory for those who worked directly for Uplift Adventure and Rescue and didn't extend to her, though sometimes she came to see everyone.

"No, not today. I need to get several things checked off my to-do list here before heading out to tackle those home vet visits this afternoon. I only have a handful, but they're spread out, so I'm assuming it'll take me several hours to see everyone."

A swell of concern for her going out alone had my brows pulling in tight. Baylee was just so tiny, in stature and weight, and Alaska was dangerous—the animals, people, and landscape. I'd noticed, based on the few pictures framed in her cabin, that she'd lost significant weight since Dean's death, giving her an almost frail look. Which was when my slight fixation with feeding her as often as possible began.

Even though I knew she was capable and smart, I never wanted her to be in a situation where she felt like she had to handle everything alone. It was my job now to protect her and keep her safe. To eliminate all threats so she didn't feel so damn abandoned in this life.

"Will I see you later?" Blush stained her cheeks as she peeked up through blonde lashes.

"If you want to see me, Little Bit, I'll be there. Want me to come to your place?"

She nodded, biting her lower lip as her gaze slowly worked its way down my body. Oh fuck, this woman and her blatantly proving my point that the attraction went both ways might kill me by the worst case of blue balls in history.

Shaking off the idea of pressing her against the rough wood wall and kissing her until she begged for my hands to explore every inch of her tiny body, I thrust the packed cooler between us. "Before I head out, I wanted to give you this." I massaged the back of my neck and cleared my throat, suddenly anxious about how she'd react. "I made you breakfast."

Shooting me a shy grin, she pushed open the lid and peered inside.

"Two hard-boiled eggs, a sliced apple, and one of those Nutella packets you love." Baylee's wide eyes met mine. "Oh, and milk—whole milk, since, you know, it's proven to be better for you and has more calories." I stopped rambling about fucking milk—oh, how the mighty playboy had fallen —at her slight headshake and disbelieving expression. "What? Why are you looking at me like that?"

"Nothing, it's just that... well, you're all kinds of adorable, Liam."

After setting the cooler down at our feet, I folded both arms over my chest and widened my stance. "I am not adorable. That's for kittens and panda bears."

She silenced a soft giggle with three fingers pressed to her lips. "Pandas? Really? That's what you're going with? No puppies or bunnies."

I shrugged, unable to explain where the hell that came from. Clearly, I needed to limit the amount of *Animal Planet* I watched.

"And sorry to burst your tough-guy bubble, but yes, *adorable* is the perfect word." Pushing up to her tiptoes, she fisted the front of my shirt and pulled me down until our lips hovered close. "The most adorable. But don't worry, your secret is safe with me. And thank you for the food. Your slightly odd obsession with people eating healthily is a nice perk in our—" She gestured between us, making me huff. "—whatever this is." Pressing a soft kiss to my lips, she lowered down to flat feet. "Really, thank you."

I avoided her gaze at her remark. I had slightly lied to her about my passion for wanting people to eat healthily. It wasn't *all* people, just her. My fascination was firmly fixated on ensuring she was fed. I literally couldn't help it. From the first time we met, the woman triggered every protective instinct inside me, and her not eating enough to even fuel a sparrow drove me insane. So, I might have mentioned that because of my amateur MMA fighting background and the health food regimen required to keep me at top training shape, I had a need to ensure people ate healthily because of how good I felt eating right.

Desperate for another taste of her, I wrapped my fingers around her chin to hold her in place and sealed a demanding kiss to her lips. Her lids fluttered closed as I deepened the kiss, swiping my tongue along the seam of her lips, begging her to open for me, to leave me with something to daydream about while we were apart. The vibrations of her soft moan had my own growl rumbling in return. Taking advantage of the opening, I devoured her mouth, swiping my tongue against hers and exploring her like I wanted to do with my head between her thighs.

Fucking hell, did I want to taste her pussy, to lick up her sweet cum as she drenched my face.

My cock strained against my jeans, twitching behind the stiff fabric. Arm wrapped around her shoulders, I sealed us together, the pressure of her soft frame doing nothing to relieve the throbbing ache. Her small, delicate hands fisted the front of my shirt, tugging us even tighter together. With an almost feral growl, I guided her backward until her spine sealed against the wall.

But before I could act on all the fun and utterly dirty ideas I had for Baylee, an exaggerated—and fucking infuriating—cough had me pulling back with a snarl. Frustration and annoyance had me shooting a death glare toward the asshole who disrupted us, but the sound of Baylee's soft laugh turned my attention back to her, the smile on her flushed face calming the rage mounting in my veins. All irritation with Langston vanished at her shy grin. Palm pressed to the center of my chest, she urged me back a step until she had the space to move around me.

"Go," Baylee said with a shooing motion. "You two don't want to be late for the meeting. You know Brandon hates that and will find some way to get back at you if you are. Last time, didn't he make you take that Instagram influencer on that hike from hell?"

Damnit, she was right about Brandon being a petty jackass if I was late. With an agreeing grunt, I rubbed a hand down my face to clear the lust fog that clouded my thoughts, hoping I hid my disappointment at being interrupted.

With a grumbled and slightly pouting goodbye and promise to see her later, I stalked toward the asshole waiting for me at the barn door. The moment I was within reach, I slammed a hand against his shoulder, making him stumble to the side to keep from falling on his ass.

"Damnit, Liam," he shouted as he righted himself and turned, bracing for another attack. "What the fuck was that for?"

"For being a motherfucking cockblocker, you little shit. Just because the woman you want would rather sleep with a

Kodiak bear than be in the same room with you, don't take your disappointment out on those of us who aren't acting like assholes."

A stormy expression crossed his reddening face. When his lips parted, no doubt ready to lay into me for bringing up his fucked-up feelings for Juno, I waved him off and started toward the side building where the Monday morning meetings were always held.

We had ten minutes before we were late, which meant less talking and more walking. Thankfully, the barn wasn't too far away from the central area of our community, since every long stride had my still-stiff cock chafing against denim.

"She doesn't hate me that much." I shot Lang an incredulous look where he now walked beside me, keeping up with my quick pace. "Better than you and—"

Without thinking, I lashed a hand out and wrapped it around his throat, cutting off his next words. His emerald-green eyes flared with annoyance before narrowing.

"I dare you to finish that fucking sentence, Lang. I fucking dare you to say one negative thing about my Baylee. I haven't had a decent fight in a while."

I released him with a hard shove, and he stumbled to the side, rubbing at the red marks blooming around his throat.

"Whatever, fucking asshole. I wouldn't say anything bad about her, just you." He glanced down at his phone and cursed. "Shit, we need to hurry the fuck up. We don't have time for all this *Jerry Springer* drama shit."

Gravel crunched beneath the balls of his feet as he twisted around and began jogging toward the meeting. Huffing a laugh at his random comment, I sprinted to catch up with him.

"You watch a lot of *Springer* reruns, do you?" Langston

rolled his eyes, making me bark out a laugh. "You do seem one for the dramatics. I can see why it's your favorite show."

"Oh, fuck off," he snapped, but I didn't miss the slight curl of his lips in an almost smile.

Shaking my head, I increased my pace, pulling ahead of Langston, which of course the uber-competitive jackass couldn't allow, so he did the same but added a little more. A carefree smile tugged at my lips as I huffed and sprinted full speed toward our destination, with Langston keeping stride right beside me. With neither of us okay with second, we didn't slow until we were only a few feet from plowing directly into the side of the building. Langston and I slammed into the cement block exterior with a grunt at almost exactly the same time. Chest heaving from my rapid breaths, I turned a cocky grin his way, finding Lang smirking right back at me.

"I won," we both declared at the same time.

"Pretty sure that was a tie, gents. You two act more like kids than the somewhat adults your ages suggest you are." West, Uplift's mechanic, chuckled as he approached from the opposite direction. "You're both idiots, by the way, and too damn competitive for your own good. Now get inside."

With a pointed look to the man beside me, West marched up the steps and yanked open the door, muffled voices and rolling laughter pouring out as he stepped inside.

I groaned at the pain radiating from my crotch. I should not have raced in jeans with a half-mast dick. After adjusting myself to lessen the rub, I slapped Langston on the shoulder to move him along and followed West, hoping we weren't late.

Once inside, I did a quick scan around the room and cursed under my breath. We were the last two to arrive. Miles and Aiden, our motor vehicle adventure guides, sat side by side at the very end of the round table, the former giving me a nod in greeting before turning his attention back to his best friend. To their right, West flopped down onto a metal chair and leaned back on its two rear legs, fingers interlaced behind his head as he watched Langston lumber in behind me.

A bark of laughter drew my attention to Finley and Dax, both in their matching black flight suits, telling me they had either a float plane or helicopter tour later. They were best friends, having served together in the Air Force, stationed outside Fairbanks, and came here after. Dax poked Finley's shoulder, making her swat his hand away with a wide grin on her face.

I really wish the two of them would just fuck and get it over with. Neither one had an idea that the other was helplessly in love with them, and it was grating on my nerves. Though not as much as the center of a different shit show that sat beside Finley, frowning at her phone.

Juno Jones. Thorn in Langston's side and charmer of West. Those three... fuck, there wasn't enough time in the day to even scratch the surface of the toxic mess they had going on.

As I made my way to an empty chair, Oliver, Anchor Bay's deputy sheriff, and Hudson, a former LA detective Brandon knew from his SEAL days and had asked to come help investigate the missing women's cases, hitched their chins in greeting.

The metal chair groaned as I sat, making me grimace. Hopefully, it would hold. I didn't need another one breaking on me.

Brandon, the owner and founder of Uplift, stood at the head of the oval conference table, making everyone halt their individual conversations.

"I'll let Oliver and Hudson go first since I know you're all wondering what the hell happened after we caught Jasper Cain breaking into Caroline's cabin last week."

I smirked, remembering how the asshole screamed for help till he went hoarse after I caught him sneaking into a missing team member's cabin and hog-tied the asshole. He was a flight risk, and I needed a nonlethal way to keep him secure while we waited for Oliver and his idiot father, the sheriff.

Oliver cleared his throat and scanned the room, making eye contact with everyone before speaking.

"Unfortunately, it's a dead end." The room went utterly silent at that admission. "He's not responsible for Caroline's disappearance or connected to the other missing women's cases."

A beat passed before shouts of outrage and disagreement erupted from everyone around the table. Everyone except me. This wasn't a surprise. I had a feeling that weak ass couldn't have done anything to Caroline. She was capable and tough as hell. I knew if he had tried to hurt or take her, she would've kicked his ass all the way to Anchorage and put his body in the morgue herself.

No, there was something more sinister going on around our town and along the trail than Jasper fucking Cain.

Oliver raised both hands to quiet everyone down so he could finish.

"I questioned him extensively, and everything rang true. They *were* dating before her disappearance. The last time he saw her, she told him she was headed out on a solo hike for a few days to explore new cliffs to climb. That was the last he heard from her, which was two days before anyone noted that something was off. And I'll tell you, I believe him."

"He's not smart enough to pull one over on Oliver or

me," Hudson added. He and Oliver shared a conspiratorial smirk. "I was there with Oliver and his father when they questioned Jasper. I even ran him through my own interrogation."

"Then why the hell was he in there?" Aiden asked, crimson highlighting his cheeks, exposing his rising anger over this revelation.

Oliver looked at Hudson, who nodded at whatever silent question he asked. "A journal. He said he was looking for Caroline's journal."

"What the fuck?" I muttered. "He wanted her fucking diary?"

"Showing your age, old man," Dax said, leaning around Finley and Juno to shoot me a wink. "No one calls it a diary anymore."

"Except young girls," Hudson cut in. When all our gazes landed on him, he cleared his throat and adjusted the collar of his long-sleeve shirt. "Sam has one with unicorns on it. Though it's more of a doodle pad than anything, since she can't actually write her thoughts yet." His eyes narrowed into slits. "If any of you shitheads have something to say about my girl having a unicorn diary, you can come to me about it."

No one said a word. The fucker was just as scary as the rest of us—well, except me and Langston.

"Good. If we're done talking about what to call it, I can tell you about this journal." Hudson gripped the back of the chair in front of him, knuckles going white. "Apparently, your friend and colleague Caroline was running her own investigation into the recent disappearances and documented her findings in that journal."

Miles stood abruptly and slapped both palms to the table. "So, where is it, then?" he demanded.

"That's the thing," Oliver stated. "Jasper didn't find it, and neither did we after our own search. It's gone."

So it seemed their one lead in Caroline's disappearance wasn't a lead at all, and any clues she might have documented regarding the women going missing on the trail had vanished.

Wasn't that fucking fantastic.

**3**

---

MEMPHIS

The rubber soles of my black combat boots gripped the wet, slime-covered wooden planks as I stepped off the boat and onto the dock. Through the Aviator's dark lenses, I scanned the busy marina before turning my focus back to the asshole who captained the enclosed passenger boat I took from Anchorage to Anchor Bay.

With a cutting glare, he grabbed my two worn duffel bags from where they were stowed and tossed them onto the damp wood by my feet. Lips pursed, I scowled at the jackass who'd almost pitched everything I brought from Florida to Alaska into the murky water lapping below us. My annoyance eased when he helped my best friend, Elvis, off the boat with much more care.

Though who wouldn't with that smiling face and a tail that wouldn't stop wagging. The massive yellow lab could win over even the worst human's heart.

Like now.

"Elvis," I called with a sharp whistle.

With a reluctant look at his new friend, who distracted the cheerful dog with head scratches, Elvis trotted closer and sat at my feet, leaning his heavy body against me. Wet nose in the air, dark eyes locked on me, his thin tail slapped at the wood in happy thumps.

Smiling at my friend, I ran a hand over his head and glanced back at the captain—Langston or something like that. "We good?"

Instead of responding like a normal person, the massive man just continued to glare at me like I had somehow offended him during the trip, which I knew I hadn't, since I was preoccupied with plotting out my first few days in Anchor Bay.

Never one to back down from a fight, I folded both inked arms over my chest and met his stare straight on. The man's intense gaze scanned me up and down, from my styled, long, dirty-blond hair to the shaved sides that exposed the tattoos on my scalp. The designs didn't stop there—hell, there wasn't much of my body that wasn't decorated with either tattoos or piercings.

When his narrowed eyes focused on the dark tattoos decorating both hands and all ten fingers, I lifted one between us and flipped him the bird. "Do you give everyone this kind of inspection when you drop them off, or am I just fucking special?" I snapped.

Sure, I was used to it, but I figured a man with tattoos of his own trailing down both arms wouldn't judge me too hard. It was unnerving. His probing gaze left me feeling exposed, which I fucking hated. I focused on not reaching down to pet Elvis, my nervous tell.

"Maybe," he said with a shrug, uncaring that he'd pissed me off with his judgmental stare. "What are you doing in Anchor Bay?" he asked. Squatting low, he looped a rope around a metal tie-down and tightened the line, securing the boat to the dock.

Well, fuck. He just had to ask the one question I sure as hell didn't want to answer.

I hitched my chin in defiance. "What's it to you?"

"Just answer the damn question, kid."

Both brows shot up my forehead in surprise. *Did he just call me kid?* There was no way I looked that young to the guy. After what I'd been through and survived, I thought it had aged me, giving me a hard, weathered edge—the tattoos not helping, of course.

Adjusting the full pack on my shoulder, I watched as a fisherman passed by, lugging a cart behind him. "I'm visiting a friend," I muttered, hoping he wasn't an asshole *and* a human lie detector.

Not waiting for more questions I wouldn't answer truthfully, I wrapped my fingers around the handle of each duffel and hauled them into the air. Ignoring his shouts for me to come back, I strode along the creaking planks, Elvis happily trotting beside me with his nose in the air, catching all the unique scents. Apparently, rotten fish, oil, fuel, and salt water was a heavenly blend for a dog, based on his wagging tail and tongue hanging out of the side of his smile.

It took no time to reach the parking lot where the resort instructed me to wait for a complimentary ride to The Nest. The fancy-ass resort wasn't the typical accommodations I'd normally book, but it was the only fucking place to stay in Anchor Bay unless I wanted to secure a camping spot for me and Elvis way outside town. That wouldn't be terrible—we had slept worse places—but I didn't pack all the gear that would be needed.

Turning in a slow circle, I took in everything around me, from the mountains piercing the sky to the brightly painted buildings lining the street. This was my first time in Alaska

—hell, on this side of the States—and it felt like a different country.

With a quick glance at my phone to check the time, I slipped it back into my pocket. The ride was scheduled to pick me up soon, and then my reason for flying out to Anchor Bay on a whim, unable to resist the pull once I found her after all these years, would kick into gear. Anxiety over what was to come twisted my gut and constricted each breath. Her reaction to me not only searching her out but flying to see her with no warning had the potential, and likelihood, to be terrible considering the circumstances and years that had passed. Which was why I'd decided to start with a bit of recon work before letting her know I was in town.

Maybe wanting to prolong the inevitable made me a coward, but I had to consider my mental health and what her reaction had the potential to do to me and my recovery. Her rejection would shatter the part of my soul that still clung to our shared past. Plus, there was the chance that seeing me could rip open her emotional wounds. The last thing I wanted to do was cause her more pain than she'd already been through the last two years.

"This was a dumbass plan," I muttered to Elvis just as a late model Land Rover with The Nest's logo on the side pulled into the parking lot. "But it's too late to turn back now."

Not that I wanted to.

I had to see her, even if it was only from the shadows without her knowing, to gauge the woman Baylee Smith had grown into. Was she different or still the same genuine, fun-loving girl I remembered?

Once I figured that out, spent enough time watching and waiting, then I'd decide my next move.

**4**

---

BAYLEE

A stifled breath burned in my lungs, teeth digging so deep into my lower lip that I worried they'd puncture through. With the sleeve of my lab coat, I wiped away the rolling drop of sweat that threatened to fall into my eyes and blinked several times to clear my vision. A pained whimper sounded above me, echoing through the small exam room, but I didn't shift my focus, not when it was all needed right in front of me.

Smooth metal slipped between my sweat-slicked fingers as I inched the pointed tip toward the thick wooden sliver causing my panting patient pain. Careful to not pinch too hard and break the splinter in two, I gently pulled back, plucking it free from the swollen paw.

My relieved exhale brushed past my dry lips as I grinned, pride swelling in my chest at the accomplished task. Sitting up straight in the chair, I praised Jubie for being so patient and brave only for the words to turn into a high-pitched squeal as her thick, slobbery tongue swiped from my chin to right ear.

"Thank you for that, sweet Jubie," I said, wiping the

layer of sticky saliva off my cheek. "You give the best slobbery kisses."

A soft male chuckle had me twisting to face Aiden where he leaned against the far wall of the exam room, his attention on the phone in his hand. A tiny smirk tugged his lips upward.

With an exaggerated eye roll, I turned back to the large Bernese mountain dog that was literally smiling at me and leaned in to whisper conspiringly, "We don't have to guess at *who* he's texting based on that mischievous smirk, do we?"

Her soft, floppy ears shifted as I stroked my nails across the top of her head. Aiden shot an amused expression my way with a slight headshake as he put the device into the side pocket of his black tactical pants.

"How's our girl Jubie here?" He shoved off the wall and stepped beside me, raking a hand through his unruly hair as he studied Jubie, concern creasing his features. "My boy Miles has been acting like an overbearing helicopter parent since the incident. I swear the dog can't take a piss without the grumpy asshole right beside her, making sure she doesn't get hurt."

"Based on this exam and the four others she's had in the last week"—Aiden chuckled at my incredulous tone as he scratched Jubie's chest, who raised her head up high to give him better access—"Jubie is healthy and doing great despite what happened. Whatever was used on her didn't cause any prolonged issues from what I can tell. We've run her blood work multiple times, and there isn't anything that shouldn't be there."

As if to thank me for the clean bill of health, Jubie lunged forward and ran her thick tongue along my cheek once again.

"How's Aspen?" I asked, rubbing the slobber off with my

shoulder while storing the few instruments I'd used during the exam that didn't need to be sanitized. "If Miles is this fixated on Jubie after what happened, I can't imagine how he's being with her."

At his nonresponse, I glanced over my shoulder, finding him frowning at the ground, seeming deep in thought. I whirled around to face him, clutching the small counter behind me in a death grip. "What? What happened? Is Aspen okay?"

My heart raced at the thought of my new friend being injured, or worse, suddenly ripped from my life like Dean had been. One of my ongoing trauma symptoms was always assuming the worst had happened to someone I loved or cared for.

Aiden held up his hands, surprised at my outburst. "Easy there, Baylee. She's fine. It's not Miles or her that's the issue." My grip on the counter eased a fraction, allowing some blood to flow to my fingers again. "It's her family, actually, that's giving us problems."

*Ah.* I blew out a breath and nodded. "She finally told her parents about you three being together. She was worried it wouldn't go over well." Sensing Aiden's distress, Jubie released a high-pitched whine and shifted on the table, knocking her large head against his side. "And by your reaction, I'm guessing that was the case."

His fingers absentmindedly ran through Jubie's fur in rhythmic strokes. "Saying it didn't go well is putting it fucking lightly. Her mom told Aspen she's destined to burn in hell for all eternity." I winced at his words and cutting tone. "And that neither she nor Aspen's father would ever accept her back into the family if she didn't fly home immediately and marry someone they deemed an acceptable match for her."

"Wow," I mouthed.

He scoffed. "Yeah, tell me about it. It's like she doesn't give two shits that Aspen is happy." The worry lines faded from his face as a goofy grin appeared. "Really, really happy in all the ways. Miles and I make sure of that."

When Aiden waggled his brows suggestively, I giggled, grabbing a rag and chucking it at his face. He caught it midair before it could hit him.

"I do *not* want to hear about that." Turning, I prayed he didn't catch the pink that highlighted my cheeks at his suggestive statement. Blowing out a slow breath, I pressed a hand to my stomach to calm the nausea the mix of heat and guilt triggered. "Well, I'm happy for you three."

And I really was.

That wasn't the lie.

Was I a little jealous? Sure, but it had nothing to do with them—well, not exactly. It was more about their ability to love and live so freely, unlike me. There wasn't a day that passed that I didn't wish the heavy baggage I carried wasn't there so I could live a life unburdened of that constant weight. But then as soon as I wished that, more guilt would pile on, adding to the oppressive burden that sometimes prevented me from taking a full breath.

Miles, Aspen, and Aiden were allowed to be happy—everyone around me was—and I wanted that for them. But I had that easy laughter and soul-altering love once until it was ripped away. I wanted it again, but I wasn't sure that was possible with how utterly broken I was on the inside.

"Baylee."

I jolted, jumping a bit at Aiden's shout.

Whirling around, I narrowed my eyes at the man who was staring at me with worry and concern.

*Great, just what I need—more pity for the broken girl who can't get her shit together.*

"You're all good to take her home. Tell Miles if he wants me to see her again next week and the week after that, you know I'm here Tuesdays and Thursdays, or I can swing by on my way home one day. It's not like your place isn't two cabins down from mine."

"Come on, Baylee. Look at me."

I tensed at his gentle tone. He rested a wide palm on my shoulder and squeezed, drawing my focused stare away from Jubie. His honey-brown eyes searched my face, a small frown out of place on his normally cheerful expression. "Don't hide your sadness from me, or any of us. We're here for you, always."

My shoulders slumped as I nodded. Aiden was a good man, considerate, and had enough trauma in his own background that it wasn't a surprise that he'd picked up on my sudden mood shift.

Grabbing Jubie's chart, I clutched it against my chest, using it as a makeshift shield from the memories his concern dragged to the surface.

*Do not cry, Baylee Smith. Do not fucking cry because your friend is being nice to you.*

"Thanks, Aiden," I rasped around the unshed tears burning down my throat. "But I'm... good. Promise."

"Good," he responded skeptically.

I shook my head, strands of long blonde hair sliding over my shoulders with the movement. "I'm...." I swallowed hard to clear the emotions clogging my throat. "I'm okay. Some days are worse than others, but I'm used to it at this point." I offered him a shaky smile.

Placing both hands on my shoulders, he pulled me in for a brief hug before stepping back out of my personal space.

Tipping my chin up, I focused my watery gaze on his sternum, not wanting him to see the tears I was barely holding at bay.

"And that's normal, Baylee." I blew out a trembling breath through pursed lips. "As long as you don't let those bad days win and you keep fighting for the good ones. Because they're coming. I know they are. You're too good of a person for there not to be."

I nodded, unable to look up. "I know," I whispered. "And I'm trying. It's just that all this going on with Liam is...." I couldn't finish the sentence. How did I explain the jumbled mess my feelings were around the amazing man, and feeling like I was cheating on my late fiancé? It was nonsensical, I knew that, but I couldn't stop. I wanted Liam, desperately, but I felt guilty for that in the same breath. I loved our time together, but the sadness and anguish rushed back in afterward, filling me to the brim when he wasn't there keeping it all away.

Aiden's brows pulled in tight and both corners of his lips dipped. "Wait, Liam what? Did he fucking push you before you were ready for something? Make you uncomfortable?"

My blue eyes snapped up to Aiden at the anger shaking his tone. "What?" I gasped, shocked that he'd think that about my adorable cowboy. "No, that's not—"

"I will kick his ass." I couldn't help the snort that escaped. Aiden grimaced and nodded in agreement of my skepticism. "Right, he is a massive fucker who used to nearly kill people for a living." His features turned thoughtful. "And I guess killed people for a living in the Army. Fine, Miles and I will attempt to kick his ass if he did anything to make you feel uncomfortable. We might need more volunteers, though."

The corners of my lips pulled upward as I huffed a laugh at his ridiculous words.

"Ah," he exclaimed and pointed at my face. "There's a smile. No more tears, okay? They hurt my sensitive heart. Now, what were you saying about Liam?"

My lips parted, but no words would come out. This was not something I wanted to talk to Aiden about. This was girlfriend-level conversation.

As if sensing I needed a distraction, Jubie barked and leapt from the exam table, enormous paws slapping to the floor before padding over to the closed door.

I gestured to her with the chart. "I think that's her saying she's ready to go home." Stepping back, I gave Aiden a soft smile. "I'm sure I'll see you guys around later tonight. Let Miles know if he has questions about Jubie, he can call me."

Opening the chart, I laid it on the counter and pulled out a pen to write my notes from the procedure, more to have something to do than needing the documentation. My practice wasn't large, so I remembered everything regarding my patients and their care.

"Just do me a favor, Baylee." I glanced over my shoulder with an arched brow. "Don't let your past take away the future you have ahead of you. I've stayed in that kind of purgatory before and know it's hard to find your way out."

"How did you?" I asked before I could think better of it.

"I followed the light that stumbled into my life." His gaze went unfocused as he smiled. "And she's been guiding me and walking beside me ever since."

I swallowed hard. "Aspen is a lucky woman to have you, Aiden. Both you and Miles."

He shook his head and ran a hand through his longish hair. "Nah, we're lucky to have found each other. Just don't overlook all the people willing to be that guiding light for you, Baylee. We're here, all of us, day or night. We're a family, and that's what families do."

With a forced smile and nod, I waved them out the door, his words running on a loop in my mind.

Tapping the laptop to bring it to life, I checked the fancy scheduling system that Juno added to the website she built me one night after realizing I didn't have one. Who knew too many glasses of cheap wine at book club would turn my small practice into something that now covered the more remote towns close to Anchor Bay? My schedule wasn't booked solid, but more and more new patients and appointments popped up every day.

Noting that Jubie was the last patient despite it only being a little past one in the afternoon, I closed the laptop, tucked it under my arm, and exited the exam room to pack up for the day. I plopped down into the uncomfortable chair in my office and slid my phone out of the side pocket of my navy scrubs.

Twenty missed calls from a blocked number. My stomach dropped with dread. The strange, unnerving calls started a few months ago, only one a week then, but recently had escalated to dozens a day. If I picked up, the person on the other end of the line didn't utter a word. The only sound heavy breathing, the caller's anger almost palpable with each breath.

I didn't who the calls were from or what the hell it meant. Until I did, I had convinced myself there was no reason to tell Liam or any of the other overprotective men in my life. They would just blow it all out of proportion, especially considering everything going on around Anchor Bay.

I wasn't worried or scared, not really—more confused and curious. Shaking my head to redirect my thoughts back to my real issues, I cleared the missed calls and few voicemails without listening to them, knowing it would only be the enraged heavy breathing, and slouched back in the chair staring at the now blank screen. Aiden's words ran on a loop, urging me to take his earlier advice. Something needed to change in my life, because I couldn't live like this anymore. I wanted to be free, wanted to live.

Saying yes to Liam when he asked me out was that first step; now I just had to keep moving forward and not let my past hold me back.

Mind made up, I opened the messaging app and pulled up the most recent text from Liam.

> Me: Hey, you free later?

> Liam: For you, always. Everything okay?

How the hell did I answer that? Physically, yes. Emotionally, fuck if I knew.

Apparently, I took too long to respond, because Liam's next texts came through rapid-fire.

> Liam: Answer me, Baylee.

> Liam: Are you hurt? Where are you?

> Liam: Fuck, please write me back, Little Bit.

My heart clenched at the clear worry in his messages.

> Me: Calm down, big guy, I'm fine. Just wanted to see if you were free to talk later.

The little bubble popped up and disappeared several times before the message came through.

> Liam: Your place or mine?

> Me: Yours.

> Me: I'll get cleaned up after work, then head over. Sound good?

> Liam: I'll make dinner. Chicken or beef?

I bit the corner of my lip as I smiled at my phone. His obsession with feeding me should put me off, but instead I found it endearing. Not that he found me lacking because of my slight weight and nonexistent curves but because he was worried about me. Honestly, sometimes when I looked in the mirror and saw how much weight I'd lost, I worried about me too.

After responding to Liam, I set the phone down and twisted the chair side to side, deep in contemplation. If I really planned to have the much-needed awkward conversation with him tonight, push myself past my comfort zone, I needed a solid plan.

The problem was, I did not know where to start.

Good thing I knew someone, or a few someones, who could help.

---

ALMOST THIRTY MINUTES LATER, still in scrubs but having changed into a clean pair that didn't have a layer of Jubie fur, I stood outside our favorite local dive bar, Dave's, which had the best Alaskan beers on draft and the most delicious nachos ever. My stomach growled as I tugged open the heavy, weathered wooden door, the scents of fried food and beer immediately wafting over me.

Just before I stepped over the threshold, the hairs on the back of my neck stood on end as an unsettled feeling raced down my spine. Palm sealed to the center of the door to keep it open, I turned, scanning the sidewalk for what set me on edge, but noticed nothing out of the ordinary. As if knowing I was unsettled, my watch vibrated with an incoming unknown call, amplifying my paranoia.

Blowing out a calming breath, I ignored the call, shrugged off the sensation of being watched, and stepped into Dave's, immediately spotting my friends toward the back corner, already seated around a table. Weaving through the few high-tops, I waved at Finley, whose hand shook wildly in the air to draw my attention.

"I've already figured it out. You're pregnant," she said smugly and high-fived herself.

I froze halfway between standing and sitting in one of the open wooden chairs to gape at her. "Um, what?" I fell the rest of the way into the seat and dropped my backpack to the floor.

Finley nodded and pointed at me. "I knew it. You're not denying it." She swung her gaze across the table to Aspen and Juno, who didn't look convinced. To my right, Amy, Brandon's wife, tried to muffle her laughter behind a loose fist. "Told you that was the reason for the emergency book club meeting."

"I'm... what? Finley, what the actual fuck? Do I look pregnant?" I shrieked while patting my stomach and pulling the scrub top tighter.

Her wide smile faded.

I waved off her panicked expression, knowing she meant nothing by her very inaccurate guess for my 911 text. "No, fuck, I'm not pregnant. No way for me to be," I grumbled at the end, not expecting anyone to hear me.

But Amy must have by the way she snorted into her pint glass. "Give her a second to breathe, Finley, for fuck's sake.

She doesn't even have a drink yet." She eyed me before nodding at whatever she'd just decided in her head. "I have a feeling a round of duck fart shots is in order for whatever this is all about."

I started to protest, but she'd already pushed back from the table with a determined expression, and I knew any effort to stop the upcoming shots would be futile. With a groan, I massaged both temples, wondering if I'd only made everything worse by reaching out to them.

"Okay, Baylee," Aspen said, folding both arms on the table. "Calista can't be here, something about not having a babysitter and not wanting to bring a kid to a bar. So, with us all here who answered the emergency call, this book club meeting is now in session. What's going on?"

"I don't know where to start," I complained, suddenly nervous. Not once since I moved here had I really opened up about my life before Anchor Bay. Sure, the women around the table and the guys in our community knew of Dean, that he was my fiancé and died in combat, but that was it. It wasn't until talking with Aiden today that I realized keeping all my worries, fears, and confusing emotions inside was actually doing me more harm than good.

I knew these women, trusted them. Not a single one around the table would judge or gossip about me. We were family at this point, and I needed to lean on them for support if I had any hope of surviving.

"Then start from the beginning." Five full shot glasses were carefully placed in the middle of the scuffed wooden table. Grabbing one, Amy motioned for the rest of us to follow suit. After tapping the rim of her glass with all of ours, she pressed the edge to her lips and tossed it back.

Knowing this was a terrible decision but doing it anyway, I downed my shot, wiping the remnants from my lips and using the few moments while the others did the same to get my chaotic thoughts together.

"I knew I wanted to marry Dean the moment I saw him," I said, staring at the empty glass twirling along the table as I twisted it between my fingers. "We were just stupid kids at the time, but I still knew he was it for me. But...." I grabbed Amy's half-full pint glass and took a sip, knowing she wouldn't mind. "I also wanted to go to college to one day become a vet. From my first pet, I knew that was what I wanted to be, and I also knew it would take years to reach my goal."

Appearing out of nowhere, a pint glass filled to the brim with liquid gold was placed on the table in front of me. I shot Finley a thankful smile as she folded her tall, lean body into the chair beside me.

"I was the one who wanted to wait to get married," I shared. The words just bubbled out of me, no hope of stopping now that I had started. "I was so focused on my goals, what needed to be done to get there, and thought we had a whole life, a long future together to make up for the wait." Tipping the glass back, I downed half the beer before setting it back on the table. "Dean didn't know what he wanted to do out of high school, so he decided to join the Army, thinking it would be a good way for him to make some money and get his future college paid for, all while waiting for me while I went to school in Texas." Unshed tears burned in my throat. "He didn't want to follow me to A&M, something about not wanting to be a distraction while I worked hard for my dreams. Dean was great like that, always thinking about me first.

"The long-distance thing was hard on both of us, but we made it work. I saw him when I came home during breaks if he wasn't deployed, but then I got a steady internship during the breaks and stopped coming home altogether. Even still, he understood and didn't resent me doing what I needed to do. He wanted my lifelong dream to become a reality. He was so supportive of everything. Even the sex thing," I whispered while flicking my gaze around the table.

Juno, who had been quiet up to this point, raised her hand with a confused expression. "Um, am I the only one lost right now? *What* sex thing?" Her gaze darted to the other women, no doubt hoping everyone else was as confused as she was.

"I wanted to wait until we were married," I admitted quickly, then took a gulp of cold beer to calm my nerves.

"To have sex?" Finley probed. At my hesitant nod, she pressed her lips into a tight line. "Um, okay, that's your choice. You do you, boo, and nothing to be ashamed of like you look right now, but why?"

I raised my shoulders in a noncommittal shrug. At this point, I even questioned myself, knowing now what I didn't then. If I would've known our time would be cut short, I wouldn't have waited for that intimate connection with Dean, but I didn't, and now here I was, a late-twenties virgin.

"Dean and I came from a small town in Kansas, about the size of Anchor Bay, actually. It's super old-school, very religious, and there was a piece of me that was too afraid of...." I trailed off and looked away, not wanting to finish the statement. It made me sound as selfish as I felt now.

Amy reached out and placed a comforting hand on my forearm. "You were afraid of what would happen to your goals if you got pregnant," she finished for me, clearly understanding.

I dipped my chin in a hesitant nod. "I was terrified of it. My high school had one of the highest teen pregnancy rates in the state because there was literally nothing else to do on the weekend but hook up. I watched as too many girls my age had their dreams of getting out of our Podunk town shattered or altered because they got pregnant. I swore I wouldn't end up like that, like my mom had. Sure, she's happy with my dad, but I know she wanted more but couldn't because she had a baby to take care of."

"No matter the reason, you wanting to wait isn't a bad thing, Baylee. Sounds like you were both on the same page, so what are you—"

"Because he died," I said, the hot tears I'd been holding back breaking free to leak down my cheeks. "Taking our future, that chance with him. Everything I had pushed aside, everything that should've taken priority, was ripped away from me. I never got a chance to have that intimacy with him, never got to sign his last name as mine, and as soon as all of that was taken away, I realized everything I'd poured my focus into didn't actually matter. Not really, not as much as him. As us. Who gives a shit if I got out of our town, that I became a vet like I always dreamed. I don't have him."

Snatching a cocktail napkin from the center of the table, I used it to wipe my wet cheeks.

Amy squeezed my forearm, drawing my avoidant gaze to her. "I'm so glad you're telling us all this, not keeping it in. We know you're hurting," she whispered. "But please know, you do still have a future that wasn't taken away by his death. Sure, it might look different from the one you planned, but...." She bit her lower lip, as if debating her next words. "Dean's gone." I choked back a sob, pressing the napkin to my lips to quiet the sound. "But you're not. Sweet girl, you still have a full life ahead of you."

"I don't know how to let go," I admitted. "I don't know if I want to let go of him."

"Then don't," Aspen said, her own eyes glassy with unshed tears. "You don't have to forget about him to keep living. He will always be a part of you, but do you really think he'd want you to be sad, to stop living because he isn't here to live it with you?"

"No," I rasped. "And I'm trying. I really am. You know how me and Liam are—" I waved a hand in the air. "—whatever we are. But what if I'm always this broken? What if I can't move on?"

"Have you talked to him about any of this?" Juno asked. "What's holding you back from going all in with him?"

I shot her a sheepish look. "No. I don't want all this mess inside me, all my mixed-up emotions, to push him away." That thought terrified me, that I'd make him realize I wasn't worth the trouble as I worked through my shit. "And if I don't open up, don't let him get close, and things don't work out, then I'll still be okay because I never really let him in." There was no way I could survive someone else leaving me if I allowed myself to let him in, to offer him a piece of me that not even Dean got.

"Girl, that man is head over heels into you," Amy stated, smacking my arm to emphasize her point. "Talk to Liam. Nothing you say or do will push him away as long as you're honest about how you're feeling and why. Just don't freeze him out of everything that's bothering you. You think that will protect you from getting hurt, but it'll only make you lonely. He can't support and help you if he doesn't understand what you're going through."

Inhaling deeply, I nodded. Grabbing my beer, I finished it and gently set the empty glass back on the table. "That's where you guys come in, why I called this emergency meeting. I think I'm ready to stop hiding from him. I just don't know how to take that first step."

I startled when Finley slapped both palms on the wooden surface, drawing all our attention as she stood. "Good thing you called us. We can figure it out together." She glanced at Juno and winced. "Well, maybe you should've just called Aspen and Amy, since they're the only two who know how to do the healthy-relationship shit. I'll go get another round of shots and beers. I think we'll need them."

Despite it all, my lips curved upward as I watched my friend weave through the high-top tables, headed for the bar. Not sure how, but I already felt better. Lighter in my soul in a way I hadn't in a long, long time.

Which meant maybe, just maybe, I wasn't the lost cause I believed I was after all.

## 5

LIAM

**B**alancing the pan in one hand, I reached for the oven door only to freeze at a demanding knock at the front door of my cabin. Grumbling under my breath, I dropped the metal pan on the stovetop just as the door vibrated again from whoever pounded on the other side.

*What the fuck?* The heels of my boots slammed against the hardwood floor, my irritation rising with every step.

Whatever was going on better not mess with my night. Just thinking about Baylee's text had the unease gnawing at my insides all over again. It had calmed down while I distracted myself by making dinner.

Hand wrapped around the metal handle, the smooth edges digging into my palm, I yanked the door open, lips parted to tell whoever was on the other side to fuck off, only for them to snap shut. Pretty sure yelling at your boss when he already looked irritated as hell wasn't the best idea.

"Get your shit," Brandon barked. Not waiting for my reply or giving further instructions, he turned on his heels and stormed down the porch steps.

"Fuck, give me a second," I shouted, making him pause.

He glanced over his shoulder with an arched brow. "I was in the middle of making dinner. I need to put it in the fridge so I don't give us both fucking food poisoning later. What the hell is going on, and what shit do I need to bring?"

Turning to face me, he folded both thick arms over his chest and released an exasperated sigh to the cloudy sky. "Miles called me. Said we needed to get down to Dave's right away. Apparently, our girls are there, hammered out of their minds from one too many duck fart shots. Fuck knows that was mine's idea," he grumbled under his breath, even though humor laced his tone.

It took a second for his words to register.

"Wait, *our* girls? Baylee is there, too, drunk?"

Brandon dipped his chin in acknowledgment.

My heart raced, knowing she was out there vulnerable and unprotected. Sure, Miles was there, but I wasn't, and that wouldn't do.

"What the hell? What are we doing standing around here for?"

Fuck the dinner I'd planned. I'd figure food out later. Right now, getting to Baylee and ensuring she was safe was all that mattered.

Grabbing the keys from the hook by the door, I slammed it shut behind me, locked up, and rushed to catch up with Brandon, who was already halfway to the gravel lot where we all parked our personal vehicles. The trucks, SUVs, ATVs, and various other motor vehicles owned by the company were in a shed, the toys all sorted out by the season they were used.

"Why is Miles there?" I asked, tightening my grip on the keys until the teeth bit into my palm.

"You know how paranoid that fucker's been since the incident. Like he would let Aspen out of his or Aiden's sight if she's off our property." He shot me an unreadable look as we approached my late model Ford truck. "You doing okay with all that, by the way?"

I shrugged, very much feeling nonchalant about the whole thing. "Yeah, I'm fine. It's not the first time I've witnessed someone dying."

His eyes went wide. "You mean dead," he corrected. "Not the first time you found someone dead."

Fuck, did not mean to let that slip. My mind was too wrapped up in getting to Baylee to monitor my words. I leaned forward, pressing both forearms to the hood of the truck.

"Yep, dead. That's what I meant." Brandon huffed a laugh and shook his head, knowing full well I was lying out my ass. "We've all been around it enough in our past that it didn't bother me as much as it should, I guess." Especially not after what happened, and the reason why that person was injured and dying in the woods. Nope, I did not feel bad about it, not even a sliver. Karma and all that shit always comes around. "Meet you there?" I asked, shoving off the cold metal.

He held up a finger for me to wait. "I called the others. They're coming with us. They should be here—" His words cut off when Langston and Dax jogged around the corner, the former griping about something. "You two take Langston's 4Runner. Liam is driving his truck, and I'll ride with him, then drive Amy's Explorer back here once we round them up."

The truck shook as our two large frames climbed into the cab. Shoving the key into the ignition, I gave it a hard turn, firing the engine to life. Arm draped over the back of the bench seat, I twisted to watch as I reversed out of the spot, barely missing Langston as he peeled out of the parking lot, dust and rocks flying in the tires' wake.

"We just might witness World War III if Dax can't calm him down," I muttered as I shifted the truck into Drive.

"Yeah, well, you know Langston. He shows he cares by being an overbearing asshole. Though I don't think Juno's caught on to that just yet."

I felt his stare burning into the side of my face.

"So, you were making you and Baylee dinner?"

I tightened my grip on the wheel and responded with a clipped nod.

"How's it going with her?"

A single broad shoulder rose in a nonchalant shrug even though I was tense as fuck about our current mission and his line of questioning.

"Fuck, Liam. We're closer than that shit. You don't have to do that with me. I know you care about her. More than you let on."

My knuckles went white around the steering wheel.

"Yeah, well, it doesn't really matter if I do or not. It won't ever be enough for someone like her. I should just back off and let her find someone who deserves her, but I'm a selfish bastard and won't." Fuck, it sucked saying those words out loud. When Brandon started to respond, I cut him off, not wanting to hear it. "I know the shitty man I am." Hell, I'd just admitted to watching a person die and not being affected by it, and that was one of my better fucking qualities. "She deserves way more than I can ever give her, what I can actually give." Which was why the idea of someone else, the multiple-partner side of our community, intrigued me. Maybe someone like me could actually have a healthy relationship if there was someone else to fill in the gaps where I lacked. Because those gaps were fucking canyons. "But unfortunately for her, I'm too much of a selfish bastard to not go after what, or who, I want, and that's her. Even if I know she deserves better than a man like me."

The rest of the short ride was quiet, Brandon's digging into my love life thankfully done.

The small bay downtown wasn't busy no matter the time of day, which made finding a place to park close to Dave's simple, right next to Langston's 4Runner. The sound of four doors slamming shut at almost the same time echoed down the sidewalk. Stepping up onto the walkway, I marched along the wooden planks at a fast clip, eager to get my eyes on Baylee and ease the worry tightening my chest.

Not waiting for the others to keep up, I moved around a local leaving Dave's and stepped into the bar, the other three right behind me, nearly slamming into my back in their own impatience to locate the group. Quickly scanning the open area, the tightness in my chest making it difficult to breathe eased at hearing Baylee's distinct laughter over the music playing through the crappy speakers.

I pointed toward the back, catching sight of her white-blonde hair and Amy sitting beside her. Weaving through the high-top tables, I looked around the bar, suddenly feeling like something was off, but turned my focus back to my girl as I neared.

My girl.

Fuck, if only she thought that too.

Soon, hopefully. Though I would wait patiently as long as she needed. Grief was a fickle bitch, making you feel okay one day and almost too damn heavy to get out of bed the next. Everyone's grieving process was unique, and I refused to rush Baylee.

Mid-cackling laugh, Amy's gaze moved our way, making her do a double take, eyes wide when she saw the four of us approaching. Snapping her lips shut, she shoved the shoulders of the two women sitting beside her, almost pushing Juno and Baylee off their seats.

"Uh-oh," she said, eyeing Brandon when he stopped behind her. "We're in trouble now, girls."

Aspen shook her head with a wide smile spread across her face. "Not all of us. My personal protection detail has been sitting at the bar for the last hour. After that fourth shot, I knew there was no way I was driving home, so I texted him and Aiden."

As though he'd been summoned by her words, Miles stepped up behind her, wrapped his hand around her dark ponytail, and tugged until her face tipped up to his. "Good girl."

"Holy fuck, that's hot," Finley whispered, not so quietly.

I shot a quick look at Dax to see what he thought of that comment. Lips pursed and nose scrunched, he looked like he'd eaten something sour. Seemed he didn't appreciate his best friend's remark.

"This was my fault, babe," Amy said while attempting to stand, only to stumble right into Brandon's arms. "It was an emergency book club to talk—"

"First rule of book club, Amy, is don't talk about book club shit," Finley whisper-shouted, flicking her gaze around the table. "We are sworn to secrecy about all things discussed."

"Yes, exactly," Baylee said, nodding with a smile so wide it made my heart ache with happiness for her. Fuck, I loved seeing her radiating joy when it was so often dampened by her grief. "Which means no talking about me being a virgin."

And... pretty sure the entire bar went silent at that declaration.

As if not realizing she said the words out loud, Baylee finished her beer and gently set the glass down on the table, adding to the collection of pint and shot glasses stacked there. Fuck, was that a highball glass too?

I scrubbed a hand down my face to keep my smirk hidden. My girl was too damn adorable for her own good.

"Um, Bay," Juno said after a few seconds of the uncomfortable silence and the other women all flicking nervous gazes around the table. "We won't say anything, but you just told the entire bar yourself."

Baylee's blonde brows furrowed before shooting up her forehead, almost hitting her hairline. Eyes as wide as dinner plates, she turned her petite face up to mine, scrunching her tiny nose.

"Did I really?" I nodded, losing the fight with my growing smile. "Well, fucknuggets."

Several deep chuckles cut through the silence, and the usual sounds of other conversations and laughter filled the bar. Squatting low to put us at eye level, I scanned her rosy cheeks, bright eyes, and wide smile.

"Looks like you had fun," I said, noting the other guys were doing the same with their women. "And about what you just announced, don't be embarrassed about that, Little Bit. I kind of assumed you were more innocent than me."

A mischievous grin spread across her face as she did a slow once-over up and down my body. "But I am very experienced at other things."

*Oh fuck.*

Her gaze once again dipped, sliding down my chest and pausing on my crotch. "I can do this thing with my tongue that—"

Standing with a grunt, I hauled her out of the chair in the same movement. I shifted her in my arms to carry her bridal style to the truck since I didn't trust her not to hurt herself walking, but the gorgeous drunk had other plans. Both her arms circled around my neck while her legs did the same around my waist. Her flushed face pressed between my neck and shoulder, a soft, content sigh brushing against my skin.

Damnit. I was a strong fucker, but even I didn't have the willpower after her tongue comment to not palm her ass, loving the way it molded beneath my tightening fingers as I carried her toward the exit. Behind me, I could hear Juno and Langston's loud argument, followed by an ear-piercing, pissed-as-hell screech that cut through the bar noise. Twisting to look over my shoulder, I barked out a laugh at Langston storming my way with Juno tossed over his shoulder. Her legs kicked wildly while she screamed some pretty damn creative insults at the fucker.

Behind him, Dax attempted to guide a stumbling and very chatty Finley through the tables, his lips pressed in a tight line as if attempting not to laugh at whatever she was going on about. The others were behind them, but not wanting to be run over by a furious Lang on his hurry to get out of the bar, I strode to the door, waving at Gus and the barback on my way out.

Outside, the sun still sat high in the sky, making me squint at the sudden shift from the dim bar.

"I'm sorry," Baylee said against my neck, her soft lips teasing the skin.

"For what?" I murmured while holding the door open for the others as they filed out.

"For being such a fucking mess." She leaned back, and her glassy eyes met mine. "I understand if I'm not worth it."

My stomach dropped. What the fuck was she talking about? That was *my* line, how *I* felt about her being too good for me. Which she was, but again, I was a selfish bastard, and I wouldn't let her go.

"My highs and lows, crying and then laughing, angry, then sad." She shook her head, blonde hair shifting along her back, and buried her face against my neck again. "I understand if I'm too much trouble, but...."

"But what?" I rasped when she didn't finish.

"I don't want you to give up on me."

I grunted, the pain in her tone almost like a physical punch to my gut. "Never, Little Bit. You listen to me. You are not a mess. You're perfect, and there isn't a chance in hell that I'll ever even think about giving up on you."

"You fucking bastard, put me down or I will cut your balls off in your sleep." Juno's threat echoed down the walkway, but Langston kept marching toward the 4Runner like she hadn't spoken. "I will make you pay for manhandling me, Langston. I'll... I'll... fuck, I can't think up something sinister and painful upside down like this, but I'll come up with something really awful."

"You tell him, Juno." I turned to find Finley smiling at Juno's swaying head, giving it a sweet pat as Langston stormed past. "I'm glad we're best friends."

"I thought I was your best friend," Dax said, arm wrapped around Finley's waist, attempting to keep her from falling over the railing into the bay. "Damn, woman, I've never seen you *this* drunk."

"I'm fine," she said, shoving him off, or at least attempting to. "I've never felt this good in my life. No worries in the world—" She slapped a palm over her mouth, and a sickly green tint overtook her face. I grimaced as Finley spun out of Dax's hold to pitch over the railing, vomiting everything she drank and ate into the water.

Concern tightened Dax's features as he fisted her black

hair and held it away from her face while Finley emptied her stomach.

"Uh, Liam?" The hesitation in Baylee's voice had me looking down at her, brows pulled in tight. Skin more pale than fair, she chewed on her lower lip. "Now would be a good time to let you know I'm a sympathetic puker."

I blinked, not understanding a word she just said. "A what?"

"It means if she hears or sees someone else throwing up, so will she," Dax shouted over his shoulder. "Go on, get her out of here. We don't need two pukers on our hands." Finley swatted a hand blindly behind her, smacking Dax in the chest. "Woman, stop it. I'm just kidding. Take her home, Liam. I've got this. I won't let anything happen to Finley unless she keeps hitting me, and then I'll dunk her in the freezing water to sober her up a little."

Not waiting to get puked on or wanting Baylee to get sick, I headed for the truck, pausing at the hood where Miles and Langston stood, heads bent together. Movement in the 4Runner drew my attention, and I huffed a humorless laugh at Juno pouting in the back seat, arms folded over her chest, lips moving as if talking to herself.

"Yeah, I noticed him too," Langston said. "He got here yesterday or the day before that—fuck, I can't remember, but I can check the bookings. I think he's staying at The Nest and brought his dog with him."

Miles looked over his shoulder at Dave's. "He didn't strike me as someone here to make trouble or who would be harmful to us or the town." He ran a hand over his mouth. "If we see him around town again, I'll have a little chat to see what he's doing here. He doesn't look like the outdoor enthusiast we normally get visiting here."

Langston grunted in agreement. "He pushed back when

I pushed him, but it felt more self-protective than anything. I got the feeling he's been through shit and is coming out the other side."

"Like we all were when we got here," I stated, joining the conversation. "Who are you two talking about? Do we need to go back—"

"Guys, I need to get Finley home now. She's done puking for the moment, but I'm not sure how long that'll last." Dax didn't even stop as he guided Finley to the 4Runner's back seat and opened the door.

I turned to Dave's, the urge to go back and confront the man my friends were discussing almost too strong to ignore. That was until a soft kiss pressed to my neck, followed by a gentle hum, refocused me on what was important.

"Come on, Little Bit," I muttered into her hair, inhaling the sweet coconut scent. "Let's get you home."

"Home," she repeated. "He used to be that for me, you know." I knew exactly who she was talking about, no explanation needed because I had that at one time too long ago. "Now I don't know where home is."

I sucked in a breath, her words and sad tone a punch to the balls. "Home is always with the people you love, who support and protect you. Your home is with me, Baylee, with all of us. We might not be a family by blood and are super fucked up, but we *are* family just the same. Let us in and you'll see."

Her crystal blue eyes searched mine. "What will I see?"

"That you're safe, every part of you. It's okay to be vulnerable, to open up and let us see the good, sad, and ugly. We'll be here for you, but you have to take that first step to letting us in for us to be your safety net."

"I'm trying," she whispered, tears filling her lower lids.

"I know you are, and I'm so damn in awe of your

strength. So fucking proud of what you've survived and that you're still able to smile and give so much to others. But you don't have to do it alone, not anymore. Not with me, not with the others."

A small smile curved the corners of her lips upward despite the tears leaking out of her eyes. "See, you're proving me right. Adorable. You're just a big softy, you know that?"

Shaking my head in disagreement, I stepped up to the passenger door. Before pulling it open, I inspected the area around us, noting how quiet it was now that the others had left.

"Anyone who has ever met me would disagree with you on both counts." Especially the bastards I nearly killed during my MMA days, the insurgents I handled while serving my country, and the bulls I fucking owned during that rodeo stint in high school. "If they were conscious after, at least."

It was terrible of me, but I couldn't help the cocky smirk that formed. I loved the fight, the thrill of your life on the line, sure, but mostly I loved fucking winning. That glorious high that came from knowing you were the biggest and baddest shit in the arena was epic. Never again would I be the scrawny kid who got his ass beat over and over when he tried to stand up to the bullies fucking with those smaller than them.

Even back then, I was a protector. I just couldn't do shit about it.

Not now, though. Now I could handle my own, either hand to hand or with most weapons.

"Nope." Her sweet voice pulled me out of those dark memories. "You're my sticky-sweet cinnamon roll." Her head popped off my shoulder as I gripped the chrome door handle. "Do you have cinnamon rolls at home that we could make? Oh, or cookies?"

Pressing a smiling kiss on her forehead, I pulled the door open and gently sat her on the bench seat. Grabbing the seat belt, I stretched it out wide and buckled it around her lap, double-checking she was secure. A small, warm palm cupped my cheek, freezing me on the spot. Ever so slowly, I angled my face toward the smiling Baylee.

"I changed my mind. You're a Tootsie Pop." *Oh fuck.* She leaned in close until our lips brushed. "You're something I want to lick and suck on to get to the yummy center."

Closing the minuscule distance between us, I sealed my lips to hers, unable to hold back after that strangely erotic metaphor. Fingers wrapped around the back of her neck, I held her in place as I deepened the kiss, tasting every inch of her mouth before reluctantly pulling back.

"Holy fuck, you're good at that," she whispered, eyes wide. "Every time we've made out, I have been so turned on, but I couldn't...." She trailed off and flicked an avoidant gaze toward the driver's seat.

"Hey, it's okay. I—"

"Dean is the only guy I've ever done anything with." She peeked at me out of the corner of her eye. "Anything," Baylee emphasized. She paused, waiting for me to catch on to something, but I had no fucking clue what she was alluding to. "I'm saying you're only the second guy I've ever kissed, Liam." Pride swelled in my chest, and I fought the instinct to pump my fist in the air like an idiot. "And you're fantastic at it."

She bit her lip, clearly not done sharing. Careful to not break the moment, I stayed perfectly still, only my nostrils flaring with each deep breath. Maybe it made me a terrible asshole, allowing her to spill all this while intoxicated and vulnerable, but... no one ever said I was a good guy.

"I don't deserve your patience," she said with a heavy exhale. "But I need it for a little longer."

"You'll have it as long as you need," I promised.

Her eyes rolled to the roof. "Guys have needs that need to be met. Hell, *I* have needs."

My brows shot up over my forehead at that tidbit. "Oh yeah?" She nodded. "Do tell, Little Bit. Tell me about these needs of yours."

Yep, it was official. I was a terrible asshole.

"After you leave my place, I have to take care of myself with these—"

*Nope.*

*Fuck. Abort mission.*

No man on this planet had enough resistance to hear his girl talk about playing with herself and not fuck her right then.

I jerked back, the back of my head connecting with the edge of the roof with a loud thump. A string of curses flew out as I rubbed at the sore spot while squinting up at the clouds like they were the ones that caused me pain. Fuck the long-ass daylight hours here in Alaska. I never needed the cover of night like I did now to hide my flushed face and tented jeans.

A honeyed giggle had me narrowing a fake frustrated expression at Baylee, who hid a wide smile behind a couple of fingers hovering over her curved lips.

"You think that's funny?" I grumbled, still massaging the pain away from my skull.

She nodded. "Just my yummy Tootsie Pop."

Groaning, I made sure she was fully tucked into the truck before slamming the door shut. I needed that physical barrier before I bent her over the tailgate and fucked her until her screams echoed through town and everyone knew she was mine.

My footsteps stuttered at that thought. I gave my head a hard shake and forced myself to continue to the driver's side. Nothing good would come from giving in to temptation tonight.

She needed to feel safe with me while she was this vulnerable and so damn adorable. I'd rather carve out my heart with a rusted spoon than do anything to jeopardize how she viewed me.

A Tootsie Pop and cinnamon roll.

My chest vibrated with a deep chuckle as I folded my tall frame behind the wheel.

Only the amazing, brilliant, and utterly precious woman beside me would ever say that about me. If I were honest with myself, I fucking loved it.

But more than anything, it made me want to be the man she believed me to be.

---

## 6

## MEMPHIS

Shoulder pressed against the side of the faded pink building, I watched as the cool-as-hell late model Ford disappeared down the road, taking Baylee with it. I shook my head, still chuckling to myself at the entertaining shit show that I enjoyed the last couple of hours. And that grand finale when all their drunk asses were hauled out by several men was unexpected and hysterical. The women appeared to trust the men who came for them, or I would've figured out a way to take them on. Considering most looked like former military, even special forces, it would've been a slaughter since I'm a lover, not a fighter. I hoped to meet Baylee's friends if it got to that point. They were hilarious and loud, especially after the fourth round of weird Alaskan shots hit their systems.

I was so entertained that I didn't have time to be envious or crave their drinks or something other than the gallons of Sprite I sipped on throughout the night. From a two-top table tucked in the back corner of the dive bar, I heard everything they talked about—which, holy shit, women had a lot to say—and could watch Baylee out of the corner of my eye without being too damn obvious.

Her revelation to the table about her and Dean never fucking wasn't a surprise. He'd mentioned it a time or two when we were still friends. Never with resentment or annoyance, just a blanket statement with a shrug. What was a shock, though, was that she hadn't moved on even once since his death.

Especially considering how the big-ass angry fucker acted around her. The two were clearly closer than friends. Dating, maybe, but not sleeping together.

Odd.

I raked my fingers through my hair, tugging at the long strands to distract me from the insistent urge to follow them. Tucking a hand deep into my black leather jacket pocket, I freed the pack of smokes. Cigarette filter pressed between my lips, I ignited the end. A moan rumbled in my chest at the first deep inhale, the tension keeping my shoulders up near my ears easing. I had sat inside the bar for over an hour observing Baylee and her friends to gather more intel on Baylee, then more to ensure no one harassed the table of chatty, clearly drunk women. I never once stepped out to smoke, hoping to stay as unnoticed as possible.

It worked until the one friend of hers texted her boyfriend. Or was it boyfriends, because she said she'd messaged two guys? Which made sense, I guess, after hearing bits and pieces of stories told by two of the women. It seemed the company most of them worked for and the community the owner built just outside town was very open-minded regarding the number of people in a committed relationship.

At one point, I almost got up and asked them where the sign-up sheet was to join.

Sucking in another drag, I ambled along the walkway toward the docks. Hips pressed to the wooden railing, I stared into the bay's dark, choppy water. That poly lifestyle was intriguing, and I ended up googling the gist of it on my phone. While it wasn't anything I'd ever taken part in, the idea of multiple partners centering on a single female was something I wouldn't be against. Hell, I dared hope for it a long time ago.

Back in high school, Dean talked about Baylee all the fucking time, so it was hard not to fall for the amazing woman, too, based on his stories. Plus, there were those times when she caught me watching them make out or hoping for a peek of what Dean's hand was doing beneath the blanket covering her lap. I never broached the subject of being added to their relationship, but I sure as hell daydreamed about how that conversation would go down and the fucking amazing things that would happen after they agreed.

I cocked my head to the side as a thought filtered through. Was that why she moved here in the first place, to be somewhere that accepted the unconventional lifestyle she wanted?

Lead formed in my gut while fear wrapped its tight fingers around my chest and squeezed. If she was already with the big angry fucker and others, did that mean she wouldn't consider me for... hell if even I knew how to finish that thought. I had no expectations when I came to Anchor Bay, just that I needed to be here to see her. Once I saw her picture, face squished next to a big fat cat, on her clinic website, I was packing for Alaska.

Now I just needed to grow a set and approach her. Let Baylee know how much I'd missed her, and him too.

Maybe that desperation to fill the space in my heart

where our close-knit friendship used to live was why I needed to come here. Seeing her even from a distance made that deep, vacant cavern inside me feel less bottomless somehow.

Palms to the railing, I pushed off and turned toward where I'd parked the borrowed Nest SUV. Passing by the bar, I took one last hit of the nearly spent cigarette and extinguished the lit end in a plastic bucket of sand by the door.

The weathered wood swung open, almost clipping my shoulder, making me stumble back. A man I recognized as one of the bar's employees stepped outside, hand already raised and lighting a cigarette dangling from his lips.

Seeing me, he paused, eyeing the tattoos along my skull and neck while holding the door open wide. Tempting scents and laughter poured out onto the walkway, begging me to step back into the bar for one drink. Not that it would ever be just one drink, and I wasn't ruining my sobriety now. Even still, my mouth watered at the thought of cold vodka sliding down my throat, calming the anxious energy that thrummed through my veins. I fisted both hands at my sides and shook my head to disrupt the tempting thoughts.

I stepped around the guy, who was still eyeing me with suspicion, and forced my feet to move down the wooden planks, hurrying to put distance between me and my ultimate temptation.

Almost two years sober was close, and I would not fuck up all that progress. Especially when the woman I couldn't stop fantasizing about was close as well. Baylee didn't know how far off track my life went years ago, the dark hole I barely clawed my way out of. I sure as hell didn't want to relapse into that self-destructive behavior for her or for me.

Tonight was what I needed, seeing Baylee and gauging

the woman she grew to be all these years later. She was exactly the same, though now a little more sadness darkened her smile.

It was time to man up and talk to her. To stop stalking her, daydreaming of approaching her and her reaction.

Tomorrow.

It had to be tomorrow before I lost the nerve and pushed it off another day. It was time to let her know I was here.

There was a ray of hope that bloomed within me after hearing about the poly community. A spark of anticipation flickered inside me that maybe, just fucking maybe, Baylee could be mine like in those dirty dreams I never confessed to anyone.

If I only had a sliver of someone like her, that would be enough for me. A piece of Baylee Smith in my life would be better than being on the outside, having to watch and witness what I was surely missing out on. Like I did those years with her and Dean.

No more waiting, no more watching.

Tomorrow was the day to step from the shadows.

My lips curled into a smile as I twirled the SUV keys around a single finger. Thankfully, I had the perfect plan.

## BAYLEE

The scent of something delicious yet sent my stomach rolling dragged me awake. I tried to swallow the bile slipping up my throat but couldn't with my desert-dry mouth. A thin sheen of sweat slicked every inch of my skin, the heat adding to the building nausea.

Desperate for a reprieve, I kicked off the too-heavy blankets, sighing when cool air swept across my damp cheeks. A combination grown and whimper escaped my cracked lips when I rolled to my side, the mattress dipping beneath me, praying the new position would ease my nausea. The pounding headache reminded me why eating while drinking, and not mixing alcohols, was a life lesson I learned a long time ago and should've abided by.

Lids squeezed shut, I slapped a hand over my eyes, hoping to erase the sun's bright rays peeking through the blinds that felt like ice picks to the brain. Tongue stuck to the roof of my mouth, I attempted to swallow in a desperate effort to generate a drop of moisture.

*Fucknuggets.*

*Did I eat sand or gravel at some point between the bar and...
wait, where am I?*

The waft of cooking food had my stomach growling, distracting me from that very important—and concerning that I didn't know the answer to—question.

My palm fell on the pillow, allowing the sunlight to pierce through my closed lids in my lame attempt to ease my eyes into what I knew needed to happen next. Almost like someone glued them shut while I slept, it took several attempts for me to peel both heavy lids open. After rubbing the heels of both hands against my eyes to clear my fuzzy vision, I relaxed when details of *my* room, not some stranger's, came into focus.

The metal bedframe creaked in protest when I flopped onto my back and stared at the ceiling while flickers of memories played like highlight footage of the embarrassing moments. This time, the sound that escaped was a true whimper from sheer humiliation. Why did I share all those personal and TMI things with my friends—and bonus, continue after Liam and the other guys showed up?

It was official. I only had two viable options.

Either allow this brutal hangover to kill me like I was almost certain it was or move out of the beautiful state so I would never have to face anyone from yesterday again. At least those were the only logical choices to avoid everyone from Anchor Bay.

Tossing a forearm over my eyes, I rolled my head side to side in slow, disapproving shakes at my dumb ass.

"What in the hell were you thinking, you oversharing twit?" My arm slid off, and I blinked at the ceiling. "Not only did you tell everyone in this tiny, gossipy town that you're a virgin, because fuck knows you said nothing quietly last night, but bonus"—I held up a single finger in the air—"you told the hottest man you've ever known and have a massive crush on that you wanted to lick him like a Tootsie Pop. Who says that?" I squeaked. "Unstable people, that's who. Fucking hell, woman, you should be put out to pasture where you can't embarrass yourself and others."

Squeezing my eyes shut, I attempted to remember any details after we left Dave's in Liam's truck, but I couldn't remember a single thing. Awesome.

Peeking open a single eyelid, I scanned the familiar bedroom and the empty spot beside me on the bed. A heavy weight sank in my stomach, and tears gathered in my lower lids. Why the hell was I disappointed that Liam wasn't here beside me?

That disappointment quickly morphed into pulse-racing anxiety. What if my oversharing and calling him a piece of candy displayed my brand of crazy like he'd never seen before, and he decided I wasn't worth it? Which would make sense, except the aroma of cooking meat told me someone was here, and who else would be cooking me breakfast but Liam? Maybe I was jumping to conclusions and Liam didn't leave me all alone last night, uncaring about my intoxicated state.

Elbows pressed into the soft mattress, I eyed the baby blue scrubs I clearly slept in. That meant Liam was either an utter gentleman and helped me to bed, not wanting me to feel vulnerable this morning knowing he undressed me, or he was so fucking annoyed at my drunk ass that he got me into bed and left.

I absentmindedly rubbed my cracked lips together. Liam leaving me dangerously drunk and alone didn't sound like something he would do, even if I was irritating as fuck in my inebriated state. So why would that scenario even come to mind?

Realization dawned even through the brain fog and lingering alcohol, making my brain sluggish.

Because in the past, that was the way Dean treated me and made me feel in comparable situations. In high school and during those breaks when I came home while in college, if we were together and I drank a little too much, Dean would ensure I got to bed safely, then leave to keep hanging out with our friends. My stomach soured at those memories of being alone and so sick or feeling like a burden who was just deposited in bed and left alone with the bare minimum of care given. Not sure why I just realized that when he did that, I subconsciously felt like an obligation instead of someone he loved or cherished.

Blowing out a heavy breath, which I immediately regretted when my toxic breath singed up my nose, I mustered up the energy to swing both legs out of the bed. As the tips of my toes brushed against the soft rug that protected my feet from the cold floor all year round, a loud, inhuman growl rumbled around the room and physically trembled my gut. Apparently, my stomach demanded that I locate the source of the yummy smells immediately. Greasy food would cure me like it had countless times in the past. Well, except for the mortification that would no doubt take a lifetime to recover from.

Grumbling under my breath about never drinking again, I raked my fingers through my long hair, wincing when they snagged on a rat's nest of tangles that somehow formed while I was passed out.

*Okay, first things first: Brush my teeth because my mouth is disgusting, then do something with my crazy hair before hunting down food.*

Palms to the mattress, I pushed off the bed and shuffled toward the adjoining bathroom. A flick of the switch doused the dark bathroom in light, and I instantly regretted the decision.

One look at my reflection made leaving Anchor Bay and never returning my only viable option. Fucking hell, it looked like I'd pulled all-nighters for a week straight. I scrambled away from the mirror, slapping at the light switch as if that would solve all my problems.

Thankfully, the sunlight pouring from the bedroom into the bathroom offered enough light that I was able to get ready without having to stare at my horrifying reflection. Waiting for the faucet water to heat, I brushed out my long hair with one hand and attacked my grimy teeth with the other, ensuring both were decent before cleaning up my raccoon eyes and smeared lipstick. By some Alaskan miracle, the lukewarm water I splashed on my face helped clear the lingering brain fog while the few sips straight from the faucet started to settle my rolling stomach.

Soft cotton absorbed the drops rolling down my cheeks and jaw as I patted my face dry. I glanced at my reflection and winced. I didn't look like death anymore, but I sure as hell didn't look great.

Knowing it was as good as it was going to get for now, I started for the kitchen, hoping my assumptions were right about Liam being the one cooking and not some random person. The hardwood floor chilled the bottoms of my bare feet, each step barely making a sound as I padded across the bedroom.

The second I opened the slightly ajar door, the delicious smell of bacon wafted over me. Fingers still gripping the knob, I squeezed my eyes shut and then opened them wide, fairly sure I was seeing things. Great things. Sexy things.

*Fuck, maybe I'm still passed out, and this is a dream.*

But no matter how many times I blinked, the scene in

front of me didn't change. The sexy-as-hell Liam was truly in my kitchen, an apron tied around his waist, standing in front of the stove and flipping sizzling bacon in a pair of Wranglers that hugged his oh-so-perfect ass and the red flannel shirt he had on last night, unbuttoned with no undershirt.

Gray eyes met mine and a smirk pulled at his lips, no doubt loving that he caught me staring. I wiped at my lower lip to make sure no drool had escaped since my mouth was literally hanging open while I eye-fucked him.

"Good morning." He chuckled when I winced at his loud, deep voice.

"Shhh, too loud," I rasped, allowing my fingers to slide off the doorknob as I shuffled toward the kitchen.

"I plugged in your phone last night; it's on the counter. Looked like you've missed a lot of unknown number calls." He eyed the phone with suspicion before looking up, his features softening. I could see the lingering questions he wanted to ask about the calls, his past making him wary not his trust in me. "How are you feeling?"

I gave him a thumbs-up at his lower volume and sighed in relief that he didn't push the missed calls. "Like death run over? That's the best way to describe it." Knowing food would make everything better, I sat on one of the two stools in front of the island. Elbows on the smooth concrete countertop, I propped my head up with a hand beneath my chin. "I am never drinking again."

Liam's soft laugh floated through the small kitchen. "That's the lie we tell ourselves, then forget the next time we're out having a good time with friends."

I slashed a hand through the air in disagreement. "No. I'm for real this time. One beer from here on out, that's it. Oh, and I'm never taking another duck fart shot again."

Feeling my stomach roll, I pressed a hand to my stomach to calm the fresh wave of nausea that the drink's name conjured.

With a slight shake of his head, Liam turned back to the stove, giving me a breather from his observant gaze.

"Hey, Liam?"

After setting aside the tongs, he turned, leaning against the counter, giving me his full attention. Fuck, why did that alone make me swoon?

"Yeah, Little Bit?"

I cleared my throat and shifted my focus to the fridge. "I'm drawing some blanks from last night. So, could you fill me in on what happened *after* we got in your truck?"

When I chanced a look, humor sparkled in his gray eyes and a smile slowly spread across his face. "Do you remember telling me you wanted to lick me like a Tootsie Pop?"

My features pinched with a wince. Yep, I totally remembered that part of my embarrassing verbal vomit. "That, yes, but nothing after."

His smile slipped as he scanned my face. "You really don't remember anything?"

"Not a single thing after you buckled me in and closed the door."

Liam's lips pressed into a tight line, and his dark brows pulled in tight. "Even without the suspicious shit going on around Anchor Bay, getting that drunk is dangerous, Baylee." Ah hell, he used my name. He must be really worried or pissed. "You're a grown woman. I won't tell you that you can't, and I'm not saying this to control you, but I want you to be safe." His hands tightened on the counter beside his hips. "I need you to be safe."

My heart stuttered at the worry in his tone and expression. "I know," I admitted, running a hand through my hair and gathering it into a low ponytail at the base of my neck while giving him a pleading look. "It was dumb. I 100 percent agree with you on that. But I really didn't expect yesterday to go the way it did. It wasn't smart, and I am definitely paying the consequences this morning."

His features softened as he released a heavy exhale. "Next time, just give me a heads-up. That way, I can be there to make sure you and your friends are protected while you have all the fun you want."

I swallowed down the urge to vomit. "There will be no next time. I'm never drinking again, remember?"

With a huff, he released the counter and turned back to the sizzling bacon. "You fell asleep in the truck and snored the entire drive home." His shoulders and back shook as if he was holding in laughter.

I gaped in a mix of annoyance and horror. "I did not! I do not snore."

"Passed-out Baylee does, apparently," he chuckled over his shoulder.

"I don't snore." Faking a pout, I folded both arms over my chest with an exaggerated huff.

"I carried you out of the truck and into your cabin—which was unlocked, I might add." A grumpy Liam shot a faux glare my way. "Got you into bed, took off your shoes, covered you up with a blanket, and sat in that girly-ass chair in the corner of your room to watch you sleep."

"Well, that's a little creepy."

Liam grinned and shook his head before twisting the knob on the stove, shutting off the burner. "I was worried you'd get sick and wanted to be there if you needed help."

Okay, well, that was sweet, not creepy. It was hard to wrap my head around the fact that he sat in that uncomfortable chair all night watching over me just to be close if I needed him. Liam wasn't annoyed or frustrated with my actions or crazy talk, nor did he just drop me off like a delivered package, fulfilling the obligation to take care of me, and leave to sleep in his own bed.

No, instead Liam gave up his own comfort and sleep for me.

Inhaling deeply to keep my swelling emotions in check, I stood from the stool and rounded the island to wrap my arms around his waist, pressing my forehead against his spine.

"Thank you," I whispered. "I'm sorry I was such a fucking mess that you had to—"

Liam whirled around, somehow keeping my arms where they were, so when he stopped, my cheek rested on his taut chest. "Baylee, I didn't *have* to do anything. And you're not a fucking mess." I huffed in disagreement and shook my head. "Okay, fine, maybe last night you were kind of a mess." I shifted, placing my chin on his sternum to look up into his gray eyes, finding him gazing down at me. "But you're *my* mess. My perfect, smart-as-hell, naïve, gorgeous mess."

Hot tears filled my lower lids at him claiming me as his —and his very inaccurate description of me. "I don't deserve you, Liam."

A large, hot palm cupped my cheek, thumb stroking along my skin. "I think you have it backward, Little Bit. You deserve the world, and I'll do everything I can to make sure you have it."

For several seconds, I stared up at his handsome face, memorizing every small scar until the moment was shattered by my stomach growling like a bear coming out of hibernation.

"And bacon," he said after planting a soft kiss on the top

of my head. "You deserve crispy bacon to help with that hangover I'm sure you're feeling. Though you're young enough that it won't last multiple days like it does for me now." Spinning me around, he guided me back around the island and easily lifted me to set me down on the stool I vacated earlier. "I wanted to make eggs, too, but there weren't any in the fridge. Hell, there isn't much of anything in there other than condiments, cookie dough, and some moldy fruit. When was the last time you went grocery shopping?"

I watched his movements like a hawk as he slid the perfectly cooked bacon from the sizzling pan onto a paper towel–covered plate. "Last week, the week before, maybe. I'm shocked I even had bacon, honestly." I pointed at the empty package on the counter with a wince. "Did you double-check the expiration date?"

The plate clinked against the concrete countertop, and a folded paper towel was placed beside it. Grabbing a piece, I broke it in half before shoving the fried goodness into my mouth, almost crying at how perfectly crispy it was.

Perfection. Absolute perfection.

Halfway through inhaling a third piece, its magic working instantly on my headache and upset stomach, I realized he hadn't said anything. Peering up through my lashes, I caught him watching with a satisfied smile on his face.

"Now you enjoy watching me sleep *and* eat?" I tsked, pointing a piece of bacon at him. "I'm sticking with my creepy comment from earlier."

His barked laugh had a smile growing as I chewed.

"Yes, I checked the expiration date. You know I wouldn't serve you something that could hurt you."

Pinching a piece between two fingers, he held it up to my

lips and arched a brow in silent command for me to take a bite. Our eyes locked. I pitched forward on the stool to seal my lips around the food, barely grazing his skin. His heated stare followed me as I leaned back, tracking the movement as I chewed and swallowed.

Maybe I was still a little drunk, or his all-consuming, desire-filled stare just had that dazed effect on me. Before his hand dropped, I wrapped my fingers around his wrist and guided the grease-coated digits close, sealing my lips around the tips.

"Holy fuck," he rasped, lids hooded.

He dared a step closer, only for the moment to shatter at a sharp squeak, followed by the distinct scratch of tiny claws on the hardwood floor. Sighing at the poor timing of my little friend, I sat back on the stool and turned to watch the slinky white ball of fur dashing around the living room.

"BamBam," I called out as the ermine I rescued as a baby skidded to a stop near my feet. "The reason I had bacon." I scooped him off the floor with one hand and placed him on my lap, where he immediately lifted onto his back feet, sticking his nose toward the last piece.

Before I could snag the meat for the hungry little guy, Liam snatched it off the plate with a disapproving expression aimed at BamBam.

"Don't worry, I saved him a few raw slices." He tilted the piece of bacon in my direction in silent question. At my headshake, he pushed it between his lips, chewing as he moved toward the fridge. When he turned back around, shutting the metal door with his hip, he held BamBam's dish piled full of raw bacon. The ermine practically vibrated with excitement.

Acting more like a relative to a flying squirrel than a weasel, BamBam leapt off my lap, diving toward the meal waiting for him in the dish Liam set on the floor. A small smile curled the corners of my lips as I watched him attack his food, remembering when I found him as a baby, injured and abandoned in the snow. It was by luck that I caught his slight movement that morning when pausing to stretch along my normal running trail. After I nursed him back to health and mothered the shit out of the little guy, he refused to leave.

Which I was totally okay with. It was nice having something to look after that was somewhat my own. I wasn't to the point of delusion in my grief that I thought I could truly own and tame a wild animal like BamBam, but I rejoiced every day when he came back to me—even if deep down, I knew it was just for the easy food supply. What animal wouldn't want their food delivered to them in a porcelain dish instead of hunting for hours in the cold?

The sound of the water running pulled my attention to where Liam stood in front of the sink, washing the dishes and utensils he used. Shaking my head, smile wide, I hopped off the stool and padded across the cold floor.

"I'll do that," I admonished, snuggling up against his side. "You cooked, I clean. That's how it works, right?"

His returning sweet grin made my heart hammer painfully in my chest and my stomach do this weird flutter thing that seemed to happen a lot around him. This massive man who towered over me and could snap me in half with hardly any effort, a literal badass from his fighting days and military training, was the sweetest, most considerate man I'd ever met.

Even more than Dean.

That disparaging thought about my late fiancé had the awe of my sweet giant evaporating, leaving me hollow like it always did. But something was different this morning. As I watched his massive hands gently wash the fragile plate decorated with blue flowers and vibrant birds, the sadness and guilt lifted almost as quickly as it appeared.

I was different. Stronger, maybe, was the right feeling. There must have been healing magic in those drinks, or maybe it was the hours of talking through my jumbled feelings out loud with friends, but this morning I *wanted.*

Wanted him and not the sorrow that had clung to me like a second skin.

Wanted hope and not regret.

Yesterday tipped me over that edge from surviving to truly moving on.

Gazing up at his handsome face, I couldn't resist tracing a finger along his scruff-covered jaw. Those gray eyes cut my way, scanning my face. For what, I wasn't sure. All I knew was the overwhelming desire and need to show this man how much I appreciated him, wanted him, was too much to ignore.

Like I had done for weeks now. Why? I could blame it on the heartache that still weighed heavy on my soul, but that wasn't all of it.

Fear.

Fear of letting myself fall for someone again, giving away what was left of my heart. That thought was terrifying. There was also the dread of his rejection, of me not being enough, and of allowing this feeling welling in my chest to swallow me whole, forever changing me.

After last night's drunken confessions, acting like an idiot, and Liam still being here this morning taking care of me, wanting me despite my actions and words, I was done being afraid. Tired of running from...

Actually living and not just surviving.

This wasn't a switch that had flipped, cutting off the

trauma that held me back before. This healing process was a winding road that would be filled with setbacks and mountains to climb. And that was okay because I knew, after yesterday with my friends and this morning with him, I had company on the difficult journey.

It might be a long road, but I wasn't walking it alone.

# 8

## LIAM

The soft brush of her fingertips caressing along my jaw and throat sent heat surging through my veins. My lids fluttered closed as I inhaled deeply, hoping it would help strengthen my fraying restraint. After her dirty revelations and analogies of wanting to lick me like a piece of candy, I was left with the worst case of blue balls. Which meant I was keyed the fuck up, and her simple yet intimate-as-hell touch pushed me toward my breaking point. If she wasn't careful, Baylee would find those wrinkled scrub pants ripped off, her chest sealed to the counter, and my dick buried balls-deep in her virgin cunt.

Fuck.

I swallowed down the desperate groan that thought alone had rumbling in my chest.

I never gave a shit about a woman's sexual past—fuck knew I didn't want anyone judging me because of mine—but knowing her tight little pussy had never been stretched wide with a cock, that it was no doubt soft and snug, almost had me coming in my damn jeans.

Fingers gripping the counter until every knuckle went

white in an effort to keep from grabbing Baylee and playing out all the dirty fantasies I'd imagined over the last few weeks, I leaned into her touch, savoring the scrape of her short nails through my rough facial hair.

"What are you doing, Little Bit?" I somehow got out around gritted teeth.

A mischievous gleam flashed in her big blue eyes, making my cock twitch uncomfortably. A single finger changed course to trace along my lower lip in soft strokes. Back and forth with her gaze locked with mine, that tempting motion unraveled me faster than I could fight back the temptation.

Unable to stop, I dipped my chin so that a single digit slipped between my parted lips, then nipped at the tip before licking away the slight bite.

Her soft gasp only spurred me on.

Gripping her delicate wrist in a firm but tender hold, I guided her finger free. "What do you want, Baylee?" I asked while directing that slick digit to her own mouth and pushing it inside to the second knuckle.

Seeing her lips wrap around her finger, cheeks hollowing as she sucked, I fucking snapped. Releasing my hold, I gripped her narrow waist and hauled her up onto the counter, pushing her knees wide so I could step between them. Palms to her soft cheek, I cupped her face, angling it higher until glassy blue eyes met mine. "I'm a strong man, Baylee, but even I have a limit to my restraint. I refuse to hurt you by pushing you too fast, further than you're comfortable."

I sealed my lips to hers, sucking on the soft, plump flesh and taking a quick nip before pulling back and standing tall. "I don't trust myself with you right now, so I'm going to go before I do, fuck, all the erotic fantasies I've fucked my hand to lately that you're not ready for."

Forcing myself to turn, I ripped off the apron, tossing it onto the island, and took one reluctant stride away from the ultimate temptation—only to pause at the feel of a tiny hand gripping my forearm. I squeezed my lids shut, nostrils flaring with a deep inhale, before I looked over my shoulder at the little temptress who had no idea what demanding beast she was teasing to the surface.

"Don't go," she murmured, a slight plea in her tone. "I don't want you to leave just yet."

Blowing out a controlled breath through pursed lips, I gave in to her request despite my better judgment. Her small hand slid to my wrist when I turned to face her, this time keeping some distance between us for my sanity.

I wouldn't hurt Baylee—hell, I wouldn't hurt any woman —but I was afraid the need pumping through my veins would make me hear meaning in her words that maybe wasn't there. That was the last thing I wanted, to think she wanted me to fuck her against the counter when she only wanted company, not her pussy stretched around my thick cock....

*Fuck.*

Face tipped to the ceiling, I forced those thoughts to the back of my mind to deal with later when I was alone in the shower.

"Little Bit." Her pet name was more of a pained hiss than words. "If you don't want this to go any further than me hanging out so you're not alone, then—"

"What if I don't?" she said, cutting me off. Pressing her small feet to the floor, she moved forward until she stood right in front of me, looking up with those innocent blue eyes. I swallowed a groan as my cock hardened to the point of actual pain. "What if I want it to be more than just hanging out?"

Two cold palms pressed to my bare stomach, exposed by the unbuttoned shirt I'd tossed on earlier. My abs flexed at the gentle caress, breath hitching as she slid her hands higher, exploring my chest all while never looking away from my heated stare.

"You need to be specific on what 'more' means to you, Baylee." I swallowed hard. "*Very* specific."

"I don't know how to be brave, to talk about this without alcohol," she admitted, blush staining her fair cheeks. The tip of her tongue swiped along her lower lip. "Be patient with me, okay?"

I nodded. "Are you wanting me to take the lead? Because I'll be honest, I will take until you tell me to stop. I want it all, sweetheart. All you're willing to give me."

Her lips parted as her breathing grew erratic. Instead of responding, she let her hands drop, making me hold back a pathetic pout, and turned to tiptoe toward her room. I followed the sway of her ass the entire way, only looking up when she stopped at the doorframe.

My muscles bunched with the need to close the distance between us, to rip off her clothes and take and take and take. To taste every inch of her amazing body, imprint the feel of my cock buried so deep inside her cunt that she'd always feel fucking stuffed full even when I wasn't there, making her scream my name.

"Liam." I jerked out of the fantasy, finding her smiling at me with a knowing look, as if she knew exactly what I was thinking. "Are you coming?"

*Fucking hopefully.*

"Where?" That was the safer and smarter response.

With a smirk, she disappeared into her room, crooking a

single finger over her shoulder for me to follow. Which I immediately did like a trained dog following its owner's command.

Paused at the entrance to her bathroom, she spun to face where I stood, hands gripping the doorframe above my head. I needed that grounding, feeling the wood creaking beneath my hold, until I knew exactly what she wanted from me.

"I need to get ready for work, and I'm pretty sure you didn't shower last night since you were babysitting me."

More like watching her sleep like a fucking crazy person, imagining sleeping beside her, curled up against her, feeling her soft body molded against my hard muscles.

I missed that the most about marriage.

The comfort of holding the one you loved in your arms all night, protecting them and keeping them safe. There was a peace that came with feeling them beside you, breathing deeply in sleep, knowing they were okay. A good fuck was easy to come by, but that, the intimacy that came with holding someone, only came with a genuine connection.

"So, what do you say?" she asked. The hesitancy in her tone snapped my gaze from her unmade bed to where she stood, fingers twisting nervously in front of her stomach.

"To what?" I hedged, not wanting to put words in her mouth. "I need you to be very clear about what you're wanting, sweetheart."

Baylee's head tipped toward the bathroom behind her. "Showering." I followed the movement as her throat worked with a hard swallow. "With me."

Every muscle bunched, and my lungs froze. "Showering with you," I clarified. "To...."

Get clean?

Get dirty?

Break me into a weeping baby at seeing her perfect naked body and not being able to worship it the way I desperately wanted?

Fucking hell, I was pathetic.

"Well, I was hoping to repay you for being so sweet last night and—"

I dropped a hand from the doorframe and swiped it through the air, cutting her off right the fuck there. "If I ever," I growled, my bubbling anger burning through the earlier desire, "hear you say you need to repay me for making sure you were safe or taking care of you, I will spank your fine ass so fucking hard you won't remember what it's like to sit without those sweet cheeks stinging."

A flush spread along her throat and crept over her cheeks.

"Oh, yeah, okay. But that was easier to say out loud than actually admitting what I want," she said, shifting her gaze to the side like she was embarrassed.

In three quick strides, I was in front of her, cupping her face in one hand with enough pressure to make her look up at me.

"You're an amazing woman, Baylee. Smart, beautiful, kind, and so fucking strong to survive what you have and still find the strength to smile every damn day. Tell me what you want. Be brave for me, and I'll give it to you. I can guarantee you there isn't anything you'll ask of me that I won't do or find a way to."

She squeezed her eyes shut. "Okay."

"Eyes on me, sweetheart. No hiding from this, from me."

Both lids popped open as she exhaled. "I want you in the shower with me."

"That's my girl. Now tell me—"

"With me on my knees." *Oh fuck.* I almost swallowed my

tongue. "And your fingers in my hair." Damnit, I was seconds from coming in my jeans like a teenager. "Your dick in my mouth—"

I couldn't take another dirty word from her sweet lips. Bending forward, I captured her mouth with mine, thrusting my tongue inside as I urged her backward until her spine pressed against the glass shower door. Her hands snuck between us, fingers fisting the sides of my shirt as I yanked at my belt, the clink of the metal echoing around the bathroom.

"Are you sure?" I asked, lips moving against hers, unable to fully pull away.

"Yes," she rasped.

Hands on my shoulders, she pushed the soft flannel down my arms until it fell free, pooling at my feet. Her fingers tangled with mine as we worked the top button free of my jeans. When she started tugging at the zipper, I stopped her with a firm hold around both wrists in one hand and stretched her arms high above her head.

"I think that's enough until we shed some of your clothes."

A soft, dark chuckle escaped at her eager nod. Her hooded gaze slowly scanned my broad chest, no doubt taking in the various scars that littered my golden skin. A flash of hesitancy came and went, knowing she was so much younger, innocent and perfect. I was all hard muscles with scars that spoke to the tough and violent life I'd lived.

"Oh my goodness, you're so hot," Baylee rasped. Her gaze slid up to mine. "I'll admit I'm nervous."

"About?"

"Look at you," she said, nodding to my bare chest. "You're older, more experienced, sexy as sin, and then there's me."

"You mean perfect?"

"I'm not perfect, Liam."

"True, no one is, but I'm sure you're damn close. Now let me get back to unwrapping you like the gift you are."

Releasing my hold on her wrists, I fisted the hem of her scrub top and worked it over her head. A desperate groan rattled in my chest at the sight of her small tits spilling from the top of a snug sports bra.

"I know it's not fancy lingerie. I didn't know—"

"Damnit, Baylee," I hissed, making her wince. I shook my head hard to cool my temper. "Will you stop talking about yourself that way, like you're not living up to every fantasy of mine by just being you and allowing me to be here with you?"

Seconds ticked by with her simply staring up at me with wide eyes.

"Really?"

"Really what?"

"Me, like this, is enough?"

"Yes, sweet girl. Even if you have on granny panties"— her soft giggle took the hot edge off my temper—"haven't shaved in weeks, or whatever else you think makes you not desirable to me. I'll still be here feeling like I won the damn lottery that I'm the man here with you."

There was no way I could've expected what she'd do next. It actually took me a second after her knees hit the tile floor to react.

"Baylee—"

"This is what I want." She shook her head as she unzipped my jeans and worked them down my hips. "No. This is what I *need* right now. Please." She stared up at me with a pleading expression on her petite face.

A firm tug on the stiff denim made my very hard and

leaking cock pop free. Her tiny hand wrapped around me, making me hiss. With a smirk, she ran her tongue along her lips, wetting the plump skin, and then pressed a kiss to the crown, licking the precum dripping from the slit.

"I like that you go commando. Something I'll be thinking about every time I see you from now on."

"Fuck," I groaned, head tossed back as I fought the urge to shift forward until I was buried in her throat.

"Soon," she said while licking around my crown. Stars sparkled behind my lids as I worked to not come on her face. "But not today. We'll work up to that."

At her pause, I forced my lids open to gaze down. Damn, she was a glorious sight—on her knees with my dick in her hand, lips barely brushing against the sensitive skin.

"Okay?" she said softly.

Running a hand through her hair, I fisted it in a makeshift ponytail at the base of her skull. "I'd wait forever and a day just to have you in my arms, Little Bit. This is all just a fucking bonus. But one thing." Blonde brows shot up in question as she sucked me between her lips, smirking at my groan and the rattle of the glass shower door when I slapped my hand to the smooth surface. "Lose it." I hitched my chin at her sports bra. "I want to see your tits while my cock is down your throat."

My disgruntled grumble echoed through the room as she sat back on her heels to do as I asked, causing my dick to pop free from her lips. With a quick tug and some wiggling, the bra dropped to the floor, exposing her peaked pink nipples to the cool air.

"Grip your heels," I rasped while fisting my cock and squeezing until a hiss pushed through my clenched teeth. "Pull your shoulders back so those tits are on full display for me." When she did as I ordered—which was a whole different turn-on—I worked my hand up and down my shaft in slow strokes, imagining painting her chest with my cum. "While my cock is in your mouth, I want you playing with those needy nipples."

Her desperate whimper had me smirking.

"Now, sit up." She immediately obeyed, making me almost purr in delight. "Good girl." I threaded my fingers through her white-blonde strands, fisting a handful tight enough to make her lips pop open on a gasp. "This is what you want?" I arched a brow, letting her know it wasn't a rhetorical question.

"Yes," she pleaded.

"Then open wide, sweetheart."

Her lips widened in the most erotic invitation I'd ever seen.

Inch by inch, I slid into her hot mouth, gliding along her tongue. I sucked down gulps of cold air to keep from losing control and fucking her mouth hard. It would happen soon —maybe not today or tomorrow, but I would take her devilish mouth hard and fast, slipping down her throat at some point.

Using my hold on her hair, I guided her forward and back, keeping pace with my own thrusts while her fingers plucked and twisted at her tight nipples. Teeth sunk into my lower lip, I kept my gaze locked on her mouth, savoring and memorizing the way it stretched around my thick cock. After only a minute of her very talented tongue and hot mouth pushing me closer and closer to the edge, a familiar zing raced down my spine, right to my balls.

I sucked in a breath. My rhythm turned frantic and aggressive as I chased that high only a mind-blowing orgasm could give someone.

"Fuck, I'm going to come. If you don't want me to—"

Her hands gripped my ass, nails digging into both cheeks, cutting my words off as that little bite of pain shot me straight over the edge with a barked curse. My grip tightened in her hair while I fucked her mouth with utter desperation as my orgasm rocked through me, keeping the demanding pace until she'd milked every drop of cum from me.

Chest heaving with my chaotic breaths, sweat slicking my bare chest and back, I watched in wonder as the tiny beauty swiped a few missed drops from her lips before licking her finger clean.

"Damn," I rasped, throat dry and scratchy. "Hot damn, woman."

Desperate to touch her, feel her in my arms, I gripped her shoulders, lifting till her bare feet pressed to the tile floor, immediately sealing my mouth to hers.

"I taste good on your lips," I murmured while kissing along her jaw. "I bet your hot cunt will be fucking addicting."

Circling an arm around her waist, I crushed her bare tits against my chest while my free hand worked the elastic band of her pants over her hips until they slipped to the floor and pooled at her feet. My jeans were a little more difficult, as they had fallen around my shins, but a few kicks freed one leg, followed by the other, and I flung the denim across the bathroom.

Her plump lips sucked and kissed along my chest, a light bite sneaking in every so often, making my cock stir to life again. Fuck, this woman was even more tempting in real life than in my fantasies. Wrenching the glass shower door open, almost ripping it off its feeble hinges, I turned the handle to heat the frigid water that sputtered from the showerhead.

Soft skin slid against my own as I eased my hold around her lithe frame. My knees cracked when I squatted. With an almost feral growl, I pulled one stiff peak between my lips, sucking while flicking my tongue against the tip. Her beautiful gasp echoed around the small room. Blunt nails scraped along my scalp as she urged me even closer to her chest.

Teasing her other tit with my fingers, I pinched and pulled at the stiff nipple while looking up through my lashes, watching the way her face tensed and relaxed with the mix of pleasure and pain. I released her with a loud pop to kiss my way down her flat stomach, pausing at the edge of her pale pink panties.

Her delicious scent had me burying my nose between her thighs and inhaling a lungful, focusing on memorizing the smell of her arousal. My dick, once again hard and ready, twitched, tapping against my inner thigh. Fuck, I wanted to lick her, to suck down every drop waiting for me behind the thin cotton, but first I needed to ensure we were still on the same page.

"You good with me eating your pussy, licking you clean, and fingering your tight virgin hole?" Damn, saying it out loud had cum leaking out.

Her loose blonde hair slid over her shoulders as she looked down at me and gave an eager nod.

"Good girl." With a mumbled curse, her head tipped toward the ceiling, causing her hair to cascade between her shoulder blades. "After I take these off, my plan is to eat this sweet pussy here and in the shower until the water runs cold."

That had her head snapping forward. Wide, glassy eyes stared down at me. "I have one of those endless hot water tanks, like your cabin."

My smile turned devilish. "Oh, sweet Baylee. I am well aware of that."

The ultra-soft cotton slid along my thumbs as I hooked them on the sides of her panties and tugged. They slipped down her narrow hips, thighs, and calves. Offering my hand for assistance, I helped her step out of the drenched cotton before tossing the damp material over my shoulders toward my jeans. You'd better believe those were going home with me after all this. I knew after being this close to her drenched core, her smell embedded in my lungs, that I'd need that scent close to me at all times.

Creepy? Maybe, but fuck if I cared.

Tongue rolled tight, I slipped it between her soaked lips and slowly dragged it upward, capturing the evidence of how fucking turned on my girl was after sucking my dick dry.

My girl. Fuck yes, she was, especially now that I'd tasted her.

Swallowing her delectable flavor, I spread both lips apart with my thumbs to suck on her swollen nub like I did her nipples.

"Liam," she cried out, hand pressed against the back of my head, pushing me closer to her hot center. "Please."

The desperation in her tone snapped the last thread of restraint I had. With an almost guttural groan, I flicked my tongue against her clit, knowing she was close. Then I teased the opening of her pussy before pushing a thick finger inside.

My cock jerked, anticipating the day I'd feel those hot, snug walls wrapped around me. In and out, I slid the single digit while driving her need higher until both legs trembled and her hips bucked into my face.

At her loud gasp, I buried my finger deep in her pussy,

stroking that magical spot, making her scream as she pulsed around it. Only when she slumped against the steamed glass, flushed chest heaving, did I reluctantly pull free.

Hooded eyes gazed down, only to widen at my hard cock bobbing between my thighs. A feral smile tugged at my lips as I gripped my stiff shaft tight and gave it a slow pump.

"Don't worry, sweetheart. I won't destroy your cunt today with this. But we're just getting started on all the other ways I want to hear you scream."

My needs would wait forever if necessary. Getting my girl off, hearing her scream my name and knowing I did that, was the only thing that mattered in life going forward.

# 9

## MEMPHIS

Tucked between two colorful, though weather-beaten, businesses that lined the small downtown street, I raised the nearly spent cigarette to my lips, full focus on the familiar Ford truck idling in front of Baylee's clinic, where it had sat for the last two minutes. With the sun barely cutting through the billowing gray clouds, it was difficult to see the two people inside the cab, making my imagination run wild with possibilities. My free hand groped at my stiffening cock as the mental porno of what they could be doing in there played on repeat, each scene even more vivid and erotic than the last.

I wasn't attracted to men, or at least never had been before, but there was always a blistering heat that filled my veins those times I had watched Dean and Baylee making out. Now, after seeing her with the new guy, their size difference alone made it a fucking turn-on to imagine them together. Knowing Baylee was as innocent as she seemed, just waiting to be corrupted in all the right ways, added to the fantasy.

Shifting my weight, I angled an ear toward the truck,

straining to hear any moans or even sounds of distress. It was obvious last night that the big fucker was her boyfriend, or at least wanted to be, and someone she was comfortable with, which was why I wasn't storming up to the driver's door and pulling the asshole out onto the sidewalk. What I would do after that, hell if I knew. The guy was scary as fuck, which made me wonder why that drew me in. Anyone who watched him for half a second could tell he knew how to handle himself. It was the way he moved with purpose and ease. Add in his height and stacked build....

*Damn, am I into guys?*

A low growl at my side snapped my focus down to Elvis, brows pulled in tight. He never growled. Elvis was the happiest fucking dog you'd ever meet, which meant something was very off. Sitting absolutely still, his intense gaze was locked down the wooden walkway in the opposite direction of the truck. I scanned the darkened alleys and alcoves, hiding places similar to the one I stood in, searching for what the hell had set him off.

Another low growl rumbled from his chest, and he stood on all fours, the fur along his spine standing on end.

"What the hell do you sense?" I muttered under my breath, gaze flicking between my tense-as-fuck dog and the direction his head was trained. Unease filled my chest as I watched the few people dipping in and out of the various storefronts. A dangerous chill raced down my spine and had me reaching for the knife secured to my thick belt.

Lungs tight with a final inhale, I dropped the spent butt to the crumbling asphalt and ground it beneath the heel of my black combat boot.

A soft, lyrical laugh jerked my focus back to the truck, where a tiny bundle of sunshine leapt out of the cab. Her tennis shoes slapped the pavement, and she wavered on her feet, grasping at the hard metal edge of the door to keep her upright. My stomach jumped at the thought of her slipping, falling to the wet street and hurting herself, but she stayed standing, turning to shoot a wide smile and a few words I couldn't hear over her shoulder before slamming the door closed.

I continued to watch, hand gently running across the top of Elvis's head to calm my racing pulse.

The truck idled until Baylee disappeared into her clinic with a last wave. Even still, the driver waited a full minute before pulling away from the curb and heading out of town. I watched until it disappeared from view, hating that she had someone so focused on her safety who wasn't me, but also appreciating that the man was diligent in watching over her.

Anxiety about the approaching appointment had me pulling another cigarette free from the hard pack. I stuck it between my lips, lighting the end while inhaling deeply. The past month had all led up to this pivotal moment. The uncertainty around the outcome suddenly felt too much. Waiting a few more days, watching from the shadows while not knowing if she'd reject me—or hell, even remember me —was almost more enticing than showing up for Elvis's appointment and finally knowing how she would react.

Even before seeing her picture on her website, Baylee had always been in my thoughts. It was the memories of our friendship and the hope of having her in my life that kept me from pouring a drink or returning the calls of my previously well-used dealers during my bad days while in rehab and after. If I didn't have that hope, I wasn't sure what would happen to me. Not that I'd ever tell her and put that pressure on her. Fucking never. She didn't need to know that the memories of our friendship and the few times I saw her when she came to visit during college were what I clung to during my darkest moments. The thought of being a man who deserved her one day helped me get sober so that maybe I would be in this exact spot at some point, begging for the opportunity to be a part of her life.

It was heavy shit, but Baylee was my light then and continued to shine brightly even during all these years apart. Now here I was, hoping for a chance. So much balanced on this, and fuck, now that I was yards from the woman of my dreams...

I just wanted to run away like a coward.

As if sensing my building anxiety and worry, Elvis shifted to put his full weight against my leg in unspoken support. I smiled down at my best friend, finding his gaze still locked down the street, but his demeanor had returned to his happy, relaxed self. I knew for a fact that Elvis was an excellent judge of character. He hated all my so-called friends who had only hung around for the drugs and booze, and the dealers who stopped by late at night to offer a variety of fixes for any mood I found myself in. So whatever had him raising the alarm was bad.

Really fucking bad.

For that kind of reaction, I had to wonder if something or someone who radiated evil was too close for comfort. Either way, that response from him meant I needed to be on alert.

My gaze slid back to the vet clinic door, the glowing red Open sign now blinking brightly in the overcast light.

If there was someone or something evil out there lurking around Anchor Bay, then this meeting had to happen. No backing out and trying to find my balls again tomorrow. It had to be today so I could be there for Baylee, protect her from whatever threat Elvis sensed.

Sure, she had that big fucker, but someone like Baylee needed all the protection she could get.

She was perfect.

She was innocent.

Though that last part I couldn't help but groan at, imagining all the ways I wanted to defile that innocence. On my own or with her boyfriend. I was game either way as long as she was safe and satisfied. And if she only gave me a chance, I knew I could give her both.

Only time would tell if I'd leave Anchor Bay brokenhearted and head back to a life of using and drinking or stick around the somewhat picturesque town with her as a friend, or maybe in my arms and bed.

If that included that boyfriend of hers too...

Maybe then I'd finally have a relationship that would last.

## 10

## BAYLEE

I blinked at the computer screen, reading the same schedule that I'd been staring at for the last ten minutes. Who knew multiple orgasms by one man's talented tongue and fingers could scramble one's brain like this.

I sure as hell didn't.

Until now at least. Which was crazy, since Dean and I weren't completely innocent when we were together. Many times he'd done just as Liam, yet the results were vastly, magnanimously different. And I sure as hell didn't remember feeling like my brain was scrambled eggs after. Did that mean Liam was that much more talented than Dean, being older and having more experience?

I ground my back teeth as a flash of jealousy flickered at the thought of Liam giving that kind of pleasure to someone else despite knowing the reality. He was married once and had multiple partners before me.

I just didn't want to think about it.

The truth was, Dean and I *were* so young, together since high school, so maybe that was the difference between my lackluster response then and explosive reaction now. He hadn't had time or multiple previous partners to grow his skill set like Liam. Which somewhat made me feel like shit for comparing them, considering my insides were still turned inside out from the mind-blowing orgasms he pulled from me hours ago.

Soul-shattering, knee-weakening orgasms that Liam easily wrenched from me.

That alone was a shock. There were many times when Dean and I had fooled around that I never fully got off, just enjoyed the overall experience of playing with him. Back then, I assumed there was something wrong with me, but now I wasn't sure.

Guilt filled my chest with the familiar dull ache. With a hard headshake, the tip of my ponytail flicking back and forth, I shoved those negative feelings away. Not now, not today. I wouldn't allow my regrets and past to diminish what Liam and I did before the shower, during the shower, and again after we were clean by feeling guilty about it. I could move forward with my life and still miss Dean. Those two did not have to be mutually exclusive.

Or so I hoped.

Blowing out a steadying breath to clear my mind of those distracting thoughts, I rubbed the heels of both hands against my eyes and refocused on the schedule for the day. It was a light one, thankfully, because I had little energy after waking up hungover, stuffing my face with crispy bacon, and then, well, the aerobic shower.

The first appointment was someone visiting Anchor Bay and his companion coming in for a basic wellness visit. Why he couldn't wait until he went back home, I wasn't sure, but I would do the checkup all the same. It was a nice change of pace, like the husky I saw a few days ago before he and his owner went out on the trail, considering most of the locals didn't bring their animals in for regular care, only basic vaccines or if they were injured.

Grabbing a new patient chart from the file cabinet, I slid the paperwork inside. Once everything was ready, I pushed off the armrests to stand only for black spots to dot my vision.

The entire room spun, and my hearing faded. I stumbled to the desk and gripped the edge to keep me on my feet. I squeezed both lids shut and opened them wide several times, hoping it would help remedy the unexpected wave of dizziness.

Between the lingering hangover and the active morning, my equilibrium must've been off. That was the only logical explanation. I ate more for breakfast than I had in months and was on my second Stanley of water for the morning.

Vision back to normal and balance restored, I grabbed the file once again and moved to the exam room to get it ready for the first patient. Lost in the list of things that could've caused the random dizzy spell, I almost missed the ring from the bell above the front door.

*Time to get to work.* Slipping on a clean lab coat, I headed for the front to meet my first patient.

Focus on the chart, I started to welcome the client to Anchor Bay, but the words froze in my throat when I finally glanced up, finding the hottest real-life bad boy standing in the middle of the room. My brain went offline, and my lungs forgot their one job, making a stalled breath burn in my chest. I swallowed hard, hoping that would kick me out of my frozen state.

My calculated, slow inspection started at his edgy dirty-blond hair, the long portion on top slicked back, exposing the tightly shaved sides. An eyebrow ring snagged my focus to his mint-green eyes that swirled with so many emotions, I had the urge to drop the chart and hug him until he couldn't breathe. With a broad nose, full lower lip that shone like he'd been licking it, and sharp jawline, he was a perfect balance of masculinity with a dash of softness that clashed with the dark tattoos decorating his skin.

The detailed designs curved down his neck, shifting as his Adam's apple bobbed with a thick swallow. He wore a lightweight Army green jacket that didn't appear nearly warm enough for the cooler morning and a black shirt beneath. Dark wash jeans hung on his narrow hips and hugged his thick thighs, the bottoms tucked into unlaced black combat boots. His style was a unique mix of edgy grunge and trendy that you'd never see around Anchor Bay.

As I was checking out his cool-as-hell boots, the other set of feet—paws, rather—caught my attention. Apparently, I was too busy ogling the owner to notice the gorgeous yellow lab sitting beside him, tail swishing along the lobby floor.

Clearing my suddenly dry throat, I slid my gaze back to the man's, casually wiping at the corner of my mouth since it was literally hanging open. When our gazes met, unexpected recognition swirled. I squinted as if that would help place the stranger. My heart squeezed painfully, almost making me gasp, but I didn't understand why. This time I scanned his striking face to determine how I knew him rather than admiring his sharp, model-like features.

When I came up blank, I shook my head in annoyance with myself and forced a smile, clutching the chart to my chest.

"Hi, welcome in. I'm the veterinarian here, Dr. Baylee Smith, but please call me Baylee." I couldn't help but gawk at the sexy-as-hell tattooed hand and fingers he stretched out between us. Swallowing hard, I slid my much smaller hand into his and squeezed before pulling back quickly. My heart raced, breaths turning choppy at the small touch, which made little sense.

When he didn't offer his name, which I had already forgotten even though it was on the appointment booking, I turned a strained grin to his adorable companion. Finding the large yellow lab practically smiling at me, my own turned genuine, the tension and confusion melting away.

"And who do we have here?" I squatted low, putting my face right in front of his.

"Elvis."

I shivered at the mysterious man's deep voice. Tipping my chin up, I found him staring at me with an intense expression that I didn't understand.

*Shit, maybe too many orgasms scrambled my brain.*

*Oh well, it was worth it.*

Another wave of recognition, a little tickle in the back of my brain hit me then, making my smile drop.

"Do I know you?" I asked before I could stop. Fingertips to the floor, I pushed to stand. "Sorry, I just... it feels like...." I stared at him, slowly shaking my head in confusion. "Anyway, sorry, I'm not feeling great this morning—"

A squeak escaped, and I clutched the folder tighter to my chest when he cleared the distance between us in a single step. The toes of his boots stopped a centimeter from the tips of my tennis shoes. Staring at his chest, I tipped my face up, finding his green eyes full of concern.

"What's wrong?" he murmured, hand hovering beside my face as if tempted to touch me.

"What?" I breathed. I was certain I should feel uncomfortable or scared with a stranger standing so close, but I didn't. I really, really didn't. The way my pulse raced, and my stomach trembled with desire and not unease spoke to a very different feeling than fear. If I had more than a few seconds to process it all, I'd probably feel terrible at being attracted to the stranger after my morning with Liam.

"You said you were sick. What can I do? Do you need to sit down?"

Before I knew what was happening, his hand pressed to my lower back, and I was guided to a basic plastic chair in the waiting room. Eyes still locked on his, I lowered into the seat, and he followed, crouching in front of where I sat.

"What is going on?" I couldn't even react when he grabbed my wrist, pressing two fingers to my pulse while lifting his other wrist, exposing a traditional watch.

"Tell me your symptoms. Did you eat something this morning?" he asked while staring at his watch, lips faintly moving as he counted my pulse. "You should drink some water. I'm sure you're dehydrated after last night."

"I had—"

He froze when I did, and his green eyes caught mine. This close, just a short distance separating our faces, that flicker of recognition turned into an unrelenting beat.

"Who are you?" My voice shook, but it wasn't exactly from distress, more confusion and worry.

A soft tongue swiped at the back of my hand, drawing my attention to Elvis, who laid his large head on my thigh and whined.

"What is going on?" I repeated a little more urgently. The longer this went on, the more freaked out I became.

"Fuck," he cursed under his breath at whatever he saw flash across my face. Sighing, he gently laid my arm down on my thigh, his fingers sliding away like he was reluctant to stop touching me. "Your pulse is fine, though a little weaker than I'd like. We should get you something with electrolytes."

The slight accent mixed with a voice so deep and familiar had me leaning in, brows pulled in tight as I studied the man's features. Then it hit me like a punch to the stomach. I sucked in a breath and jerked back, fingers flying up to cover my gaping mouth.

He gripped the armrests, boxing me in. "Hiya, Bay. It's been a while."

Overwhelmed by too many emotions to identify, tears welled in my lower lids before spilling over. "Memphis?"

His chin dipped in a hesitant nod, features frozen as he studied me, waiting for my response.

Without questioning my gut reaction, I threw both arms around his neck, the motion sending me sliding forward in the chair. Warm breath brushed past my ear with a grunt at the unexpected attack. He rocked backward but somehow caught me, regaining his balance to keep us from falling to the floor.

"Memphis," I whispered, not fully believing he was here, in Anchor Bay, in my waiting room. As the shock wore off, a million questions bombarded me. Pulling back, I gripped his shoulders, almost to reassure myself that he was actually here and not a figment of my grief and confusion. "How? Why? What?"

A corner of his lips curled upward in a familiar smirk. I stared in shock that I hadn't recognized him instantly. Sure, the tattoos and piercings were new, but he was still the shy yet cocky, sexy and sweet Memphis. Mine and Dean's Memphis.

"I'm sure you have a lot of questions. I do, too, but first" —his tattooed hands cupped my face—"I need to know that you're okay. You said you didn't feel well." When he stood, I tried to do the same, but he kept my ass sealed to the seat with a firm hand pressed to my shoulder. "I'll get you some water—"

A low, menacing growl rattled out of Elvis and cut him off. We both watched as he stalked toward the glass windows, the hair on his back raised.

"That's the second time today," Memphis muttered to himself.

"He doesn't normally do that?" He shook his head, not looking away from the dog. I frowned. "Okay, but what are you doing here—"

"I'm not leaving you up here exposed."

Before I could process his words, I was lifted out of the chair, one arm supporting my spine, the other beneath my knees. Striding toward the back like he owned the place, Memphis inspected the first exam room and then the other, stepping inside and carefully sitting me on the chair pet owners normally occupied while I helped their furry family members.

After making sure I was comfortable, Memphis and Elvis strode back out of the room, leaving me alone and utterly confused. I gaped at the empty doorway, jaw hanging open, not sure what the hell was actually going on.

"I must've fallen over earlier and hit my head. This is a concussion dream. It has to be."

Memory after memory after memory floated to the forefront of my mind of Dean's best friend, Memphis. It had been years since I last saw him—at least that was the excuse I was giving myself as to why I didn't immediately recognize him even with the drastic appearance change, though it seemed he still had a flair for style.

My lips quirked at that as a soft laugh escaped. There was no mistaking the kindness in his eyes, the shyness in his smirk, and the way his presence made me feel safe and taken care of. That was exactly the way I remembered him in my dreams.

Before I left for Texas A&M, the three of us were inseparable. Yes, he was Dean's best friend, but he was also mine too. When Dean was working at his job as a part-time mechanic and I wanted to go out, Memphis would take me. Sometimes if I couldn't get a hold of Dean and needed help, Memphis would come instead.

My thoughts came to a screeching halt as other, hotter memories surfaced. I swallowed hard as warmth filled my veins and my core throbbed. Recalling those moments, it seemed I'd been curious about the multi-partner relationship since high school, though I hadn't correlated our unique friendship to the community's lifestyle I currently lived in. Not that anything happened between the three of us, but there was always that unspoken spark, an intensity between Memphis and me, that I refused to acknowledge at the time. It felt wrong then, like I was cheating on Dean by being attracted to his best friend.

Loving that he was part of *us* and added to our relationship.

Just thinking about Dean and all those good times in high school had me slumping back in the chair and rubbing at my tired eyes. Fuck, these up-and-down emotions were exhausting. But unlike the past several months, the familiar punch of guilt didn't knock the air out of me. It was there, of course, but not like before.

Earlier with Liam, I jumped off that healing cliff, diving headfirst into a new chapter of my life. One where I wouldn't allow what happened to dictate how I moved forward in the future.

"We need to have a discussion about the food supply situation here." I peeked one eye open, finding Memphis filling the doorway, Elvis at his feet, that sunny smile back on his sweet muzzle. "You have one apple that's on its last day and a half-drunk Gatorade bottle in the fridge."

I pursed my lips to stop the growing smile as I shook my head in disbelief. How had two overprotective and obsessed-over-my-health men made their way into my life? Hell, the only reason there was an apple in the fridge at all was because of Liam.

Extending my hand, I motioned for the half-full Gatorade bottle dangling from his fingers. After removing the cap, I tipped the drink back and finished what remained from the other day.

"It has to be lingering issues from my hangover," I murmured to myself after wiping my lips. His words from the lobby had me jerking my gaze to him and narrowing my eyes in accusation. "Is that why you said I was probably dehydrated? How did you know about last...?" My cheeks heated and my stomach rolled with renewed embarrassment. "Oh fuck. Were you there?"

"I was," he said, stone-faced.

I pitched forward, burying my hot face in both hands, and groaned.

*I should just move to Hawaii.* I needed to run far, far away from the shit show that was yesterday and the results of my inebriated behavior.

"That's it. I'm dying of embarrassment. It will be a new discovery in future medical journals of how someone actually died, while at work, of embarrassment from their drunken stupidity."

A soft chuckle had me dropping my hands to glare at Memphis, who at least had the decency to hide his laughter. How dare he laugh at my misery?

"You weren't that bad," he said, still clearly amused. "Your friends were worse."

I scrunched my nose. "Not sure if that makes me feel any better."

He eyed me with an unreadable expression, pale green eyes scanning my face as if waiting for something. Then it hit me. Right, the reason he was here.

Slapping the tops of my thighs, I stood, thankful that the room didn't spin, and tossed the empty plastic bottle into the garbage can.

"Sorry, I got so wrapped up in seeing you and the mess from last night." Memphis's soft lips pressed into a thin line at my blubbering and waving both hands like an idiot. "I'm sitting here talking, and you just came to have your furry friend checked over."

Of course he wasn't here for me, to reminisce about the good times. But why did it feel like he was and wanted to surprise me? Memphis wasn't listed as the owner's name. I would've remembered that because it was so unique.

I really wished he was here for me, not just for Elvis's health, because a little piece of my heart that had yet to heal mended upon seeing him. It was like my childhood home had suddenly found me, offering the warmth and happiness that I hadn't felt in a long time. My life here was great, but I still missed home sometimes, and now a piece of that was here at my clinic.

When I reached for Elvis's leash, Memphis's tattooed fingers interlaced with my own, stopping them. Confused, I studied our joined hands before blinking up at him.

"The appointment wasn't real, Baylee."

I shook my head, knowing I saw it earlier in the scheduling system. "No, you're mistaken. It's in the system, but under a different name, I think. I can show you where—"

A wide smile spread across his face, making him appear exactly how I remembered him from high school, minus the new bad-boy look he had going on. Which, holy shit, was a good look on him.

"I mean I'm here for you, Baylee. I made up the appointment and name—sorry about that, by the way—as an excuse to come see you. Elvis is fine. Besides his very recent growling episodes, he's perfectly healthy."

All I could do was blink at Memphis as his words went in one ear and out the other.

Seeing my confusion, he blew out a slow breath and squeezed my fingers. "I came to Alaska for you. To talk to you. I was just chickenshit and didn't know how to approach you, and I figured this was the easiest way."

"What! That's amazing and confusing and I don't know what else," I said, meaning every word. "You came all the way to Alaska just to see me?" I furrowed my brow. "Um, why exactly?"

Memphis looked away with a chuckle and raked his fingers through his hair. "I was hoping we could talk about the why later, but yes, I came all the way from Florida to Alaska to see you."

I froze. "Are you the one who's been calling me nonstop, leaving those empty voice messages?"

His features hardened, and his eyes seemed to darken with anger. "What calls? What messages?"

My brows pulled in tight as the realization hit me like a freight train that I knew nothing about the man standing in front of me. Again, I scanned his tattoos, the small scar along his cheek, and the one that cut between the brow without the ring.

I might've grown up with Memphis Thomas the boy...

But I didn't really know this man.

## 11

LIAM

"They don't know shit," Aiden grumbled from where he paced on the other side of Harry. I nodded, agreeing with him as I continued to clean out his hoof. "And our only lead wasn't a lead at all."

Carefully releasing the gelding's leg, I patted his side in silent communication that I was moving on to the next one.

Noting that Aiden had paused, I glanced over the horse's back. He glared at the ground, both hands on his hips, no doubt thinking about Caroline. No one had heard from or seen her for weeks now. We didn't want to assume the worst, but it wasn't looking good for our friend.

"What about that notebook or whatever Jasper said he was looking for when we caught him going through Caroline's cabin?" I asked as I lifted Harry's back hoof and set it on top of my knee. "Though that sounds sketchy as shit, like something he made up as an excuse for him being in there."

"Hudson and Oliver worked him over pretty good." A huffed laugh escaped at the happiness in Aiden's tone. "They believe him, and while we haven't known Hudson that long, he seems like the kind of guy who can smell bullshit when it's given to him." His brows pulled in tight. "Why didn't Caroline tell us she was doing her own investigation for the missing women? Why did she keep it a secret and write it all down in some mysterious journal instead of coming to us?"

I stood straight and faced Aiden, absentmindedly running a hand along Harry's back.

"Because every single one of us is an overprotective asshole who would've made her stop because it was dangerous." Aiden's noncommittal grunt made me chuckle as I shook my head. "You know it's true. Look at the way we acted last night. We practically stormed into Dave's and dragged the women out like the fucking cavemen we are."

"I'm sad that I missed out on being there. From what Miles and Aspen told me, it sounded... entertaining." A wide grin spread across his face, erasing the earlier concern. "I heard you took Baylee home, though, and didn't go back to your place until this morning." A single brow lifted in a silent question. "I'm assuming that means you two are...."

"I'm not telling you shit," I muttered. "But yes, I stayed the night to make sure she was good. I was worried she'd get sick considering the amount of alcohol she consumed and mixed too." He winced, and I nodded, knowing that was a fucking death sentence for hangovers. My hand paused on Harry's spine, and I narrowed my eyes. "Wait. How in the hell do you know about me staying the night with Baylee?"

Hands in his jeans pockets, Aiden shrugged, but there was no missing the smirk he attempted to smother. "Come on, you know my best friend and roommate is basically the neighborhood watch." Clearly wanting to change the topic, he gave a pointed glance at the horse I was almost done grooming. "You have trail rides today?"

"None scheduled for today or tomorrow, which is good.

The horses need a few days off. We were booked solid last week." I didn't need to mention that I fully intended to spend the downtime over the next couple of days worshipping Baylee. My cock twitched in my jeans, remembering our earlier time in and around the shower. "What about you and Miles? Any ATV or dirt bike excursions booked?"

His hair shifted as he tilted his head to one side, then the other. "A few, but instead of doing them together, Miles and I asked Brandon if we could alternate so one of us could be out with the search party looking for Caroline." His worried gaze shifted to focus over my shoulder to the open barn doors and mountains beyond. "What are your suspicions about what's happening on the trail? I don't know what to make of it besides someone taking the women and killing anyone who stands in their way, but why?" He ran a hand through his hair. "And what is that person doing with them?"

Harry swung his head around and chuffed, demanding I get back to my job. I gave his long neck a few comforting strokes as I debated my answer.

"Those are my thoughts, too, and everyone's at this point, I think. It makes the most sense that some fucked-up psycho has been snatching women off the trail. The who and why and what the fuck is being done with them, I don't have a clue." Anger vibrated through me, making me want to punch something repeatedly. "Worse, I can't even think about someone in our town being responsible, but that's what makes the most sense too. Though I guess since women have gone missing from the fjord's end of the trail as well, it could be someone there."

"I hope she's dead." My head snapped around so fucking fast my neck cracked. With a devastated expression, Aiden shrugged. "Tell me you don't want the same for Caroline.

I've seen enough crime shows. There are some sick fuckers out there. *If* she was taken, me hoping she's dead is more merciful than her being alive."

A grimace tightened my features as I dipped my chin in reluctant agreement.

*That* was the quiet part no one wanted to say out loud. Hudson and Oliver probably discussed it in their private meetings, but around Anchor Bay and those in our community, no one gossiped about what could be happening to the missing female hikers.

Aiden was right. The most merciful outcome was they were dead and not out there alive, subject to who knew what. We humans were brilliant at creating new ways to hurt each other, each more depraved than the last.

"I know what you mean. If what happened to Caroline is the same as all those other missing female hikers and not just some bouldering accident...." I trailed off, not wanting to finish the statement. The other part no one mentioned was that the ongoing search parties for Caroline had changed from rescue to recovery focused. Hell, some went to help now as moral support for our group, knowing how hard this was on us, because this time the person missing wasn't some unknown tourist.

Caroline was a friend to all of us and an important part of the Anchor Bay community. She was basically a native to the wild state, having grown up in various areas of Alaska. People respected her, appreciated the care and concern she had for the delicate ecosystem and animals.

And now she was one of the missing.

Yet another victim of someone out there literally hunting unsuspecting women on a trail so many flocked to Anchor Bay eager to explore. There was still a remote possibility that she went looking for alternative rock-climbing locations, like she told Miles and Jasper before going missing, and suffered a fatal accident, but we would've found her body by now if she had.

It all pointed toward the horrible conclusion that we had one sick fucker living among us.

"I came by to see if you wanted to head over to Dave's for lunch. Aspen is hungover as hell and said their nachos would save her life."

I tugged off my cowboy hat and swiped a forearm over my sweaty forehead. "Thanks, but I think once I'm done here, I'll head over to the clinic to see if Baylee wants to grab something together."

Aiden's laugh rolled through the open barn. "You're so fucking whipped over that woman."

I flipped him the bird and gathered the brushes and tools I used on Harry to store back in the tack room. "You're one to talk, asshole. You and Miles won't even take a piss without asking Aspen first."

"I'm not saying it's bad, Liam, just pointing it out. I'm happy for you two, especially her. Since you two have been doing whatever you're doing, she seems to have more good days than bad." Pride swelled in my chest at his compliment. "She deserves to be happy, and I think you're helping her get there. Keep doing whatever you're doing, and don't break her heart. The woman's been through enough of that for several lifetimes."

With a wave, he strolled toward the barn entrance, whistling like he had no cares in the world, and disappeared around the corner of the metal building. I checked my watch, noting that it had only been two hours since I dropped Baylee off, but fuck, I wanted to see her again.

I *needed* to see her, to feel her body mold beneath my hands and kiss the fuck out of her. What we did that morning lit an all-consuming fire inside me, making me even more needy for her than before. I craved her pussy tightening around my fingers, her delicious flavor coating my tongue, her screaming my name as an orgasm ripped through her tiny body.

A frustrated groan vibrated in my chest, and I adjusted my rock-hard cock where it pressed against the zipper of my jeans.

Fuck it.

The chores could wait, my insistent craving to see Baylee wouldn't.

The anticipation of surprising her made me hustle faster than normal. It took less than an hour to secure Harry in the pasture with the other horses, grab a quick shower, change into clean clothes, and get over to downtown Anchor Bay. Fingers wrapped around the metal key, I turned off the truck's engine and shoved open the driver-side door. My boot heels clicked along the walkway as I strode past the various businesses, tipping the brim of my cowboy hat at the few locals who waved.

As I passed Sips, movement inside slowed my steps to a halt. Brows pulled in tight, I watched through the large glass window as Paul McGravey paced behind the counter, one hand holding a cell phone pressed to his ear while the other rubbed at his sweaty forehead. His movements were jerky, agitated at whoever was on the other end of the call. At the next turn of his pacing, our gazes collided, and he froze like someone had just hit a pause button.

Or caught him doing something wrong.

I glanced down the boardwalk to the vet clinic, wanting to keep walking but curious about whatever was going on inside the coffee shop. Curiosity winning, I swung my atten-tion back to Paul, who was no longer behind the counter or anywhere in the front area of the small business. With a frustrated grumble, I retraced my steps to Sips's front door and jerked the metal handle. The thick aroma of coffee instantly engulfed me, followed by the sweet scent of something delicious baking in the back.

Every table was empty, though a few dirty coffee mugs and plates with half-eaten pastries indicated customers had been in recently. Catching a hushed conversation, I silently stepped deeper into the coffee shop, rounding the counter to access the swinging door that led to the kitchen. I hesitated, hoping to catch some of the conversation being said on the other side, but the door swung open. Only my quick reflexes kept it from slamming into my face instead of catching on my foot, stopping it mid-motion.

A surprised shout sounded from the other side when I assumed Paul smacked into the door, not expecting it to stop halfway.

Taking a big step back, I gripped the thin edge, pulling it wide. A frustrated Paul grumbled under his breath while massaging his forehead where a red mark had already formed.

"What the hell, Liam," he snapped, narrowing his eyes at me. "You're not supposed to be back here. It's against health codes or something."

"Or something," I grunted and released the door, turning on my heels to make my way back to the customer side of the counter. "Everything all good?" I asked, eyeing him with suspicion. "You seemed upset when I saw you through the window."

"I'm fine, yes. Why wouldn't I be?" he said, though the quick and defensive tone made me think I was right. "What were you doing back here anyway?"

I studied his fingers that fidgeted with the edge of his

shirt and the slight sheen of sweat glistening on his bald head. But it was the dirt and debris coating his black tennis shoes and jeans that had me arching a brow with a pointed look.

"You go on a hike this morning?" I questioned.

Paul's eyes widened in what looked like fear before he forced his features into a pissed-off expression. "What's with the twenty questions? Do you want coffee or not? Because I have some shit I need to do in the back."

"No, I'm good. Already had some at the cabin. You seemed—" I angled my head one way, then the other. "—frustrated earlier. Wanted to check in, make sure all is good."

Paul huffed and tossed both hands in the air in exaggerated exasperation. That movement drew my calculating gaze to the hand white-knuckling his cell phone. "All well here, no need to worry. You can go back to minding your own damn business. Now, if you don't mind, I need to get back in the kitchen." Without waiting for a response, he stormed into the back, shoving the swinging door so hard it crashed against the wall.

I waited a few seconds, stare locked on where he disappeared, trying to put the puzzle pieces together on what the hell just went down. Paul was hiding something, but what and why, I wasn't sure. Or maybe because of everything that was going on in our small town, I was teetering on the edge of hypervigilant and paranoid more than normal.

I scraped my calloused palm across my mouth as I debated whether following him to demand answers was worth the additional time away from Baylee. It didn't take but a second to conclude that it wasn't any of my business, and I exited the quaint coffee shop.

Outside, I inhaled deeply through my nose and held it,

hoping to ease the tension knotting my gut, then started toward Baylee's clinic, only to freeze mid-step at the distinctive click of a lock being engaged. Glancing over my shoulder, I found Paul on the other side of the glass door, his face barely visible through the sticker of the coffee shop's logo, flipping the Closed sign around. Frustration and anger had my muscles tightening and my hands curling into fists at my sides, knowing he'd just closed his store so I wouldn't return to ask more questions.

Mentally filing the strange incident away to figure out later, I forced my feet to keep moving. By the time I stepped inside the clinic, the incident with Paul was forgotten, replaced with anticipation of seeing Baylee. But it quickly turned to fear, my heart stopping in my fucking chest when a scream rattled through the waiting room from the exam room area.

Storming down the hall, bloodlust thrumming through my veins, I slammed a shoulder into the closed exam room door, busting it off its hinges. Hand hovering over the holstered gun on my belt, I took in every detail of the small space.

A wide-eyed Baylee kneeled on the floor with a large yellow lab hovering over her. Her shocked expression leveled my way, and the dog's behavior, his long whiplike tail going back and forth as his tongue hung out of his mouth, told me she wasn't being attacked. After another once-over to ensure she was unharmed, I slid my stony stare to the stranger in the room.

He returned my glare like *I* was the danger and held a long-ass knife out in front of him as he slowly inched to stand in front of Baylee. Years of training took over as I advanced on the man to neutralize the threat to my girl. The knife clattered to the floor at the asshole's feet a second before I had him pinned face-first against the wall with both hands secured behind his back.

Baylee shouted my name as I fought to maintain my hold as he did everything he could to break free.

"Damnit, Liam, stop hurting him," she shrieked, now pulling at my arm.

"Who the fuck are you?" I snarled in the asshole's ear, slamming him against the wall when he pushed back into me. "Fucking stop."

"*You* stop," Baylee screeched, tossing up both hands before placing them on her hips. "If you'll give me two seconds to explain, I'll tell you who this is and why he's here."

"You screamed when I walked in," I said, taking my eyes off the threat for half a second to look at Baylee, only to grimace at her furious expression zeroed right on me.

*Well, fuck.*

"Because Elvis here kissed me, tongue and all."

Red coated my vision once her words processed.

As if sensing his imminent death after that statement, the fucker bucked against me at just the right angle to break free from my hold and then turned, fist swinging right at my face. With a malicious smirk, I ducked and followed through with my own to his stomach, which connected exactly where I wanted.

The guttural pain-filled grunt had a manic smile spreading across my face as I pulled back, ready to knock him the fuck out with one punch to the temple. But a flash of white-blonde hair and glaring crystal blue eyes froze me in place.

"What the hell are you doing?" the stranger gasped, trying to catch his breath while attempting to pull Baylee behind him. "Never do that again. You could get seriously hurt, Bay."

*Bay?*

My eyes flicked between the two, my brain attempting to catch up to reality since it seemed my initial assumption was wrong.

"Liam won't hurt me," she huffed, trying to get around the guy, but he kept shifting side to side to prevent her from getting between us again. "Damnit, how is it possible to now have two overbearing, protective assholes in my life?"

I slowly dropped my fist but stayed alert just in case.

"I think most women would consider themselves lucky to just have one," the guy said with a shy smile as he looked down at my girl. A low growl built in my chest at the soft look he gave her, but it silenced when he reached between us, initiating a handshake. "Memphis Thomas. I was a friend of your girl's and Dean's back in high school."

*Well, fuck.* Feeling guilty as hell, I reluctantly shook his hand while taking in every detail of the guy.

Trendy haircut, shaved on the sides, exposed tattoos on his scalp and neck. Not as tall as me, maybe six feet even, which meant he still towered over Baylee. He had more tattoos on his forearms, down to his hands and even his fingers. And they were good tats, too, making me want to ask who his artist was and how to get a booking.

Movement in my periphery had me sliding my gaze to the dog.

"And this is Elvis." Memphis ran his hand along the top of the lab's block-shaped head, which earned him a lick from the panting dog.

I squeezed my eyes shut and groaned at my asshole tendencies when his dog's name registered.

"The dog kissed you, not him," I muttered, running a

hand down my face. Gripping the top of my cowboy hat, I pulled it off and tossed it onto the exam table.

"Exactly. If you would've given me two seconds before going all crazy—" Baylee started.

"To his credit, he walked in, heard his girl scream, and found her alone, behind a closed door, with a guy he didn't know." I arched a brow at Memphis, who shrugged. "I would've done the same."

"Unbelievable," Baylee grumbled while pinching the bridge of her nose. When she looked up, her gaze went to the destroyed door.

I winced. "I'll have it replaced by the end of the week—"

"Today," she corrected, pointing an accusing finger at the door before swinging it to me, then Memphis. "You can work on it while the three of us talk. Like adults, not toddlers fighting over their favorite toy."

I swallowed my response and simply nodded, feeling completely chastised by the tiny woman who had me by the balls. Aiden was right, I was 100 percent whipped—but ask me if I fucking cared. I'd be anything she wanted me to be as long as I had her.

And the way the Memphis guy kept staring at her... it seemed like I wasn't the only one who thought that way.

"Sorry for slamming you against the wall," the angry fucker I now knew was Liam grumbled as he assessed the damage he did to the door.

"Twice, which fucking hurt like hell. What are you made of? Steel?" My joke, attempting to ease the tension in the room, just earned me a glare over his shoulder. "And no hard feelings. Like I said, I get it."

He just nodded, letting me know he heard me. "Earlier, you said 'heard *his girl* scream.' How did you know that?" Liam asked, attention on the doorframe, but I knew he was watching me for my reaction too. The man didn't trust me, which I somewhat understood since I was a literal stranger.

My lips parted to respond with the truth of my slight stalking when Baylee spoke up, cutting me off.

"Memphis told me he was at the bar last night, which means he saw you carry my drunk ass out." She shot me a wink. Guess that meant if I wanted to stay on Liam's good side—if he had one—I shouldn't tell him about the unannounced or noticed observations from the shadows the last couple of days. "I've known him for years. Dean, Memphis, and I all grew up together."

A wash of sadness engulfed me, making my lungs freeze at the mention of Dean's name. By the downturn of the corners of Baylee's lips, it seemed a similar feeling hit her too.

Pursing her lips, she forced the forlorn expression away with a tight grin. "Memphis was Dean's best friend. The two were inseparable when Dean and I started dating. I felt more like the third wheel with the three of us than Memphis because he was there first, I guess," she teased. Her light eyes sparkled when they connected with my own. "We did everything together."

"Well, not *everything*," I added. Longing dipped my tone, which of course Liam picked up on, based on the curious, single eyebrow-raised expression he sent over his shoulder.

Baylee studied me, too, with a furrowed brow before shaking her head as if clearing her thoughts. "Before you burst through the door like a mad bull, Memphis was filling me in on what he's been up to since I last saw him. Which was, what, that time I came home to visit Dean the summer after year two of veterinary medicine at A&M?"

Lead formed in my stomach, making it drop to my feet. That visit was right before Dean and I had our falling-out. After he distanced himself from me because of that fight, I started hanging out more with a group of so-called friends who led me down the toxic path I wished like hell I'd never taken. It took years for me to find my way back on the right track, sober and holding down a fulfilling job as an EMT.

"That was a long time ago. What brings you here now?" Liam asked, rotating to lean against the wall to face me straight on with an unreadable expression.

Fuck, he was intimidating.

Giving myself a second to work out an answer, I picked up the knife from the floor, which reminded me of how quickly Liam had disarmed me of the weapon. I eyed the sharp blade, then him. "Where did you learn to do that?" I asked, sliding it into the sheath that was normally covered by my jacket.

"The Army."

"Liam was a Ranger for years before retiring and coming to Alaska." Baylee smiled at Liam, whose features softened with her attention on him.

"Baylee, you asked where I've been the last few years. I guess a little bit of everywhere, but most recently Florida is where I call home. After my stint in rehab—"

"Rehab?" Bailey asked, head tilting to the side.

I nodded, hating having to fill her in on all the shit in my past. "I got mixed up with some not-so-great influences who, unlike you and Dean, didn't have my best interests in mind." Liam's assessing stare intensified as I spoke. "Alcohol and prescriptions were my downfall, fueling one party after another. That continued for years before I was ready to get the help I needed. My life was in shambles. I was barely surviving day to day."

"Memphis," Baylee murmured. Her hand found mine, interlacing our fingers, and squeezed. "I'm so sorry. I didn't know. I didn't realize you—"

I shook my head to dismiss any thoughts of her feeling guilty. I ran my free hand along Elvis's head in cathartic strokes. "I did it, all of it, to myself, Bay. I didn't realize how deep in it I was until it was running my life. I woke up needing a drink, wanting a pill to quicken that escape from reality."

"Barely surviving?" Liam asked, sounding genuinely interested. "What does that mean?"

Disappointment in myself and embarrassment over how bad it had been pumped through my veins, making a hot flush creep up my neck. Thank fuck for the tattoos.

"I couldn't hold down a job, so I lost my car, my apartment—hell, everything except for Elvis here." Squatting low to put us nose to nose, I scratched behind both of his ears in a silent thank-you for always being there for me. "We lived on the streets for a while. Not a single person I went to for help took us in when I needed them most. That's when I realized the friends I thought I had weren't actual friends, and I was fucking alone." A hollow feeling grew in my gut, but one look at Baylee had it vanishing. "So I did what I swore to myself I'd never do and asked my parents for help. They got me into a treatment facility that I took seriously, knowing it was my one chance to get out of that life alive. I completed the program and was determined to never sink that low again."

Streams of tears poured from the corners of Baylee's eyes, trailing down her freckled cheeks. A sharp pain had me pressing a loose fist to my sternum, knowing I was the cause of those tears. I hated her being upset, but she needed to know, and I needed that weight lifted. Speaking about the trauma and past to someone who cared had healing repercussions. Step five of the twelve and all that was legit.

Arm draped over her slim shoulders, I guided her to my chest, curling her smaller frame in a crushing hug.

"I'm okay, Bay," I whispered into her soft hair while stealing a whiff of coconut shampoo. "It's a struggle that will always be there, but I got help when I needed it most and realized I was wasting my life."

"I'm so proud of you," she rasped with unshed tears in her lower lids. "What made you ready to get help?"

"Dean's death." She winced like my words were a physical blow but quickly schooled her features. "After I found out, I lost days drunk and high. When I finally came out of that bender, I realized life was too short and I didn't want to spend one more minute dependent on the contents of a bottle or pills. I lost years of my life, put my parents through hell, and for what? A brief reprieve from reality, but it being so much worse when I came to." I shook my head in disappointment at myself. "It will always be a temptation, but every day is easier. I'm sorry I wasn't there for you at the funeral, Baylee. I'm so fucking sorry."

I hated not being there, especially since it was my doing, but it hurt even more after my mom told me how awful Dean's mom had been to Baylee at the memorial service and burial.

"But you were at the bar last night," Liam stated with the hint of a question in his tone.

"Drinking gallons of Sprite helped, but yeah, the bar scene isn't ideal for a recovering alcoholic. But their food...." My stomach vibrated with a loud, rumbling growl just thinking about the nachos. "I've tried other places around town, but no one has food like *that*, so I powered through. And to answer your earlier question about what brings me here now." I inclined my head toward Baylee, who was still tucked against my side. "I randomly looked her up one day and found her clinic website here in Anchor Bay. The memories of us three together, the good times we had, are some of my best. I guess I wanted to find Baylee and—" I lifted a single shoulder in a noncommittal shrug. "—maybe see if we could be friends again. I miss Dean. Fuck, do I miss him, and seeing her reminds me of the good times, which makes that pain of losing him forever sting a little less."

Liam continued to stare, not saying a single word, just studying me as I brushed comforting strokes down Baylee's spine as she worked to stop her tears. As if confirming a thought only he heard, he gave a clipped nod and pushed off the wall.

"I don't need to replace the whole door. It's structurally sound enough. Just the latch and hinges are bent and need replacing." He pointed at my chest. "You're coming to the hardware store with me to get the parts I'll need. We'll grab lunch for all of us on the way back here."

"That's perfect," Baylee said around a sniffle while wiping at her damp cheeks with the sleeve of her lab coat. "I need to prepare for my next patient. Mittens, Mrs. Jones's cat, is an angry beast with supersharp claws, meaning I need to gear up to keep from getting scratched. Elvis can stay in my office until you get back."

My dog shifted his weight to Baylee's legs, making her stumble to the side with a soft giggle.

Liam stared into my soul and hitched his chin toward the door in a not-so-subtle request to give him and Baylee a second alone. As I walked down the hall, I couldn't help but replay the events after the door burst open. I was pissed that he got the upper hand so easily, though now knowing about his military background, I wasn't too torn up about having my ass handed to me. I had never been a fighter, though I learned to keep myself armed at all times after living on the street in those few months.

Back in the waiting room, I paused in the middle, facing the large window, watching the people hurrying past, when an older, bald man stormed down the walkway speaking animatedly to the guy beside him, who looked pissed as hell.

"Ready?"

I jumped in surprise, a curse slipping out at Liam's deep

voice directly behind me. "Fuck, you're quiet for someone your size."

I swore his lips twitched in an almost smile before his normal deadly expression settled on his face, aimed directly at me. "Remember that about me, because if you do anything to hurt Baylee, and I mean any-fucking-thing, you'll never see me coming."

I swallowed hard and nodded. Holy shit, the guy was intense. I figured that after watching him and her the last couple of days, but it was worse this close to him.

We didn't say another word as we left the clinic, him holding the door open for an older woman who carried a cat carrier with a yowling animal inside.

It wasn't until we were several buildings away that he spoke again.

"I can tell she cares about you still, which is why I'm not asking you to leave Anchor Bay immediately and never come back."

"I don't think I could even if you told me to leave. I didn't realize how much I missed Baylee, having her in my life in any capacity, until I saw her picture online. I wasn't exaggerating in there. She, Dean, and I were always together. Where they went, I was there too." Which sucked because I had a front-row seat to their make-out sessions, only tapping out when it became too much for me, not them asking me to leave. "I miss her."

He shot me a strange glance out of the corner of his eye. "I can understand that. If something were to pull Baylee and me apart, I'd miss that woman every day of my life until I could find my way back to her. Tell me the truth. Are you here for her, to take my Baylee away from me?"

Even if I was, I sure as hell wouldn't tell this silverback

gorilla of a man that. Fuck, did he know how that tone and question almost made me shit my pants?

I eyed him, taking in the smirk he tried to hide. The fucker absolutely knew.

Asshole.

My fingers reached out for Elvis, needing his comfort, but they only danced in the air. "I'm not here to take her from anyone, so please don't kill me."

He barked out a laugh and shook his head like he wasn't just imagining tossing my lifeless body in the bay for the fish to take care of.

"I can see you make her happy," I continued. "She's been through enough shit in her life. I'm not going to do anything to add to that pile by taking her away from the people and friends who make her smile, who help her forget for even just a second who she lost."

With a clipped nod, Liam ripped open the hardware store door and stepped inside, chuckling when he released the door so it almost smacked me in the face. He grabbed a plastic handbasket and shoved it against my chest before turning on his heels and marching down the aisle. I rubbed my chest and eyed the now-cracked basket.

"So, what now?" I grumbled to his back. "I'm supposed to just follow you around and hold your shit?"

"Yep." He rounded the end cap to stroll down the next aisle, stopping in front of the small selection of hinges. "Tell me, will any of the shit from home follow you here?"

I furrowed my brow until it registered what he was referring to and why he asked the question. "Nah. First, that was over two years ago. I don't know those people anymore. Second, I'm in fucking Alaska. No one has a grudge against me that fucking big to come to basically Russia." Liam snorted as he inspected the different door hinges in each hand. "And I know what you're thinking—"

"Fucking doubt it," he mused, "or you'd be running home right about now."

Not sure why, but I felt like the constant death threats meant he liked me.

"You're terrifying, you know that?" I nervously joked. "Fucking hell, man, stop coming up with ways to murder me or get me to run. I'm not here to take your girl."

Liam just nodded, not looking away from the display. "You're an unknown. You two have a history, one I don't have. There's also the fact that you remind her of Dean, who she still grieves daily. Your presence, those memories you stir up, have the potential to add to her grief." He pursed his lips. "Or help. I can't watch her slip back into more bad days where she couldn't even eat because she was so damn sad rather than the good where she could see the hope of happiness."

"I don't want that either," I stated, wishing like hell he believed me. "I'm not here to cause her pain, I fucking swear. If I did, I'd run away like my ass was on fire to prevent that from happening."

With a confirming nod, he tossed three identical hinges into the basket. "Good. Then we agree. Where are you staying while you're here?"

Walking past the rope section, I paused to feel the different textures. "The Nest," I said to where Liam stood beside me, watching like he was trying to figure out a puzzle. Dropping the nylon rope, I gestured with the basket for us to keep moving. "It's a bit too fancy for me and Elvis, but it was the best option. The resort isn't too bad if you don't account for their douche general manager."

Liam's booming laugh rumbled through the store. A few

people turned our way, eyeing him, not that he seemed to care. With his size, it appeared he was used to people watching him everywhere he went. It was that size and the way he moved, all thick and powerful muscles, that spoke to how capable he—

*Um, what the actual hell, Memphis?*

"I fucking swear I'm straight," I muttered to myself while rubbing a hand down my face. "Right?"

Liam snorted and shook his head. "How the fuck should I know if you don't?" At the next aisle, he turned to me with an arched brow, scanning my face and studying my tattoos. "I'm fairly certain that's your decision and not something someone else should choose for you."

"Right. Damnit, I did not mean to say that out loud." I gestured between us with the basket, making Liam jump back with a curse when I almost clipped his balls. "I was thinking about you and—"

He pressed a palm to my chest, forcing me back a step. "I really don't need an explanation, but if that is something you're into, that's fine, just not the way I swing." He shoved both hands into the pockets of his jeans. "You'll find that the community Baylee and I live in, that encompasses the employees of Uplift Adventure and Rescue, doesn't view relationships as traditionally as most. So you do you, and don't be afraid of what Baylee or any of us will think, because they're the most accepting group of assholes you'll ever meet."

Heat flickered in my veins as I remembered what I'd seen and heard yesterday in the bar.

"About that," I said, clearing my throat. His gray eyes cut my way before focusing back on the packaged door handle in his hand. "I noticed those interesting relationship dynamics last night when I was at the bar and also overheard some of the women's conversations about their boyfriends, as in plural."

His massive shoulders rose and fell in a shrug, like living in a poly community was a run-of-the-mill occurrence. "Yep, it's what we do, and everyone accepts everyone for what they want. We're all consenting adults."

"Agreed, just different. How did it come about? I've never heard of a poly community, and the fact that it's in a random small town in Alaska...."

The basket shifted in my hand when the heavy door handle in its thick plastic packaging landed on the bottom.

"*That* would be our owner and his two partners' doing. They were tired of being judged and the negative comments people made to Amy, so they started their own community. It started as a well-run, family-centered company and turned into what it is now. We work hard to keep it that way too. We pull our own weight, and not just in our respective jobs with clients. We help anywhere needed around the compound to keep it thriving and everyone happy."

Longing swelled in my chest at the idea of that kind of utopia. "It seems too good to be true," I mused, following him to the front of the store. A few women scanning the shelves blatantly checked him out, but a guy two aisles over glared at Liam like he wanted him to die a horrible death.

"Hey, who's that guy two rows down, and what did you do to make him that mad?"

Liam didn't even look up, apparently already knowing exactly who I meant.

"That would be Jasper Cain. You might have seen him around town or at Sips, where he works. I'm sure he's still fucking pissed that I tackled his scrawny ass and hog-tied him with his own belt." A surprised laugh snuck free, making Liam smirk. "Yeah, pretty sure that's what the death glare is for, not that he can do anything about it." His features turned contemplative. "Actually, I wish he would. I'd love a reason to knock that fucker out."

Um, okay. Baylee's boyfriend was fucking intense.

*And why do I like it so much?*

"Did he deserve it?"

His cocky smirk fell when he pressed his lips into a tight line. "Yeah, he did. I caught him in our friend's cabin." He snatched the basket out of my hand to set it on the counter for the cashier to ring up. "We're all on edge." Credit card in hand, he swiped it through the reader and took the full plastic bag from the young woman's outstretched fingers. Tipping his hat in thanks, he strode to the door with me hot on his heels. "Food, then back to the clinic. You okay to go into Dave's again, or do you need to wait outside?"

"And here I thought you wanted to kill me," I said with a sarcastic smile. "How considerate of you." He flipped me the bird, making my smile grow. "I'm fine. Thanks for asking, though. Seriously."

Liam walked off like his concern for my sobriety wasn't the most considerate thing anyone besides my parents had done in years.

"Has anyone told you about what's going on around here?" he asked while nodding to someone across the street.

I shifted to the side to let a woman with a baby pass without her feeling crowded. "Sure, the amazing fishing, fun outdoor shit, and trails. The Nest also has information on your boss's company, Uplift, to book through."

"All that brings tourists and hikers, but that's not what I'm talking about. Have you heard about the Soul Trail?"

I nodded, remembering a few articles about the highly difficult trail that connected the small town of Anchor Bay to the fjords.

"Over the last year—hell, maybe even longer and we didn't realize—female hikers have been disappearing from that trail."

My brows pulled in tight, trying to understand. "Disappeared as in got lost?"

"As in we don't fucking know." He snapped his hand out and grabbed my shirt, yanking me hard. As I started to shove him off me, he inclined his head to the post I almost ran into, too focused on him and engrossed in his story to notice. "You're welcome. And the missing, we're well into the double digits. In a couple of cases, the women's male companions' dead bodies turned up, looking like they were attacked by an animal."

"But you don't believe it," I stated, suddenly feeling paranoid. Checking over my shoulder, I watched everyone with suspicion.

"No one does, except for the lazy-as-fuck sheriff who just doesn't want to make a big deal out of it all. That means more work for him apparently." Liam's hands fisted at his sides, indicating exactly how he felt about the sheriff's actions. "Women have also gone missing from the fjords side of the trail. Either way, it's all the same. Besides the males, no other bodies have been recovered. That's what I meant by fucking disappeared."

"And now a woman from your community is missing too?" He dipped his head in a clipped nod, face tight with tension. My heart dropped when realization hit me like a punch to the stomach. Like he did me moments ago, I fisted his shirt, yanking him to a stop. "Baylee, is she safe here?"

He stared at where my fingers bunched his button-up denim shirt. "I suggest you release me." The intensity in his tone and glare made me instantly relax my fingers and step back. "And yes, as safe as I can keep her. That independent woman doesn't think about her safety enough."

A snort escaped as I shook my head. That sounded like something I would've said about her back in high school. "You mean like stepping between two men to break up a fight?"

He huffed a humorless laugh before he started walking again. "Exactly. She likes to run in the mornings, alone, which I fucking hate but can't do anything about."

I nodded absentmindedly, memories of years ago filtering through and making me smirk. "She's always been a runner and independent, so I'm not surprised she's still doing it, no matter the risk or what you say. Back in high school, neither Dean nor I could change that woman's mind once she decided on something. Drove me batshit crazy, but one of us was always there, hidden in the background, making sure she was safe."

The delicious aroma of fried food assaulted me as I stepped into Dave's right behind Liam. I followed him to the bar, where he perched a boot on the lower rung of a stool and waved the bartender over.

I eyed the slightly heavyset man as he ambled toward us. His judgy eyes were locked on me like they had been the night before. Judgmental prick. Just to piss him off, I slid a pointed gaze up to the few strings of hair he'd slicked back in a desperate attempt to cover up the bald spot and ran a hand through my thick strands.

"Hey, Ches," Liam said in greeting when the disheveled man paused in front of him, wiping both hands with a rag. "I need two orders of the elk nachos fully loaded, two burgers medium well with everything, and a side of onion rings." He turned to me and gestured toward Ches. "What are you ordering?"

A sudden swell of emotions filled my chest, making my heart hammer. For the first time in too long, I felt companionship, not so fucking lonely. Maybe it was his quick acceptance, the easy back-and-forth conversation, that reminded me of the friendship I had with Dean before the fight. And damn did I miss that, more than I'd realized until now, missed having a genuine friend so fucking much.

Was it too much to hope that coming here meant I not only would have Baylee in my life again but gain a genuine friend in Liam too?

Or was today the start of something much bigger than the three of us could ever imagine?

## BAYLEE

The truck rumbled down the road, vibrating beneath me where I sat between Liam and Memphis. Since the fun lunch, I hadn't stopped smiling. The two men had gotten along better than I'd expected, Liam seeming to have acknowledged that Memphis wasn't a threat to my safety or our relationship.

"Bay," Memphis sighed. "I don't mind staying at The Nest."

I cut him a fake glare and shook my head like I had the last few times he suggested going back to the resort instead of staying with me. He blew out a controlled breath and leaned forward to see around me, eyeing Liam in the driver's seat.

The resort was not only expensive, but the distance would be annoying now that I knew Memphis was in Anchor Bay. We had too much catching up to do and reminiscing about old times, and that couldn't happen with him there and me at home. I wanted to laugh about the dumb shit he, Dean, and I did as kids, about his life and mine. Lunch together was just a preview. I had laughed harder than I had in much too long. Somehow, seeing Memphis and talking about the good times made missing Dean a little less heavy. Not sure why or how, but I didn't want that peace his presence brought to end.

"You're okay with this, Liam?" Memphis asked, studying him.

Liam draped an arm over my shoulders and sealed me even tighter to his side. "I already explained what would happen if you hurt her," he responded as he turned the wheel, directing the truck down Main Street. "Plus, I'll be there too."

"What?" I exclaimed, choking on my spit. I coughed to clear my throat, staring wide-eyed at Liam's profile. I didn't mind that he'd be there too. I actually loved the idea. As long as he slept in my bed and not on the couch with Memphis.

Liam's gaze slid from the windshield to me. I swallowed down the soft gasp that wanted to escape at the heat and promise in those gray eyes. Flush warmed my cheeks as desire slithered through my veins. With that single look, I knew he planned to repeat our morning, which I was totally down for even with Memphis on the couch. Or maybe *that* caused the surge of desire, making my panties damp, knowing Memphis would hear us, that he'd know exactly what was going on in the bedroom.

"You good with that, Little Bit?" His deep voice rumbled through the truck, distracting me from the dirty fantasy. He chuckled and sent a knowing glance to Memphis. "Thought so."

A sheen of sweat coated the back of my neck. I squirmed on the seat, an uncomfortable throb pulsing between my thighs as memories of those times in high school when I caught Memphis watching Dean and me flashed in my mind. More than once, I'd held Memphis's intense stare with Dean's lips on my own and his hand between my thighs.

And more than once, I'd hoped he'd join us.

It had made me feel horribly, being in love with Dean but also attracted to his best friend. But things were different now. *I* was different, and I lived in a poly community that supported those desires, the need for more than one partner.

"You have a girlfriend back home?" Liam asked out of the blue.

The tip of my ponytail whipped me in the face with how fast I twisted to see Memphis's reaction to Liam's probing question. His pale green eyes searched my face as he shook his head. A relieved sigh escaped as I slumped against Liam's side.

Both men chuckled.

"You seem pleased that I don't, Bay," Memphis murmured, a knowing smirk pulling at his lips.

*Fuck, what did these two talk about when I wasn't around?* It was one trip to the hardware store, for God's sake.

"How long do you plan to stay?" I asked, my voice squeaky from the tightness in my throat and the rapid pulse that pounded in my ears.

Liam's question and Memphis's response had threesome fantasies playing out in my head. I didn't know if I should be upset with Liam or kiss him for making my thoughts go down that path. His suggestive tone and questions threw gasoline on my roaring desire. That morning had flipped a switch inside me; all my thoughts now revolved around the need pumping through my veins.

This craving and desperation for his touch was like nothing I'd ever felt before.

Memphis searched my warm face, his grin growing. "Not sure." He offered me a wink before glancing over his shoulder to where Elvis rode in the truck bed. Paws on the edge and face in the wind, he seemed to be living his best life.

"Maybe you should've asked that before you invited him to stay with you." Liam's wide palm engulfed my thigh, fingers tightening in a reassuring squeeze. I studied the single finger that traced circles on the inside of my leg, leaving trails of heat in its wake. "What do you do for work back in Florida, Memphis?"

Memphis relaxed against the door as if the question put him at ease. "I'm an EMT in Orlando County." A wicked gleam made his eyes sparkle. "You'd be shocked as hell what crazy places people stuff those damn mouse ears."

The cab was silent for half a second before Liam and I erupted in loud, genuine laughter. Memphis watched us with a soft expression and longing behind his eyes. Without second-guessing the urge, I rested my palm on top of his leg and squeezed.

My gaze shifted back to Liam's hand still wrapped around my thigh to my own wrapped around Memphis's, and instead of guilt, a flood of need had that earlier desire surging back to the surface. Pulse racing, my lips parted to accommodate my quick breaths.

Both men's attention zeroed in on me, making the blush from before come back with a renewed vengeance. Forcing my focus out the windshield, I pressed two fingers to each hot cheek and blew out a slow breath. Liam hummed a response beside me while Memphis continued to stare at my profile like he was attempting to solve a puzzle.

"What?" I demanded.

"So, you're in a poly community now?" I nodded in

response to Memphis's question, unable to speak. "And you're happy here?"

I blew out a slow breath, hoping it would keep the trembling out of my voice. "Very happy." Liam's hand gave my leg a reassuring squeeze. "I still have bad days when I miss Dean so much that it physically hurts. But thankfully—" I shot Liam a smile. "—those days are few and far between lately." I chewed on my lip and peeked over at Memphis through my lashes. "You apologized for not being at the funeral. Why weren't you there?"

Memphis ran a hand through the long section of his hair and turned to look out the window. "Besides being too fucked up to travel or even remember the date," he bit out, his anger and frustration at that clear, "Dean and I had somewhat of a falling-out." He shook his head. "I really thought I'd have time to make things right with him, thought we'd work it out and go back to being best friends, but we never got that chance. Three years later, after our split, he was gone, and in some ways, so was I."

"I know what it feels like when that time you thought you'd have later is taken away." His misty green eyes met mine. "Not regret but also not guilt, more just sad to your core that all the stuff you thought you had time for would never happen."

My voice broke at the end, and it was Memphis's turn to lend a comforting touch. He laid his hand on top of mine that still rested on his jeans-covered thigh and threaded our fingers together.

"I'm sorry you had to go through that alone," he rasped. "I'm sorry I wasn't there for you when you needed a friend, that I was too fucked up to even show up."

I could only manage a nod in response. Because I had needed a friend, anyone besides my parents, to lean on in my grief and as a buffer to the words and looks from Dean's mom.

The rest of the drive to our compound was quiet, the three of us lost in our own thoughts. When Liam parked the truck and cut the engine, no one moved.

"What was it about?" Liam probed, twisting to lean against the driver's door.

Memphis blew out a breath, sealing his lids shut and tapping the back of his head against the headrest with a frustrated groan. "It's a long fucking story. One that started way before that night when our friendship ended." He turned to me with a forced smile and pointed to our community out the windshield. "Ready to show me around?"

I eyed Liam, whose features were tight, clearly not liking Memphis's response. It was curious for sure, but nothing that needed to be uncovered within the first few hours of Memphis being back in my life. We had time to figure out his evasive answer later.

With a smile and nod, I stretched across Memphis and pushed the heavy metal door open.

"A tour of the compound will happen, but first stop, the cabin so you can drop your stuff off and meet BamBam if he's around."

"BamBam?" Memphis questioned as he stepped out of the truck and stretched his arms high into the air, exposing a sliver of his inked abs.

I slid across the bench seat and followed him. "Yes, he's an ermine that I rescued—"

"Kidnapped," Liam cut in around a fake cough as he rounded the hood.

Once he was beside me, I gave his shoulder a hard shove. "I did not kidnap a wild animal. I would never.

BamBam would've died out in the elements, so rescued *is* the perfect word for how he came into my life." I scrunched my nose and stuck my tongue out.

Liam's thick fingers gripped my jaw, holding me in place. "Little Bit, don't show me that tongue unless you're planning to use it."

I snapped my lips shut. Renewed heat filled my veins, shooting straight between my thighs and making that insistent pulse return. Behind me, Memphis grumbled a string of curses, but I didn't dare break Liam's intense stare.

"Say you understand." I nodded, but his grip on my jaw tightened. "Words, Baylee."

"Yes, I understand. I'll only show you my tongue if I plan to use it."

"Good girl," he praised.

With a goofy sigh, like I was made of wax and he was the blistering sun, I melted against him.

Movement out of the corner of my eye drew my attention to Memphis helping Elvis out of the truck bed, his lips moving like he was talking to himself or the dog.

"Come on." Liam interlaced our fingers and lifted my hand to his lips, pressing a gentle kiss to each knuckle. "If it's okay, I'll head to the barn while you show him around. I put off some chores earlier to come see you at lunch."

My cheeks burned with the wide, genuine smile I angled up at the considerate man. "See, you're the sweetest." Pushing up to my tiptoes, I wrapped both arms around his neck and pulled him down to me. "Thank you for being cool about this, about him being here."

His gaze scanned my face. "He seems to make you happy. Does he, or do I need to kill him?"

Rolling my eyes at that last part, I gave myself a moment to come up with the right response. "At first, I was shocked that he was here and looked so, so different. I'll have to find pictures of him from high school. You'll be surprised at the difference. Then I was confused why he was here, then excited *and* confused. I guess that's where I am still, confused but loving that my old friend is here meshing with my present."

"What's your take on his explanation of coming to Alaska to see you? Did you two talk about that before I got there earlier?"

I pressed my cheek against his hard chest, allowing his steady heartbeat to soothe my nerves. "Yeah, I honestly think he's lonely and needs a friend. *Lost* may be a better word. I don't think he came with malicious intent. And, Liam." I pulled back to gaze up at him so he could see my sincerity. "Nothing will happen with him, between him and me. I know what happened with your late wife is a trigger, so I want you to know and be reassured that I wouldn't do that to you. Go behind your back, I mean."

His lids fluttered closed, and he released a heavy sigh. "Thank you, Baylee." A slow smile pulled at his lips. "And yeah, he doesn't have any malicious intent. I would've made him disappear if I sensed that," he remarked offhandedly. "I'm just not buying his being here for just a friendship." I angled my head to the side in confusion. "Based on what I've heard from those stories of you three, I think he wanted you back then and is here to see if there could be an opportunity now."

"Really?" I breathed. "Well, that's... something."

Liam's chest vibrated with a chuckle. With a soft kiss to the top of my head, he stepped out of my hold but kept an arm draped over my shoulders. "Just know one thing, Little Bit. I'm yours as long as you'll have me. While you're trying to figure out how you feel about him being here and him in general, I'll support whatever you want. I know you won't go behind my back and keep anything hidden like she did." He looked at the sky. "What I'm trying to say is, if you find you have mutual feelings for him *and* want me, too, I'm here."

"Whatever I want?" I mused, tapping a single finger against my chin. "That's a lot of things after this morning." I waggled my brows, then pulled them in tight. "Don't take this the wrong way, Liam, but you seem a little—" I bit my lip as I searched for the right word. "—possessive for an open relationship."

"I am, but I'll also do anything to keep you in my life, and I want you happy. Being around the others here has taught me that as long as it's a good fit for everyone, it makes sense. It's difficult because this guy is an unknown to me, but for you, Little Bit, I'll do anything to make you happy."

"How did I get so lucky?" I whispered, meaning every word.

A wet tongue swiped along my palm, drawing my focus down to the panting Elvis. Memphis hovered by the back of the truck doing something on his phone, giving us a bit of privacy.

"All right. You go do your chores, and we'll see you back at my place later for dinner. Not sure what we'll eat, but I'll figure something out," I said.

"I can cook." Memphis sauntered over, hands tucked into the front pockets of his dark jeans. "Depending on what you have at your place, I'm sure I can figure something out." Blush stained his cheeks. "While in rehab, I became obsessed with cooking shows. It gave me something to do and kept me out of places that served alcohol once I was out on my own."

"Works for me." With a quick kiss to the top of my head, Liam raised a hand at Memphis and started toward the barn. I didn't hide the way I ogled his fine ass as he walked away.

"Damn, you have it bad," Memphis chuckled, leaning against the truck beside me.

"You would, too, if you appreciated a fine ass like Liam's. We can come back for your bags. They're safe in the truck while we walk around." Shaking my head, I looped my arm through his and started toward the main road. Gravel crunched under our shoes as we walked. "It's crazy that I'd be attracted to someone like him, right? Dean was such a...."

"Scrawny fucker," Memphis finished for me with a laugh. "Yeah, those two couldn't be more different physically."

He sealed his lips shut like he had more to say but didn't know how. Not wanting to push him if he wasn't ready to share just yet, I shifted topics.

"So, this community was built by the owner of Uplift Adventure and Rescue. Brandon and his two partners, Amy and Carl, started this place from the ground up. They all worked for some shady excursion place in Montana before they moved here."

We strolled down the center lane that separated the cabins. As we passed Miles, Aspen, and Aiden's place, the sound of laughter poured out of the open windows, making me smile.

"We're a tight-knit family here, all with our own responsibilities. Almost everyone here works for Uplift in some capacity. While I don't take clients out on hikes, ATV rides, fishing excursions, or helicopter tours, I take care of the animals. We have goats, chickens, and horses—all have some purpose. Then in my off time, I run the vet clinic in town, and I also make house calls to those who don't want to come into town or can't."

Memphis nodded along as I spoke, his assessing gaze roaming over the well-built cottages, animals running amok, and gorgeous backdrop. A flash of white followed by a massive dog darted across the street several feet in front of us.

Elvis barked and raced off to join the fun with happy yips. Memphis cursed and started after him, but I tugged him to a stop.

"He'll be okay. Jubie is a great dog. She's just chasing after BamBam. Those two are friends, I guess." I shrugged, not sure how to explain the dog and ermine's relationship. "We're very animal friendly here if you can't tell."

"I'm sure you had something to do with that," Memphis murmured as he leaned forward to see where Elvis had run off to.

"Yes and no. Me being a vet makes it easy for everyone who wants an animal to get the proper care for their furry family members, but most here love animals just as much as I do. And dogs like Jubie are crucial for rescue missions." I paused. "Well, if BamBam is out playing, then we don't have to go to my cabin, since you'll see that later. How about I show you the greenhouse and then the barn?"

Memphis slowly nodded, seeming a little taken aback by it all, and reached inside his jacket pocket, pulling out a pack of cigarettes. "Cool if I have one on our way?"

With my nod, he lit the end and inhaled deeply. I suddenly found myself fascinated by the way the smoke swirled out of his pursed lips, or maybe it was just his lips in general.

"Sorry. Smoking is a bad habit, I know, but it's the one addiction I just can't kick. The lesser of all the evils and all that, I guess."

Watching him smoke was just one more reminder that

the man beside me was no longer that boy I knew and now very much a man. The tattoos on his throat moved as he stretched out his neck.

"How are you doing, Baylee?" His question jolted me out of my daze. "Dean's death was a shock to everyone, but you're the one whose future was just gone one day."

I swallowed down the emotions attempting to clog my throat. "It's been difficult, and I'm not over it, honestly. The people here, my friends and Liam, are patient with me, helping me understand that I don't have to heal alone. I miss him every day, but it also gets a little easier each day to breathe when he crosses my mind. I've struggled with a lot of guilt, which has made the healing process tough."

"Guilt?" he questioned after taking a long drag. "About what?"

"That I made us wait for me to graduate to be together, that I put school before him, that I stopped going to see him as much when he wasn't deployed. The list could go on and on. I know I had nothing to do with his death, but what if I would've asked him to move to Texas with me? What if—"

He slowed to a stop and grabbed my hand.

"You'll drive yourself crazy with all the what-ifs. We all could. You know Dean. He wouldn't have messed with your dream of becoming a veterinarian even if you had asked him to move to Texas. You both did what you needed to do separately for your future." He searched my face. "Dean really never told you we had a falling-out?" I slowly shook my head. "That's... surprising."

"Why? What was it all about anyway?"

Memphis dropped the cigarette to the ground and crushed it beneath the heel of his black boot. "That's a conversation for another time, Bay. Right now, I want to remember all the good times we had with him, not the one moment I wish like fuck I could take back."

Despite my curiosity begging me to push him on the topic, I smiled and gave his hand a slight squeeze.

"Remember that time he wanted to see if he could outrun a bull?" Memphis's lips curled upward, and a spark shone in his green eyes. "And found out real quick that he couldn't."

His deep rumbled laughter had my heart swelling with joy and hope.

This.

This was exactly what I needed. To remember Dean and all the good times we had without immediately falling into mourning for him in the same breath.

As Memphis recalled another idiotic idea Dean had in high school, I tipped my face up to the low gray clouds and said a silent thank-you. I'd asked Dean for a sign that it was okay to move on, to let go of a future that would never happen the way I'd imagined.

The man from my past who'd walked into my present was just the sign I needed.

It was officially time to move on.

## LIAM

My content grin hadn't dropped since the sounds of her laughter and the scent of something delicious cooking met me when I opened her cabin door. Baylee had turned to me when I walked in, joy radiating off her, and beckoned me over, pulling me into her arms to kiss me like she hadn't seen me all day. While I sipped on a glass of water, wishing like hell it was a cold beer, she and Memphis traded crazy memories from high school while he cooked, and she watched from her perch on the island counter.

The whole fucking thing was homey, warm, and damn amazing after working my ass off all day. Dinner was fresh, healthy, and fucking delicious, and I wasn't the only one who thought so. Baylee ate more in one sitting than I'd seen her eat before, maybe ever.

Drying my hands on a towel after finishing the dishes, I headed for the couch to join the other two. Heat radiated from the fireplace, flames casting a relaxed glow over the living room from the small fire I started before dinner to chase away the damp chill brought in by the storm raging outside. Rain had been battering on the metal roof and pelting the windows for the last hour, adding to the cozy evening.

The cushion dipped beneath me, the motion causing Baylee to press against my side. At her content sigh, I glanced at Memphis in the single armchair and inclined my head in silent thanks for his part in making my girl so damn happy and relaxed. The serene smile tugging at his lips as he watched her contradicted the tatted hardass his outward appearance made you want to assume he was.

"I need to get cleaned up," Baylee announced while pushing off the couch to stand. She stretched both arms high into the air, making the scrub top lift, exposing a sliver of soft porcelain skin. "I won't be long."

Both our gazes followed her out of the room until she disappeared into the bedroom and we heard the click of the bathroom door. I studied him out of the corner of my eye, still unsure of his real reason for being in Anchor Bay. Memphis stared into the fire, tatted fingers loosely interlaced and dangling between his spread knees, as if lost in thought.

"Shoot me straight, Memphis. Why are you really here?" I asked, my deep voice cutting through the fire's peaceful crackle.

His eyes didn't leave the dancing flames. "I wish I could tell you, but I honestly don't know myself. I saw her picture, and I knew I needed to see her. There was this insistent pull to this place that I couldn't ignore." The leather groaned when he leaned back in the chair and rested his ankle over the opposite knee. "Baylee is the woman no one else could live up to in my mind. I guess I'm here for some closure regarding Dean and to see if she'd want me in her life again. I miss my best friend, but after today, I realized maybe I missed her more."

I hummed in agreement and shifted on the couch to get comfortable. "I can see that. Now that I've known her, had her in my life, I'd miss her too. Do anything, including fly across the country, to see her again."

He nodded, running a hand through his hair, disheveling the styled dirty-blond strands. "I wasn't sure how she'd react. It'd been so long since we last saw each other, but I'd hoped that she'd remember me the way I remembered her, want that connection again. Fuck, I don't know."

"Were you hoping for more than a friendship with her?" I asked carefully. I didn't want to push either of them, but it was clear they each still had unresolved feelings for the other. Now they were both in a position to explore that connection—with me directing it all, of course.

Fuck, just thinking about that had my cock twitching.

His odd, light green eyes met mine. "I hoped for anything that she would give me. If that was just friends, then that was what I'd be. But yeah, a part of me wished that the spark we had back then, even with Dean in the mix, would still be there."

"Is that what the fallout between you and him was about?" I leaned forward, not dropping his intense gaze. "You told Dean how you felt about her?"

He bit his lip and shifted his stare back to the flames. "No. Though he threw that in my face, saying I was trying to break them up so I could have her for myself."

"Were you?"

"Fuck no. I wanted to be a part of the relationship, not the rift between them." He shook his head and dropped it back to regard the ceiling. "I wanted what they had so fucking much, wanted them to want me even if that was crazy talk. Dean liked to fuck with me since he knew I liked her, would start shit on the couch with Baylee while I sat right there. And hell yes, I'd watch. She knew I was, too, which made it all so fucking hot."

"Have you ever tried it?"

"Tried what?" he asked, sounding exhausted.

His dog pushed off the floor from where he lay beside the chair and rested his large head on Memphis's leg. Long tattooed fingers brushed over his fur before scratching behind each ear, causing the dog's tail to rapidly thump on the hardwood floor.

"A poly relationship, more than one romantic partner, like in our community. Have you ever tried it?"

He shook his head, not looking away from Elvis. "No, though I'll admit after being here, I'm intrigued. What about you?" He peeked over through his light lashes. "Was this all new to you, or were you in this lifestyle before?"

"I was in one but didn't realize it," I grumbled, and his brows rose. That single ring glinted in the firelight. "Before moving here, I was married, faithful to her even though we hardly saw each other because of my deployments. She was killed in a car wreck, head-on collision. Later I found out she wasn't the driver—her fucking boyfriend was."

"Oh fuck. I'm assuming he died in the crash, too, or you killed him with your bearlike hands."

I snorted a laugh, which was shocking considering this topic always fueled that undercurrent of anger running through me. "I figured out she was having an affair with some guy for a while behind my back. The cops relayed all the information on the accident investigation, and I also did my own, uncovering a lot of other shit I really wish I hadn't."

"Like?" He leaned forward, clearly engrossed in my fucked-up past.

I rolled my eyes to the ceiling, trying to remember some

of the worst of those discoveries. "Like the fucker wasn't her first boyfriend and probably wouldn't have been her last. She told her friends she was unhappy in the marriage but didn't want to leave me, so she just fucked around while I was away, then acted fine when I was home. That fucked with me for a long time. How she could act happy but was doing that behind my back. Everything felt so fucking fake, and I hated it."

The dog's head swiveled my way with a whine. I tapped a single finger on my thigh, and he trotted over and rested his muzzle on my leg, with big dark eyes gazing up at me like he desperately wanted to soothe me.

"Is he a therapy dog?"

"Not trained, but he picks up on moods. Elvis has been with me through it all—the rehab program even let him come with me. I think he's more hyperaware of strong emotions than most dogs. He likes his ears scratched," Memphis added. "What happened after all that?"

"A funeral that I didn't even want to attend because I felt so fucking betrayed, but I still went out of loyalty to our marriage. After that, I lost myself for a while. Went back to the rodeo circuit in Montana, picked up amateur MMA fights, too, but none of it helped the"—I pressed a fist to my chest where the pain used to live—"anger and grief. Someone knew a guy named Brandon who started an adventure and rescue company in Alaska and needed help. I had one conversation with the guy and knew it was my shot at breaking out of the misery I'd fallen into. I packed up my shit and moved here." A small smile pulled at my lips. "Then she came."

"Baylee." At a whine and pressure on my thigh, I resumed running the tips of my fingers through Elvis's short coarse fur. "She moved here right after Dean's death?"

Memphis questioned, watching me and Elvis with a goofy grin.

"A while after the funeral, yeah. Even in her utter grief, the sadness that wrapped around her, she was breathtakingly beautiful. Every aspect of her felt real, no agenda or manipulations. It was the complete opposite of what I knew before, and it instantly drew me to her. But knowing she was mourning and vulnerable, I didn't want to take advantage, so I waited."

"And waited and waited and waited."

Both of our heads whipped around at the sound of Baylee's voice. She tiptoed into the room, rounding the couch to stand in front of where I sat. I swallowed the distressed groan that wanted to escape at the sight of her in the oversized shirt that hung down her thighs, covering up whatever sleep shorts she wore beneath. If she even wore any.

She looked down at me. "You're a good man, Liam, and I'm sorry I made you wait so long, that my grief—"

Hands around her hips, I guided her onto my lap, her legs falling to either side of my hips. Over her shoulder, I smirked at finding Memphis's heated stare locked on her ass.

"You're allowed whatever time you need, Little Bit. My biggest fear was you getting stuck there. You deserve so much more than that dark, sad state of living."

"I don't know if I do."

"Please tell me you don't believe that, Bay." She shifted to glance at Memphis. "Dean wouldn't have wanted you to mourn him forever, to not move on and be happy."

"It just feels so wrong to be here, to be happy when he's not. He's gone." Her voice broke and her head fell forward, allowing her blonde hair to curtain around her face.

Pulling her even closer, I wrapped both arms around her back until she buried her face against my neck.

"But you're still here," Memphis stated, pushing out of the chair to stand in front of the fire. His fingers twitched at his sides, as if fighting the urge to rip her out of my arms. I curled my lip in a silent snarl that had him holding up both hands in surrender. "You didn't die with him, Baylee. Maybe the future you wanted, but not your actual future. There is so much more to look forward to. If all the group therapy in that rehab program taught me anything, it's that we learn from our past, but don't let it dictate your future."

Silence filled the cabin for several long seconds. Her gentle breaths brushed along my neck, making me relax into the cushions as the tension drained from my tight muscles. If I could have her in my arms every day, maybe I wouldn't be so fucking angry or have the urge to kick the shit out of someone just because I needed a release.

"I asked Dean to give me a sign that it was okay. Time for me to move on." She pressed her small hands to my chest, pushing back to find Memphis with her watery blue gaze. "Then you showed up, and I feel...." Memphis's shoulders rose to his ears, the tension in his frame almost palpable. Elvis trotted over to where he stood and nosed a clenched fist. "Relieved. Happy. Settled even." Her gaze flicked to me, and she licked her lips. "Though that could also be from the fun we had this morning too."

I squeezed my eyes shut and pressed the back of my head hard into the couch. Memories from earlier flickered behind my lids, making my cock twitch in my jeans. My nostrils flared with every deep inhale.

"Must have been good with that reaction," Memphis mused.

"All I'm saying is, I'm glad you're here, Memphis. It's

great to see you. Today was so fun showing you around, introducing you to the people I call family now, and talking about Dean." After a couple of failed attempts to turn herself around on my lap, Baylee released a defeated sigh and peeked up at me through her lashes. "Help me turn around, please."

"But I like you straddling me." I grabbed a handful of her ass and squeezed.

"Please," she repeated. "I can stay sitting on your lap, just the other way."

Like I could ever deny her anything she asked, even if what she wanted was my last breath. Hands on her waist, I easily lifted her slight frame in the air, holding her up while she twisted around. Her round ass came down hard on my stiff cock, making me grunt. Baylee sent me an apologetic smile over her shoulder before turning her attention back to Memphis.

"Instead of making me sad, talking about Dean and us three back in high school made me happy. It was like with every story we told, a little more of that exhausting grief vanished, leaving me feeling lighter. I'd already decided it was time to move on, to let the past go, but you being here helped solidify that decision."

Memphis's shoulders slumped in seeming relief. "While he and I lost touch the last few years, he was still my best friend. I miss him all the time and enjoyed talking about him today, too, so whenever you're in the mood to walk down memory lane...."

"You're my guy," she finished for him.

Wrapping an arm around her waist, I tugged her back until her spine pressed to my chest. With a single finger, I swept her long hair away from her ear and pressed my lips to the shell.

"Is that all he's your guy for?" I felt her breath hitch and heart rate increase. "From what I've picked up on, there was more to your friendship back in high school."

"Liam," Memphis cursed, though his curious gaze was locked on Baylee, gauging her reaction. "Don't push her."

I hummed a noncommittal response while trailing a single fingertip up her thigh, brushing the hem of the T-shirt up with each lazy stroke. His gaze followed the movement while Baylee's breathing picked up.

"I'm not pushing. I'm reading the fucking room. She said you make her happy. I want her happy and taken care of." I nibbled at her earlobe, making a sweet whimper leave her lips. "Taken care of in all the ways. If you say stop, I stop, pick you up, and finish this in the bedroom alone. Or...."

"Or what?" she asked, the words more of a pushed breath.

"Is it still there, Little Bit?"

"Is what still there?"

"The attraction," I murmured while stroking my finger even higher along the inside of her thigh, loving the feel of the goose bumps pebbling her soft skin. "Seemed like you were back then, but what about now? What about the guy standing in front of you, looking like he would fight me to the death just for the opportunity to be in my place right now."

"Fucking hell," Memphis cursed, running one hand through his hair while the other reached down to adjust himself.

"See what you're doing to him," I whispered. "So, what will it be, sweetheart? Are we staying out here to have a little fun, something to take the edge off what's building here, or am I carrying you into your room to worship you in private?"

Her quick pants mixed with my heavy breaths as I waited for her response. I'd been patient for a long time, and I sure as hell wouldn't rush her into something now. But the crazy fact was, this wasn't forced on my end. Hell, I was so fucking turned on at the idea of that fucker watching me play with her that my dick throbbed.

I hadn't tried the poly lifestyle, so I didn't realize I would be *this* into it. But since this afternoon, watching them laugh, seeing her so fucking happy, the image of us three as a unit wouldn't go away. There was something about him specifically. Maybe it was their history, or the way he looked at her like he'd stab himself in the dick to keep her safe. That made this all not only okay in my mind but fucking hot as hell.

An attraction to other men had never been my thing, though I had to admit, Memphis had something about him that made me wonder if he'd be the first. Not that I wanted to fuck him like I wanted with Baylee, more like I wanted control over him. To dominate him. Make him do whatever the fuck I wanted him to do, and if he pushed back, which I hoped he would, then do whatever it took to make him obey.

I swallowed a groan, picturing me ordering him to please Baylee while I watched, driving them both insane with need before allowing them to fall over that edge.

"Bay?" Memphis hissed as he tightened his fingers around the outline of his cock over his jeans.

"Yes."

My gaze snapped to Memphis's. "Is that a yes to staying out here or a response to him saying your name like a damn plea?"

"Yes to staying out here." She shifted on my lap, her tiny button nose brushing against the tip of my own. "Are you sure you're okay with this? Just because I want it, am attracted to both of you, doesn't mean you have to accommodate my wants—"

I shut her up with a hard kiss, palm pressed to the back of her head to keep her right where I wanted her until I made my point. Fingers threaded through her hair, I tugged until our lips pulled apart.

"I'd give you my damn heart on a platter if I knew that was what you wanted, what would make you happy. I'm not the type of man who would do anything he didn't want to do, you know this. If I'm asking, being the one to start this, then you know I want it, too, and it's not just for you, sweetheart." Her eyes flared as she searched my face. "I don't know what this will be tomorrow, but right now, it's fucking hot as hell, and I've never been so damn hard in my life."

"I want you," Baylee whispered as she squirmed on my lap, making me groan. "All of you."

My nostrils flared with the restraint it took not to rip off her clothes and slam my cock into her virgin hole.

"Maybe later, alone. Your first time doesn't need to be with me rutting you like a damn animal like I would be right now, or with an audience. That will just be for us."

Stealing another kiss, I shifted her back in place, using my knees to spread her legs open wide. The long T-shirt rose up her thighs, exposing her to Memphis.

"Right now, though, let's see just how much your friend can take."

"Before what?" she asked, breaths coming in quick pants.

I sent a sharp smile to Memphis, who cursed at whatever he saw on my face. "Before he breaks."

## 15

## MEMPHIS

That sneaky, brilliant, pushy motherfucker. If this was the game he wanted to play, I was fucking ready. It was as hot as I remembered, watching Baylee squirm from the touch of another man. Heat from the fire warmed my back where I stayed rooted in place, unwilling to move, afraid it would disrupt whatever the hell he had planned for us.

I'd fucking stop breathing to ensure neither of them changed their mind about me watching.

My cock jerked in my snug boxer briefs, desperate for my touch, or hers—or hell, with how turned on I was, maybe even his.

"Sit down," Liam ordered. His commanding tone had my feet moving before I even knew what I was doing. "Good boy."

I arched a brow as I sank down into the chair. "I don't have a praise kink, but thanks."

He kept his gaze locked on me as he ran the tip of his nose over her arched throat. "What is your kink, then, hmm?" he asked.

"You first." Heat scorched beneath my skin, making me twitchy. Heart racing and breathing labored, I shot a glare at the fire, wanting to blame it for my sudden hot flash even though that didn't explain why my cock hardened at his voice.

Liam's responding deep chuckle was full of menace and danger. "I thought it was obvious by now. Control, and recently, watching this one eat." Baylee smiled up at Liam, which he returned, losing all the harsh lines and intensity as he gazed down at her. "And one other that I'll keep to myself for now."

*Color me intrigued.* My eyes narrowed on him.

"Pain?"

He shrugged with a knowing smirk.

"Ass shit?"

That made him bark out a laugh.

"Gerbils."

"You want to keep running your mouth or watch me play with Baylee's drenched pussy?" One hand threaded through her hair as he tugged her head to the side to kiss along her neck. "And I know it's drenched because I can smell how wet she is."

Her responding whimper had me slapping both palms to the armrests, fingers clenching the soft leather to keep from launching off the chair and diving between her spread thighs.

"Bondage," I rasped, making them both freeze. "And exhibitionism, especially if there's a high probability of getting caught."

Baylee's crystal blue eyes were so wide it would be comical any other time. "You like tying up your partners?"

I dipped my chin. Forcing my grip to relax, I interlaced both hands behind my head. "Nothing too kinky or extravagant, but yes. It could even just be my hands holding them down." I licked my lower lip as I studied her flushed face. "Like holding your wrists hostage against your spine with your face pressed to the mattress and ass in the air."

"I'd like to see that," Liam mused as he ran a finger up her inner thigh, raising the hem of her sleep shirt even higher. "What about this?" His other hand released her hair to gently clasp around her throat, holding her head to his shoulder.

I felt my pulse in every fucking inch of my body. Sweat collected on the back of my neck as I resisted the urge to stick a hand down my pants and squeeze my throbbing cock. Warmth rose along my neck and up to my cheeks as arousal blistered through my veins.

"I'll take that as a yes," Liam chuckled. "Let's see about her, see if she likes it as much as you do. And me, if I'm honest. It scratches that control itch that I crave too."

"Do it," I rasped. "Show me."

With a sharp smile, Liam gripped the hem of Baylee's long tee and dragged it higher, first exposing her lavender lace panties and then her bare tits.

"Fuck, she doesn't have a bra on." No longer able to hold back, I worked my belt buckle free, the metal clinking together, mixing with our combined harsh breaths. My fingers trembled as I undid my jeans. Shifting on the seat to give me room, I shoved a hand down into my boxer briefs, palm immediately wrapping around my cock, though it offered little relief.

Tucking the T-shirt under her arms, Liam stroked a finger from the center of her breasts down to her belly button and back up to circle one peaked nipple, then the other.

"Can you see how wet she is from there?"

I nodded, biting my lip to silence a guttural groan as I stared at her lace-covered center.

"Tell me," he demanded, voice harsh, exposing how affected he was too.

My gaze zeroed in on the glistening wet spot darkening the center of her panties. Tracing the tip of my tongue along my lips, I fantasized about doing the same to her pussy. I jerked my cock and tightened my hold. "There's a wet spot that covers the entire area of her pussy. She must be fucking soaked. Fuck, I can smell her too." A grunt escaped as I fought against my urge to dive between her thighs. "I want to taste her so damn bad. It's all I can do to stay here."

"I can tell you from experience, she tastes even better than she smells. And if you think your restraint is at its max now, wait until you hear the sounds she makes. The soft pleas and desperate begging followed by beautiful whimpers are enough to make any man break."

As if to prove him right, she released one of those desperate whimpers. Baylee's hooded gaze locked with mine.

"You still with us, Bay?" I asked to gauge if this was too much. The buildup was fucking fantastic and not how I'd expected the day to end, but I was grateful that it did.

"I need more," Baylee begged. The fingers wrapped around her throat moved with each word. "Please, Liam."

Liam's finger stilled where it hovered just over one peaked nipple at her plea. With the barest touch, he flicked the tip, causing her to squirm on his lap. Pinching it between two fingers, he pulled it taut. Baylee's back bowed off his chest with a hiss that quickly morphed into a moan.

Palm on her sternum, he slid his hand down to her stomach, then continued to move lower, his hungry gaze tracking every inch just like my own. Each breath hurt, like my lungs were too tight. Jerking my hand up and down my length, I waited, barely breathing, as he traced the top of the lace. His fingers dipped beneath the delicate material, stretching it out when he cupped her pussy, Liam's lids fluttering shut as he cursed.

"Fucking hell." The fingers around her throat flexed, making me choke on my tongue. "Do you know how easy it would be to slide inside you right now, sweetheart? With how wet you are, even that virgin pussy wouldn't offer my dick any resistance."

"Liam," I grunted.

It was the only word I could get out, but he understood what I meant, what I silently needed. Pulling his hand free, he gripped one side of the lace and yanked, almost yanking her off his lap with the force. The material snapped. Baylee's lips parted, probably to complain about the ruined panties, but Liam silenced her by directing her mouth to his in a demanding kiss.

As their lips moved together, each hungry and devouring the other, Liam snapped the other side of the lace and flung the ruined material over his shoulder to land somewhere in the kitchen. With his hand on her throat and the other on her hip, I had an unobstructed view of her spread pussy. Even with the dim light from the fire, I could see every perfect pink inch. Her dripping entrance and swollen nub called to me, demanding my mouth and tongue.

Unable to resist another second, even knowing it would probably end with my death at Liam's hands, I jerked my hand free and stood. In two quick strides, I stood between their combined spread thighs. Not looking away from her center, I dropped to my knees and pressed a palm to each inner thigh, spreading her even wider.

"Holy fuck, you're beautiful everywhere, Bay." I peeked up through my lashes, finding both their hooded gazes locked on me. "Do you know how many times I dreamed of being right here, of kneeling between your thighs while...?" I shook my head, not wanting to bring up Dean's name. Not now. He was in our past for sure, but he didn't get to be here now. Liam was here; he didn't deserve to be in the shadow of a dead man.

"I didn't say you could move," Liam growled. "But now that you're here, you might as well make yourself useful. Sweetheart, wrap your arms around my head and hold them there."

I almost choked on my spit when she complied, hooking both hands behind him, which forced her tits into the air as her back arched. He released her throat to slide his hand lower, cupping one breast in his massive palm.

He reached his other one out and threaded it in my hair, making me jerk back, but his grip held me in place.

"What the fuck, man?" I growled, fighting the urge to escape.

"I told you I like control, and you took that away when you got out of the chair without my approval. So now, this is what we do. You want to eat her cunt, then I'm going to guide you."

I stopped fighting. "Oh. I thought you were going to make me take your cock or something."

He arched a dark brow. "Not my thing, remember. Though based on your statement at the hardware store, it sounds like you might be questioning if it's yours."

My lip curled in a snarl, but I didn't refute his statement.

The corners of his mouth tilted upward, and I fucking knew the next words out of his mouth before he said them. "Good boy."

"Fuck you."

"Again, not my thing," he chuckled as he kissed the side of Baylee's neck, making her squirm. "Now, this is what's going to happen. You're going to lick her from entrance to clit, lapping her clean until I tell you to stop."

Before I could respond, with his hold in my hair, he yanked my face right to the center of her thighs. A feral moan rattled in my throat at the first taste of her on my tongue as I did just as he instructed. Sweet and tangy, her flavor was now embedded in my cells, one I'd never forget and would crave the rest of my life.

Reaching into my pants, I fisted my cock in a punishing grip and jerked in time with each slow swipe of my tongue. Baylee squirmed on Liam, his feral grunts filling me with smug satisfaction, knowing he wasn't getting out of this without some pain-filled restraint either. Soft, quick pants made her chest rise and fall in quick succession as the porcelain skin of her chest all the way up to her cheeks flushed a perfect pink.

I hissed in protest when he yanked me back by my hair. I bit my tongue to keep from cussing out the asshole as his hand dipped between her thighs.

One thick finger slid inside her dripping pussy to the first knuckle before retreating, repeating the motion each time, sinking deeper. I stared, mesmerized, as his finger disappeared inside her, barely breathing except for the harsh grunts that escaped with every jerk on my cock.

"Describe how her pussy takes my finger, how she stretches around it like a good girl."

I forced my focus from her weeping cunt to Liam's face. His eyes were sealed shut as if in pain, teeth digging into his lower lip. When his lids fluttered open and his gaze locked on me, the firm grasp in my hair tightened in a not-so-gentle reminder of his demand.

"She's fucking perfect. I could come just watching her pussy suck your finger in like she's desperate. I bet she could take more," I rasped, holding on to my sanity by a damn thread. This was by far the hottest, most erotic thing I'd ever done, and I fucking loved it. "She'll need help to relax to fit two inside her."

Without warning, he jerked me forward until my lips were hovering over her core while his finger continued to slowly thrust in and out.

"Suck on her swollen clit, then. Help her relax enough to take more." He leaned in close to her ear. "We need to get this pretty pussy stretched and ready to take me at some point, sweetheart. Stretch your cunt so I can fuck you in all the ways I've fantasized these last few months without hurting you."

"Yes," Baylee begged. "I want it now, please," Her head rolled side to side along his shoulder as tears leaked from the corners of her eyes. "I need it."

"Don't worry. We know exactly what you need." His gray eyes met mine in a silent demand to help ease her pain in the best way possible.

Fucking gladly.

A slight sting radiated along my scalp from his tight hold as I inched forward to wrap my lips around her swollen nub. At the first flick of my tongue, her rasped scream echoed around the cabin, making me smirk. Below my lips, Liam's hand moved back and forth. The grunt that came from him and the following sweet mewling from her told me he'd added another thick digit.

"Fucking hell, just two of my fingers can barely fit," Liam hissed.

Humming, knowing that small vibration would send her over the edge, I sucked hard and nipped. Her body shook, chanted curses filled the air, and the delicious sound of Liam's fingers pumping in and out grew louder as she gushed with her orgasm. As she slowly came down from her high, I gave a last lick and gentle kiss to her pussy before sitting back on my heels.

Liam's hold fell from my head to cup her breast, keeping her tight against his chest. Not wanting to waste a drop, I licked my lips clean, still staring at the obscene way his fingers stuffed her pussy full.

"Fuck, that's hot," I grunted as I squeezed my cock to keep from coming in my pants. My balls fucking hurt, and my dick was almost raw from jacking off with no lube.

Liam's hooded gaze met mine. It felt like he read everything going through my mind.

"Go take care of yourself," he ordered, voice tight from his own unfulfilled need pulsing through him.

My legs trembled when I stood, barely holding my weight as I stumbled to the side. "You've got her?" I didn't want to be a dick and walk away to focus on me after that perfect scene he controlled for us. Baylee's aftercare was more important than me finding relief.

"Yes, of course." He angled a disbelieving, awed smile at Baylee, who looked so damn relaxed that she very well could be asleep. "Go."

Elvis stood and stretched from where he lounged in front of the fire, but I waved him off, not wanting my dog to watch me fuck my hand in the shower. Thank fuck he didn't react to Baylee's screams or my tortured grunts.

Not bothering with the overhead light—the open door allowed enough light to filter through—I immediately stripped, eager to get rid of the constricting material.

Gripping the lever, I twisted it all the way to the left, waiting just outside the freezing-cold spray until it warmed while teasing my cock and gripping my balls, too keyed up to stop. Water pounded from the showerhead, soaking my hair first, dripping down the sides of my face as I pumped my fist from base to tip, flicking the barbell pierced through the head until a hiss whistled through my clenched teeth from the perfect pain.

Blinding light had my lids popping open at the sudden burst that filled the bathroom. Through the fogged glass, I found Liam standing in the doorway with Baylee in his arms. The shock at the disruption quickly changed to an unrelenting craving.

"Sweetheart here wants to watch you." His voice was so tight, I almost couldn't hear the words over the shower. "You good with that?"

Good with her wanting to watch me jack off? Was that a trick question?

"Fuck yes, she can watch me any time she wants." I ran a palm down the glass to clear the steam, allowing her to see me clearly. Her wide, crystal blue gaze took in every inch of my inked body. "Like what you see, Bay?"

"Yes," she breathed.

I looked down at the swirls of black designs that covered my chest to the Mexican sugar skull tattoo decorating my rippled abs. The small barbell pierced through the head of my dick glinted in the light, and a devilish smirk pulled at my lips. Wiping away the steam right in front of my cock, I stepped closer to the glass, almost pressing the sensitive skin to the smooth surface in my desperation for her to see it. I knew the second they both noticed the piercing.

"Fucking hell," Liam muttered, eyes squeezing shut.

"Wow," Baylee mouthed.

Taking in her bare tits and exposed center, I bit my lower lip hard as my hand moved in quicker pumps. But when she wrapped her fingers around Liam's wrist to guide his hand back between her thighs, my movements stuttered.

Liam's eyes flew open. "Are you too sore?" he asked, though there was no hiding the hopefulness in his tone.

Her white-blonde hair shifted, cascading over her shoulders with the quick headshake.

His lips moved, almost like he was saying a silent prayer as he cupped her mound. His gaze met mine. "Watch as my fingers disappear inside her and imagine it being your cock stuffing her perfect cunt."

The glass rattled beneath my palm when I slapped it to the smooth surface to keep from falling over. Widening my stance to stay upright, I zeroed in on his two fingers as they pushed inside her.

"Move closer," I grunted as my balls tightened.

With her cunt as a handle and the other hand palming her breast, Liam lifted her slight frame off the floor and guided her to lean against the glass. With his hand gone, her tits pressed to the shower door, and it was all I could do not to lick where her nipples strained against the glass.

I moved my palm to press where hers did on the other side. Our hooded gazes clashed. Lips parted, she dipped her face to watch my hand move along my dick.

"What will it feel like?" she asked.

"It's different for everyone, but fucking mind-blowing, that's how it will feel." I barely got the words out through my gritted teeth. I was so close, but I didn't want the moment to end. It was better than anything I'd ever dreamed, and I wasn't even touching her. Going forward, this would be a memory when I was alone and needed release from now until I died.

"Oh fuck," she moaned, pressing her forehead to the glass. "I'm close."

"She's squeezing the life out of my fingers," Liam bit out. "You better fucking come with her."

It was as if his command snapped something inside me. A tingling sensation raced down my spine straight to my balls. Curling my hand into a fist, I resisted punching the glass as my body shook with the soul-shattering orgasm that rolled through me. I swayed, leg muscles trembling, but kept my hand sliding along my spent cock to prolong the almost painful release.

When I finally forced my eyes open, I found hers staring at me through the glass with wonder in her content gaze.

This. This was my life now.

There was no going back.

It was death or being here with Baylee, which apparently included Liam. And I didn't hate it.

Tonight confirmed that having a third in a relationship could be better than I'd ever imagined.

## 16

BAYLEE

I swallowed a whimper at the loss when Liam pulled his fingers free. With a hand on my hip, he whirled me around, pressing my sweat-slick back to the warm glass. Chin tipped up, I studied the tension lines on his face, the tight set of his lips. But all that quickly disappeared, morphing into a euphoric expression when two glistening fingers slid past his lips.

"You taste like heaven, sweetheart. I think I could survive on your cunt alone and be happy forever."

I swallowed hard, throat working with the movement.

"Baylee." I glanced over my shoulder at where Memphis was lathering up beneath the spray. "Pretty sure your man is in pain after all our fun, something you could help relieve."

I whipped back around, brows raised, feeling bad for forgetting about Liam's needs. I had felt how hard he was against my ass on the couch, then again where it dug into my back, keeping me pressed to the glass just now.

"I'm fine," Liam said around his fingers while shooting a death glare over my shoulder. "Don't make her feel bad, asshole, if she doesn't want—"

I pressed a hand to the center of his chest. "But I do want to. I really do."

And that was the truth.

For the first time in years, I finally felt free. Uninhibited by the heaviness, the guilt and pain that weighed me down. This bold, playful Baylee was the real me. Earlier in the day with Liam, and now tonight broke me free from whatever held me back from fucking living. Sure, I had toys, but all those orgasms felt hollow, leaving me even more lonely. But with them, I was loved, cared for, their only focus.

And that was everything.

My sluggish mind shifted through all the possibilities. I needed to feel him between my thighs. After having his hard cock pressing against me all night, I longed to feel it where I wanted it most.

Fingers wrapped around his wrist, I guided Liam into the bedroom. He didn't utter a word but followed obediently, which had a small smile pulling at my lips. After tonight, it was clear Liam needed control, but he allowed me to take over now.

It was comical, me maneuvering the massive man, positioning him exactly where I wanted him on the bed. The mattress dipped as he sat, his gaze never leaving mine. A single dark brow arched, but he still didn't say anything as I worked the buttons of his shirt, exposing his wide, muscular chest. Standing between his spread knees, I slipped the shirt off his shoulders, my fingers exploring every dip and curve of his corded muscles.

His belt took several tries to loosen, but he didn't get frustrated or take over. After working it off and then undoing the buttons of his jeans, I pressed my index finger to the center of his sternum, urging him to lie back on the soft duvet. Wearing a cocky smirk on his kissable lips, he complied, interlacing both hands behind his head, posing like a sexy calendar model. Fisting the stiff denim, I inched his jeans over his hips, exposing his huge, hard cock.

I'd seen it earlier that morning, had it in my mouth and hand, but still blinked in shock at how big he was. Memphis's cock was long and thick, but Liam was so wide it was almost intimidating thinking about it fitting inside me.

Almost as if he heard my internal thoughts, a calloused palm cupped my cheek and forced my gaze up to his.

"Not tonight," he whispered, gray gaze flitting across my face. "But when we do, it will fit."

A pitiful, desperate whimper escaped. I wanted him so fucking bad, wanted to feel that stretch if it was anything like how it felt with his fingers inside me.

I nodded. "I want to feel you there, even if it's not all the way."

His eyes widened a fraction. "Baylee." One knee on the bed, I froze at his guttural tone. "I don't trust myself to not take it further than we're both ready for. Not with your cunt that close, so easy to take with one hard thrust."

"I'll be here." My head jerked up. Memphis stood in the doorway with a towel wrapped around his waist, fingers clutching the top of the doorframe. "I won't let you hurt her."

Angling his head back, Liam stared at Memphis upside down. "Good. Thank you."

With a confirming nod, Memphis strode into the room and came to stand beside me. "We've got you, Bay."

Blowing out a breath, suddenly self-conscious, I continued crawling onto the bed. Straddling his hips, I gazed down at Liam in wonder. How had I gotten so damn lucky to find a man like him, protective and growly but utterly sweet and patient with me, and who understood my needs so effortlessly? I didn't deserve him, not even close, but I couldn't walk away. Not when he made me feel alive.

Palms pressed to his firm pecs to steady myself, I let my knees slide out wide. A whimper sounded in my throat when I settled over him, his cock nestled between my slick lips. Large hands wrapped around my hips and tightened, fingers digging into my skin.

"Holy shit," Liam panted as if he'd run a marathon. "Your cunt is so fucking hot and slick, and I'm not even inside you."

The desperate urge to move had me shifting along his thick shaft until the swollen head tapped against my clit. My arms trembled as an electric bolt filtered through every cell at the contact.

"This feels so good," I moaned, head tipped back and hair brushing along my spine. "Way better than my toys."

A second later, the sound of a drawer opening and things being shifted around had me looking to where Memphis rummaged through my bedside drawer. He held up a tiny vibrator, one I loved for a quick release, in one hand and a purple dildo in the other.

"Our girl has been taking care of her own needs." He clicked his tongue. "No more."

"Unless it's with us, those toys stay in that drawer, you hear me," Liam growled. Using the tight hold on my hips, he helped me slide along his cock faster. His chest rose and fell in quick succession as his movements grew erratic. One slide up had the head of his cock bumping against my entrance, almost pushing inside.

We both stilled. Our gazes locked.

With the slightest shift of his hips, the thick head of his cock pushed into my opening. A bolt of pleasure had me trembling and sinking even farther down to push him deeper.

"Memphis," Liam snapped.

"Oh fuck, sorry. Distracted by toys." He dropped both to the bed and moved to stand behind me. "None of that, Bay." I whimpered as desperate tears flooded my lower lids. "None of that. This isn't what you want."

"Yes, it is," I begged and shifted to push more of Liam into me.

Liam's hold tightened, only to fall away completely and be replaced by Memphis's. He lifted me with ease, hovering me in the air. "It's not. Not for your first time, Baylee," he whispered into my hair. "Don't talk us into that, please. We'll do anything for you, but let us make your first time better than now. So, can you be Liam's good girl and just slide along his cock?"

Fuck if I knew, but I wanted to feel him again, so I nodded.

"I'm in control," Liam said through a tight jaw. "But stay right there, just in case."

"Oh, I will, because I have an idea that will help our girl get off one more time and forget all about needing your dick stuffed inside her."

Liam's growl vibrated around the room. "Fucking hell, man, don't say shit like that right now."

"Sorry." His tone said he was anything but. Though I totally forgot about all that when Memphis lowered me back down to Liam and shifted me so his stiff length was nestled between my lips again. "Let's see how this thing works."

Before I could process his words, a familiar vibrating sound came from the small silver bullet in his hand. Liam cursed and gripped my hips, starting the frantic sliding motion all over again, but this time not letting me move too far up to keep us out of dangerous territory.

"I'm fucking close," he snapped. "Help her."

My lids fluttered closed when Memphis positioned the toy over my clit and pressed down. My body jerked with the sensation that zipped up my spine from the contact. Head tossed back, I focused on the feel of Liam moving against me while the vibrator catapulted me toward another mind-blowing orgasm.

With a rasped scream, I came for the third time that night, though it was just as devastating as the others. Liam's hold turned almost punishing as he ground me against him, his own release hitting him hard. Panting, unable to catch my breath, I jerked away from the vibrator, the sensation too much on my sensitive nub.

When Memphis moved it away, I fell forward, burying my face in Liam's neck. I pressed a soft kiss to his skin as gentle fingers slid up and down my spine.

"You're perfect, Baylee. In every way, you're perfect. And mine."

A throat cleared. "Ours?"

Liam's grumble made me smile.

Ours.

I liked the sound of that, even if I had no idea of how it would work.

That was a worry for another day.

BROW FURROWED, I searched the shallow cabinet for a third time. "Where the hell is that bottle?" I mumbled under my breath.

Glass clinked together as I shifted things around, but

still the missing bottle of antibiotic didn't magically appear. I studied the mostly full one in my hand, knowing I opened it last week but had made a mental note that there was another bottle behind it. Being where we were, supplies were often hard to get, and I kept at least one extra of everything stocked.

But where was that unopened bottle now?

"I finally feel human again." I turned at Amy's voice, distracting me from the mysterious missing antibiotic. "I swear I'm never drinking again." She paused beside me and leaned against the barn wall. "Well, for this week anyway."

"It's Saturday," I laughed.

"Exactly, so tomorrow I'm game for anything. Except duck farts." She bent over with an exaggerated fake gag. "No shots for a while."

My stomach rolled at the mention of the delicious but dangerous concoction. "Agreed, no shots." Reaching inside the cabinet, I grabbed a fresh syringe, unwrapped the plastic, and removed the cap from the needle. Jabbing it through the rubber seal, I pulled the plunger to the measurement needed.

"So, rumor mill is going wild this morning," she said, curiosity in her tone.

"Oh?" I replied with a smirk, knowing exactly where this was going. "About?"

"Don't play dumb with me, Baylee," Amy chastised, giving my shoulder a shove. We both looked up when the noise from the pounding rain on the roof increased. "Man, we're getting a ton of rain." She shook her head and pointed at me. "Not only did a certain cowboy who's been infatuated with you for months stay the night, but so did some mystery bad boy who showed up in Anchor Bay a few days ago."

I hummed a nonresponse while double-checking the

dosage I needed for Carla. The silly cow tried to escape—again—and cut her thigh bad enough that I worried about infection. Putting the vial back into the cabinet, I shut the metal door and put the cap back on the needle, shoving it into my lab coat to administer later.

"What are you wanting to know?" I asked, moving to sit on a bale of straw meant for the goat pens. We'd need a ton to cover their pens and others, since none of the animals could go outside because of the out-of-season heavy storm.

"I want to know if you're still a virgin," she stated with a straight face.

My lips popped open, and I gaped at my friend in utter shock at her bluntness.

My obvious shock made her serious expression break into a wide grin as she shoved my shoulder. "Just kidding. Kind of."

"I never should've told you guys," I grumbled in exasperation mixed with embarrassment while picking at the straw to distract myself.

"No, I'm only kidding with you, Baylee. I'm glad you told us. We're here for you. That was wrong of me to joke about." I shot her a small smile and nodded. "So, who is this mystery guy? Are his hands really fully tattooed?"

I followed her stare to where Memphis and Liam stood on opposite sides of a horse, brushing it down while talking in low voices. I couldn't help but smile at the sight of them, even if we'd been together all morning.

"Please tell me that goofy smile has something to do with those two."

Liam tipped his head back in what I assumed was a laugh, but the pounding rain on the roof swallowed the sound. Damn, he looked good in his Wranglers and boots. In true Liam fashion, he had on his customary button-up flannel shirt and cowboy hat too. The man looked down-right edible.

And rideable.

I squeezed my thighs together to calm the building throb. One would think after yesterday's activities, I'd be good for a while, but instead all those mind-blowing orgasms had the opposite effect. I craved release. Desire flooded my veins more than ever before. Sure, I'd been horny in the past, but never like this all-consuming need. And there were only two men I knew who could sate me.

A sliver of guilt weaved its way through my desire.

Did I ever crave Dean like I did Liam and now Memphis?

Noticing our stares, Memphis shot me a wink while Liam licked his lips like he could still taste me there. I relaxed against the wooden beam with a dreamy sigh.

"Oh hell," Amy laughed. "You have it bad." She tilted her head. "Wait a second. Did you guys...?" She waggled her brows.

Elbows pressed on both knees, I hid my face in my palms. "Amy," I groaned.

"Baylee." Her pouting tone had me peeking through my fingers and smiling at her expression. "I'm not asking for details—unless you're willing to give them, of course. I just... was it good?"

I sat up straight and blew a raspberry. "It was better than good. Great even. And what was even better, I didn't feel guilty about it."

She nodded, though she looked confused. "Because of your former fiancé."

"Yeah. Before, any time I'd kiss Liam or feel that rush of butterflies in my gut, it would turn to lead because of the guilt. Last night, though, with them both—"

"Oh shit," she muttered while fanning herself, making me laugh.

"—I didn't feel it once." I chewed on my lip and turned my focus to the piece of straw I was anxiously shredding. "Memphis is from my childhood. He, Dean, and I were best friends. And a part of me now recognizes that I had more than platonic feelings for Memphis back then, but I didn't know what to do with it because I was in love with Dean. Him being here now, it's like the final brick tied to my feet, keeping my head below the surface, has been released." I looked up through my lashes at Amy. "It's like I'm free."

With a high-pitched squeal even the rainstorm couldn't drown out, she launched herself at me, wrapping both arms around my neck and pulling me in tight.

"I don't think I've ever felt this happy for someone else, Baylee." She pulled back and held my face between her small hands, squeezing my cheeks. "Ever. You deserve every bit of happiness that you can wring from this life, and I'm so fucking glad you're in a place where you see that and can believe it."

"Thanks," I said, the word muffled because of her hold on my face.

Her hands dropped to mine. Tears flooded her lower lids as she smiled at me. "When we built this place, we didn't want it to be just somewhere to work but a family. When you came on board, my heart ached for you, but I knew there was a life waiting for you on the other side of your grief. You showed me that our community, Uplift, is so much more than I could've ever imagined. I've watched you heal, little by little, and seeing you like this"—tears leaked from the corners of her eyes—"is such a gift, a reminder of what a special little haven we're a part of."

"This place has been a godsend. I don't even want to

think about where I would be if it weren't for you and everyone else. There was no way I was going back home, and I was just so damn lost after the funeral."

Amy's brows pulled in tight. "Why couldn't you go home? I thought it was because you didn't want those memories, but the way you just said it makes me think there's more to it than that."

I chewed on the corner of my lip. "Well, yeah, there was that. I didn't want to drive around our hometown where everything reminded me of Dean, and now thinking about it, I didn't want to remember Memphis either since he was gone from my life too. But there was also his mother."

"Dean's," Amy clarified.

"She didn't take his death well," I said slowly, knowing that was putting it lightly. Psychotic break was a more accurate description based on my parents' recent emails. "She was great to me before he died, but after...." I shook my head to clear the memories of her at the funeral, the cold shoulder, hateful looks, and muttered awful, awful things when we'd pass each other, plus the lies she spread to everyone who attended. "I knew I couldn't be around that negativity while still reeling from his death. It was at the funeral that one of Dean's Army buddies mentioned Uplift, and, well, the rest is history."

"Everything okay over here?" The heels of Liam's boots clicked against the concrete as he strode toward us, his gray eyes locked on me.

"Damn, you're perceptive," Amy said with a forced smile. "Just because she's talking about something that makes her uncomfortable doesn't mean she's in danger or that you need to fix something."

"Who do we need to hurt, Bay?" Memphis questioned when he came to a stop beside Liam.

"Oh good, there are more of you." Amy groaned good-heartedly. "I guess this type of job, and Brandon using his military past for recruiting new hires means we'll only get over-the-top protective men."

"We're not over-the-top," Liam grumbled with a half smile to Amy.

"Right. I only have about a hundred instances to back up my statement." Pushing off the bale of straw, she stood and patted Liam's shoulder with one hand while the other reached out to Memphis. "I didn't get a chance to meet you yesterday. I'm Amy, Brandon and Carl's wife. Well, technically, just Brandon's on paper, since this state doesn't allow poly marriages."

"Memphis Thomas," he responded with a quick shake before pulling his hand back.

After eyeing him, then Liam, she whirled around to me. "You'll need a bigger cabin." I choked on my spit. Memphis gently patted my back as I coughed into a loose fist while staring in disbelief at my friend. "You have a single, and so does Liam." She tapped her cheek with a single finger while studying the ground as if it held all the answers. "Miles and Aiden's old place would work. It's only a two-bedroom, but it's bigger than what you have now."

I held up a hand, stopping her organizing a living situation I wasn't even sure the three of us were ready for. "Give us more than twenty-four hours to figure this out, okay."

"Fine. But just think about it. All remnants of the *incident* are gone, just in case that's what you're worried about."

"Incident?" Memphis asked, glancing between us. "What remnants?"

Amy, Liam, and I looked at each other, sharing a silent conversation.

"Fill you in later," Liam said, running a hand down his

face before focusing on me. "Right now, it's time for me to feed Baylee. Come on, Little Bit, let's get you some lunch."

Taking his offered hand, I allowed him to tug me against his chest. His lips pressed against my ear. "And while we're there, I can eat you for my dessert."

Yes, fucking please.

# 17

## LIAM

Someone yelling and the repetitive smack of feet sloshing through the mud and rivulets running along the perimeter of the barn drew our attention to the open barn door. Unsure of the threat, I tucked both Amy and Baylee behind me at the same time Memphis shifted so we stood shoulder to shoulder, widening his stance.

A pulse of relief had me breathing a little easier, knowing he was ready to protect the women with me. Sure, I was a trained fighter and could take out almost any threat, but it was a reprieve knowing I had backup.

I straightened to full attention as Ethan, Uplift's survivalist trainer and all-around outdoor badass, sprinted into the barn. He skidded to a stop when his frantic gaze landed on the four of us.

"Help," he rasped, chest heaving. "It's West. He's hurt."

We all snapped into action, taking off in a sprint to follow when Ethan turned and ran back out into the pouring rain. My muscles tensed at the cold drops, and goose bumps pebbled my skin as soon as we stepped out into the storm, soaking us within seconds. Keeping Baylee in my periphery, catching Memphis doing the same, I sprinted down the main road, noting when Ethan took a hard right and headed in the direction of our aircraft hangar.

"What happened?" Amy shouted, running toward the small huddle of people near the touring helicopter once we were all inside. Her words were almost swallowed up by the rain thundering against the metal roof.

My stomach dropped as I slowed my approach, unsure of what exactly I'd be walking up on. West was laid out beside the helicopter, passed out cold, his head resting in a sobbing Juno's lap. His face was pale—too fucking pale. I didn't realize I'd stopped in my tracks until Memphis shouldered past me.

Dropping to his knees beside West's head, Memphis gently pressed three fingers to the man's throat. "Where is he injured?" He eyed the streaks of blood on the concrete floor and growing puddle near West's ribs.

"His hand," Juno whispered through her tears. "He was working on something inside the engine, and then suddenly —" Her voice broke, and she squeezed her lids shut. "He just started screaming. I don't know, I don't know...." She repeated it over and over while stroking West's shaved head. Her tearstained face turned to Memphis. "Please help him."

He just nodded. "His pulse is fine. The pain must have made him pass out. Which is good and bad." He assessed me with a critical eye. "Know where I can get some basic field medical supplies? You guys have a first aid kit—"

"Langston does," I said, already turning in the direction that would get me to Langston and West's place the fastest. "He has a bag. I'll be back."

By the time I returned, Lang's medic bag in hand, West was awake, his screams and curses cutting through the storm's noise. Both Baylee's and Amy's cheeks were wet with tears, same as Juno, who looked almost sick. I dropped the bag beside Memphis and squatted low.

"How bad is it?" I murmured as he ripped open the clasp and started rummaging through it.

"Bad. I'm not sure—" He cut himself off and shook his head. "Baylee." She appeared on his other side. "We have to do something for his pain or his body could slip into shock. This is too much for his body to process, and that's not what we want. Do you have any pain relievers in your cabin or something for the animals that you know is safe for humans?"

"I can't risk that," she rasped. "I want to help, but—"

"I have some at our place from when Brandon hurt his back last year." With that, Amy bolted out of the shed that had suddenly gone deadly quiet.

"Fuck, he must have passed out from the pain," Memphis snapped, more to himself than at anyone. He grabbed Juno's hand and pressed her fingers to West's throat. "Monitor his pulse. If it races or dips, let me know." He swallowed hard. "While he's out of it, I'm going to look at his hand again, see if I can get a better idea of what we're dealing with. Any chance there's an ambulance in this town?"

"No. We don't even have a true emergency clinic, just the doc at The Nest," I said, already pulling out my phone to warn the doctor that we had an emergency case. But instead of me giving him a heads-up about my friend's injury, the call went straight to voicemail.

"Looks like three fingers are smashed to the point that I don't know what's left." My stomach churned, and I turned away, unable to stomach the sight. Baylee gasped and curled against my side, burying her face in my soaked flannel shirt.

"I need to wrap them, stop the bleeding, but not until we get some pain meds in him. I'm more worried about shock than him bleeding out."

"Where the fuck is Langston?" I asked Ethan, tapping Lang's contact on my phone.

"He made a run to Anchorage for the doc. The last shipment of some medicines didn't come in, and he ran out of critical shit like antibiotics and gauze, so he asked Lang to make a quick run." Ethan ran a hand through his black hair, tugging at the ends as he looked up. "Fuck, this is bad."

I nodded, fully agreeing with him. This was bad. If West lost his fingers.... I shook my head to clear that dark line of thinking.

Amy ran in, Carl right behind her. They skidded to a stop on the other side of West, and Amy extended the prescription bottle toward Memphis.

"Here. Brandon is a big guy, so I'm not sure how much you should give West to be effective."

"Thank you." Memphis held the bottle close, inspecting the table. "This is perfect. He can have one now. That should help with the pain enough to—"

"Guys, I don't know," Juno said, voice shaking. Memphis's head snapped her way, no doubt hearing the same terrified tone we all did. "His pulse is crazy fast."

Memphis dropped the bottle between his knees. Reaching inside the medic bag, he pulled out the stethoscope, situating it in his ears before placing the opposite end on West's heaving chest. With a curse, he ripped the equipment down so it draped around his neck.

"The pain is too much. He's on the verge of having a heart attack if we can't get his heart rate leveled out." He eyed the medicine bottle for half a second before grabbing it off the floor and unscrewing the top. Dumping the contents into his awaiting palm, he poured all but two back into the bottle.

"I thought you said—"

"I know what I said," Memphis snapped over his shoulder, cutting me off. "But this is still safe. I just didn't want to do it unless it was necessary. Which it fucking is right now. I need help to make him swallow these."

Dropping to my knees beside him, I took the offered water bottle from Ethan. "Tell me what to do."

With a little fumbling, Memphis and I worked together, getting both pills down his throat with only a few curses and half the water spilled.

Memphis wiped at the sweat dripping down his forehead with the sleeve of his black Henley. "I have to wrap his hand," he mumbled to himself as he dug through the medic bag, tossing things to the ground that he didn't need. Placing a package of quick-clot gauze and a roll of bandages beside his knees, Memphis hovered a hesitant hand over West's mangled one.

"I need you to keep him calm," he murmured softly to Juno, who nodded. "Talk to him. Even if he's passed out, he can hear you." He ripped open the packaging with his teeth. "Liam, I need you ready to hold him down if he wakes up and fights me. The last thing I want to do is cause more damage if he jerks his hand out of mine. I'll do this as fast as possible, but I have to be careful too."

As Memphis counted, he inhaled and exhaled in deep, controlled breaths. At his muttered "Three," he slid his fingers beneath West's wrist and started wrapping the destroyed flesh. West flinched, and a pain-filled sound almost like a howl escaped, but thankfully he stayed passed out. My intense focus was zeroed in on West to catch any movement, ready to hold him down if needed.

And thank fuck I didn't. To Memphis's credit, he did what he promised, his work efficient and quick. A few minutes later, he gently rested West's bandaged hand on his chest and sat back on his heels with a relieved exhale.

"That's the best I can do to keep him stable." He swiped his forearm across his sweaty brow. "Now, how do we get him help from an actual doctor?"

Carl stepped forward, attention on his phone. "Lang is on his way back. We need to get West to the docks so the second he's here, Langston can turn around and get him to the hospital in Anchorage. That's the best chance out here of saving that hand."

The roar of a truck engine and the splash of tires had us all turning to the old-school Ford skidding to a stop outside the metal structure. Engine still running, Miles leapt from the driver's side and jogged our way.

"Let's go," he said, staring at Juno. "You're going with him and Langston. I have someone from the hospital on standby for you to call when you're close, and they'll meet you at the docks to transport West to the emergency room."

She nodded, wiping at her cheeks and nose. Miles carefully lifted West's limp body into the air and strode toward his truck. Without another word, they hurried out into the rain, situated West inside the cab, and sped away. For several seconds, we stood in utter silence, watching the taillights as they faded into the massive downpour, before someone spoke up.

"That was intense," Ethan rasped. Memphis grunted when Ethan slapped a palm between his shoulder blades. "That was fucking awesome, guy I don't know. I'm Ethan Carthage, one of the employees here at Uplift."

It looked like Memphis tried to smile, but the adrenaline high was wearing off, so it was more of a grimace. "Memphis

Thomas, and thanks. The last year working as a medic in Orlando helped prepare me for shit like this, but"—he grabbed an alcohol wipe from the bag and started cleaning his hands—"having no hospital close by is throwing me. How do you guys do it?"

"Most of our injuries can be treated by Dr. Richards, but if they're too severe and you don't have someone like you or Langston around, then you're fucked," Carl said, his tone distant as he stared at the puddle of blood on the cement. "Which isn't okay. Not for our community or anyone in Anchor Bay. Yes, everyone understands the risks when they move here, but I still wish we could do more."

I nodded while rubbing the back of my neck with one hand, holding Baylee tight to my side with the other. "Maybe we need someone dedicated to responding to trauma. Langston is great from his time in the military, but like now, he's not here all the time. He has a full-time job to manage."

"We'd need someone who could do the job, be available at any time, and understand the complexities of being this remote," Amy said, cutting her eyes over to Memphis, who was busy scrubbing at his nails with a clean alcohol wipe. "Yeah, let's think about that."

Baylee looked up at me, brows raised. Pitching forward, I kissed the top of her head and gave her hip a squeeze.

"This isn't going to work," Memphis grumbled. "I need a shower to get clean."

"Or just stand out in the rain," Ethan said, inclining his head toward the steady downpour. "Fuck, this is a lot of water in a short period."

"Come on," I said to Memphis. "I'll walk back with you to Baylee's place. I need to change into dry clothes before I can finish my chores." I winced when I shifted, the wet jeans rubbing against my damp, cold skin. "You want to come with us, Little Bit, or should I bring you a change of clothes and lunch to the barn?"

"I'll, um, meet you back in the barn," she said distractedly. She motioned to the ground where West had been lying. "That was a lot, and I need a second to process it."

I furrowed my brow when she stepped out of my hold and started in the direction of the barn. Not liking the idea of her being alone, I went to follow her, only to have a gentle hand wrap around my wrist.

"Let her go," Amy said softly, watching Baylee jog through the rain. "I think seeing West made her remember that even we're not immune to accidents and how quickly things can change. I'm sure it's dragging up old feelings of how one day things were fine, then the next... her world imploded."

"Then I should be with her," I grumbled, hating the idea of Baylee hurting and me not being there for her. "She shouldn't have to process all that alone."

"She's right," Memphis said while tossing everything he didn't use back into Langston's medic bag. "Let her have some time to think through her thoughts. When she's ready to talk about it, she'll let us know. Until then, I'm not sure she even knows how she's feeling right now, much less how we can help her. We can check on her after we get cleaned up."

With a reluctant nod, I raised a hand in goodbye to Ethan, Amy, and Carl, and followed Memphis, who was already striding through the rain.

"Great job back there," I said over the sound of our boots sloshing in the rivers running along the main road through the community.

"Thanks." He smiled and tipped his face up to the rain.

"I love it, that high from the intensity and stress. I guess I switched out one addiction for another."

"But this one isn't killing you and is helping others. I say it's a good trade." He nodded in agreement. "As long as this keeps scratching that itch and you don't go back to what was hurting you." And had the potential to hurt Baylee.

"It's a daily struggle—I won't lie about that. Especially the alcohol because it's everywhere. I can handle it, though, and it's only just being surrounded by alcohol, like in a bar."

"And that was where we went for lunch yesterday." I ran a hand down my face. Even though I asked him if he was good, I should've made sure, should've double-checked he wasn't just saying yes for me. "Fuck, this will take some getting used to."

"It's fine—"

"No, it's not," I snapped before I could reel in my temper. "My job, my focus, is to protect those around me, keep them safe, even if that means from themselves. Which means it's on me to think through my actions and how they'll affect us." The term *us* came easily, which scared the fuck out of me but was comforting too. "I don't want to put you in a situation again where you're uncomfortable. That's not what protectors do."

His smile grew, and he shot me a look I couldn't read.

"What?" I asked.

"She's right, you know."

"Who?"

"Baylee," he said with a laugh as we climbed the stairs to her cabin.

I beat him to the door and unlocked it, swinging it open for him to walk through first. "Fuck, we'll get her place soaked."

Memphis turned, scanning the area. "I'll just strip out

here. I'm not shy." Without a word from me, he pulled off his wet shirt, then toed off his boots and started on his jeans.

With a shrug, I followed suit, not caring who saw me, but when I got to the button of my jeans, I grimaced.

"What?" he asked, already down to his underwear and standing inside the cabin, holding the door open for me.

"I don't like underwear, and I don't want everyone out here seeing my dick," I mumbled under my breath. Memphis barked out a laugh. "Fuck off. Go get in the shower."

When he held up both hands in surrender, the door started to close. Slapping a hand to the center, I kept it open. "What was Baylee right about?"

"Yesterday when we were walking around while she showed me this place, she said you're just a big softy. I didn't believe her, thought it was just her you were that way with, but now I'm thinking she's right."

"I could kill you a dozen different ways right now with my bare hands," I snapped.

He just nodded, that damn smile not dimming. "Okay, okay. I won't bring it up again, tough guy. You're a big scary cowboy who could kill me."

"Damn right, I am," I muttered, feeling a little better at his words.

"Though I think her description of you as her...." He tapped a finger against his cheek, pretending to think. "Oh, that's right. Her Tootsie Pop. That's much more accurate."

With a snarl, I lunged for him, making him curse and bolt through the cabin, his laughter cutting off when the bathroom door slammed shut.

But as hard as I tried, I couldn't stop fucking smiling.

---

## 18

## MEMPHIS

My feet slid around in the too-large muck boots I'd borrowed from Liam with every step through the deep puddles on the way to the barn. The rain finally let up, though the dark clouds hinted that it could start up again any minute. A small smirk pulled at my lips, recalling the earlier easy banter with the asshole despite feeling numb after the accident. Digging into my front pocket, I pulled my phone free to see if there was an update on West's condition. Scrolling through the group text I was added to, I pursed my lips, disappointed that there was nothing new.

Flipping to the text string with my mom, my loud laugh rumbled through the air as I watched a dumb cat video she'd sent earlier. Shaking my head at her quirky antics, I hovered both thumbs over the screen to respond.

> Me: Hilarious. Love seeing a kitten with a hat on.

> Mom: Hope that made you smile! I miss you! How is your day?!

Me: Mom, what have we talked about with overusing exclamation marks?

Mom: Well, how else will you know I'm excited to hear from you?!

Mom: How is Alaska?! Have you seen Baylee yet?!

I groaned in good humor at her frivolous use of the excited punctuation but knew I had to let it go because it really was just Mom being Mom.

Me: Saw her yesterday.

Me: She's just as great as she was back in high school.

Mom: Baylee was a doll! She should come over for family dinner one night!

Mom: I'm glad you went out there to see her! I know you've been missing Dean!

Me: If we weren't a boat ride, three plane trips, and a long drive from the airport, we totally would, Mom. You know I miss your cooking on the daily.

Mom: Ha! You're lying because I can barely cook soup, and now you're this super chef!

Me: Not super. Not a chef.

Mom: To me you are!

Me: Thanks, Mom.

Mom: And I know it would be hard for you both to come home. I just want to see you two.

Look at that. It took her mentioning the tense relationship between me—and I suppose Baylee too—and Dean's mom to not use an exclamation mark.

I stopped outside the barn, giving myself a second to respond before dipping inside to see Baylee.

Me: I know, Mom, and at some point I will come home. I'll leave that decision for her to make for herself if she wants to come with me.

Me: Right now I'm just soaking up the time with her and her friends.

Mom: Friends?! You're making friends?!

Me: Don't sound so shocked, Mom.

Mom: Not shocked! Happy! If they're friends of Baylee's, then I'm sure they're good people! Unlike those rascals who you hung out with before!

Me: Rascals. Really?

Me: They are good people. Everyone works at the same adventure and rescue company.

Me: It's only been a few days here in Alaska and a day since I met everyone, and it feels good.

Mom: Good?!

Me: I feel happy. Settled. Secure.

Mom: I'm crying! Happy tears!

Mom: Your dad sees the tears and is worried! Need to go! Bye for now!

Pocketing the device, I stepped inside the wide-open barn doors and paused, searching the vast space for Baylee. My heart stopped upon finding her backed against the goat pen with some guy I didn't know standing way too fucking close.

"Hey," I bellowed, already storming in their direction. Their heads whipped my way. My fingers tightened into fists at the look of relief that flashed over Baylee's face. "What the hell is going on here?"

The guy took me in before holding up both hands and stepping away from her. I didn't stop until my body was between them, Baylee safely at my back. Her small hand dipped under my shirt and pressed to my bare skin, helping me calm down from a murderous rampage to being willing to hear this guy out... before going on the murderous rampage.

"I'm Dr. Richards." Instead of sticking his hand out, he tucked both into the front pockets of his slacks. The motion drew my attention to the white gauze wrapped around his forearm from wrist to elbow.

"You okay?" I asked over my shoulder, not taking my eyes off Dr. Douche.

Baylee nodded. "Yes. Taylor here stopped by a few minutes ago. He heard what happened to West and came to see if he could help."

I eyed the man suspiciously. "Did that need to be discussed so fucking close to you?"

The idiot rolled his eyes and huffed like I was the one being ridiculous. "Oh good, another one." His lips dipped into a frown as he scanned the tattoos on my neck and forearms where my sleeves were pushed up. "Anchor Bay will need a tattoo place soon to keep up with all the... people"—his tone said he wanted to use any other word than that—"that Brandon is bringing into town."

Baylee pushed me aside and shifted to stand in front of me. I was too shocked by the sudden move to stop her.

"Actually, he was brought here by me," she said, tipping her chin up to glare at the doctor. "He's my friend."

My chest swelled with appreciation for the tiny yet mighty woman defending me. I rested a hand on her shoulder as I fought the need to pull her to my chest.

The doctor's expression morphed from shock to disgust. "*Friend*, huh?" He shook his head and glared down the bridge of his nose at my Baylee. "I'm disappointed in you. I thought someone with your higher education would have better sense than this."

"Than what?" she snapped, stomping her foot. I almost told her it was adorable, but she was literally vibrating with anger, and I didn't want to get kicked in the shins or something. "Working for a place that allows me freedom, housing, and a family?"

"This isn't a family," the soon-to-be-dead man—not by me but my big-ass fucker of a friend—bit back. "This is a cult, and you're too blind to see it."

Baylee looked over her shoulder with both blonde brows raised. "We're a *cult*, he says."

"I'm not the only one," he continued, voice rising. Okay, maybe I didn't need Liam to handle this. I could take care of him easily, based on the anger pumping through my veins. How dare he talk to her like that? "There are others in town who are disgusted with the type of characters that—"

My lips parted to tell the asshole to die in a fire, but Baylee spoke up first.

"Stop it, right now. Don't you dare say another word, you judgmental, high-and-mighty prick. You and your little band of ultraconservatives can talk all you want, but this company brings in tourists, which brings in money for everyone in Anchor Bay. So you might not like our lifestyle, but you sure as hell take the money this business brings to town. I will not stand here and let you talk down about this family, here on our own fucking property." Her tiny fists clenched at her sides. "I don't know what's gotten into you today, Taylor. You need to leave. Now."

"Or what?" he scoffed and gestured toward me. "Your delinquent boyfriend here will beat me up?"

"No," she said, taking a challenging step toward him. "I will."

*Oh shit.* I was so entertained, ready to clap at the verbal lashing she gave the prick, that I didn't realize it was about to escalate to violence.

"Whoa, whoa, whoa." I snaked an arm around her waist to tug her against me. "Calm down there, Kitten," I said against her ear for only her to hear. Standing to full height, I inclined my head toward the open barn doors, sending a death glare to the asshole. "I suggest you leave. Last time I saw West, he was passed out but stable. I'll let them know you stopped by to check on him."

*Look at me being diplomatic.*

*Until I put arsenic in his drink one day soon.*

My tone brooked no argument, and thankfully the guy understood it for the thinly veiled threat that I meant it as. With an annoyed huff and a last glance at Baylee, he stormed off, mumbling under his breath about criminals and tattoos.

I didn't release my hold on Baylee until he was out of the barn and gone from sight. With an adorable foot stomp and a frustrated groan, she molded against me.

"I totally could've taken him," she huffed, tipping her head all the way back to look at me upside down.

"Oh, I have zero doubts, Bay. You would've kicked the shit out of his shins." Knowing that would set her off, I was prepared when she whirled around, fingers poised to tickle my ribs. I gently batted her hands away and dodged her advances. "You're not playing fair, Kitten."

"I'm not a kitten," she hissed, then stuck out her tongue while scrunching her nose in fake disgust.

My head tipped back as I laughed so hard my stomach hurt. "Fuck, I missed you."

When I finally got control of my laughter, I looked down, finding tears flooding her lower lids. *Oh shit.*

"What's wrong?" I asked, slightly panicked. I'd hurt her feelings somehow.

"Nothing is wrong, Memphis. It's just that I missed you too," she rasped. Wrapping both arms around my neck, she jumped up, legs squeezing around my waist. "I really missed you. Missed the laughs, missed the happy times and the simple conversations. And I really, really miss him."

Her first sob felt like a stab to my heart. So did the second and third. Tears dampened my shirt as she wept in my tight, comforting hold. There was nothing I could say or do to ease the pain of her loss, which made me feel utterly useless. Swallowing down my own tears, I squeezed her even tighter, wishing like hell I could physically absorb her pain.

"I'm terrified I won't survive something like that again," she whispered when she pulled back. I searched her splotchy, tearstained face, adjusting my hold to swipe the drops dripping off her jaw. "For things to be normal one day, then... the rug is pulled out from under me and my world shatters. That's why I waited so long to move forward with Liam." She sniffled and wiped both palms across her damp cheeks. "And why I'm terrified of letting anyone in, even you, Memphis. What if I start to live again without reservation, without holding back, and then one day it's ripped away from me again? I barely survived that agony and devastation the first time. I'm not strong enough to do it again."

Her lower lip trembled, and all I could think of doing to make it stop was to press my own to hers. She instantly melted against me, lips parting, allowing me access. Carrying her a few steps, I carefully pressed her spine against the tack room wall, savoring our first kiss. It wasn't passionate but more intimate at a soul level. It was healing, as if I could kiss away her worry and fear.

"I can't promise you that I'll never leave. I don't have control over destiny or when it's my time to leave this earth, but I can guarantee that if I go anywhere, it will not be voluntarily. That doesn't give you the reassurance you need, especially after seeing West's accident, but it's what I can wholeheartedly promise you. You tell me to leave, that you're sick of me, and—" I pressed a kiss to the tip of her button nose. "—I probably still won't go. I'll just watch from the shadows, grateful to see you happy and safe."

"You'd stalk me?" she asked, brows pulled in tight.

"The good kind of stalking." A huff escaped her perfect lips, drawing my attention. "Sorry I stole our first kiss."

The shy smile that tugged the corners of her lips up and the blush creeping along her cheeks made pride and relief swell in my chest.

"Yeah, you did, though it seems kind of silly to be blushing over a kiss after what we did last night."

"You mean how I ate your delicious pussy and licked you clean before I claimed your mouth?"

She smacked her small palm against my shoulder while rolling her eyes, but my smile only grew. That joyful expression dimmed. "Yeah, but what does that say about me? I didn't return the favor, and you had to—"

"Don't you dare cheapen or lessen last night because you think you owed me something in return, Bay," I demanded. Her crystal blue eyes met mine and held my imploring gaze. "Last night was fucking amazing, and I was honored to be involved in worshipping your body. Liam didn't have to invite me to play, but he did, and that was... a huge fucking relief. I had watched before, but last night, finally participating, was everything. You not touching me doesn't diminish what happened between us in my mind, and it shouldn't in yours either."

Her gaze broke away with a reluctant nod, as if she heard me but didn't quite believe my words.

"Now, what was all that about with the doctor douche?" I stepped back, allowing her the room to slide down my body. Her shoes squelched when they pressed to the concrete floor, reminding me that she was still in her drenched clothes from earlier. "We need to get you changed," I said, more to myself.

"He, um, came by to check on West, or so he said." Her darting gaze was looking everywhere other than me.

I tapped the end of her nose, making her swat at me with a hiss. "But you don't believe that?"

A single slim shoulder rose in a half shrug. "It's just that when I came back from giving Carla her medicine—"

"I haven't met her yet, have I?" I asked, brows pulled in tight as I searched my memory.

Baylee's light laughter filled the small space between us. "No, you haven't, because Carla is a cow, and I haven't gotten around to introducing you to the animals. Didn't want to overwhelm you on day one."

"Thank you?" I chuckled. "So, you gave Carla her meds and...." I gestured for her to continue the story.

"Right, so when I came back, I found Taylor messing around in the medicine cabinet. It has a lock, but I've never used it because I've had nothing stolen or misused."

I eyed the metal cabinet. "Sounds like there's a 'but' in there."

She nodded. "I'm missing a full bottle of antibiotic, which is really odd. Out of all the other medicines in there, that was the only thing taken." She gnawed on her lip, brow furrowed as she followed my line of sight to the cabinet. "Now that I think about it, gauze is missing too. Anyway, when I caught Taylor, he seemed surprised to see me. I asked him what he was doing looking around in the cabinet, but he avoided the question completely, shifting the conversation to West's accident."

"That sounds shady as hell," I muttered.

"Yeah, and then his arm...." She searched my face with a thoughtful expression. "Carl mentioned the reason Langston wasn't around was because Taylor was out of antibiotics, which is what's missing here. None of it makes sense."

"We'll get to the bottom of it," I reassured her, kissing the top of her head. "Do you still have stuff to do around here, or can you take a break?"

"I'm good." Pinching her damp, teal long-sleeve T-shirt with two fingers, she pulled it away from her skin with a grimace. "I might head back and change. Where's Liam?"

I hooked a thumb in the direction of her cabin. "He's back at your place getting cleaned up. He took a shower after me. Why don't you head there now? I'll be right behind you. I need to pick up the brushes and shit we used earlier, then will head back to the cabin for lunch."

She pressed a hand to her stomach when it growled at the mention of food. "Yes to all of that, it seems. Want me to stay and help?"

I shook my head with a lopsided smile. "I think Liam could use some alone time with you. He was frustrated when Amy talked him out of following you earlier. He knew you were upset and didn't like the idea of you being alone. She convinced him you needed time to process what happened and to give you some space to work through it by yourself."

Baylee blew out a heavy breath. "Yeah, she was right, I did. But I can see how that would cause my big cinnamon roll distress. I'm sure he's worried about me changing my mind about us after—"

Movements quicker than she could react, I gathered both of her wrists in one hand and pushed her back against the wall, securing her hands high above her head. Eyes wide with surprise, she gaped up at me.

"He wasn't thinking about himself, Baylee. He was worried about you. Worried that you were sad and hurting and doing it alone. It had nothing to do with the relationship you two are building." A look of guilt fluttered across her face. "He's not that kind of guy, which is shocking as hell. Liam looks like he should be the biggest asshole on the planet, but he's not. Even a day with him has shown me just how much he cares about you, and it's not related to how you feel about him in return."

Her throat worked with a hard swallow as she nodded. "You're right." Pulling her hands down, I kissed each palm before releasing my grip. "And holy hell, that was hot," she rasped, eyes a little glassy.

"The restraining part or standing up for your boyfriend?"

Lower lip between her teeth, she attempted to stifle a sly smile. "Both, I think. But wow, I can get on board with at least one of your kinks for sure."

"And the other one I mentioned?" I murmured, dipping a hand under her damp top, caressing her ribs with a single knuckle.

I gazed down at her in wonder. How the fuck was this my reality and not some dream that I'd be woken up from soon? I'd fantasized about this, pinning her to a wall with my hips as I touched her soft skin. Though those visions never stopped with the innocent touch like I needed to now. If things continued the way they were with the three of us, I would hopefully have Baylee pinned beneath me soon, and then I wouldn't have to hold back.

"Guess we'll have to wait and see, won't we," she said, breathing harder than she was seconds ago.

Forearms pressed to the wall on either side of her head, I leaned in until our lips brushed. "Looking forward to it, Kitten."

With a smirk, she dipped under my arms, but she didn't move fast enough. My hand connected with her firm ass, the smack vibrating through the barn. Her responding squeal and following giggle had my heart seizing. Baylee was the most amazing woman I would ever meet.

If she'd allow me the honor of being a fixture in her life, not a day would go by when she would question how much she meant to me.

---

## 19

BAYLEE

Despite the fact that my tennis shoes were already soaked from earlier, I still dodged the various puddles on the road as I hurried toward the cabin. My heart was hammering against my ribs from both the adrenaline and desire rush from Memphis pinning me against the wall. After that, my damp underwear had nothing to do with the prior downpour I'd sprinted through.

Bounding up the few porch steps, I toed off my shoes and pushed the front door open. Elvis leapt up from where he lay at Liam's bare feet as the man stood in the kitchen wearing a pair of snug Wranglers and nothing else. I blew out a steadying breath through pursed lips to chase away the building nerves.

Not allowing my insecurities to take hold, I strode across the living room. Liam looked up from the sandwich he was constructing, turning to face me just in time to catch me as I jumped into his arms. He shifted to the side at the surprise attack.

"Well, hello to you, too, Little Bit," he said, planting a kiss where my neck and shoulder met.

Every press of his lips to my skin ramped up the throb between my thighs that Memphis started. Squeezing my legs around his waist, I shifted to seal my core against his stomach and ground against him. Both large hands cupping my ass tightened.

"I was worried about you," he whispered against my skin, the concern in his tone clear. "You all right?"

I pulled back just enough to gaze into his worried gray eyes. "I am. No need to worry. It took me by surprise how West's accident affected me. I needed some time alone to sort out my feelings and reaction."

"And did you?" he asked, searching my face. "Why the hell does it look like you've been crying?"

"Because I have been, which is okay. Memphis was there to hold me while I snotted all over his shoulder." I wrinkled my nose in disgust.

"Lucky bastard," Liam said with a pout, clearly not agreeing with it being gross.

A wide grin split my face at his response. "Do you *want* my snotty nose on you?"

"I want all of you, Baylee, the good and the snotty. Memphis was there for you, and I'm jealous of that, even though I'm also thankful you had someone you trusted there to hold you."

My heart swelled, making it hard to breathe. I knew he was telling the truth, not just saying it to get in my pants or cover his jealousy. This type of emotional vulnerability and strength was both perfect and confusing—it was hard to comprehend that this amazing man wanted me for me.

A shiver slid down my spine, making my shoulders shudder. Between the sexy time with Memphis in the barn and now Liam's hard body pressed against mine, all my focus went to the urgent, throbbing need pulsing through my veins. Running my blunt nails along his scalp, I guided him closer until our lips brushed.

"I need you, Liam," I whispered, a bit of whine leaking to my voice. "Now." His dark brows pulled in tight, as if unsure of what I was truly asking for. "I'm done waiting for the right moment, done worrying about getting too attached in case something tragic happens. I want to let go with you."

"Now?" he asked, studying my flushed face.

"Right now."

That was all the confirmation he needed.

Striding to the bedroom, Liam paused in front of the bed and slowly lowered me to the floor. The damp clothes suctioned to my clammy skin as I slid down his chest. Fisting the cotton, he pulled it over my head, tossing it to the floor once I was free. I struggled with the urge to apologize for my basic black sports bra. But the way he traced the edge of the material, leaving goose bumps in his wake as he gazed at my chest, told me he truly didn't care.

"You need to get warm."

My protest turned into a squeak when he wrapped me in his arms and hauled me into the bathroom. My toes curled into the plush bath rug outside the shower. First my sports bra, then my pants and underwear were carefully tugged free and tossed aside in a pile of wet clothes.

On his knees in front of where I stood, Liam gripped my hips and yanked me to him until my core pressed against his face. The guttural groan that vibrated around the room had me shivering from the influx of desire that pumped through my veins.

"Fuck, woman, you'll be the death of me," he said, placing a quick kiss to my slick center. Running a finger through my slit, he held it up for me to see it glistening in the light. "Is this all from the idea of me taking your virgin pussy, or did you and Memphis start something in the barn?"

My cheeks heated and my stomach flip-flopped. "Both," I breathed. My pulse raced and blood pounded in my ears as I watched him lick my arousal off his finger.

"Tell me, in detail, what Memphis did to get you this soaked for me. And don't be embarrassed, sweetheart. It's all good. I'm the one getting to reap the tasty benefits."

Throat dry, I tried to swallow while holding his fiery gaze. "Memphis pinned me against the wall with my arms restrained above my head." Just thinking about his grip, not being able to move because his hips held me against the wall, had an achy throb pulsing in my core. "Liam," I begged. "Please."

Popping the top button of his jeans, he shoved the denim down his thick thighs and stepped out of the puddled material. Not giving myself the chance to second-guess myself, I wrapped a hand around his hard cock and brushed the pad of my thumb over the smooth head. His responding hiss made my breath hitch as the building desire scorched through me.

Keeping his gaze locked on mine, he reached between my thighs and slid a single finger inside my dripping center. My lips parted on a gasp at the sudden yet incredible intrusion. But it wasn't enough. I needed more. A whole fucking lot more than that single digit. My body vibrated with need, feeling like I would combust.

"More," I breathed, only to choke on a breath when he immediately complied, pushing another wide digit inside me. "Yes, but no," I whined. It was good, but not enough. "I need you." I tightened my hold on his cock for emphasis.

The loss of his fingers thrusting into me had me swaying forward, but an arm snaked around my waist, pulling me against his bare chest. My peaked nipples rubbed against his sweat-slick skin, causing more desire to leak from my core.

Liam hauled me into the shower, his back taking the brunt of the initial cold spray as he turned the lever. His deep grunt when the water sputtered and splashed against him made me giggle. I tried to hide my growing grin behind the three fingers holding down my curving lips.

"You sure about this?" he asked. I locked eyes with him and nodded, all humor fading at his serious tone. He hummed in a content response and smirked. "Good girl, but we need to get your pussy nice and relaxed to take all of me. Do you have condoms?"

I arched an incredulous brow. "Really? I'm a virgin, so...." He huffed a laugh and ran a hand through his wet hair. "But we don't need one as far as I'm concerned. I had an IUD put in a few years ago to solve some period issues, and I trust you to not endanger my health."

Unable to resist, I dragged the edge of a nail along his bobbing, stiff shaft.

His entire body shivered, his lids fluttering shut at the delicate touch. "I haven't been with anyone since my last health test," he grunted through clenched teeth.

"Okay," I murmured. "I trust you, Liam. I know you wouldn't put me in any kind of danger, whether that's emotional or physical."

Instead of responding, he grabbed my shoulders and lifted me. Both legs immediately wrapped around his waist, and he sealed his lips to mine, our mouths devoured each other. His tongue danced with mine as I rubbed my drenched core against his rock-hard abs. Already turned on, the slight friction sent bursts of pleasure sparking through me, driving my movements faster.

With one hand palming my ass cheek, Liam slid the other between us and pinched my swollen clit between two fingers. I tossed my head back, shouting his name. My hair slid between my shoulder blades as I came apart from the minimal touch.

Breaths coming in quick pants, I straightened, finding Liam smirking.

"Good girl," he praised while moving those two fingers to my entrance and pushing inside. "I said you needed to be nice and loose for my cock to fit into this virgin pussy without hurting you, so we'll need a few more of those with me stretching you with my fingers."

A pitiful mewl escaped at the thought of him pushing inside me, of feeling something other than fingers or a toy. Last night was a tease, a preview of that amazing stretch I knew would come when he finally thrust inside.

Liam added another finger, the angle and pressure making my breath hitch at the mix of pleasure and pain. Grunting something I couldn't understand, he lowered me, urging me to lean back while spreading my legs wide with gentle taps with his foot against one ankle and then the other.

Kneeling between my legs, the now-hot water soaking his dark hair and slipping down his handsome face, he thrust those three fingers back inside. My sharp inhale turned into a moan when he pitched forward, sealing his lips around a peaked nipple. The back of my head tapped against the wall and rolled against the white tile. The pump of his fingers mixed with his sucking on my nipple had me inching higher toward that perfect bliss. The addition of his thumb flicking my clit shot me over the edge with a nearly silent scream.

Panting through the aftershocks, my lids fluttered open,

only to find him staring in awe at where his fingers were buried inside me. When he leaned in closer, I gripped what I could of his hair, stopping his movement. Gray eyes met mine through dark, wet lashes.

"Enough. I want this, Liam. I want you now. Stop playing with me and fuck me."

A determined expression overtook his face as he slowly stood and swooped me up in his arms. I wrapped mine around his neck, holding my drenched body against his. After shutting the water off, Liam stepped out of the shower, grabbed a towel, and strode into the bedroom. He carefully lowered me to stand on my own, untangling my arms so he could kneel in front of me.

"Liam," I protested as he swiped the towel along my skin, soaking up the streams of water.

"I'm giving myself a second here, sweetheart. That way I won't take you too hard the first time. You don't deserve that."

I stilled his hand with a firm grip on his wrist. "I might be inexperienced compared to you, but I decide what I do or don't deserve, Liam." His brows shot up, no doubt surprised at the conviction in my tone. "I want you exactly the way you want me, so stop treating me like I'm made of fucking glass."

It took all of two seconds for him to process my words before he dropped the towel to the floor, lifted me into the air, and tossed me onto the bed. The mattress gave beneath my slight weight, bouncing me an inch in the air. Liam trailed soft kisses up one inner thigh, then the other, along my stomach, and between my breasts as he moved up the bed to hover over me.

Anticipation had my heart hammering, my breaths shallow and erratic as I waited, focused on his face, the concentration in his eyes. Forearms pressed into the mattress on either side of my head, he shifted his hips, sliding his cock between my slick lips. A depraved groan escaped, my eyes squeezed shut as he nudged at my entrance, the thick head pushing inside like it had last night. Sparks danced behind my lids while my body adjusted around his girth.

"Wrap your legs around my hips," he murmured. "I need you to open for me."

Adjusting on the duvet, I did as instructed, gasping in surprise when the new position allowed him to slide in deeper.

"Good girl, that's it. Feel how your virgin cunt stretches for me, a perfect fit."

Gripping the back of his neck, I urged his mouth down to mine, needing a distraction as he pushed in deeper. Our lips moved, tongues dancing while he worked his thick cock into me inch by inch. The slight burn from my body accommodating his girth had my lids flying open. His gray eyes were already locked on me, no doubt studying my reactions.

"You okay?" he panted, placing gentle kisses along my cheek and jaw.

"Yes," I breathed. "Keep going. I'm good."

He shifted his hips, thrusting all the way in, stealing my breath. My spine arched, rubbing my nipples against his chest as wave after wave of pleasure and stinging pain rolled through me.

"Fucking hell, woman," Liam gritted out, his jaw tight. "I'm doing everything I can not to come right now, but your pussy is squeezing me like it never wants to let go."

Sweat beaded along his forehead with the restraint to stay buried inside me, unmoving while my body adjusted to the fabulous intrusion. When my breathing evened out and the sting faded, I rolled my hips, testing out the movement.

Our mingled moans filled the bedroom. Never looking away, he slid out until only his head remained inside me, the motion itself leaving me breathless, before thrusting back in in one stroke. With every slide of his thick cock stretching and filling me almost to the point of pain, my body relaxed, and roaring need consumed me.

Sweat glistened on every inch of skin as we moved together, both of us eager to fall over that edge into pure bliss. Gripping an ass cheek in each hand, I urged him faster, deeper, to hit a spot that had black dots filling my vision. Releasing a fierce growl above me, he picked up the pace, slamming into me with quick, hard thrusts.

"Oh fuck," I breathed, that familiar flutter in my lower belly telling me I was close. "Liam," I cried, not knowing what I needed, but knowing I needed something.

"I've got you, sweetheart." The mattress shifted when he adjusted to lean on one arm, keeping his full weight off me, to sneak a hand between us.

A couple of rough flicks to my clit, and I shattered. My thighs clamped around him as my back bowed off the bed, mouth open wide as I called out his name. Above me, he grunted a string of curses that I barely heard through the blood pounding in my ears, his movements stiff from my tight hold. One more powerful thrust, going as deep as he could, and I felt him swell even more inside me.

My name fell like a prayer from his lips as he came, muscles quivering with the effort to keep from dropping on top of me. With a final relieved grunt, Liam dipped to the side, taking me with him. With his still-hard cock inside me, I lay sprawled out on his sweat-slick chest, working to calm my rapid breaths and racing heart.

"Fucking hell."

My cheek moved along his chest with my growing smile

at the sound of his words rumbling in my ear. A wide palm cupped an ass cheek and squeezed.

"I knew it would be amazing with you." I shifted to rest my chin on his sternum. His soft, relaxed expression made him look years younger and perfectly content. My heart swelled, knowing I did that. That I gave him a few moments of peace. "But it was beyond anything I could've imagined."

I sighed, utterly content as a single scarred knuckle traced down my cheek.

"I don't want to move," I admitted, but like the traitorous bitch it was, my stomach growled loud enough for Liam to hear.

"I want to stay buried in your warm, tight pussy for the rest of my life—"

"That's called cock warming."

Both our heads snapped toward Memphis's voice.

"Lunch is done and on the counter." I felt my cheeks heat, though I wasn't sure why. "I'm happy for you—both of you. And even though I wasn't here for it all—" He reached down and adjusted himself, drawing my attention to the way his jeans tented. "—what I saw was hot enough for me to almost come in my pants. Come and eat when you're ready. No rush." A smirk pulled at his lips. "If you want to do it again first, just let me know, and I'll park my ass on that chair in the corner to watch the full show."

I relaxed against Liam with a relieved sigh. It wasn't embarrassment that he'd caught us, but worry, maybe. I wasn't sure how he would respond to Liam and me, knowing he'd taken my virginity and we did it alone, without him. Seeing how calm Memphis was—turned on, actually—eased the lingering concern and allowed the possibilities of the three of us to flood my thoughts.

Liam's grunt had me turning my focus to his strained expression.

"What? Am I hurting you?" Palm to his chest, I pushed away only for him to stop me with an arm around my waist, holding me hostage.

"Whatever you just thought about had your pussy squeezing the life out of my dick." He peeked one eye open to scan my face. "What was it?" When I sealed my lips shut, he lifted a hand and slapped it against my ass hard. "Answer me."

"Us three together," I rasped. "Liam," I hedged. "I think I need...."

"I fucking know, Baylee. I can feel you getting wetter and fluttering around me. All that because you thought about us three?" He threaded a hand through my loose hair, pushing it out of my face as I nodded. "Tell me." When I started to respond, he pressed a finger to my lips, dipping the tip inside my mouth. "No, actually tell *us*. Memphis," he yelled.

Memphis appeared in the doorway and leaned a shoulder against the frame. "You called?"

"Seems like our girl here thought about us three together and made her needy for more of me taking her perfect pussy."

A smirk pulled at his lips as he studied me, gaze sliding over my naked body like a gentle caress. "Oh, really?"

Lips parted, cheeks hot, I gave in to the need to move, slightly shifting my lower half that was connected to Liam. The hand in my hair tightened, pulling at my strands as his hiss sounded through the room.

"Really," Liam groaned. "Sit in the chair like a good boy," he commanded, "and let's hear all the dirty thoughts Baylee has about the three of us."

"Fucking gladly." On his way to the chair, Memphis

paused by the bed to run a single finger down my spine and along the curve of my ass, lingering there. "Wait until you try to take both of us."

I whirled my head toward him. "Have you done that before?"

"With the help of a dildo, yes."

I pressed my lips into a tight line, not liking the idea of him with someone else, which immediately made me feel guilty. Another man's dick was literally inside me right now. How could I be jealous of someone from his past?

A wide smile split Memphis's face. "I like you being jealous, Kitten, but no one has ever compared to even the idea of you. They were all just mediocre stand-ins."

My heart raced as he leaned down, kissing me. I moved along Liam's shaft, attempting to push him even deeper to relieve the pulsing need once again filling my veins.

"Looks like you'll be participating after all," Liam said. "Keep kissing her and playing with her tits while I take care of her needy cunt."

Memphis stood straight and shrugged out of his jacket, then knelt on the bed.

"Best day ever," he said before devouring my mouth.

I couldn't agree more.

Though with the way things were going, I had a feeling the best days were just beginning.

# 20

## LIAM

"I'm glad you two enjoyed the ride. Thank you for booking through Uplift."

I took the reins from the woman's outstretched hand, careful not to touch her, though she apparently had different plans. It was minuscule but clearly deliberate when her pinkie finger stroked against the side of my hand in a teasing touch. Her batting thick black lashes and high-pitched giggle when I said nothing remotely funny also signaled that the unwanted touch was intentional.

Throat working, I swallowed down the string of curses that sat on the tip of my tongue. But like a good Uplift employee, I kept my mouth shut to not offend the paying client. Instead of offering her the forced smile I usually gave clients, I settled my features into a blank mask, not inviting any hope that her blatant flirting would work and turned to lead the last horse to the trailer. Today's ride was on a trail far from town but easy, which was why I chose it for inexperienced riders like the woman's ten-year-old son.

"I've heard rumors about the company you work for and the unique community," the woman said, following me to the trailer. With my back to her, I rolled my eyes to the blue sky, knowing she couldn't catch me. "I'm intrigued and...." She paused, making me look back at her, hoping she'd passed out or bitten her tongue off, but she was just checking over her shoulder where her son played in a small stream, throwing rocks and cheering at the big splashes. Her smile widened, thinking I was actually interested in what she had to say. "A lot turned on at the idea of multiple partners. Is that something all of you participate in? Even you?"

*Well, fuck.*

Grumbling under my breath, I turned my back to her again and started walking. "It's good to see your son enjoying the outdoors," I said, blatantly ignoring her questions. "Most kids these days only want to play on their devices."

Catching up, she walked beside me, her wide, pearly white smile still in place. "Yes, well, my husband loves to take him camping and all that." She waved her hand dismissively, the huge rock on her hand glinting in the sun. "I never found it interesting. I much prefer activities in the bedroom with men who can keep up with my needs." She licked her lips as she gave me a slow once-over. "I'm sure you could, cowboy."

After loading the horse, I backed out of the trailer and closed the doors. Lock secured, I turned only to curse, back slamming against the metal with a bang at her being right in front of me with a hopeful expression.

Annoyance and resentment churned in my gut. The woman reminded me too much of my late wife. Perfect makeup, though thick and unattractive to me, uncaring about upholding her marriage vows, and only fucking thinking about herself. She didn't even notice that her son had wandered farther down the stream, almost out of sight.

When her hand hovered over my chest, I sidestepped like I was dodging a viper to avoid the contact.

"Do not touch me," I snarled. "And back the hell up. We appreciate your business, but we are done here. You can follow me back to The Nest in your car, where I will leave you to head home to my amazing girlfriend."

As I spoke, her sultry smile fell until her lips were pressed into a thin line.

"You're missing out on a good time," she snapped. "I could be so much better than your girlfriend."

"No, what I'm missing out on is time with her because you're delaying me getting home to her. Please grab your son and load up. I have somewhere I want to be, and it's not fucking here."

Turning, I stormed to the truck and yanked the driver's door open, slamming it shut after I folded into the seat. Hands curled into tight fists on my thighs, I watched as the woman helped her son into the back seat, then stomped around the back of her rental and climbed inside.

Chest heaving from the ball of anger and rage filling my chest, I did the only thing I knew would help. After tapping Baylee's contact, I put the phone on speaker and tossed it into the cupholder. She picked up right as I cranked the engine, the roar almost drowning out her sweet voice.

"Hey, you." The tension in my shoulders instantly eased a fraction. "You on your way home?"

"Yeah," I breathed. Putting the truck into Drive, I eased off the brake. "Should be back soon."

"Everything okay?" Her tone was tight with concern. "You sound like something's wrong or you're about to snap someone's neck."

I huffed a laugh at that last part, knowing the joke was her attempt to ease my tension. "Just a difficult client after a long ride," I responded, not wanting her to worry. After what happened with Miles and Aiden, I didn't need her thinking this woman would turn into a stalker.

I shifted my gaze to the side mirror to make sure the rental SUV was still following me.

"I'm sorry. Anything I can do to help?"

"You already did," I answered honestly. "Be home in a little while."

I ended the call and focused on the road. Hauling a trailer full of horses down the narrow and winding road wasn't anything new or difficult, but keeping my head in the game kept me from making mistakes, which could easily be life-threatening out here.

Two hours later, I had the trailer unloaded, tack removed and cleaned, and horses taken care of with fresh oats in their feed buckets. Closing the barn door, I lifted my cowboy hat and swiped a forearm over my sweaty forehead. The sun shone high overhead, a nice reprieve from the storms. The trail was muddy because of all the rain, but the horses didn't mind, happy to be out of the barn.

Irritation still simmered just under the surface from the woman's advances, distracting me to the point that I didn't notice the small crowd hanging around Baylee's cabin until their muffled conversation reached my ears.

Shifting to a jog, I rushed to the group. My heart dropped into my gut, finding Langston's arms wrapped around Memphis. With a curse, I shoved the others aside, bounded up the stairs, and forced myself between the two men. Lang stumbled back with a grunt, falling against the railing with a confused expression, while Memphis sailed backward, slamming against the front door.

"Shit," I cursed, rushing to help Memphis off his ass.

"What the fuck are you doing, Liam?" Langston yelled at my back.

"Saving his ass and your life," I snapped, turning around to face the asshole.

Keeping my body positioned between them, I searched the group to get a read on why no one else had intervened. Baylee sat calmly on the porch swing beside Amy, both failing to hide their laughter and wide smiles behind loose fists.

My brows pulled in tight, utterly confused why she thought Langston fighting Memphis was funny. "What am I missing?"

"They weren't fighting," Ethan offered from where he leaned against the railing near the swing. "Though, knowing Langston like we do, I can see why you thought that instead of what was really happening."

"Which was what?" I asked, looking around. At the base of the steps, Brandon and Carl stood side by side, heads together, talking in low voices. "What's going on?"

The earlier irritation made me jittery, the urge for a fight an insistent itch beneath my skin.

"Langston, the grumpiest asshole you'll ever meet, was actually attempting to hug your third." It took a second for Ethan's words to register. Memphis grabbed my shoulder, drawing my attention, and nodded. "Apparently, the tatted newbie is officially a welcomed and protected member of our community thanks to him saving West's life."

Then it clicked. West and Langston were in a complicated relationship. They shared women but also had their own version of fun if an interested female wasn't around. I wasn't sure how much they actually cared for each other, but if Langston was here hugging Memphis for saving West's life, then it was more than I suspected.

Memphis stepped up to Langston and held out a hand. "I'm glad to hear your friend is all right, and I was happy to help." He leaned back against the side of the cabin and turned to me. "Langston stopped by to let everyone know West made it to the hospital safely and the doctors think they can save his fingers, including regular mobility."

"Really?" I questioned, hope lifting my tone.

Langston ran a hand over his short dark hair, appearing more exhausted than I'd ever seen him. "He's scheduled for surgery in the morning. They had to call in a special surgeon."

"We'll help cover all the medical bills," Brandon chimed in before turning his attention back to Carl, his expression bleak.

"What's this about?" I motioned between the two of them, but Langston was the one to respond.

"West was out of it from the pain meds, but before I left to grab clothes and shit, he dropped a fucking bomb on me and Juno." It didn't go unnoticed that Langston didn't have the same snarl when mentioning Juno. "He said only one thing made sense for why the chopper was such a damn mess inside. It was sabotaged."

Either the entire world went quiet or my hearing went out, because there was only silence as that unexpected word repeated over and over in my head.

"I know what he said, but that doesn't make any sense. It had to be the pain meds," Amy said beside Baylee, who grabbed her friend's hand and squeezed. "Who would want to sabotage our shit?"

"What about that guy?" Memphis mused, hitching his chin at Baylee. "The doctor guy who gave you a hard time yesterday."

I stood up a little straighter at that fucking news. "What is he talking about, Little Bit?"

A flush crept up her neck and flooded her cheeks. "Taylor—Dr. Richards—came by yesterday, and when Memphis intervened, Taylor got a little mouthy."

"Mouthy, my ass. The asshole spewed vile shit about this group. Hell, I could almost taste his disdain." Memphis huffed and reached into his jeans pocket, pulling out a pack of cigarettes. He lit the end and took a deep inhale. "But I think it was more about Baylee calling me a friend, and me intervening, than his resentment for you guys."

"How do you mean?" Brandon asked, joining the conversation. Out of the corner of my eye, I caught Dax jogging our way.

"Just a feeling that he's interested in her. He mentioned her 'being smarter' or something similar. Makes me think he sees her as an equal to himself, maybe the only equal in town."

"Huh," Amy said. "You know, now that you say it, I can totally see that asshole thinking he's better than everyone because of his fucking degree."

"Hey," Dax said, slightly out of breath as he paused in the middle of the group. "Finley and I just got back from flying over Caper to assess the damage. The main road to their settlement is completely gone from the landslide."

"What?" This was the first I'd heard of any issues from the storms.

"We received a call on the emergency line this morning while you were out," Carl clarified. "They need supplies, which we can air-drop, but they also said the slide damaged the homes, and their animals were caught up in it too."

Baylee stood so fast, the swing rocked backward from

the force. She came to stand at my side, fully engrossed in the conversation at the mention of injured animals.

"From what we could see, the main road and even the ATV trails are all impassible, which means there's no way for us to get someone in there to assess the damage except on foot. I can't land the floatplane. The helicopter would've been our best bet, but it's out of commission." Dax's gritty tone spoke to how frustrated he was.

"And I have to get back to Anchorage," Langston added, rubbing at his beard. "I can't go as the medic."

Memphis raised the hand holding the cigarette. "I'd be happy to help where I can."

"I want to go too," Baylee added with a determined nod.

I shook my head. "No, I don't think that's a good—"

"There could be injured animals, Liam. I'm going."

I pursed my lips, wishing like hell I could smack her ass for that sassy tone even though she was right. I just didn't fucking like it.

"We can take the horses," I sighed. "They're our best way into Caper if everything else is blocked, and it's quicker than going on foot. Dax and Finley can air-drop supplies like water and nonperishable food. We three will assess the damage from the ground and render aid however needed."

Brandon eyed me as he contemplated my plan. It was a solid one, even if it would take over a day to get there on horseback. Caper was a tiny, multigenerational compound of sorts, a grouping of houses all owned and occupied by the Leech family. It was rustic as hell, but the Leeches had always lived off-grid and wanted to stay. The fact that they'd reached out to us for anything was a testament to how bad the situation was.

"I don't know," Brandon said, taking out his phone and coming to stand at my side. He pulled up a satellite view of the area. "It's rough as hell out there, but there might be some animal trails you could ride along." At that, he gave Memphis a skeptical glance. "Have you ever ridden a horse before?"

Pink stained Memphis's cheeks. Clearing his throat, he responded with a reluctant nod. "Once or twice. There were horses at the rehab facility."

I pointed at the marked trailhead for the Soul Trail. "We could start there, then veer off a few miles in. There's a big drop-off somewhere around here, but I'm sure we could find a way around it." My gaze went to Baylee at the mention of the Soul Trail, stomach sinking, knowing it was where all those women had gone missing. "If we leave soon, we can get several miles in before having to camp for the night. We would get to Caper early tomorrow, if everything goes according to plan."

"There are a lot of risks."

I clapped Brandon on the shoulder. "There always are in these types of rescue assignments. You know that better than anyone. But we still help anyone who needs it, hence the 'adventure and rescue' part of the company you three started."

"He's not wrong," Amy chimed in. "We'll make sure they have satellite phones, since there's no way in hell their personal cells will work out there, plus enough supplies to get them through several days in case things don't go as planned." At Amy's comment about no cell service Baylee deflated, almost seeming relieved. Odd. "We have to send someone, babe. They called us for help. You know how hard that had to have been for old man Leech."

Brandon's resigned sigh was all the approval I needed.

"Carl, bring three sat phones to the barn." He nodded, turned on his heel, and started toward the main office where we kept the equipment and had our weekly meetings. "Baylee, get your personal bag and kit packed for what you'll need to treat the wounded animals, but remember, we're on horseback. Lang, take Memphis to your place and help him pack up your medic bag. I'll run to the general store with Amy to grab some jerky and other nonperishable food items that aren't heavy or bulky."

With a loud clap to get us all in motion, I gestured for Amy to head down the stairs first. Before Baylee could follow her, I wrapped an arm around her waist and yanked her back against me.

"I don't like you being in danger," I said into her ear.

"I won't be. You and Memphis will keep me safe." She turned her head to brush her lips against mine. "I trust you, Liam."

After one more quick kiss, she shimmied out of my hold. I sighed, watching her perfect ass as she walked toward the barn. Running a hand over my head, I started after Amy.

"If anything happens to her," she said when I caught up, "I will cut off your balls and serve them to you as grilled hors d'oeuvres." The smile she shot me made me blanch. Fuck, she was scary. "Also, have so much fun and be safe, okay?"

I could only nod in response, because what else could you say to a remark like that? Though Amy didn't have to worry about her friend. I'd protect Baylee with my life. And after earlier with Memphis and Langston, it seemed I felt the same way about the recent addition to our community. That made the unexpected add-on to my relationship with Baylee way fucking easier than I ever expected sharing her could be. Baylee trusted and wanted Memphis, and I trusted him to take care of her and keep her safe.

Now all we had to do was make it official. Me, Baylee, and Memphis. Plus Elvis, too, I guess.

Something deep inside me settled at that thought, like everything was finally falling into place. But like Baylee, I'd had my expected future yanked away and shit on, so it would be hard to trust that this wasn't fake or short-term. I just had to trust them... which for someone with my past was a big fucking ask.

But for her—for them—I'd sure as hell try.

# 21

---

## MEMPHIS

I looked fucking ridiculous, and from the way Baylee kept eyeing me over her shoulder and giggling, she 100 percent agreed. With an annoyed grumble, I shifted in the uncomfortable saddle to ease the growing ache in my ass—and we'd only been riding for thirty minutes.

Baylee slowed her horse until we rode side by side. "Don't look so petulant. The clothes don't look bad. They're just not your typical trendy style, that's all."

No fucking shit, this getup wasn't me. I eyed the Wranglers and flannel shirt I'd borrowed from Carl with disdain. I had to put my foot down when he tried to make me wear a pair of cowboy boots. That was a step too far. My go-to motorcycle boots weren't ideal for horseback riding, but the style was all me, and they fit like a glove on the off chance we needed to get off the massive beasts to hike at some point.

"The jeans make your ass look bitable." For emphasis, she leaned back in the saddle, eyes going to my ass, and snapped her teeth.

"I feel like a fraud," I groaned, jumping slightly when the horse jerked its head. Yes, I had ridden before, but horses and I didn't get along like Liam, the horse whisperer who rode several yards ahead of us. I had a healthy respect for the enormous animals, sure, but that was about the extent of my feelings for them. "Maybe I should walk."

"There is no way we can cover enough distance on foot, so suck it up like a good boy," Liam shouted ahead of us.

I flipped off his back, making Baylee giggle.

"I saw that, Memphis. You can count on paying for that later."

Desire slithered through my veins at the vague promised threat, which once again confused the hell out of me. Out of habit, I looked down to check on Elvis only to deflate. We were unsure of the terrain we would encounter, and I ended up agreeing with Liam that it was best to leave Elvis at home. It was the safest decision for my best friend, but that didn't mean I didn't regret leaving him behind.

"Has Liam filled you in on this trail and the missing women?" Baylee asked.

I dipped my chin in a slow nod.

Lips pursed, she blew a raspberry and nervously scanned our surroundings, making me do the same. "It's terrifying that they have no leads, zero clues to indicate what's going on out here." Her features tightened with worry as she gnawed at her lower lip. "Did he also mention that one of our friends went missing several weeks back?"

Fuck, her concern killed me.

"They've sent out search parties, hoping to find her or even something of hers, but haven't found anything. It's slow going because Alaska is so fucking wild." She gestured to the towering mountains and dense trees lining the narrow trail. "There are millions of acres where she could've easily fallen or gotten hurt, and we wouldn't have a clue where to look." She swallowed hard and looked at me with tears in her lower lids. "I don't like thinking of the alternative, that someone took Caroline or the other missing women."

Up ahead, Liam swiveled his horse around and leaned against the saddle horn, eyeing us. "What's more concerning to me is all the places someone could hide out, live completely off-grid," he said, inclining his head toward the vast, treacherous landscape. "But everyone needs supplies, even sociopaths."

"Okay," Baylee drawled, brows pulled in tight.

A huff escaped when I understood what he meant. "You're saying everyone needs supplies, and the closest place for that is Anchor Bay. You think it's someone you know or have at least met before?"

Baylee gasped in surprise, covering her parted lips while her crystal blue eyes flicked between us.

"That makes sense to me, and I'm almost positive it's what Oliver and Hudson are considering too. But there's no way to know who. Most of the 'locals' to Anchor Bay live outside town and only come in when absolutely necessary to stock up on necessities."

"So, in your mind, anyone who comes to town is a suspect." I blew out a heavy breath. "Damn."

"Oliver and Hudson just need one fucking lead, a clue to point the investigation in the right direction." Turning his horse, he clicked his tongue to get the beast moving forward again.

"I know I brought it up, but can we *please* talk about something else?" Baylee pleaded. "I'll have nightmares tonight if we don't."

"Don't worry, Kitten," I said with a wink. "I'll be pressed up right beside you, keeping you safe all night long."

A pink flush stained her fair cheeks, making me wonder if the memory of me watching Liam slowly fuck her while I kissed her like my life depended on it kept flashing on repeat in her mind like it did for me. Her face when she came on his dick was burned into my brain, a memory I'd remember for the rest of my life.

"Fuck," I grunted when my cock twitched in the tight jeans. "Horseback has to be the worst damn place to get turned on."

"Maybe for a guy, but for a girl?" She slowly rotated her hips back and forth, rubbing herself against the leather saddle. Baylee's lips parted slightly, and her lids fluttered shut with the sensual movement. "It's a fucking tease, that's what it is."

"Is that so?" I rasped, watching her move again.

"Good, it'll get you ready for us tonight," Liam said, smirking over his shoulder. "I can't wait to take you under the stars, Little Bit."

"Well, this just got a hell of a lot more fun," I quipped while adjusting my now semihard cock so it didn't get rubbed raw. "Makes the sore ass and awful clothes worth it."

Liam barked out a laugh, and Baylee shot me a wide smile.

*A lot more fun indeed.*

---

NOT FUN.

Not fucking fun at all.

My inner thighs were so sore it hurt to walk. There was

legitimate concern that I would walk bowlegged forever. Plus, both ass cheeks were numb and had been the past two damn hours. Hand pressed against my lower back, I bowed backward like some old fuck in a nursing home, groaning as my spine cracked.

Lifting both arms overhead, I angled my face up to the cloudless sky, taking in the golden sun as I stretched out my tight muscles. A forceful smack landed between my shoulder blades, propelling me forward a few steps.

"You did good today." I arched an incredulous brow in Liam's direction, making him chuckle. "Right, good is a stretch. You were decent. At least you didn't fall off."

"True, way to think positive. I didn't take you as a glass-half-full type of guy."

The corners of his lips curled in a smirk as his intense gaze slid to Baylee, busy brushing down her horse. "Me either, but things change when the right people come into our lives."

"That's fucking deep, man. Must be the fresh air or something,"

He snorted, motioning for me to follow him. "We need firewood. Help me find anything somewhat dry. I have some starter blocks in my pack, but wet wood smokes something terrible, and I don't want that shit in my face all night."

"What about Baylee?" I didn't like the idea of leaving her alone for a second, considering the topic from earlier.

"I'll keep an eye on her, make sure she's never out of my sight. Just stay close to camp."

Camp was quaint, a single tent that made me happy as hell knowing I'd get to sleep beside Baylee.

Keeping close to the clearing, like Liam asked, I nudged a somewhat-dry branch before bending down to add it to the growing stack in my arms. Just as my fingertips brushed over the moss-covered wood, the sense of something being off had the hair on the back of my neck standing on end, making me pause. Attempting to stay subtle, I gripped the limb and slowly stood, twisting one way and then the other, pretending to stretch out my back rather than scanning the dense trees for danger.

Nothing moved between the thin trunks or rustled through the thick underbrush except for Liam, several yards away, with a large stack of wood bundled against his chest. Shaking out the paranoia, I resumed scouring the ground for firewood, though this time I kept attuned to my surroundings too.

Back at camp, I dropped my armful of mostly dry wood on the ground beside the makeshift fire ring. At the noise, Baylee popped out of the tent—well, it was sort of a tent, more a tarp held up by paracord, configured to keep the elements off us.

"Everything good out there?" she asked, eyes nervously flicking around the clearing.

The strange moment from earlier had me striding to her side. "Why?"

Rubbing at her arms, she curled against me. I wrapped an arm around her shoulders, securing her even tighter.

"I don't know. Maybe it's knowing we're only a few miles off the Soul Trail, but I'm just...."

"Nervous?" I finished for her when she trailed off.

"Yeah." Baylee buried her face against my chest. "It's probably nothing. It just feels off out here. I can't put my finger on why, though."

I started to tell her about my similar feeling when Liam emerged from the trees, a stack of firewood almost twice the size of mine in his arms. His gray eyes took us in, lips pulling into a frown as he deposited the branches beside the ring of stones.

"What's wrong?"

"Baylee is nervous about being out here, and I don't blame her. I don't think we should leave her alone, so she doesn't worry." Her smooth hair slid beneath my palm as I moved it over the top of her head, then pulled on her ponytail to tip her petite face up to mine. "That work for you, Kitten?"

At my tug, she gasped and her pupils dilated, clearly liking the action. "That's perfect," she breathed.

"Yes, you are, Baylee." I pressed my lips to hers, reluctantly pulling back at the sound of the firewood being moved around. Liam squatted beside the ring of rocks, creating a teepee of sorts out of the smaller sticks. "Want help with that?" I eyed the horizon. "We have what, another hour or two of light left?"

He shook his head, but a knowing smirk pulled at his lips. "I've got this covered. You and Baylee go distract yourselves from worrying about this place."

I arched my pierced brow at Baylee, finding her eyes already on me. "What do you say, Kitten?" I teased as I toyed with the tip of her ponytail, tugging on it sharply. "Do we need a distraction?"

"Depends." She licked her lips. "What do you have in mind?"

Swallowing down a groan at her breathless tone, I examined the clearing, zeroing in on a cluster of boulders and rocks several feet away. Fingers wrapped around the back of her neck, I guided Baylee in that direction. With every stomp of my boots, my need for her swelled as I pictured her pinned against a smooth rock while I showed her just how amazing my pierced dick would feel sliding along the walls of her pussy.

Pausing at a smooth boulder that came up mid-thigh, I sat in front of her, shifting my hand around from the back of her neck to lightly grasp her throat. A guttural groan escaped her parted lips, and my lids slammed shut at the erotic sensation of her throat moving beneath my palm when she swallowed hard. With her between my spread thighs, I moved my free hand beneath the hem of her long-sleeve T-shirt to skim up her stomach, then trace a single fingertip along the band of her sports bra.

Peering up through my lashes, I wordlessly begged for approval. At her permission, I slid my hand higher to palm one full breast, squeezing and scraping a nail against the tight material where I could feel her peaked tip underneath. Her lids fluttered closed at the small contact, breath whooshing from her lungs as her head fell back.

"Take it all off for me," I demanded, releasing her throat to lean back onto my elbows, eager to watch the striptease.

Heated gaze locked on me, she pulled the shirt off, setting it on the rock beside me to keep it off the soggy ground, followed by her sports bra, leaving her naked from the waist up.

Bits of rock dug into my palms when I pushed off to sit up straight. Hands around her narrow waist, I tugged her even closer to seal my lips around her pebbled nipples. Her fingers slid through my hair, holding me there as I sucked and nipped.

Switching sides, I played with the saliva-covered nipple, twisting and tugging while I sucked on the other. My name fell from her lips like a prayer and curse woven together. Releasing her with a pop, I gripped the back of her neck and guided her face to mine so I could devour her lips.

The hand around her waist dipped beneath her jeans and panties, fingers sliding to her slick core. A pleasure-filled groan rattled from my chest and escaped to vibrate between our lips.

"You're soaked for me, Kitten." I flicked her swollen clit, making her entire body shudder. "Tell me what you want."

"You," she panted, eyes open wide and locked on me. "I want you, Memphis. Here, right now. Like you like it."

My already stiff cock pressed even harder against my zipper at her words.

"You just had that virgin pussy fucked yesterday, Bay. You're sore and—"

She gripped my chin, shocking the hell out of me with both the move and firm hold.

"It's my body. I do with it as I want. I know what I need, I know what I can handle, and I know how I feel. Now, if you don't want to fuck me, fine, I'll go find Liam and—"

I batted her hand away and stood, towering over her petite frame. Rotating our positions, I gently pushed her to sit in the space I just vacated. Big blue eyes full of heat and trust gazed up at me. A breath caught in my chest as I took her in. This was real, a moment I dreamed of for years was playing out right before me. Unlike the unreal moments in the days previous, it was just us, only me and Baylee.

"You're still wearing too many clothes," I said, trailing a finger between her breasts to her belly button. When her fingers went to the top button, I pushed them aside. "Allow me the pleasure of unwrapping the gift you're giving me."

I took my time, treasuring each brush of my fingers along her soft skin as I slowly undid her jeans and worked the denim and panties over her hips. After removing both boots and socks, I pulled her pants free, tossing them to the side, careful to keep them off the soggy ground.

I ran the tip of my thumb along my lower lip, mouth literally watering at the beauty before me. Adjusting myself, I reached between her thighs, sliding a single finger into her hot pussy. Baylee groaned, back arching off the boulder when I added another.

"Does that feel good, Bay? You like my fingers stroking you from the inside."

"Yes," she breathed. Her hand wrapped around my wrist and added to the movement making it more forceful, thrusting my two fingers deeper. "Fuck, I'm so worked up, I'm close."

"Well, that makes two of us," I chuckled. With my free hand, I worked the buckle loose on my belt and popped the button of the borrowed jeans. With a bit of room, I shoved my hand into my briefs and fisted my throbbing cock. A hiss whispered through my teeth when I flicked the piercing. "I can't wait for you to feel this bit of steel slide along your walls, feel it stroking you in a way you'll never forget."

"Oh shit," she panted. "Please, Memphis."

"I've got you, Bay." Twisting my angle, I flicked her swollen nub with my thumb while adding a third finger, stuffing her full. "Come for me, Kitten."

Baylee's lips parted as her head fell backwards and an elicit moan rattled through the trees. Birds chirped and fluttered into the sky at the erotic sound. Not me though, I didn't even fucking blink, wanting to memorize every second of our moment.

Slowing my movements, she relaxed along the stone, murmuring my praises. When those light lashes fluttered open and her hooded gaze locked with mine, I tightened my grip on my cock to keep from exploding in my pants.

That look was a perfect mix of love and lust, intoxicating and a damn aphrodisiac, if my pulsing cock was any sign.

And then she went and amped up the already electric moment.

Raising her hands, she pressed both wrists together in a type of offering and flicked her gaze to my belt.

"Want to put that thing to good use?" she asked, licking her lower lip.

"Fucking hell, woman, are you trying to get me to come before I'm inside you?" Her slow sultry smile contrasted the shake of her head. Huffing in fake annoyance, I freed my hand and slid the leather free of the loops, allowing it to dangle from my fingers.

"Are you sure?"

"Yes, please." I hesitated. "Fucking hell. I'm not delicate, remember. Now tie me up and fuck me like you want to."

Well shit. Seemed Baylee turned bossy when she was denied cock. Good to know because I fucking loved it.

"Like I want, huh?" She nodded, her blonde hair swaying with the movement. "Then flip around, Kitten, and push that perfect ass into the air, hands behind your back." My fingers twitched at my side, wanting to help her as she did as I instructed, but watching was part of my fun.

Cheek resting on the smooth rock, legs spread giving me a barely-there glimpse at her glistening cunt, ass lifted, and the cherry on the erotic moment was both hands resting on her lower back like I asked.

"Such a good Kitten, aren't you? Now let's tie up those hands so I don't get clawed when things get rough." Wrapping a hand around both of her wrists, I leaned in close, lips brushing against her earlobe. "Because that's exactly how I plan to take your tight pussy. I'll make you scream my name so loud and long that there won't be an animal left in these woods that won't run at the sound."

The leather slid along my palm, making me shiver as I

wrapped it around her delicate wrists, careful to keep it comfortable for her first time. Later I'd add in the slight mix of pain that came with a tighter binding but not now. Not when I was seconds away from losing it at just the sight of her tied up and waiting for me.

And only me.

Not Dean.

Not Liam.

Me.

Only me.

Stepping between her thighs, I gripped both hips and hiked her ass higher in the air to give me the angle I needed. Shoving the jeans and boxer briefs down to my thighs, I guided my pierced head to her dripping entrance. My teeth sank into my lower lip, quieting my groan as I pushed forward, her pussy stretching around me so perfectly.

A garbled curse met my ears as I continued to push deeper, fascinated at the way she took all of me.

"Damn, Kitten, you were made to stretch around my cock, weren't you? Born to be here, just like this with nowhere to go but take what I'm giving you."

"Yes," she cried out. "That feels... that feels so...." Her head shook. "Unreal. It's so different. And amazing," she sighed as I slowly withdrew.

Her soft flesh molded around my fingers where they dug into her hips, which had me smirking at the possibility of leaving bruises. Good. I wanted to mark her, for me and her to see later and remind us of this moment.

I slowly worked my cock in and out of her cunt, thighs trembling with the restraint to not slam into her hard and find the orgasm that I held at bay. Which was working until that fucker Liam called out, knowing his words would trigger the other kink I admitted to the other night.

"Memphis, Baylee," he called out, making me still. "You two better not let me catch you or there will be hell to pay. I'm coming to find you."

His deep voice rolled through the clearing, making a sensual shiver slide down my spine.

Fuck, what was it about that bastard that did something for me, added that edge of danger and the forbidden? Either way, the suggestion of Baylee and I being caught like this, with our pants down and my dick balls-deep inside her had me slamming into her hard.

A pleasure-filled moan floated between us as I drew back and thrust forward again. Baylee cried out my name, begging me to move faster, to hit deeper. Dropping my hold on one hip, I wrapped my fingers into her silky strands and tugged, pulling her face off the boulder.

"You want it rough, Kitten, then hold the fuck on."

The sound of crunching leaves, of squelched footsteps spurred me even faster. A familiar zing radiated from my balls, telling me I was close, and by the way Baylee squeezed around me, she was too.

"You're so fucking perfect, Kitten. Come with me, scream my name for him to hear."

And that she did, her voice cracking at the end as she trembled in my hold and my own orgasm raced through me, making my thighs tremble, and head swim from the force. Drawing out every last drop of cum to ensure she'd be leaking me all night, I stayed inside her, leaning forward to press my chest against her back.

Our labored breaths were the only sound I could hear. For several seconds we savored the moment, until a large shadow crept over us. Looking over my shoulder, I smirked at Liam behind me, his gaze locked on where I was buried deep in our girl.

"Seems I caught you," he muttered, rubbing at his scruff. "You ready for more, sweetheart? Or did our boy wear you out?"

"More," she muttered, lids closed but a smile on her lips. "Always more with you two."

Damn straight.

More, always more with these two.

## 22

BAYLEE

I woke with a gasp, my pulse racing despite having been asleep. Soothing warmth engulfed me on both sides while the cool air brushed against my exposed cheeks, enticing me to fall back asleep. The faint golden glow highlighting the sky outside the makeshift tent signaled it wasn't quite morning.

It was way too early to be awake after the exhausting day and late-night fun with Liam and Memphis. So why was I, and with my heart pounding in my chest?

Lids heavy, I started to nod off again, assuming it was my internal alarm from my early morning runs before the busy workday. Inhaling the crisp, clean air, I scooted closer to Liam's radiating body heat.

Almost asleep, my eyes popped open again at a rustling sound outside the tent. Fully awake now, I slid away from Liam, careful not to rouse either him or Memphis, who lay sprawled out on my other side, and pushed up to my elbows.

With the heels of both hands, I rubbed the sleep from my eyes and then squinted out at the clearing, searching for the cause of the noise. A quick movement in the thick trees, barely noticeable in the early-morning sun.

Running the tip of my tongue along my dry lips, I glanced between the two men. I wasn't positive about what I saw, the silhouette too small to be a large predator, and they needed their rest for the long day ahead. No need to wake them yet.

"Where are you going?" Liam's husky voice froze me where I'd shimmied out from between him and Memphis.

I scanned his closed lids and chest, rising with deep, even breaths. He looked seconds away from falling back asleep.

"Bathroom. I'll be right back," I whispered.

It wasn't technically a lie. Now that I was up, I needed to pee. It just wasn't the sole reason I was leaving the tent.

Pushing to stand, I straightened the loose T-shirt I'd packed to sleep in and tiptoed to the edge of the tarp. Forgoing socks, I slipped one bare foot into my boot and then the other, all while keeping a watchful eye on the area where I caught movement minutes ago. Grabbing Liam's discarded flannel from the day before, I pulled it on, the sleeves long and baggy. Nose pressed to the collar, I inhaled, loving the manly scent that filled my lungs, reminding me of him.

Out in the dawn glow, I paused, taking a precious moment to appreciate the utter peace that came in the mornings. These moments were why I treasured Alaska. There was freedom for me in the vast silence it offered, as if the world stood utterly still and all that mattered was that moment.

A deep, threatening growl broke the tranquility, freezing me in place. The horses stomped their hooves, snorting and shifting along the line, fully aware of whatever animal was out there.

The hair on the back of my neck stood on end, alerting me to the threat somewhere behind me. Heart slamming against my ribs, breaths quick and shallow, I slowly twisted around. That was when I saw it, the shadows no longer concealing the animal as it prowled out from between two thick trees. The massive wolf snarled, the fur along its spine raised.

No. Not a wolf.

Eyes squinted and head tilted, hoping to see farther, I studied the somewhat familiar dog as it drew closer. It watched me, studying my reaction as I did the same, attempting to remember why the particular husky seemed familiar.

Recognition hit me so fast and out of nowhere that I actually stumbled back with a gasp, hand coming up to loosely wrap around my throat. At my sudden movement, the dog's ears went back, coupled with a painful whimper as he slowly lowered to his belly and laid his head between his paws. Nothing signaled a threat from the dog; instead, he seemed terrified and vulnerable.

My heart sank, knowing that meant he was probably injured.

"Henry?" I whispered. When the dog continued to watch me, not responding to the guessed name, I racked my brain. "Damnit, Baylee, think. Harvey?" The dog huffed, and I swear he rolled his eyes. "Okay, so clearly not Harvey."

I chewed on my lip while gazing at his rust-covered muzzle. My stomach churned, realizing it was probably dried blood.

"Hank?"

His ears went up, and he shifted to stand on unsteady legs.

"Hank," I breathed in relief. "Are you hurt, buddy?" I started toward him, only to freeze with a single boot in the air. "Wait, where is she, your owner? Fuck, what was her name?" Hand out, I dared another step toward the frightened animal, but he turned and bolted back the way he came. "Hank," I whispered. "Come back here so I can help you."

He paused at the edge of the clearing and looked over his shoulder, a pitiful whine cutting through the quiet morning. Without thinking of the consequences, only Hank, I started off after him, leaving my two protectors behind. When I was within a few feet of him, Hank slipped into the trees, trotting along a somewhat-worn animal path.

Thin branches and brush scraped my exposed legs while prickly Sitka spruce needles poked at my cheeks as I weaved through the trees, keeping Hank within sight as I followed him deeper and deeper into the forest. Each heavy breath fogged in front of my face, the morning chill even colder in the dense trees.

"Hank," I whisper-shouted, head whipping every which way to make sure someone didn't jump out and kidnap me. I swallowed hard, realizing that was a legit possibility, and I was putting more and more distance between me and camp. "I think I should get the guys, okay?"

A few feet ahead, Hank whined, his bright blue eyes pleading with me to keep going like two beacons in the faint light.

"This is a terrible decision," I muttered, pulling Liam's flannel even tighter around me to trap what little body heat I could to keep from freezing to death on this dumb, side quest.

*Oh, Liam and Memphis both will be explosively pissed about this later.*

Blowing out a raspberry, I continued on, following the dog I barely knew instead of turning around like any wise person would.

I should have but didn't because... maybe Liam was right, and I had no self-preservation skills. Or maybe after everything I'd been through, I just didn't give a fuck anymore. But with him and Memphis in my life, bringing me back from the brink of a grief-induced death with smiles, laughter, and love, that "I don't give a fuck what happens" mentality was fading.

Because I did care what happened to me.

I had a future, a happy one, to look forward to.

After tromping a few more yards, the trees thinned, shifting to more of a rocky slope. Small rocks crunched beneath my boots with every careful step. The last thing I wanted was to trip over my own feet and send myself propelling down into the shallow ravine at the bottom of the slope that was currently filled with rushing water from the heavy rains.

My teeth chattered as I scanned the area, frustration rising as the seconds ticked by. A high-pitched whine had me huffing and making my way to where Hank lay in a submissive position several feet away.

"What was so important that—" I cut myself off and staggered back, falling to my ass when the loose rocks shifted beneath my boots with the unsteady step.

Neither the pain from the fall nor the bits of stone digging into my palms and the backs of my thighs registered as I gaped at the lifeless body. Hank's big head turned from it to me and back again, his whimper even more urgent.

*Fuck.*

*Fuck.*

*Fuck.*

A gust of wind cut through the area, whipping strands of hair in front of my face. I frantically swept it away to keep my line of sight clear. Breathing hard, I pushed off the muddy ground onto shaky legs and dared a single step closer to get a better look. I regretted it immediately.

There was no way to know for sure if it was Hank's owner who brought him into the clinic—I only met her once—but the way he protected her body, brought me here, told me it was her.

Mud-coated palms up, I carefully backed away, frantic gaze bouncing everywhere, searching for the person who'd done that to her.

"I need to go get help," I whispered to Hank as if he could understand me. "Stay here. I'll be back with help— stronger help." I swallowed hard. "Someone who'll know what the fuck to do with all of this, because I'm freaking the fuck out." Every breath hurt, the cold air slicing down my throat and into my lungs as my panic grew.

The heels of my boots dug into the saturated ground as I turned and sprinted back the way I came. I ran like I was being chased and my life depended on it—it very well could. Warm liquid trickled down my icy legs as the underbrush tore at my flesh with every fast step.

Despite the cold, sweat coated my forehead and slicked the back of my neck. A few wrong turns sent my fear skyrocketing. *Fuck.* I couldn't breathe; my throat had closed up, forcing me to stumble to a stop. Head down between my legs, a lame attempt to not pass out from panic, I didn't sense someone approaching, didn't register the snap of the twigs or crunch of the leaves.

A scream ripped from my raw throat when a heavy hand

settled on my shoulder. Jumping at least a foot in the air, I wrenched my body free and spun, fist already swinging.

Only for that tiny fist to be caught in a large, calloused palm. Eyes wide, I blinked up at Liam's face, a relieved sob bubbling up. The anger and worry in his tight features vanished as he tracked the tears leaking down my cheeks.

"Baylee." His warm hands wrapped around my shoulders and squeezed gently. "Baylee, talk to me. What's going on?" His palms slid down my arms as he squatted low, gaze tracking along my body. "Are you hurt? Fuck, you're bleeding. What the hell—"

"Hank," I wheezed. Even getting that word out hurt my raw throat.

Liam's brows pulled in tight and his head whipped to the side, hearing something I clearly didn't because of the pulse pounding in my ears.

"Over here," he shouted, though it barely registered despite him being so close. "I found her." Liam eyed me. "Get your medic bag. She's hurt."

Hurt.

Hank.

Dead body.

I frantically shook my head and grabbed his hand, squeezing hard to get his full attention.

"Dead body." Raising my trembling hand, I pointed in what I thought was the direction of the rocky slope where Hank waited. "Her dog came for me."

With every word I managed to get out, Liam's expression grew more serious.

His jaw worked back and forth. "Little Bit," he practically hissed. "Are you telling me you followed a damn dog out into the woods in just a shirt and boots, and it led you to a dead fucking body?"

"What the fuck?" I turned, finding Memphis approaching, medic bag in hand, clearly having heard Liam's very accurate summary.

I nodded and stepped in the direction I came—well, thought I came—from. Fuck, I was terribly lost. Sucking in a lungful of air, I released a loud whistle and called out Hank's name, knowing I'd need his help to get back to his owner.

Memphis's worried gaze scanned my face before dipping to my legs. "Fuck, Kitten," he murmured while examining a deep cut. "Did you get into a fight with a mountain lion?"

"Who the fuck is Hank?" Liam growled.

Before I could respond, a rustle from the underbrush had us all turning to find the large husky making his way toward us. He paused several feet away and growled, clearly not expecting the guys to be with me.

"Hank," I said calmly and grabbed Memphis's hand, extending ours and the one holding Liam's toward the dog. "They're friends. They can help." Out of the corner of my mouth, I said to Memphis, "Get down low so he doesn't see you as a threat, like Liam is."

Moving slowly, Memphis did as instructed. For several seconds, Hank studied us, more so the guys, before he approved of the addition to the recovery team.

Tapping both men on the shoulder, I moved to follow Hank only to be held back by Memphis.

"Let Liam go check it out. I need to dress your wounds."

My wild hair shifted, floating in front of my face with the quick headshake. "No. He trusts me, and...." I swallowed hard to keep the tears from falling again. "I think it's his owner, the body." I met both of their gazes. "It's a woman."

Liam's brows shot up. "Fuck." He pulled his gun free and

palmed the grip. Instantly, Hank released a dangerous growl and crouched low, preparing to attack.

"He apparently doesn't like that," Memphis whispered. "Put it away. I don't want to get attacked by those teeth. I've seen enough dog bites to know they shred skin and are dirty as hell. You're almost guaranteed a nasty infection if you're not treated with heavy antibiotics."

I blinked at Memphis while Liam holstered his gun, grumbling his displeasure about the situation. "What did you say?"

Memphis studied me. "That I don't want to get bit by the dog?"

I shook my head. "About dog bites being dirty and needing antibiotics."

He repeated what he said with a questioning tone, clearly not understanding where I was going with this. Honestly, neither did I, but him saying that triggered something in the back of my thoughts. It was like a tickle or an itch I couldn't quite reach.

"Come on, let's follow the dog," Liam grumbled. "I'm not leaving you two alone out here, so we're all going on this hike."

"Don't be so grumpy," I snapped. "I'm the one who found the dead body—"

"Exactly," he shouted before closing his eyes and inhaling deeply. When he opened them, they were filled with regret and something else I couldn't read. "Sorry. I'm not grumpy. I'm fucking pissed. Memphis and I were fucking beside ourselves when we woke up and you were nowhere to be found. And now I find out it was because you took off following a fucking dog." He ran a hand over his head and looked at the treetops. "We're not done talking about this."

"Or punishing you for this," Memphis added, heat to his tone. "You can't be doing that, Baylee. It's not safe, even if there wasn't some fucker out there taking women. What if you'd fallen, or an animal attacked you? Everything out here is dangerous."

Crossing both arms, which got tangled up in the massive shirt, making the frustrated move lose all effectiveness, I glared at the men.

"I'm not defenseless or helpless. Now come on. We need to follow Hank." I looked over my shoulder where he waited for us, panting. "I think he's hurt," I whispered, arms falling to my sides. "That was all I cared about, okay?"

Strong arms engulfed me and pulled me against a hard chest.

"Okay, Little Bit. But we're still not done talking about this." Turning me to face Hank, Liam urged me forward a step but kept close to my back. "Come on, let's follow him and see what's going on."

Steeling myself with a confidence-boosting breath, I nodded.

I didn't want to go back there, see that lifeless face again, but she needed us, and so did Hank. We would do everything we could to find out what happened to them. Though, based on the other tragedies over the past year, I'd bet my life that whatever happened to her wasn't a freak accident.

Someone caused it.

Hopefully, this would offer the clues needed to help us uncover who.

## 23

## LIAM

Careful to keep my distance to not disrupt any remaining evidence, I slowly circled the body for a third time, hoping to notice something I didn't on the two previous passes. I glanced over to where Baylee sat on a rock with Memphis kneeling in front of her, tending to the scrapes and other wounds that marked her legs.

A rumbling growl vibrated in my chest. The dog, watching my every move, shifted at the sound, the fur along his spine standing up. I huffed and shook my head, running a palm down my face, and refocused on the body.

There were several deep gashes on her head and face, but her hiking gear kept me from documenting additional wounds. A thin layer of silt covered the clothes, her skin, and even clumped in her long hair where it splayed around her head.

"The way the mud is deposited, I suspect she was here through the storms, and the washout from above left this sediment."

"We need to call in help," Baylee said, meeting my gaze. "This wasn't an accident. I can feel it." She pointed at the dog. "Look at his muzzle. That's dried blood there and on his chest. My theory is he attacked whoever hurt her." She jabbed that single finger at the dead woman. "It's too close to the Soul Trail to be a coincidence."

I nodded. "But we're at least two, maybe three miles away. What the hell was she doing out here?"

"Running for her life," Baylee grumbled under her breath, just loud enough for me to hear.

Memphis chuffed. "Either way, we can't leave her here."

"Or Hank," Baylee demanded, crossing her arms that once again got tangled up in my shirt, making her huff in annoyance.

"Or Hank," Memphis repeated, grinning.

I almost did too, only to remember the sheer panic and terror from earlier when I woke up and she wasn't beside me. I ground my teeth to keep from yelling at the top of my lungs, the pressure desperate to be released.

"The satellite phone is back at the campsite. We'll go together, and I'll call it in."

Oliver and Hudson needed to see this. Baylee's theory of this not being a tragic hiking accident was a solid one. Since those two headed up the missing women investigations, they would be my first call.

I eyed the dog. "What are we going to do about him?" From what I'd witnessed as we followed him, his back leg was too injured to make the hike back down on his own. "He'll need a stretcher or something."

"I call 'not it' on loading the bloody husky onto a stretcher to haul him from his owner's body, which he has clearly been protecting."

I grimaced, knowing Memphis had a point. The body showed no signs of animal activity, which was odd unless the dog had kept watch over it to ensure she wasn't disturbed. My heart broke for the animal even though he'd lured my girl into the woods alone.

I rubbed at my chest to ease the ache thinking about losing Baylee caused. Nope, not going there. Not if I wanted to stay sane or not handcuff us together.

"Would you be okay wearing a tracker?" I asked out of the blue. Memphis's hands stilled, and they both slowly turned to stare at me. "What?"

Memphis barked out a laugh, and Baylee just smirked while shaking her head in disbelief.

Not sure why they found that funny.

---

"I don't like the idea of you going back without me." Memphis cleared his throat and sent me a pointed glance from where he rolled up the tarp we'd used for the shelter. I inclined my head his way, acknowledging the poor word choice. "Without *us*."

"You've only said that a few dozen times since you called Oliver." Baylee's hand stilled on the horse's flank. "But I want to get Hank into the clinic, assessed, and X-rayed as soon as possible." She twisted to see where the dog lay. "If that back leg is fractured, the sooner I can get it mended, the better the outcome. Plus, Hank knows me, and I can keep him calm on the way down. Well," she added with a shrug, "me and the sedative I plan to give him."

"Explain to me again how you met Hank and his owner." Memphis dropped the rolled-up tarp by the rest of the gear, eyeing the horses like they might attack him at any moment.

Baylee's nose scrunched, and a deep line formed between her blonde brows. I fought the urge to kiss the tip of her nose, then take her lips with mine, nibble down her throat, and keep going until my tongue and lips were coated with the flavor of her.

"It was five or six days ago, maybe. She planned to leave the following morning to hike the Soul Trail. I told her to be careful," Baylee murmured, a sad expression overtaking her features, "but she said Hank would never let something happen to her. That was why we met. She came by the clinic to get him checked over before they headed out."

"We'll figure it out, Little Bit," I said, wrapping a hand around the back of her neck to pull her close, planting a kiss to her temple.

"But at what cost?" she asked, looking up at me, those big crystal blue eyes pleading with me. "How many more women or their male partners or dog companions have to get hurt before we figure this out, Liam? We're into double digits, and that's just on our side of the trail."

Her shoulders rounded in what looked like defeat.

With a single finger under her chin, I tipped her face up to mine. "Don't do that. Don't give up."

"I'm just sad." She sniffed. "Sad for her. She was so fun and kind. And Hank." Tears dripped from the corners of her eyes. "What's going to happen to him now?"

I started to respond, but the sound of footsteps had me spinning, gun in hand and ready to take out any threat to my family.

I slow-blinked at that thought. Family. It felt right, the word describing exactly what the two behind me had started to represent. Well, Baylee for a while now and, shocking me completely, Memphis now too.

"Put that shit away," Oliver called out as he stepped into the clearing. "You're the one who called us, remember?"

My chest moved with the annoyed huff as I holstered my weapon. Oliver, followed by Hudson and Ethan, strode toward us and then froze at the low, menacing growl that came from my side. Surprise laced through me at Hank standing on my right, stance rigid as if prepared to fight at my side against the new unknown threats.

"Easy, buddy," I murmured, the way I would to skittish horses. "They're friend, not foe."

"Is that blood on his mouth?" Hudson asked, pointing at Hank.

"Yep, so don't fuck with him. Come on." I motioned for them to follow me. "I'll show you where the body is so you can get started. Did you bring a body bag and stretcher like I asked?"

Ethan appeared at my side opposite Hank and patted the stuffed pack strapped to his back. "I have all that in here. Oliver hauled in the detective-y shit he and Hudson need to gather any evidence."

"Not sure how much we'll find considering the storms the last few days, but we figured it was worth a shot," Hudson added from somewhere behind me.

We didn't speak another word as we weaved through the trees toward the dead woman. The sound of our boots squelching in the saturated ground and the roar from the raging water below just emphasized Hudson's point from earlier. They would be lucky to get any evidence off the body, much less the surrounding area.

"Damn," Oliver murmured when we approached the woman. He took off his hat out of respect and held it over his heart. "You mentioned on the phone that Baylee met her in Anchor Bay?"

"Once. She took her dog in to see her at the clinic before she left for the hike."

"We'll need her help to identify the victim if we don't find any ID on her." Resituating his ball cap, he turned in a slow circle, inspecting the area with a trained, critical eye. "If she was hiking and fell, her pack should be around here somewhere."

"Or it tumbled down into the ravine and was swept away in the floodwaters," Hudson suggested. "But I don't think that's what any of us believe happened here."

"If not, then we need to find her campsite," Ethan stated, studying the area while actively not looking at the woman. "She wouldn't have gone this far off the trail to camp, especially not here. If she came for the Soul Trail, alone, then she was an experienced hiker and knew this entire area would be dangerous considering the weather."

"Let's spread out, gather any potential evidence, and bag it, no matter how insignificant we think it might be," Oliver commanded.

I studied the deputy sheriff for a moment, noting the dark bags under his eyes and the slump to his shoulders. Coming to stand beside him, I crossed both arms over my chest and released a heavy breath.

"You look like shit," I murmured.

"I feel like shit. We've got nothing, Liam. Nothing but more missing women, and now this innocent victim left out here like fucking trash. It's my job to keep people safe in this town, and look at me," Oliver snapped. "Fucking failing everyone."

"You're not fucking failing. You and Hudson are doing what you can. That's all you can do with what we know so far."

He nodded, but it was clear he didn't believe me.

"Did you ever find out why your dad is so against making all this public?"

Oliver released an incredulous laugh and ripped the Texas Rangers baseball cap off his head in obvious frustration. "Nope. He's sticking with not wanting people to panic, but all it's doing is allowing more victims to go out onto the trail, not knowing the danger that's out there. It's fucking bullshit, and I'm pissed but can't do anything about it."

"Pissed enough to suggest he retire and you take the sheriff's job?"

He shot me a doubtful look. "You know it'll take more than me to get him out of that seat. But I wish he would step down on his own. I used to have respect for him, when he actually cared about the safety of the residents of Anchor Bay and not how the town appeared to tourists."

"And now?" I questioned.

"Now that respect is almost gone with how he continues to hinder the investigation."

"We need to know why, Oliver. I know he's your dad, but that's shady as fuck."

He offered a reluctant nod and situated the hat back on his head. "I will, but first I need one damn lead in this investigation." He gazed down at the dead woman, sympathy filling his brown eyes. "I can't let this happen again, not to someone else."

We went silent as Hudson approached while sealing an evidence bag. He held the plastic baggie up for both Oliver and me to inspect.

"Found this over there." He hooked a thumb over his shoulder. "Must be hers."

Edge of the thin plastic between my fingers, I angled the baggie, deflecting the sun's glare to better see the silver chain and feather charm inside. I furrowed my brow as I studied the necklace, feeling like I'd seen something similar before, but shook it off when Ethan approached.

"I couldn't find a pack or campsite. Her body is here, but her stuff isn't." My brows pulled in tight as I stared at the victim. "You guys ready to get her out of here?" He shrugged off his pack and set it on the ground, pulling out everything we needed.

Oliver gestured for the black body bag in Ethan's hand. "We brought four-wheelers as far as we could and hiked in the rest of the way. Hudson and I will haul her to where we left the ATVs, then take her to the docks. Langston will take me and the body to the coroner in Anchorage."

He rolled out the body bag beside her and looked up at Hudson. "Did you already take pictures of the scene?"

Hudson held up his phone. "I did, from all different angles, plus the surrounding area."

Oliver's shoulders slumped in relief. It seemed having the former LA detective here to help him was doing just that. I was glad Oliver had someone competent and trustworthy to take a sliver of the workload off his shoulders.

"Great, then let's get her out of here so Ethan can check out spots along the trail for her camping gear. I want him to get to it before animals have more time to destroy any evidence."

We all helped carefully move the woman's body, lifting it from a thin layer of mud and gently placing her in the bag. After zipping it up, we each grabbed an edge and headed back to the main campsite where Memphis and Baylee waited for us.

Hank stuck to my heels—as best as he could with the bad leg—every step through the trees.

"My girl will fix you right up," I told the dog while adjusting my hold on the plastic as it slipped.

"You're talking to a dog," Ethan huffed while looking at the husky. "He's a pretty thing, that's for sure. Loyal too. I can't believe he stayed and protected the body. He would be an asset for any lone hiker, male or female."

"How was your last survival training group?" Oliver asked, eyeing Ethan with an intensity I couldn't read.

"The same as the last few," he grumbled while shifting to the side to not run smack into a tree. "The guys all thought they knew everything while the few women actually did and put in more work. I'm honestly not sure how much more I can take doing these. I miss the long, guided hikes that take us out for weeks, where we eat what we kill or get killed and eaten."

"This just got dark," Hudson muttered.

"We're carrying a body through the woods. It's already pretty fucking dark, Hudson," Ethan snipped back good-heartedly.

Back at camp, we carefully set the bag down, Hank lying down beside it with a heartbreaking howl. I marched over to where Memphis held Baylee tight in his arms, his chin resting on top of her head. I frowned, not liking the idea of her upset, but considering what we were doing, there was no way around it.

"They're all set to head back down with her," I said. Baylee turned in Memphis's hold and leaned back against him, gazing up at me. "You sure you want to go with them?"

"Yeah, I want to treat him as soon as possible. He has to be dehydrated and starving too." Pulling away from Memphis, she wrapped both arms around my waist, pushing her chin into my sternum to look up into my face. "I'll be okay. Don't worry about me, Liam. Hudson, Oliver, and Ethan will be with me the whole time. I already have everything loaded up on the horses for you and Memphis for the last part of the trip to Caper. Call me if there's an injured animal that needs my attention, and one of the guys will escort me there if needed."

The calluses on my palms scraped over her soft cheeks

as I cupped her face with both hands. "Please be safe, Baylee. If another random-ass dog tries to lure you away, please don't fucking follow it alone."

Her responding smile and kiss eased the frustration and darkness building in my chest from the day's unexpected events.

My girl was safe and happy.

And no matter what happened, I'd make sure that never changed.

**24**

---

MEMPHIS

"I really don't see how you wear this scratchy-ass shit all the time." I adjusted the collar of the flannel shirt, hating the feel of the material rubbing against my neck. "It's choking me."

"Layers, Memphis. Layers will be key to survival here in Alaska. It could be thirty degrees in the morning, nice in the afternoon but feels hot when you're working hard, then back to freezing at night. You need to find clothes you can put on or take off throughout the day as the fickle-ass weather changes."

I huffed in annoyance and shifted in the saddle to ease the numbness spreading across both ass cheeks. We were a mile or so from Caper per Liam's calculations, which meant I was almost done riding for a couple of days. While we rode, we crafted a basic plan for when we arrived. He would assess the manual labor aspects, and I the medical needs of the group. We would come back together, then start with the most urgent and work down the list from there.

We both wanted to get the jobs done as soon as possible, even though I knew it would mean being back on a horse sooner rather than later. Only a few hours had passed since we went in the opposite direction of Baylee, Ethan, Hudson, and Oliver, and I already missed my Kitten. The deep ache in my chest grew with every clop of the horse's hooves that took me farther and farther from her.

"I don't know how I did it for so long," I mused as I ducked beneath a low-hanging limb. "The years chained to my addictions, sure, that makes sense, and maybe part of it was drowning out how much I missed her, but after I got sober...." I shook my head and ran a hand through my dirty hair. "How did I not look her up immediately and come find her?"

Liam remained quiet for a while, making me wonder if he would respond or just ignore my rambling. Slowing his horse when we hit a gap wide enough to ride side by side, he adjusted in his saddle, removing the straw cowboy hat from his head to wipe a sleeve over his damp forehead.

"Timing is everything," his deep voice rumbled, drowning out the birds chirping happily in the nearby trees. "You found her when it was time for both of you. Until recently, she wasn't ready to see past her grief. She fought every day just to keep her head above water. Some days I had to literally watch her drown in it all with my hand held out, begging her to grab hold. You needed time to ensure you were strong enough to be with her, to not fall back into that temptation of oblivion that your addictions promised."

"I hate that she was hurting and I wasn't here to help her. He was my friend too." I eyed him, scanning his face and fit frame. "Some of the shit you say is really deep. How old are you?"

The corner of his lips quirked in an almost smile. "How old do you *think* I am?"

I shrugged and turned to hide my grin. "Young enough

to not be my grandfather, but old enough to maybe be my dad."

Liam snorted and rubbed his scruff-covered jaw. "Fair assessment. Let's just say I'm older and wiser than you and Baylee. I've done and seen enough shit that when I give advice, I suggest you listen."

"So, closer to Gramps's age, got it. I get why you're avoiding giving me a number. Don't want to let everyone know how bad you're robbing the cradle with her and me."

He arched a brow in my direction. "I'm not doing shit with your cradle." A slow smile pulled at his lips, making wrinkles spread from the corners of his eyes. "Now hers— hell yeah, I am, and I'm too much of a selfish bastard to deny what I want, even if she is too young and innocent for someone like me."

"Seriously, though, I need a number."

He sighed like I wore on his very thin patience. "Forty-three."

"That's cool, Gramps. At least you don't look it." This time, I didn't hide my wide grin.

"You're a shithead. Back to what really matters." Clearly the man was not a fan of me pointing out that he was around fifteen years older than Baylee and me. "You never explained what the fight was about between you and Dean that ended the friendship." He settled the hat back on his head and shot me a questioning glance out of the corner of his eye. "I'm ready when you are. We have nothing else to do."

I huffed, knowing he was right. It was time he knew. "Yeah." I swallowed hard, fingers curling over my leg, wishing like hell they were burying into Elvis's fur. He became my therapy-slash-emotional support dog the last couple of years, and I seriously missed him on this trip.

"The tension, what I held in, had built for years. That anger finally erupted one night when he was home for a temporary leave. You have to remember, I was there from the beginning, when he first saw her in class and told me he wanted to marry that pretty blonde." I smirked at the memory. "He was great to her when they dated, did everything he could to show her how much he cared about her. We were together a lot. She didn't want to come between him and me, so when they did something, I was invited too.

"It wasn't until after they were engaged that things changed. Maybe it was the long distance, but he lost that...." I paused, searching for the word. "Desperation for her, that fire, I guess. He never treated her bad, but he sure as hell didn't treat her well. She never came first, and I fucking hated it. Every time he brushed her off so he could hang out with his buddies instead of her, it added another layer to my anger. Baylee is fucking amazing and deserved to be treated like it."

"Still does," Liam muttered.

"The last straw was when we were hanging out one night, and she called him. I saw her face on the screen, since he was on the barstool next to me. She was in Texas. It was finals, I think, so she'd been studying her ass off and was super busy. I watched the fucker check his phone, roll his eyes at the screen as he silenced the call, and then put it into his pocket. I asked him who it was, even though I knew, fucking knew who he'd just ignored, and he just shrugged and kept drinking his beer. We were at a bar, some girl was sitting next to him who he was chatting up, and he went back to talking to her." I held up my hand to show Liam the scars on the inside of my palm. "I squeezed my beer bottle so tight, it shattered in my hand. That was when I lost it. I knocked him off his stool, sent him toppling to the ground.

Knowing I was seconds from killing my best friend, I stormed outside, leaving a bloody trail behind me."

"Hurts like hell getting all that glass out." Liam held up his large palm, displaying the streaks of scars. "Done it a few times myself."

I snorted and shook my head. "Dean followed me outside. That was when I let it all out." Grabbing a cigarette from the front pocket of the ugly-ass scratchy shirt, I lit the end, blowing out a billow of smoke before continuing. "I told him he didn't deserve her, that he needed to treat her like the gift she was. He didn't take that well. The first swing came from him, but the last was from me. Even though he had training in hand-to-hand shit, I had so much anger and resentment built up, it helped me kick his ass."

I'd never forget seeing him lying on the sidewalk glaring up at me with absolute hate in his eyes, the police sirens in the background growing closer. His words and sneer would forever be imprinted in my memory, the one I used drugs and alcohol to forget for years after that night.

"I lost my best friend for good that night. He told me if I had a problem with how he treated his fiancée, then I needed to fuck off. I said fine, that I couldn't stand by and watch it anymore, see him treat someone like her the way he did. Like she was a fucking burden." The cigarette between my fingers cracked from the pressure. Cursing, I extinguished the burning ember on the heel of my boot and pocketed the trash—I'd already learned my lesson to not toss it on the trail or I'd get a death glare from both Liam and Baylee.

"Did you ever tell her?" Liam asked. I shook my head. "Why not?"

"I had already put some distance between me and her, more for my sanity than anything. It was hard after they were engaged to be there, wanting her and knowing I'd never have her. Which was okay. I missed her like hell. She was my friend, but I didn't want to come between them."

"Except when you realized she deserved better than Dean."

"Exactly. I tried calling Dean a few weeks later, hoping we'd be able to talk through it, but every time he picked up, he told me to fuck off. He told everyone who would listen, especially his parents, that he ended the friendship because I wanted to take Baylee from him." I gritted my teeth, remembering how friends I'd had for years turned their backs on me and said all kinds of shit, assuming what Dean spewed was the truth. "So I found a new group of friends, and, well, you know about all that already."

For several minutes, only the sound of the horses' hooves stamping against the soggy earth filled the silence between us. I was so lost in the memories, debating if I'd done the right thing that night, that when he finally spoke up, I jerked in the saddle.

"You tried to protect her. She should know."

"But I also don't want to taint his memory. Despite how it all ended, he was still my best friend and her fiancé, who is dead. None of it matters now."

The sound of chainsaws cut through the air along with shouts, signaling we were close to our destination.

"For what it's worth," Liam said, turning to look over his shoulder. "I'm proud of you for trying to get that fucker to see what he had. You had my approval before, seeing how you are with her and knowing she wanted you, but after hearing that, you have my respect, kid."

My back straightened at his approving nod.

Though when he turned with a smirk, I knew I would hate whatever he said next.

"Such a good boy."

At my middle finger, he barked out a laugh and nudged his horse into a faster gait.

Funny thing was, I didn't hate it.

---

THE HARD FLOOR dug into my hip bone and shoulder. With a grunt, I rolled to my back and stared at the ceiling. To my right, Liam moved on the couch, clearly unable to get comfortable like me. He didn't find it as funny as I did when I told him someone his age should have the couch because my younger body could handle the stiff floor.

I was slightly shocked that he didn't kick my ass for the comment, actually. That spoke to how exhausted he was. We both were. Today was the first full day in Caper, and he worked nonstop from sunup to sundown to help clean up the debris and make the road passable. While he did that, I tended to the few who were injured during the landslide. One house was demolished, with two adults inside it when it hit. While none of their injuries were life-threatening, they could've been if I hadn't been there.

Thankfully, with some stitches, splints, and antibiotics, everyone would make a full recovery. I felt good about the intense work, proud even. Having the entire family thank me and Liam over and over for being there had me swallowing down unfamiliar emotions.

But fuck, did I miss Baylee.

Missed her smile, her laugh, her everything. Despite my exhausted mind, the memory of us together that evening in the clearing, with her pinned against the rock while I sank deep into her tight cunt, ran on repeat.

My cock twitched in my sweats, making me swallow a

groan as it hardened, unable to stop thinking about her. Reaching beneath the blanket, I slipped my hand past the elastic band of the soft cotton to wrap around it. An almost silent groan slipped past my clenched jaw as I tightened my grip, hoping to calm the fucker down. I was in a stranger's living room for fuck's sake, with Liam less than a foot away attempting to sleep on the couch.

Though just thinking about that did the exact opposite of what I intended. I mean, the thrill of getting caught was a kink of mine after all. Short pants rushed past my parted lips as I worked my hand up and down my dick, thumbing the head to spread a bead of precum along the piercing.

Recalling her sweet taste, the way her cunt squeezed the hell out of my cock, had my hips flexing off the floor, shoving me even harder into my firm grip. The rustle of blankets and groan of the couch's frame had me stilling, though my desire only ramped up tenfold at the deep voice that rumbled through the dark.

"Thinking about her, too, I take it."

A hiss whistled through my clenched teeth. "I don't know what you're talking about."

Liam's responding chuckle held no humor. "Right. Doesn't help that the owners of this place could walk down the stairs any second and catch you fucking your hand."

This time my guttural groan was loud, giving me the fuck away.

"I just started thinking about Bay, and then I couldn't stop. And yeah, the potential of getting caught is not helping."

Silence filled the space, and I worried I'd taken it too far, spoken my internal thoughts to the wrong person. I stared at the ceiling, unable to look toward the couch despite hearing him shifting along the well-worn cushions.

"Remember that first time when I forced you to eat her pussy, holding your face against her by your hair." I swallowed hard. Unable to resist, I adjusted my grip and started moving it up and down my shaft again. "Fucking hell, that first time, taking her virgin cunt, felt like heaven, and the second time and the third. Her face when she comes and the smell of her—" His deep groan cut off his words.

My breaths came in faster pants. "I want to be buried inside her every day for the rest of my life."

"Fuck yes," Liam grunted. "You're right, the chance of getting caught adds something to this."

I blinked in the dark. "Are you... too?"

"And close just thinking about coming inside her, staying there so all my cum stays locked inside her—fuck."

A creak of the stairs had us falling silent. Not even our earlier heavy breaths filled the living room. The stairway light turned on, and instead of stopping, all I could do was pump my hand faster. A familiar tingle of desire raced down my spine, settling in my balls.

When the light flicked off and the sound of footsteps above us faded, we both released the breaths we'd been holding.

"When we get home, let's see if she's open to me taking her sweet pussy while you fuck her hot little mouth."

That did it. The mental picture of Baylee between us, Liam fucking her from behind and pushing her so my cock slipped deeper down her throat, had me coming in my sweats like a fucking teenager. I jerked against the floor, the last of the orgasm almost painful as I slowed my hand.

Blood pounded in my ears from the intensity of the orgasm, my heart racing so fast I worried I'd be the one needing a medic. A grumbled curse had me shifting to look up at the couch to where Liam threw his legs over the side and stood.

"Haven't had to clean up like this since... hell, a long time ago. You want to go first?"

There was only one bathroom on this floor, and while it was hot as hell doing what we just did, there was no way I was cleaning up my cum in front of him. And just to make sure we were back to normal, that this didn't cause awkwardness, I gave him a smart-ass remark back.

"Nah, man, elders first and all that shit."

Liam's barked laughter had me smiling in the dark.

I had no idea what the hell just happened, but I sure as hell wouldn't mind it happening again.

## 25

---

BAYLEE

I tossed the vibrating phone into the desk drawer and slammed it shut wishing like hell that would stop it from ringing over and over. The second my voicemail picked up the unknown caller hung up and tried again. The insistent buzzing and flashing screen raked at my nerves making me constantly tense ever since I had returned.

The moment I got back in cell service range dozens of missed texts appeared and had continued to come through in addition to the calls. The messages ranged from vulgar name-calling to hoping I die and a few describing how the asshole hoped I died a horrible death. I deleted all those and reported the number as junk but I couldn't do the same with the calls since they were from a blocked number.

With the escalation of a few calls to all this I knew it was time to get someone involved. I just really, really didn't want to tell Liam, knowing he'd be pissed I hadn't told him before now and might go on a killing spree while attempting to find out who was behind the harassment.

That was a problem for later.

Pushing the unease and paranoia aside, I forced my

focus back on the task at hand. A quick click on the mouse had the next X-ray appearing on the computer screen. The office chair creaked when I leaned forward to get a better look at the film I'd already reviewed a dozen times since yesterday. Reaching down to where Hank lay beside me, Elvis by the door keeping watch, I scratched behind his soft ear.

A smile tilted my lips upward at the sound of his tail swishing along the floor. I gazed down at the slightly sedated animal, finding him looking at me with those ice-blue eyes so similar to my own. What were the odds that I could talk Liam and Memphis into keeping Hank so I wouldn't have to say goodbye?

All thoughts of kidnapping—whoops—*adopting* Hank faltered as Elvis pushed to stand on all fours with a deep growl that rumbled through my small office. The next second, the bell hanging over the front door rang. Leaving the X-ray up on the screen, I shoved off the armrests, weaved around the snarling Elvis, and strode to the front to see who waited in the lobby. A smirk formed at the click of Elvis's nails on the floor as he trailed behind me.

I released a relieved breath I didn't realize I was holding when I rounded the corner, finding Oliver and Ethan standing in the middle of the waiting room quietly chatting. Ethan's eyes flicked around the room as Oliver spoke. When his searching gaze caught me standing in the open doorway, a wide smile split his face.

"What are you two doing here?" I asked, shoving both hands into the pockets of my lab coat.

"We wanted to check on your patient," Oliver said, turning to face me. Today he wore his standard uniform, though his hat was clutched tight in the hand at his side. There was no doubt that he looked good in the uniform; it just didn't hit the same way for me as it did when I saw Liam in his Wranglers and flannel or Memphis in his trendy grunge look.

I looked at Ethan, who didn't notice, too focused on his phone. The man looked half-wild with his thick beard, long, messy hair tied up in a bun, and dirt streaked across his Army green hiking pants. But that was Ethan. He didn't care much about how he looked and would rather be outdoors than anywhere else. Hell, he spent most of his time off duty camping instead of sleeping in the two-bedroom cabin next to Liam's.

"He's in the back if you want to see him." Turning, I headed toward my office and fell into the chair. Oliver's wide frame filled the space, making it feel even smaller as he squatted to extend the back of his hand to Hank's twitching nose. "He's slightly sedated, and I have him on pain meds, so he's groggy."

"How bad were his injuries?" Ethan asked, leaning against the doorframe since there was literally no more room in my office.

"So, his right hind leg is sprained but not broken. I'm keeping it wrapped and him off it as much as possible to help it heal correctly. He also has two broken ribs—"

"What could've caused that?" Oliver asked, his voice laced with restrained anger as he ran a hand over Hank's head.

I swallowed hard. "I've seen both types of injuries before in animal abuse cases. The rib fractures probably came from him being kicked. The same with the leg."

Ethan cursed, making Hank growl at my feet. He held up both hands in surrender, closing his eyes and taking a deep breath to calm himself down.

I leaned back in the chair and studied both men. With a

confirming nod, I clicked a key to bring the screen to life. The X-ray I was studying earlier was still there. Grabbing a pencil, I used it as a pointer and gestured to the spot that was giving me so much trouble in trying to determine what the hell happened.

"Then there's this." I tapped the screen with the eraser end, drawing their focus to the X-ray. "I have no idea what could've caused this. The hairline fractures radiate from a central point, almost like it would from a bullet, but there was no entrance or exit wound."

Oliver stood and leaned in closer to the screen. I scooted the chair back as far as I could to give him and Ethan a better look.

"I need a bigger office," I muttered under my breath.

Ethan shot me a half smile before turning his full attention back to the screen. "Yeah, that's odd, though I haven't seen a lot of X-rays to say much about it."

I studied Oliver's profile. His brows were pulled in tight, lips pressed in a thin line.

"I also have some possible evidence for you, Oliver."

His eyes snapped to me. "What evidence?"

I grimaced, remembering how difficult it was to get said potential evidence. "Based on the dried blood around his muzzle and fur, I took a leap and assumed he attacked whoever hurt his owner. So I flossed his teeth."

Oliver stared at me like I was crazy. "You flossed a dog's teeth?"

I blew a raspberry. "I saw it on a crime show once where they did it with a human who had bitten their attacker. Anyway, I didn't get every tooth, but maybe there are bits of the attacker in what I found. I put it in the medicine fridge and planned to bring it to you later today. If anything, maybe we could get DNA or something. It's a long shot, I know—"

"It is, but I'll take any shot at this point. Good thinking, Baylee."

"When will we hear from the coroner?" I whispered, not wanting Hank to hear.

Oliver stood straight, bumping into Ethan slightly. He froze, the two exchanging an odd look before Ethan cleared his throat and backed up to his spot in the doorway. Oliver tracked his every move before shaking his head and turning back to me.

Interesting.

"He said he'll have the autopsy results in the next week or two. Not that I have much hope in his findings. The man should've retired a decade ago, but there isn't anyone there to take his place."

"Being a coroner in Anchorage probably isn't on the top of people's bucket lists," I said with a snort. I shifted to the side to get a full view of Ethan. "What about you? Did you find anything yesterday in your search for her campsite or gear?"

Pulling out the band tying his hair back, he ruffled the long dirty-blond strands and sighed.

"I didn't find shit, Baylee, which makes no damn sense. Even if the storm had destroyed her tent, there would be debris or her pack, or fuck, a pair of underwear in the trees." He looked down at Hank. "I was hoping he was in okay enough shape to go out on the trail with me. Maybe he could show me where they camped or lead me to something of hers."

I gazed down at Hank, who turned his eyes up to mine. "I can't allow that, Ethan." His shoulders rounded as he nodded. "I'm sorry. His injuries aren't terrible, but they could be with too much stress on the fractures, and he'd be in a lot of pain."

"We don't want that, do we?" Oliver cooed at Hank. At my laughter, he cut those almost black eyes my way. "Did I tell you I've always wanted a dog?"

My heart fluttered at his words. "Really?" He nodded. "Hank would be an excellent partner. He's already proven that, and he could withstand the cold temps here."

"Just tossing it out there." He checked his watch and cursed. "I need to meet my dad to update him on all this. I'm opening a formal investigation into her death."

Remembering the evidence, I swiveled the chair around to open the small fridge door and handed the baggie to Oliver. He nodded grimly, eyeing the contents.

With one more head pat to Hank, Oliver squeezed past Ethan, who didn't move an inch, just stared at Oliver with an arched brow.

"Later," Oliver grumbled.

Ethan leaned back as far as he could without toppling over, watching the deputy leave. When he straightened and turned back toward the office, I raised a questioning brow.

Huffing a humorless laugh, Ethan ran his fingers through the wild strands of hair, gathering it back into a bun. "It's a long story."

"Hank and I—" I stopped when Elvis trotted into the office and plopped down next to Hank. "—and Elvis have all the time. My next appointment is in an hour, and my guys are in Caper, so...." I gestured for him to spill the tea.

"You know how we sometimes go to Anchorage to...." He paused, biting his full lower lip. "Let off steam." He grimaced while looking anywhere but at me.

"You mean with women," I said, unable to stop my wide

smile. "We're adults here, Ethan. You don't have to be embarrassed to talk about sex."

"Yeah, well, it's just that he and I had never...." Ethan cleared his throat and shifted on his feet. A red tint stained his cheeks and the tips of his ears. *Holy hell, what happened to get the most even-tempered man so flustered?* "We always did our thing separate. He had his fun, I had mine, and then we would head back to Anchor Bay the next day."

I nodded, unsure of where he was going with the story. "Okay."

"Yeah, so we went to this bar, and there was this fucking smoke show. Alone. He and I started talking to her, and we both realized we were totally into her. There was just something about...." He sighed, a small smile forming. "Anyway, not sure how it all happened, but the three of us ended up together, and things got—" Ethan cleared his throat, that red tint now a deeper crimson. "—close."

"Close?" I leaned forward, pressing both elbows onto my knees.

"As in... fuck." He scrubbed a hand over his beard. "I've never been so damn close to another guy's junk before, Baylee. We're not all doctors here."

I barked a laugh, startling the two dogs and Ethan.

"First, I'm not a people doctor. The only balls I see at work are usually when I'm removing them." Ethan winced, and I swear the dogs did too. "Second, okay, I understand the awkwardness between the two of you now."

"That and...." He mumbled the rest under his breath.

"What was that?"

"There might have been some touching," he stated a little clearer this time.

"Oh. *Oh*," I exclaimed. "And you didn't want it?"

"And I didn't know I'd like it." His hazel eyes met mine,

searching as if to see if I'd judge him for the truthful admission. "The sharing piece, all of it. Fuck, what's wrong with me? After that night, now I actually want to be around people," he growled, clearly annoyed with the emotions and feelings that night evoked.

"People," I hedged, "or just one person?"

His eyes narrowed on me, and I held up both hands in surrender. Clearly he wasn't ready to dissect all those feelings just yet.

"Now we're both frustrated that we had the best fucking night, and now she's gone. Neither of us got her name or where she was from. The only thing we know is she was on the tail end of a cruise and flying out the following day. And she ghosted us, left before either of us woke up."

"And you want to find her?"

"Yes, fuck yes. I even signed up for fucking Facebook, thinking that would somehow help us magically find her. Who *am* I right now?" He tossed both hands up in the air in frustration. "I just need to get out in my element. If anyone needs me, they can reach me on the sat phone. I'm going to head out on the trail until I find something of hers."

I stood so abruptly, the chair slammed against the wall. Both dogs barked and jumped up on all fours.

"Ethan, that's not safe," I said, worry in my tone.

The frustration faded from his features, and a genuine grin tugged at his lips, making his beard twitch. "I'll be okay, Baylee. Promise. Don't worry about me."

"But I do, and I will until you're back. I can't help but worry about my friends."

"They're lucky men," Ethan said after a second. "I hope they know that. You're a gem, Baylee. A motherfucking gem."

With that, he turned and left, the front door's bell signaling his exit.

I slumped back into the chair with a groan. I really would worry about him. I couldn't help it with everything going on around Anchor Bay.

Leaning back, I stared at a blank spot on the wall, mulling over everything that had happened the last few days. From starting a physical relationship with Liam, Memphis arriving and him joining our new relationship, losing my virginity in the best way possible, to finding a dead body, it was a lot in a short amount of time. Even the run earlier couldn't settle the undercurrent of anxiety keeping me on alert.

Not sure how long I spaced out, but the need to check in had me pulling my phone out of the drawer. Grimacing, I cleared all the missed calls and clicked to the messaging app. A small smirk tugged at my lips at finding one waiting to be read from Liam.

> Sat Phone 5: Don't forget to eat lunch, Little Bit.

> Me: Don't worry, Daddy.

> Sat Phone 5: That… is interesting.

I bit my lip to stop the widening smile and shifted in the chair to ease the throb between my thighs just typing that had triggered. Fuck, what would happen if I actually said it out loud?

> Me: Interesting bad?

> Sat Phone 5: Not sure if working a chainsaw with a fucking hard-on is good or bad.

I barked out a laugh, making the dogs glance up at me like I was crazy.

Me: Ah. How is the cleanup going?

Sat Phone 5: Good. Should head out tomorrow.

Sat Phone 5: I need to see you.

Me: Miss you too.

Sat Phone 5: Go eat. I know you haven't.

Shaking my head, I set the phone down, unable to stop smiling. How in the hell did I get so damn lucky? Twice. Wait, three times?

My grin slowly slipped, and tears filled my lower lids.

It still felt a little like cheating, feeling this way about someone other than Dean, but even more than that, I felt guilty knowing I never felt this deeply for him—ever. Maybe it was because we were so young when we met and were just shallow in life. But how Liam and Memphis made me feel loved and wanted and needed, it was overwhelming.

How many times had I wished I had that with Dean when he would leave me to hang out with his friends after I said I wanted to go? The times I wished he would've shown care or concern when a wicked storm blew through College Station, and he didn't even check in to make sure I was safe. Sometimes he was deployed, but those weren't the times that stood out in my mind.

It was the nights I knew he was stateside, and he ended our call early, despite not even asking how I was or how my day went, so he could go out with his friends. Toward the end, it was all just so damn superficial.

And now I was in deep with Memphis and Liam.

Deep feelings.

Deep emotions.

Deep everything.

And I never ever wanted to lose it.

The bell over the door ringing had me shaking out those thoughts of the guys and pushing out of the chair. An alert Elvis and Hank stayed at my side as I walked toward the front. I frowned, not understanding why I needed the security escort, until I rounded the corner and stumbled to a stop.

"Can I help you?" I asked, voice strained with tension.

"Sorry to surprise you like this, but I knew this was my one chance to get you alone. We need to talk."

I swallowed hard, my heart racing with the growing panic. Both dogs inched forward, their dangerous growls filling the waiting room, clearly sensing my rising fear.

Damnit.

This was not good.

Not good at all.

## 26

LIAM

Pain radiated from every taut muscle as I stretched out my aching lower back. Between the all-day chainsaw work and making the ride from Caper to Anchor Bay in one day, it felt like I would never move again without groaning. The last scoop of enriched grain fell into the feed bucket as I smoothed thankful strokes along the mare's neck. With a final pat, I exited the stall, letting her eat in peace.

As I secured the lock, I caught Memphis out of the corner of my eye sitting on a bale of straw while staring off into space, his shoulders slumped, looking as exhausted as I felt. We pushed our bodies to the limit in an effort to return as quickly as possible, both of us hating being so far from Baylee after what we found on the way to Caper.

Well, we would feel that insistent pull no matter what, but the dead woman added to the overall stress of being away from our girl.

"You ready?" I asked, voice like gravel from the shit sleep the last three nights and stressing my forty-plus-year-old body to the max.

Memphis grunted a noncommittal response and stood, stretching both arms over his head. Our combined sluggish steps barely sounded over the animals eating as we headed to the open barn doors.

"That was fucking brutal," Memphis groaned as he twisted side to side, stretching out his back, "but worth the exhaustion. The whole extended family appreciated what we did, us being there to help them. It was a nice change of pace, being thanked."

I waved at Dax as he hurried past us, almost too distracted to notice. "Do you not get that often in your job back in Florida?"

He snorted and ran a hand through his dirty hair. "Fuck no. A handful of times maybe, but it's a high-stress, thankless job most days."

"Your compassion and skills deserve to be appreciated by those you're helping. Maybe somewhere that could use someone dedicated and knowledgeable of trauma care and would know they were lucky to have you."

He cut his green eyes my way with a slow nod. "Yeah, I've been thinking about that since Amy's not-so-subtle conversation after West's accident."

Good. I hoped it had made him really consider the ways he could affect not only our community but everyone in Anchor Bay.

At the base of the steps to Baylee's cabin, we limped up to the porch.

"I'm going to say hi to her, then head over to my place to shower so you can take hers." I turned the doorknob, but it just slid in my palm. "Good girl, Little Bit," I murmured as I knocked on the door. "She actually locked it."

"Just say hi, my ass," Memphis huffed. "Even though

we're both exhausted, we want to do more than just say hello to our girl. It's been a long, few days without her. I don't know how I survived only on memories the last few years we were apart. That shit wouldn't be enough now."

I shifted, angling my ear to the door, listening for footsteps. Hand in a light fist, I pounded on the door, the dogs inside barking as the hinges rattled.

"That's Elvis," Memphis stated, staring at the solid wood. "And I'm guessing Hank."

"Right, so where is she?"

Reaching into my pocket, I pulled my keys free. Finding hers, I slid it into the hole and twisted the metal, releasing the lock. The angry growls turned to joyful barks when I shoved open the door and we stepped inside. Hank's tail was swishing side to side along the hardwood floor while Elvis straightened from his attack position to bound over to Memphis, who hugged him like a long-lost friend.

"Baylee?" I called out as I checked the kitchen, patting Hank's head as I passed. Each second that went by with no response had my pulse inching higher and higher. I eyed BamBam on the island, nose twitching as he did the same to me. "Where is she?" I asked, not expecting a response but fucking wishing for one.

Striding to her room, I grunted in frustration at the made bed and no Baylee. Same with the bathroom. Out in the living room, I yanked out my cell and tapped her number, pressing the smooth surface to my ear.

"Where is she?" Memphis asked, hand nervously stroking the top of Elvis's head.

"I knew we shouldn't have left her alone. Fuck," I cursed when her sweet voice poured through the phone, telling me to leave a message. "She's not picking up."

"We should call that sheriff guy. He was the last one to see her, right? Or that mountain man guy."

If I hadn't been freaking the fuck out, I would've chuckled at his description of Ethan. Nodding in agreement with his suggestion, I flicked through my contacts, tapping Oliver's number.

"Liam, I was—"

"Baylee is missing," I snapped, my boots thumping against the floor as I paced the living room. Hank watched me from his spot on the floor, whining at my distress. "We need to get everyone to start—"

"She's not missing," Oliver said calmly. "She's with me."

My grip tightened on the phone and I came to a complete stop, every muscle frozen yet coiled, ready to strike.

"What?" I growled so low both dogs responded with their own. Despite knowing neither of them would hurt me like that, my trauma-triggered thoughts went to them being together behind my back. Confusion and hurt swirled in my gut, making the few pieces of jerky I ate churn as bile crept up my throat.

"There was...." Oliver paused; a heavy breath sounded through the line. "An incident involving Baylee yesterday—"

A red haze coated my vision, clearing away the earlier hurt and leaving anger and fear in its wake. Knowing it was the dumbest fucking move ever, I hurled the phone at the stone fireplace with a fury-filled roar. The device instantly smashed into a thousand pieces, bits of metal flying around the room from the force of the impact.

Every breath hurt as my chest heaved while I glared at the ruined cell in utter disbelief.

"That was fucking dumb," Memphis snapped. "What

did he say? Where the fuck is she?" He was suddenly in my face, shoving my chest with more strength than I expected. My spine slammed to the wall, too shocked to put up a fight. "Where is she?" he roared.

I stared blankly at his face while running through the normal conversation she and I had the night before. What could've happened that she didn't feel like she could tell me when we spoke?

The sound of voices and hurried footsteps on the porch had both our heads snapping that direction just as the door swung open, crashing against the opposite wall.

Baylee stumbled into the cabin, her clear blue eyes wide as they bounced around the room, finally landing on me. Palms to Memphis's shoulders, I shoved him out of my way. The momentum had his thighs clipping the back of the couch, sending him tumbling over it with a string of shouted curses. The cabin shook with every urgent step across the room until she was wrapped up tight in my arms.

"Hey, I'm here. I'm okay," she whispered, sliding two fingertips along my back in calming strokes. The boiling anger had each breath quick and shallow, sending strands of her soft blonde hair floating in the air. "I'm okay." Unable to respond, I buried my face tighter against her neck. "Liam, look at me." Her small hand pressed against my cheek and urged me to pull back. "I'm okay. I didn't realize you'd be back so soon or I would've been here to—"

I devoured her surprised squeak as I sealed my lips to hers in a searing, dominant kiss. I kissed her like it was our first and last, like she was the air I needed to fucking survive another second. Which I guess she was. Not literally, obviously, but in every way that mattered to my heart and soul.

Somewhere behind me, Memphis and Oliver spoke in

hushed voices, but I didn't pay the conversation any attention, not with Baylee safe in my arms. Except when Memphis shouted something and attempted to storm out the door, only to be yanked back by Oliver. I pulled my lips from Baylee's, narrowing my eyes at them to get a read on what the fuck was going on. Memphis's chest heaved, eyes wide and wild as he tried to leave once again.

"For fuck's sake," Oliver bellowed, grabbing him by the shoulders and whirling him around in an impressive move. "Will you two manic idiots please calm the fuck down?" He slammed the door closed and slumped against it, ripping off his hat to rub at both temples. "Baylee, I need some help right now before they kill me."

Tapping my shoulder, Baylee tipped her head toward the ground. It was only then that I realized she was in the air, squeezed tight to my chest. Grunting in reluctant acceptance, I eased my hold until her tennis shoes touched the hardwood floor.

She held up both hands in a calming gesture, gaze locked on mine as she slowly backed away toward the other angry male in the room. At Memphis's side, both arms went around his waist, and she buried her face against his chest. His palpable bubbling rage turned to a simmer the instant he wrapped her up and rested his chin on the top of her head.

"Start. Talking," I gritted out, jutting an accusing finger at Oliver, but it was Baylee who responded.

"I searched out Oliver today because I thought he should know about an uncomfortable incident that happened yesterday in the clinic after he left." My face must have shown the suspicion that churned in my chest, because she rushed out the next part. "When he came by with Ethan to check on Hank. Which, FYI, good news. He's debating adopting him once he's back to full health."

I eyed my friend—who I really did trust, but being cheated on once made you suspicious as fuck in every situation no matter the person—and dipped my chin, letting him know he was no longer on my kill list.

For now.

"While we were there, I updated Baylee on the female victim, and Ethan told us what he found on the trail." My lips parted to tell him to get the fuck on with it, but he held up a hand. "Which was nothing. Not a single damn thing. He's back out there now, searching." Oliver's brows dipped in what appeared to be worry or something similar.

"What. Happened," I snarled, inching closer to Memphis and Baylee, hating the distance between her and me while I was this worked up.

"Taylor stopped by," Baylee said, keeping a close eye on both me and Memphis.

That was all Memphis heard before he carefully detached himself from Baylee and once again attempted to storm out of the cabin, but he couldn't get past the deputy sheriff. Oliver sighed and looked to the ceiling, mouthing something to himself.

"What did he do, Kitten?" Memphis whispered softly, an edge of restrained anger lacing his tone. "We will kill him if he touched you."

"Nothing," she breathed, eyes wide. "He didn't do anything. He couldn't even get within a few feet of me." She gestured to the two dogs. "I had them with me."

"Good girl," I praised. Grabbing her hand, I guided her back into my arms and ran a knuckle along her cheek.

"Holy hell, this is too much right now," Oliver snapped,

sounding utterly exasperated. "I'll let Baylee fill you in on the details so I can get out of here before you guys"—he gestured between the three of us—"do whatever it is you're going to do."

A smirk appeared on Baylee's face. "Oh, don't act like you don't know what's going to happen." She shifted in my hold to face the deputy sheriff, whose face was now beet red. Then she turned those icy blue eyes to me, and all humor faded. "Not anything to do with me, big guy. I'm referencing a fun night he and two others had."

"Fucking Ethan," Oliver grumbled, cheeks turning even redder. Grabbing the doorknob, he yanked the solid wood open. "Thanks for filling me in, Baylee. I'll update Hudson and monitor Taylor."

"Wait," Baylee said before Oliver could bolt. "There is something else I wanted to bring up that I need you to look into." She worried at her lip, gaze flicking around the cabin. "I've been getting these calls, unknown calls. It wasn't that big of a deal at first but now—"

"Now what?" I practically growled.

"The calls are constant and when I pick up no one says anything just this creepy heavy breathing thing and—"

"Little Bit," I said voice strained. "How long? How long has this been going on?"

"The calls a month or so, maybe longer. It was just every few days at first but now they are texting me some really disturbing stuff too." Tears filled her lower lids. "I'm sorry I didn't tell you, any of you, I just thought it would go away."

"Where is your phone?" Oliver asked. Baylee pointed to the coffee table. He marched over and swiped it off the polished wood, shoving it into his pocket. "I'll look into the calls and texts. If I can't find out who is harassing you, then I'll pull Carl in to help. Until then you'll need to get a new phone, a new number too."

"And when you find out who has been harassing our girl," Memphis said, inked hands curled into tight fists at his side. "You let us handle them."

"Fucking hell no. I do not need more dead bodies around here. I'll take care of it." Clearly having had enough of our drama, he stormed out onto the porch, slamming the door behind him.

With Oliver gone, some of my tension faded, and it seemed to for Memphis too. With a sigh, he tugged Baylee into his arms, picked her petite frame up, and carried her over to the massive couch, pulling her onto his lap with him.

"Tell us everything, Kitten. From that fucker approaching you to the calls and texts."

Baylee studied me as I lowered to the couch beside them, sitting so close that my side pressed against Memphis's. She noted the lack of distance between us curiously.

"Taylor came to my office, saying he just wanted to talk—"

"Did he know you were alone?" I asked. Her lips sealed shut, telling me everything I needed to know. "Did he mention purposefully waiting for you to be alone, without us around, to have this conversation?"

"Yes," she squeaked.

"Because..." I prompted, though I already had an idea after Memphis suggested Taylor wanted Baylee for himself before we left for Caper.

"He said he wanted a chance with me, now that I was done grieving." Her eyes narrowed as she pressed her lips into a thin line, clearly pissed about something else he said.

"What else?" Those narrowed eyes looked everywhere but at me. I clicked my tongue in disapproval. "Nope." Gripping her chin in a firm hold, I tilted her face up to mine. "Tell us what else he said."

The muscle along her jaw flexed as it worked back and forth. "He said that I...." With a hard tug, she tried to break free but couldn't. "Listen, it doesn't matter."

"What did he say, Bay?" Memphis urged, his tone all business.

"That I deserved better than to be shared." Her throat shifted with a hard swallow. "To be with someone at my level." Those icy blue eyes rolled to the ceiling. "Like fucking degrees or education can determine one's character quality or what they deserve out of life. Asswipe."

"His intent was to take you from us," I stated evenly, barely able to keep my anger out of my voice, not wanting her to think it was aimed at her.

Her blonde hair slid over her shoulders with her slow headshake. "No, Liam. He wanted to take you two from me. Fuck him, and fuck his elitist attitude. I know where I belong," she whispered. "I know what makes me happy."

"Just happy?" Memphis asked, his hold tightening around her waist.

"Cared for, seen, wanted." She locked her eyes with mine. "Loved."

A deep rumble sounded in my chest at that last part. Leaning forward, I pressed a hard kiss to her forehead and then stood.

"Come on, Memphis," I growled while helping Baylee off his lap so he could stand. "We have that errand to run we talked about." I gave him a hard stare, hoping to convey that our errand wasn't anything Baylee needed to know about.

He responded with a clipped nod and pushed off the couch, storming to the front door, waiting for me there with a white-knuckled grip around the knob.

"Why didn't you tell me last night, Little Bit?" I asked, gazing down at where she sat on the couch. "About Taylor or hell, these fucking calls you've been getting."

Her lips curled in wry smile. "Really? Look at how you acted being here when I told you. If I would've mentioned it last night, then both of you would've risked your lives traveling back here as quickly as you could. You had a job to do there, and I was safe. I only told Oliver today because... it felt off."

"What did?" Memphis's voice trembled.

"His entire attitude about our community, about women in general. I don't know, it was just strange. I don't think he has anything to do with what's going on along the Soul Trail, but I wanted Oliver to know so he'd have that on his radar, I guess." She chewed on her lip, staring at the ground. "And there's the bandage on his arm. You saw it the other day." She looked at Memphis, who nodded. "What if it's a dog bite? Hank's bite?"

I stilled. "Did you ask him about it?"

"Um, no. I didn't get a chance. Halfway through his little speech about all that shit, he apparently forgot about my two animal besties and took a step toward me." She slid off the couch to kneel in front of Elvis and buried her face in his neck. "Elvis and Hank took that as an act of war and freaked out. Elvis lunged at Taylor while Hank snarled and snapped like he'd gone mad but stayed right at my side."

I gazed down with appreciation at the lab and then the husky. "Good job, boys." Both of their tails went wild, like they knew my praise was for them. "I'll pick up steaks on the way home for you both."

"He ran out of there like... well, two dogs might bite his balls off if he stayed in my clinic another second." She grinned into Elvis's fur before turning that smile up to me.

"Dogs are the best." Movement in the kitchen and a little squeak made her smile grow. "And ermines," she said louder, as if the rodent knew what she was saying. "You would've clawed his face off, BamBam."

Another squeak, this one more high-pitched, had me eyeing the ermine standing up on his hind legs on the kitchen island.

"I swear you speak fluent animal," I muttered under my breath while rubbing a hand down my face.

"What errand do you two need to run?"

Memphis and I exchanged a knowing glance before he yanked open the door and left me to answer Baylee alone. Asshole.

"Nothing to worry about, Little Bit. Plus, now I need to make a stop for these two fellas' reward." At the front door, I paused. "You'll be here, right here, when I get back."

"I might even make dinner." At my grimace, she barked out a laugh and waved me off. "I think even I can manage spaghetti."

"Remember last time when—" She threw her hands in the air in exasperation. "Right. Well, I don't expect us to be gone long, so wait for Memphis to cook when we get back. He seems to love cooking. You wouldn't want to deny him that, right?"

Hands on her hips, she cocked one out to the side. "You're playing dirty, Liam."

My responding chuckle was deep and throaty. "No, baby. That's later. Be back soon."

Locking the door behind me, I leapt down the steps, my boots slamming to the ground in front of where Memphis paced.

"You know where he lives?" he asked, lip curled in a snarl.

"Yep. First we handle this meddling asshole, then figure out what to do about the harassing calls and texts." I was frustrated and a little hurt that Baylee hadn't told me, but I couldn't focus on that now. "Let's go teach that fucker that no one messes with our girl."

And thank fuck Memphis was with me. Hopefully that meant Taylor would survive the hard lesson I planned to teach him the only way I knew how.

## 27

## MEMPHIS

I had never felt such an intense anger running through my veins, heating me to the point of sweating despite the cool breeze. How fucking dare that asshole try to take my Kitten away from me.

From us.

The way the air almost vibrated in the truck's cab spoke to a similar level of fury thrumming through Liam as we weaved through town, headed toward... hell, I didn't know exactly where. At some point, Liam digressed to only grunts and snarls, which was fine. I wasn't in a chatty mood either.

Sucking in a gulped breath, I jerked my hand up to grip the oh-shit bar when he took a tight turn too fucking fast. The tires squealed on the blacktop while my heart hammered in my chest from the building terror that the classic truck would flip with us in it, and our revenge mission would never happen.

"It's not that he wanted to talk to her," Liam said through gritted teeth as he peeled his white-knuckled grip off the steering wheel to readjust his too-tight hold. "It's that he waited for us to be the fuck out of town and cornered her in her own business. Fucking coward piece of shit."

I nodded, but a sliver of unease filtered through the anger fog. The only doctor in Anchor Bay was about to need one.

Liam turned down a side road, where a few cabins sat far off the track, several acres between them. Everything in the truck jerked and bounced down the pothole-infested gravel road, making us both fight to keep our heads from smashing against the windows.

"Ah, fuck, I should've known," Liam said, slamming a fist to the dashboard as he slowed the truck to a crawl.

"How the hell did he know we'd come here?" I muttered, gripping the door handle to jump out the second we came to a complete stop.

Blocking access to a long drive that I assumed led to the doctor's house, sat Oliver's official Jeep Grand Cherokee, with the man himself leaning against the side, arms crossed and glaring at the truck in disapproval.

"Because he knows me too well," Liam grumbled while cutting the engine.

I was out the door before Liam could say another word, storming up to Oliver, who didn't appear as concerned as he should have been. Though I had been around him a few times, so the man knew I wasn't a big threat. With the tattoos and piercings, most people put me in the scary or troublemaker box, judging me before they ever knew me. Which I guess, before I got clean, maybe I was.

But not really. I was always dead set on hurting myself through my addictions, not anyone else. That didn't make me a good man, but it sure as hell didn't make me a bad one.

"What the hell, Oliver?" Liam shouted from somewhere behind me.

Oliver just sighed and shook his head like we'd drained the last of his patience. "I knew exactly where you'd come after she told you what happened. I can't let you kill him, even if we are friends. I'm saving you from yourself, Liam."

"He cornered her," I said, crossing both tatted arms over my chest. The material of my long-sleeve shirt scratched against my skin. The sweat and dirt from the long ride back made it stiffer and more uncomfortable than it already was.

"But did nothing," Oliver said, eyeing me and then Liam, who now stood beside me, mirroring my stance. "I know it was a shitty thing to do, but he doesn't deserve to die for it. Plus, Baylee doesn't deserve to see her new boyfriends behind bars for the next twenty-plus years for doing something stupid. Hell, probably more than that since he's technically a lethal weapon with his MMA training."

I raised both brows and turned to Liam, whistling low. "Damn, man. Why the hell do you carry that pistol, then?"

His smile held no warmth. "Faster and less bloody. But tonight, I'm itching for a messy one."

"You're very scary," I deadpanned. "I'm glad we're on the same team."

"A bloody fight doesn't sound good for the only doctor the citizens in Anchor Bay have. Think this through, Liam." Oliver stood and cracked his knuckles one by one. "I really don't want to detain you."

We stood in a standoff, the two of us glaring at the deputy sheriff while he acted like this was a daily occurrence. Hell, maybe it was. I hadn't been a part of the community for more than a few days, or in Anchor Bay for that matter. Maybe Liam threatened people's lives all the time, which was how Oliver knew to come out here.

Based on what I'd gathered so far about Liam, that last one was probably the most accurate.

"If you won't let us handle it our way, then what will you do with him?" I asked, doing my best to keep a level head.

Oliver cautiously eyed us both. "Legally, there isn't anything I can do. There aren't any laws against telling a woman how you feel, even if he went about it in the shadiest way possible. Baylee only came to me so I would monitor him. I don't think he has anything to do with the missing women along the trail, but I'll check him out just to be sure."

"You need to ask him about the injury to his arm," I said, tapping my forearm for reference. "It was bandaged the other day, and we think Hank bit the person who killed the owner."

Oliver dipped his chin in agreement. "Baylee suggested that too. I promise I'm on it, guys. Listen, you're both exhausted from all you did in Caper. Go back home, for fuck's sake, and take showers. I can smell you from here. Then spend some time with Baylee. I'll handle this the *legal* way," he emphasized, "and I'll update you if I find out anything."

The muscle along Liam's jaw twitched as if he was grinding his teeth. With a clipped nod, he spun on his heels and stormed back to the truck. I watched him for a second before turning back to Oliver.

"He needs a warning that will stick," I stated. "He has to know what he did is not allowed, to Baylee or any other woman. She felt uncomfortable, and that cannot slide. If you don't make that clear, then I'll make damn sure he understands."

Oliver's brows rose, lips parted in what I assumed was shock. "Should've known that the newest addition to our town and the Uplift community would be just as violent and considerate of women as the rest of them."

I cocked my head to the side. "Them? Do you not live there?"

"Nope, just outside town, but I can see why you'd think that. I've been there a lot lately working with Hudson on the missing women's cases." He rubbed his scruff-covered jaw. "I'll admit, it's nice there. The community feels like one extensive family that supports one another."

The dip in his tone spoke to longing or sadness, making me wonder about the deputy sheriff's life, and if the lure of the community would someday entangle him in its web like it had me.

With a curt wave, I headed back to the truck, a grumbling Liam already behind the wheel and ready to go the moment I slid into the seat. The ride back was less tense than going, mostly because I couldn't help but find a pouting Liam hilarious. He caught my smirk a few times and snapped at me, but it only made me laugh more.

"I'm sorry you didn't get your bloodbath, Gramps."

The back of his hand connected with the center of my chest so hard that I swore he broke through my sternum and bruised my heart. I coughed to catch my breath, the force knocking the air out of me.

"How's that for Gramps, fucker," he said with a sharp smile. "But yeah, damnit, I needed that fight to get this buildup out of me. I'm scared of what I'll do to Baylee if I see her like this." At my shocked expression, he cursed. "Not like that, you asshole. Hell, I'd never lay a hand on her like that. I mean I might—"

"Fuck her until she screamed so loud and long from you taking her over and over that she doesn't have a voice left?"

Liam grimaced. "Shit, that sounds bad."

"I bet she wouldn't think so. Fair warning, though: Don't hold back. I tried that and got a verbal lashing from that woman. She told me not to make decisions for her, and I listened. Tell her you need it hard and fast, to fuck her until the pictures fall off the wall, and see what she says."

Liam grumbled something under his breath and shifted on the seat, adjusting his jeans with the hand not on the wheel.

"Maybe she'll even let us use some of those toys tonight," I mused while swiping a hand across my mouth to hide my smile. "I have some ideas. Though with your age, should we be worried about getting your heart rate up too high—"

"I will murder you in your sleep if you say one more word. I can outrun, outfight, outwork—hell, I bet I can last longer with her than you can, kid. Don't push me. I'm not in the mood."

I couldn't help it. It was just right there on the tip of my tongue.

"I think Gramps needs a nap. So grouchy."

The truck slammed to a stop, the seat belt snapping taut against my chest. For the second time in the short ride, the air was forced from my lungs.

Knowing my life was about to be cut short, I clicked the seat belt free with one hand while gripping the door handle with the other. His fingertips skimmed over the back of my shirt just as I lunged from the truck out onto the wooden sidewalk of downtown Anchor Bay, laughing so hard my cheeks hurt.

The driver's door swung open, and a furious Liam stepped out. With the truck between us keeping me safe for now, I waited, breathing harder than necessary from the adrenaline pumping through my veins. Liam folded his arms over the hood of the truck, and I mimicked his stance, returning his glare with a smile.

People hurried by, clearly sensing something was about to go down, though I had no idea what.

"You won't hurt me," I forced out, hoping like hell he liked me as much as I thought he did. "You like me too much."

"Debatable," he said with zero emotion, his gray eyes never leaving my face.

"Listen, fine, you're not a Gramps. Can we please get back in the truck and go see Baylee?" I lifted my shirt and sniffed. "And shower."

His gaze snapped to something over my shoulder. Afraid it was a trick to get me to let my guard down, I kept one eye on him while twisting to look down the walkway for what snatched his attention. The man from the hardware store, the one Liam said he hog-tied, stood just outside the coffee shop's glass door, glaring at Liam.

"It's that guy again," I said, turning to lean my ass against the hood of the truck, not liking keeping my back to the guy who looked ready to stab us both.

"Jasper Cain."

"The one who broke into your friend's—"

"I didn't fucking break in," Jasper yelled, clearly having heard me. "Caroline was my girlfriend. I could be in her cabin, asshole."

I furrowed my brow. "If she's missing, and no one knows what happened to her, then why is he using past tense? Why didn't he say 'Caroline *is* my girlfriend'? It's like he knows she's not anymore."

Liam's features grew stormier as I spoke. "Good fucking point."

"I know she was looking into the cases and documenting what she found," Jasper stated loud enough that people across the street slowed to listen to the tea being spilled for all to hear. "We need to find her journal." He glanced up and down the street as if afraid the wrong person would hear what he said next. Coming closer, he stopped a few feet away, no doubt thinking Liam would attack his scrawny ass otherwise. "I told the sheriff this, too, but do you know why she was so obsessed with the missing women's cases?"

"Because she was always out on the trail leading rock-climbing excursions," Liam said, like the guy was an idiot.

"She thinks they are linked to what happened to her mom."

I shot a confused look at Liam, who didn't notice, too busy glaring at Jasper.

"Nothing unusual happened to her mom. She passed just a few years ago—"

"That was her stepmom, you idiot."

"Careful," I murmured to Jasper, noticing Liam shift, his muscles bunched ready to strike.

"Her birth mom went missing from Anchor Bay when Caroline was younger." Jasper swallowed nervously and looked over his shoulder again as if paranoid someone would jump him.

"Are you serious?" I couldn't stop the words from leaving my mouth, too shocked to even try.

Jasper nodded and stepped closer to the truck. "The reports said she left on her own. Apparently, her mom and dad were having issues. But Caroline told me she never believed it, that she knew her mom wouldn't have left her."

Only the roar of passing cars and the slap of waves against the nearby docks filled the tense silence that settled between the three of us.

"You told the sheriff all this when he interviewed you?" Liam asked, his stance now more contemplative than attack-first mode.

"He said he'd fill in that LA detective Brandon brought in to help."

Confused as hell, I turned my focus to Liam, finding his gray eyes already locked on me. A lot was said silently between us, mostly *"What the fuck is going on?"* Grabbing a cigarette from the pack in my pocket, I lit the end, the building tension and information overload too much to handle without one.

As I inhaled, an itching sensation at the back of my neck had me spinning around, scanning the area for whoever caused the feeling. A few people gawked from outside Dave's, clearly having come out to witness the drama unfolding, similar to other gawkers who lined the street.

"What's wrong?" Liam questioned.

I took another hit, keeping my full attention on our surroundings. "It feels like we're being watched." Running the edge of my thumb along my lower lip, I remembered that day when even Elvis was out of sorts while we stalked Baylee. "And I don't think it's the first time I've sensed it, or Elvis when he was with me in town once."

Before I could explain, the door to Sips swung open and an angry bear of a man stepped out, hands on his wide hips in obvious annoyance.

"What the hell are you doing?" the man snapped, his anger aimed directly at Jasper. "Get back to work. I didn't give you a second chance here for you to hang out with your friends."

We all snorted in unison at that classification.

Jasper pinned Liam with a hard stare, as if trying to silently communicate something he didn't feel comfortable saying out loud now that his boss was standing close. "Just think about what I said. She thought it was connected, and I'm starting to wonder if she was right." With that foreshadowing bomb, he turned and headed back toward the coffee shop, shimmying past the angry man and entering the café.

"What's up your ass today, Paul?" Liam grumbled loud enough for the man to hear. "We were just talking."

"Then do it when he's not working." With that, he turned and stormed back into the store.

I released a loud exhale, flicking the ash off the end of the almost spent cigarette. "Damn, did you win Mr. Congeniality in the Anchor Bay pageant? Because you clearly have a lot of friends around here."

"Oh, shut the fuck up and get in the truck." He hitched his chin at the cigarette between my lips. "Without that shit."

"Glad to see this little chat put you in a better mood," I muttered under my breath after he'd slammed the driver's door. Stamping out the cherry on the asphalt, I tucked the trash into my pocket and reached for the door, paranoid gaze sliding along the brightly colored buildings.

A shiver that had nothing to do with the sudden burst of chilly wind coming off the water ran down my spine. What the actual hell was going on here?

And just how close were we all to the hidden danger?

## 28

BAYLEE

Carefully balancing the Kindle on my thigh, I tapped the screen to turn the page while continuing to thread my fingers through Memphis's soft strands. I smiled down, loving the view of his head resting on my lap, lips parted in sleep. When they returned from the suspicious errand, Memphis had stormed into the cabin, kissed me senseless, then headed to take a shower while Liam went to his place to do the same.

I swiped a clump of soft blond hair off his forehead and studied his handsome face.

How did I get so lucky?

Memories of Memphis had surfaced a few times over the years that would remind me of the friend I used to have and missed like hell, but I never took that step to track him down. Thankfully, he was braver than me, or we wouldn't be here now with me quickly falling back in love with him.

While they were gone and I had time to process the last week, I recognized that love was what I felt for Memphis then. It was platonic—though I guess not fully, or I wouldn't have enjoyed him watching me and Dean or fantasized about him joining us. What made me love Memphis then and now was how he treated me with respect, made me his priority no matter the situation, and I always felt safe with him both physically and emotionally. I could tell him things, and he would listen, then ask for more, or just hold me when that was all I needed.

Panic of the unknown, of losing everything all over again, tried to weave through the quiet moment. Even if this wasn't long-term, or ended badly, I would forever be grateful for the time I had with Memphis.

Same with how I've recently viewed my time with Dean. The grief surrounding his death and our lost future was still there, but it no longer had the debilitating choke hold on me that it once did. Instead, every day I found myself more and more grateful for the years I had with him instead of being sad about the ones I wouldn't.

My gaze slid to the front door, brows pulling in tight as I impatiently waited for it to open. Where the heck was Liam? Over two hours had passed since he left to shower, and he hadn't returned or at least called.

A noisy growl that erupted from my empty stomach had me stilling, hoping the sound wouldn't wake the exhausted man using my thighs as a pillow. After the shower, Memphis had stumbled out into the living room where I sat catching up on the book club read for the month, dropped to the couch beside me, and exhaustedly murmured that he needed to rest his eyes. He was sound asleep within minutes.

"Your stomach is loud," Memphis rasped, voice thick with sleep. He shifted on the couch, rolling to his back to blink up at me. "What time is it, Kitten?"

I checked the time on the tablet. "Almost eight thirty." A buzz came from the kitchen, and I inclined my head toward his phone. "Your phone has been going off nonstop for the last thirty minutes or so."

A guttural groan rumbled in his chest as he pushed off the cushion to sit up.

He rubbed tatted fingers against his closed lids. "That many texts in quick succession is probably my mom." I bit my lip to conceal my knowing grin. "Yes, I'm still a mama's boy. Some things will never change." My stomach released another loud growl, making his eyes narrow. I pressed a hand to my belly button, hoping to quiet the sound. "Shit, I need to feed you."

"I'm not a zoo animal," I grumbled, turning my attention back to the book. "And it's not just me. You need to eat too."

Memphis snorted like it was ridiculous that he would consider his needs before mine. Warm breath brushed along my throat as he pressed a gentle kiss just below my ear. "I could always eat you now to fill me up, Kitten. I've missed your taste on my tongue."

Heat flamed on my cheeks, no doubt flushed red, and my breath hitched with the surge of desire his words evoked. "I wouldn't be opposed to that."

Passion flared in his green eyes. "Did you miss us, Kitten?" Biting my lower lip, I nodded. "Missed us taking care of you in all the ways? Tell me, did you touch yourself while we were gone?"

"No," I breathed, pulse racing. The Kindle slipped in my grip, and I tucked it between me and the couch to keep it from falling to the floor.

"Good girl, but I'll admit that we did. Just thinking about you had us gripping our cocks at night, stroking ourselves as we reminisced on the feel of your cunt and the taste of you on our lips, while the potential of being caught with our dicks literally in our hands added to the thrill."

My eyes were so wide I probably looked like a cartoon character. "Did you touch each other?" Was the idea hot? Fuck yes. But even if they didn't, the thought of them touching themselves in the same room while talking about me had a fresh rush of desire leaking from my core and soaking my already damp underwear.

Memphis's smirk slowly spread into a mischievous grin. "We didn't, but by your reaction, it seems you wouldn't be opposed to it."

Gripping my chin, he held me in place, kissing my lips hard and pushing his tongue inside to devour my mouth like I knew he could between my thighs. I moved along the couch to ease the demanding throb in my core.

"How soaked are you right now, Kitten?"

Drenched. I was almost worried there would be a wet spot on the couch when I stood up.

Before I could respond, my stomach growled again, reminding us both that it was way past dinnertime. With one more quick kiss to the corner of my lips, Memphis stood, adjusting his tented sweats with one hand while helping me off the couch with the other. He tugged hard, making me stumble against him.

Gripping a handful of one ass cheek, he squeezed it tight. "First I feed you, then we play."

"Play?" I asked, trailing behind him to the kitchen.

"Oh yes, Kitten. Play. I plan to kiss and touch every inch of your tiny body tonight, inside and out. And I have some ideas for those toys of yours."

My knees literally went weak at the tsunami of need that flooded my entire body, every cell pulsing with insatiable desire. Thankfully, I was by the island, and I kept myself from falling to the floor by gripping the edge with both hands.

Briefly checking his phone, a soft smile forming at whatever the text said, Memphis stepped in front of the fridge. Bottles rattled in the shelves as the door swung open. A string of grumblings echoed through the small area while he inspected the nearly empty appliance. His lips were turned down when he glanced over his shoulder.

"What are the odds that Liam has food that isn't expired or growing mold?"

I folded both arms over my chest with a fake annoyed huff. "Come on. It's not that bad."

"I knew we should've gotten stuff for dinner when he grabbed the steaks for the dogs. I didn't realize it was this dire," Memphis mumbled. "Okay, let's go see what Liam has."

"Wait, let me leave food for BamBam in case he pops by later." Inside the sparse pantry, I took out the bag of organic beef jerky I bought for BamBam, the rustle of the plastic bag instantly calling the dogs to my side. "You two have already eaten your share." Both whined at my feet, their tails swishing on the floor where they sat impatiently. I chuckled. "You're right, you deserve this." After giving each a piece, which they swallowed whole, I put two pieces in BamBam's bowl and placed it in the center of the island out of the dogs' reach. "Okay, now we can go."

Taking Memphis's offered hand, we started toward Liam's place, leaving the dogs behind. A sharp gust of wind whipped through the row of cottages, rustling the few trees along the road. At my first shiver, Memphis tugged me against him, releasing my hand to drape an arm around my shoulders, keeping me sealed to his warm side.

"I can't imagine how cold it gets in the winter," he mused. "I'll have to update my wardrobe if I want to survive."

I blinked up at him, tucking a few floating hairs behind my ear. "You mean that?"

"Mean what?"

"That you'll be here through the winter?"

He paused in the middle of the road, the fading sun offering just enough light for me to see the confusion on his face.

"That's what I planned, but if you don't want me to, then—"

Instead of answering with words, I hooked both arms around his neck and jumped, securing my legs around his waist. Burying my face against his neck, I pressed a soft kiss to his warm skin.

"Yes, that's what I want," I whispered. "I just didn't want to assume you'd give up your life in Florida for me. For this."

His fingers threaded through my hair, curling into a fist at the base of my head, and guided my face away from his skin. "If you'll have me, Bay, this *is* the life I want, here with you. There isn't a life I want to live if it's not with you. I can have my things in Florida shipped here, or hell, they can give it all away. We've had too many years apart, of me denying myself the one person who makes my soul happy, to ever leave Anchor Bay."

"Yes," I choked out, the swell of emotions making my throat tight. "I want that. I want you here with us."

"Okay, then." He pressed a sweet kiss to the tip of my nose. "It's settled. I'm staying."

Sighing in utter happiness, I rested my head on his shoulder as he restarted the short walk to Liam's place. At the front door, Memphis adjusted his hold on me to pound a fist against the solid wood.

Worry wove its way into the earlier happiness when seconds passed without the door opening and Liam snatching me from Memphis's arms. Again, he knocked, this time with enough force that Ethan would hear it from his place next door if he were ever home.

Before the growing worry could turn to stomach-churning nausea, the thump of heavy footsteps came from inside the cabin. Relief swept through me when the door swung open, revealing a disheveled Liam.

A perfectly adorable, sleepy Liam. I ducked my face against Memphis's throat to hide the sappy smile that curved my lips.

"What's wrong?" Liam rasped, rubbing a hand down his face as if to wipe away the sleep. "Is she okay?"

Before Memphis could respond, wide hands gripped my waist and extracted me from his hold. Like I weighed nothing, Liam twirled me around, and this time my limbs wrapped around a thicker frame. Knuckle beneath my chin, Liam tipped my face up, eyes searching mine.

"She's fine," Memphis huffed, maneuvering past Liam, who blocked most of the doorway. "It's eight thirty, and she has nothing but wilted veggies and ketchup in her fridge for dinner."

"You haven't fed her yet?" His deep voice vibrated through his chest and against my own, amping up the simmering need Memphis stoked earlier.

"Again, not a zoo animal," I cut in, resting my face against Liam's hard chest.

"I passed out after the shower and just woke up," Memphis grumbled from the kitchen. The sound of the fridge opening reached my ears. "Oh, thank fuck you have food. I'll check out our protein options, then go from there."

He continued to mumble under his breath about sides and vegetables while Liam carried me to his living room and sat in an oversized chair, the leather groaning beneath our weight as he settled in. My head rose and fell in cadence with his deep breaths.

"I fell asleep too," he murmured into my hair. "I don't know how it happened, honestly. Pretty sure I fell asleep standing up in the shower."

"You two are exhausted." Pushing off his chest, I searched his face, my frown deepening at the dark circles under his eyes. "Let's eat a quick dinner, and then you two can go back to sleep."

"Or," he said with a smirk that had me holding a tight breath, anticipating what was about to come out of his mouth, "you can sit here on my lap, getting us both ready for what will come after dinner, while Memphis cooks and watches."

"I vote on his plan," Memphis said from the kitchen as he pulled out pots and pans. "We're having chicken, sautéed vegetables, and rice, so you have about an hour to put on a sexy show for me."

"Just sitting on your lap?" I asked, breaths coming in shallow pants, as if I'd run from my cabin to his.

He rubbed his scruff-covered jaw, heat blazing in his gray eyes. "I haven't stopped thinking about that whole cock-warming thing Memphis mentioned the other day."

A pan dropped in the kitchen, the loud bang echoing through the open space. "Shit, sorry. Keep going."

My heart slammed in my chest as I gazed at him, debating my answer. On the one hand, I wanted to say yes because it was hot and something I wanted to try, but on the other hand—

Wait. Who the fuck was I kidding? The only option was to say hell yes.

"What do you want me to do?"

Two taps to my ass were my only warning before he

lifted me off his lap and had me stand between his knees. His hooded gaze swept over my large sweatshirt to the thick leggings and Uggs.

"Keep the sweatshirt on, Little Bit, but everything else comes off."

He never looked away as I did as instructed while he tugged his gray sweats over his hips, exposing a semihard cock resting against his firm abs.

I licked my lips as I dropped my panties to the floor, shifting on my feet, unsure of what he planned next. Control was his kink, and I was 100 percent behind him directing this. I had read books with this type of scenario in them, even fantasized about it happening while using toys on myself, but I never dreamed it would happen in real life. Hell, until a few days ago, I had never slept with a man. Now here I was, standing in front of this dominant man who was too attractive for his own good, wearing nothing but my sweatshirt while practically panting for him to give that cock-warming thing a try.

With the smell of food cooking behind me, I braced both hands on each armrest when he beckoned me closer with a simple crook of his finger. He pitched forward, coming close enough for our noses to brush. Palms engulfing my lean thighs, rough hands slid up over my hips, gripping me tight around the waist and hauling me onto his lap. Our combined groans sounded through the cabin when my drenched center slid along his cock.

Liam's eyes flared when I shifted to press him between my soaked lips and then rolled my hips. My own lids fluttered closed as a soft moan escaped.

"None of that, sweetheart. This is just the preview, remember? Now watch as I stuff my cock inside my pussy."

A throat clearing behind me had Liam smirking. "Our pussy."

Movement over my shoulder had me looking at Memphis, who stalked closer. Rounding the chair, he stood at Liam's back, crossing both arms over his chest. I couldn't look away from his inked forearms or the way his tatted fingers flexed and released, like he was restraining himself from touching me.

Fuck, that was hot, knowing I made him and Liam both so damn needy.

Keeping my gaze locked on Liam's, I lifted the hem of the sweatshirt high enough for Memphis to watch as Liam pushed the first inch of his dick inside me. I gasped and pitched forward, almost slamming my forehead to Liam's if Memphis didn't catch me with a firm grip on both shoulders. It was strangely erotic feeling Liam's fingers push inside me as he worked the rest of his length into me until I was stuffed full of him.

I swallowed roughly when Liam moved his hands to rest on the armrests with a satisfied grin. Choking down a groan as he slowly hardened inside me, I gave in to the need to lean against Liam's firm chest. After helping me get comfortable, Memphis ran a hand down my head, tugging my hair just enough to send a pulse of pain through my scalp.

"Fuck," Liam snapped. "Don't do that shit. She likes it too much, and I won't be able to hold off on fucking her hard."

"Promises, promises," I whispered again, unable to stop my growing smile.

"You're going to sit still on my lap with me stuffed inside you like a good girl, understood?"

"Yes, sir," I breathed.

For several minutes, I soaked up the comfort of being in

his arms, desperately trying to not wiggle despite the insistent urge to rock against him and push his now very hard dick deeper inside me. Liam trailed calming strokes down my back, brushing against the top of my bare ass.

Remembering something from earlier, my lids popped open, and I pushed up just enough to see his face.

Eyes closed, features relaxed, I studied him for a few seconds before one gray eye peeked open.

"Yes, sweetheart? Something on your mind?"

"Earlier, at my place." His muscles stiffened with tension. "You know I'd never, ever cheat on you, go behind your back. I would never hurt you that way, Liam."

His heavy, resigned sigh sent a few blonde hairs floating between us. A single palm guided my head back to rest on his shoulder.

"I know you wouldn't, Baylee, but that kind of betrayal creates a deep wound that never really heals. Having someone you trusted wholeheartedly deceive you like that leaves scars." Nodding to let him know I was listening, I traced the tip of a single finger over his chest where I knew actual scars marked his tanned skin. "A trauma response like that can't be stopped. It just happens. But I'm better now at reasoning with myself. Like earlier, I knew you weren't like her, and Ethan and Oliver wouldn't do that to me either, but that initial suspicion sank in and gripped me tight for a few seconds before I could talk myself down."

"You've lived so many lives before now, before me," I whispered, suddenly hit with the impact of him being older. I didn't mind, had never really thought about it, but now the realization landed that he'd been through and done so much more than me. "Which has been your favorite?"

His chest rose and fell with an exaggerated inhale.

"I feel every bit of all the different paths I've taken, from the broken bones to cracks in my heart that felt like they would never heal. But my favorite? Hell, from my dumb cowboy days on the rodeo circuit to amateur MMA fighting and, of course, the Army, all have made an impact, and I wouldn't change any of them because it brought me here. Where I have a real family again, a job I love, and you." I pushed up to look deep into his gray eyes. "With all that I've done, all that I've yet to do, this, right now with you, is the favorite part of my life. Hands down, no competition. It's you and me, the way you make me feel and who you make me want to be. I never could've imagined someone as beautiful, smart, and funny with such a deep soul was waiting for me just on the other side of all the pain I've experienced."

"I love you," I whispered as hot tears leaked down my cheeks. "I'm terrified to say it because... of what happened to the last man I said it to, but I do. I really do love you, Liam. So much that I can't breathe sometimes when I think about you and the potential of losing you too."

A mischievous glint flashed in his eyes. "I'm too much of a stubborn bastard for you to lose me, Baylee. I'm yours now and forever. I've loved you from the day you told me we were going to be friends, and it's only grown deeper every day since."

Not caring about the tears coating my lips, I pressed forward, sealing my lips to his. Cupping his face between both palms, I held him exactly where I wanted and poured all the love, fear, and hope that was bottled up inside me into him.

When I pulled back, we both sucked in heavy breaths.

"I think I'm warm enough," he said huskily. Glancing over my shoulder, he hitched his chin. "Dinner can wait. Get over here so we can turn our girl's tears into screams." He turned his focus back to me with a wicked grin. "Looks like you're getting a preview of later, sweetheart. Now, I'm going to spin you around to ride me reverse while you open that perfect mouth of yours for Memphis to fuck." He leaned in to whisper in my ear. "Wonder how that piercing will feel against your throat."

Holy shit.

Whatever I did in a past life to deserve this, I'd forever be thankful.

## 29

---

### LIAM

I slumped in the cheap metal chair and leaned back, folding both arms over my chest. All around me, other members of the Uplift team talked and laughed, but I couldn't bring myself to join the conversations. My mind was stuck on the two I'd left sleeping in my bed to be here on time. I forced myself to walk away after wasting too much time staring at them cuddled together, Baylee's bare tits peeking out from the blanket, begging me to suck on them like I had the night before.

And nibbled.

And bit, leaving love marks all over her body—which, based on her pleas and begging, she liked as much as I did. Directing them all night while adding in Memphis's kink, keeping Baylee restricted with a few of my belts, was a memory I'd gladly replay all day every day for the rest of my life. Who knew seeing her struggle against the restraints would be so fucking hot? Or watching while controlling some other guy as he fucked my girl balls-deep?

I still hadn't revealed my newly gained kink that started

after meeting Baylee, shocking the hell out of me the first time I got hard fantasizing about it. Who knew the idea of her belly swollen and tits huge would make me want to keep fucking her every second to ensure it happened? Last night, I even pushed my cum back into her cunt, keeping my fingers there to hold it in, even though I knew she had that birth control contraption.

I wonder what it would take to convince her to have it removed.

She really wanted another goat....

"Shit, you have it bad," Aiden joked as he fell into the chair beside me. Miles hitched his chin in greeting from the other side of his best friend. "I'm guessing things are full steam ahead with you and Baylee."

I nodded, not wanting to get into it with him.

"And that guy, the one with the sweet-ass tattoos. I'm not into men, but if I was, it would be—"

"No, your kink is birds, remember," I remarked with a smirk, knowing that would get the entire team engaged in trolling him.

"I'm a proud ornithologist, thank you very much."

"Every time it's said out loud, it still makes me shiver. Sounds illegal and disgusting," Juno grumbled.

"Don't yuck my yum, sweetheart," Aiden responded with a wink.

I scanned the table, noting that Langston wasn't present to kill Aiden with his death glare for daring to joke with his so-called nemesis—who he also couldn't stop staring at or complaining about constantly. "Has anyone heard anything regarding West?"

Juno's smile faded. "The surgery went well, and they're hopeful he'll make a full recovery. Since we're so far from the hospital, they wanted him close for a few more days. That's where Langston is, with West until he can come home." She cleared her throat and forced a smile. "How's my girl Baylee doing? I noticed an uptick in online scheduling through the website I built for her."

I rubbed my jaw. "She's good." A small smile broke free from my normal expressionless mask. "Happy."

"Fucking finally," Juno said, her grin now genuine at the mention of her friend. "You fixed her little problem, I take it."

"It wasn't a problem," I grumbled, hating the way I felt my cheeks heat since everyone was listening to our conversation. "Not like Aiden and his bird fetish."

The man tossed both hands in the air in fake exasperation. Before we could start trolling him again, Oliver and Hudson walked in with Brandon right behind them, shutting the door hard. Oliver took a seat beside Finley, who shoved at his shoulder and started talking a mile a minute about nothing, while Hudson leaned against the far wall, brows pulled in tight as he studied the floor.

That couldn't be good.

"Amy made waffles," Brandon said, sounding exhausted, but the lift of his lips hinted that it was the kind of exhausted that made him happy, similar to how I felt. "So let's get this meeting done quick so I can get back home and eat."

"Lucky Amy," Finley chirped with a wide, goading smile that earned her a blank stare from Brandon. "Sorry."

Dax shoved her shoulder and mouthed, "What the fuck?" but Finley actively ignored him, even turning in the chair to put her back to him.

Her best friend. I narrowed my eyes at the pair. What

was going on between them? They were normally thick as thieves, but the gap between them today felt cold.

Brandon held up a hand quieting everyone and regaining their attention. "You've all been informed on what Liam, Memphis and Baylee discovered on their way to Caper, but before we address that, Liam, tell us how the rescue assignment went."

Clearing my throat, I leaned forward, pressing both forearms to the table, and rattled off everything that I accomplished, also acknowledging Memphis's hard work while I handled the manual labor side of things.

"All in all, we made a good team for that kind of assignment. He would be an asset to have on board with Uplift. Langston can't always be here, especially during the summer when most of his fishing and water activities are booked solid."

Brandon nodded, taking notes as I spoke. "I'll see what we can do about getting him on board. If that's what you want." He eyed me for a long moment, waiting for me to give him my all-in on the stranger.

"It is, and it's what our community and Anchor Bay need. We can't always depend on Dr. Dipshit at The Nest to be available."

The corner of Brandon's lips curled upward. "I heard about your failed excursion yesterday."

"Only failed because someone didn't mind their own business."

Oliver lifted both hands in surrender. "Just trying to keep you out of jail, buddy."

I huffed. "Like I would've gotten caught."

"Enough. We have more important shit to discuss like the body you found," Hudson cut in with a hard glare at me and Oliver. "As Brandon mentioned, I know you're all aware of the body Liam, Baylee, and their friend came upon while on their way to Caper. She was a hiker here for the Soul Trail but thankfully had a dog with her who actually led them to her body. I know we're all assuming this is related to the suspicious disappearances along the trail but we're keeping all options open, considering she was found so far off the actual trail itself. As far as cause of death goes, we don't have the autopsy results back yet. We did have a chance to inspect the few pieces of evidence collected at the scene. The only thing we think might be related is the silver necklace with a large feather charm that was found close—"

"What the fuck did you just say?" Miles stood up so fast, his chair toppled behind him. The former SEAL pressed both palms to the table and leveled a death stare at Hudson, who, to his credit, didn't shrink back. Probably because he was a former SEAL too. Who knew who would win if they went at it.

"We found a necklace—silver, it seems—caught in some brush near the body."

"Let me see it," Miles said, shoving off the table and storming around the chairs, everyone cursing and yelling as they shifted out of his way.

Hudson nodded and pulled out his phone. Tapping the screen a few times, he turned it to face Miles, which put it right in my line of sight. The picture was a labeled evidence bag with the necklace we found inside.

Miles leaned in closer, squinting for a few seconds before cursing and standing tall.

"That," he rasped, pointing at the picture, "is Caroline's."

I swear you could've heard a fucking cricket fart, it was so deadly quiet in the meeting space. No one even breathed aloud as we all absorbed that information for several seconds before the room exploded in a cacophony of shouted questions. Half of the room was now on their feet, hands slapping to the table, demanding to know what the hell was going on.

A loud, high-pitched whistle cut through the chaos, quieting us all down. "Shut the hell up and let us think," Oliver shouted, his commanding tone making everyone do just that. "Fuck." He pinched the bridge of his nose before grabbing his uniform hat and launching it across the room. It hit the wall hard, the bill snapping from the force of the contact. His chest heaved as he fought for control over his emotions and turned to Miles. "Are you sure?"

"I am. It was a gift from her mother a long time ago. She was always fiddling with the damn thing."

"Her birth mom or stepmom?" I asked, making everyone turn to me, various confused and shocked expressions on their faces. "It was news to me too." I explained what Jasper told Memphis and me the day before. "He said he told your dad, Oliver, but maybe he thought it wasn't relevant because that was over two decades ago."

Oliver's face had grown redder and redder as I spoke. "Did he now?" he hissed through gritted teeth. "Seems like I need to have a chat with good ole dad. And Jasper, for that matter."

"I'm right behind you," Hudson said, turning to follow Oliver out the door.

We all stared at the door when it slammed shut, the sudden quiet heavy and unsettling.

My skin itched, the need to see Baylee and make sure she was okay so insistent that I couldn't, nor wouldn't, ignore it. I shoved out of my chair, which landed in a heap like Miles's, and everyone turned to me.

"We all know what's on the schedule for the week thanks to Juno," I said to Brandon, who nodded, lips in a tight line. "I need to go check on my girl."

"Same," Miles, Aiden, and Brandon echoed.

Finley darted out the door before any of us could get there, leaving a despondent Dax at the table, staring at where she'd just disappeared. That confirmed something was off between them, but I didn't have the time or the capacity to ask Dax about it now.

We all filed out, each giving the others a nod as we broke apart and headed to our respective cabins—except Miles and Aiden, who lived together with Aspen. Down the road, Oliver's state-issued SUV disappeared, the roar of the engine slowly fading. I shook my head while I walked, trying to piece together everything that had transpired in our normally mundane weekly meeting.

The necklace we found near the dead woman was Caroline's.

What the actual fuck.

What did that mean? With all the rain, it could've ended up there from anywhere along that mountain range. There was no doubt in my mind that Miles was already putting together a search team to target that area, hoping to find more traces of his friend—our friend. Too bad the helicopter was unusable, or we could've used it to search the hard-to-reach areas.

My steps faltered at that thought. Glaring at the tips of my boots, I considered what West said to Langston about the helicopter being sabotaged. Could whoever was behind all this be one step ahead of us—hell, maybe even two to three steps? How the fuck could that happen? Didn't experts say it took a while for someone to do something like this so seamlessly, not leaving any evidence behind—to be this good at stealing women without a trace?

Maybe it had been going on for way longer—years, even—before we put the disappearances together.

With that gut-dropping thought, I jogged the last stretch to the cabin, cleared the few steps to the porch in one leap, and slid the key already in my hand into the lock. But when I gave it a twist, it didn't move, because the deadbolt was already unlocked.

I was positive I'd locked it on my way out, had even checked it twice to be sure. Fear slithered through my veins as I shoved the door open, the force causing it to bounce off the wall, cracking the drywall.

"Baylee," I bellowed. After checking the main area, I spun on my heel and rushed to my bedroom. "Memphis." His name echoed through the entire cabin.

Entering the bedroom, I stumbled to a stop at the sight of Baylee kneeling in the middle of the bed.

Alone.

Crying.

Her watery eyes met mine as those sad tears that ripped my heart open streamed down her face.

"He left," she rasped, ice-blue eyes dipping to the rumpled spot on the bed beside her. "He's gone."

Careful to keep my approach slow and calculated, I made my way to the bed and sat on the edge. The second I opened my arms, she shuffled across the king-size mattress and curled against my chest.

Her small hand fisted the front of my shirt while I stroked a hand along her back, hoping to calm her enough to get the full story, because what she said made little sense. The fucker was almost a stranger, sure, but I knew he loved the woman in my arms as much as I did. So I needed to find out, really fucking quick, what happened so I could fix it.

Even if that meant kicking his ass and dragging him back here unconscious to make her stop crying. Damn, her tears gutted me.

"Tell me what happened," I murmured.

Sniffling, she shifted to tip her face up to mine. "We were talking and laughing after you left for the meeting. Everything was fine. Then it wasn't."

"Did something happen?"

"He checked his phone, and it was like his entire demeanor flipped. He jumped out of bed and started throwing on clothes, all while deflecting my questions about what was going on." Her lower lip wobbled. "What if he doesn't come back?"

"Did he say anything when he left?" I doubted Memphis would leave her like this, even if it was some kind of emergency that needed his attention. A sliver of worry seeped in, wondering if it had something to do with his past and addictions, but I quickly shoved that down. "Were you crying when he left?"

That would determine the level of pain I'd inflict on the asshole.

She shook her head. "These didn't start until you came home." I winced, hating that I'd caused her tears. "And all he said was there was something important he needed to do."

"Did he say where he was going?"

She lifted a single shoulder. "Not specifically. He just said he was leaving. Liam, if he doesn't come back... if he leaves me, us...." Fresh tears filled her lower lids. "Why would he do that?"

"He wouldn't," I said, feeling that truth down to my

bones. "Which is why I'm going to find out exactly what's going on."

She pushed back on my chest and sat up straight. "How?"

"We're a remote Alaskan village, Little Bit. There are only so many places for him to be." Standing, I urged her to lie down and covered her with the quilts. Placing a searing kiss to her forehead, I waited for her full attention to land on me. "You stay here. I'll figure out what's going on. But have some faith in the guy. I do."

"Why was he so vague, then? Why didn't he just tell me what was wrong so I could help? I wanted to help, but he just—"

I pressed a finger to her lips. "We'll get it sorted, Baylee. I promise. Stay here while I go hunt—" Her brows flew up her forehead. "Find?" She blew out a relieved breath and smiled. "While I go find Memphis and get it all sorted. I'll be back soon."

Maybe with his head on a stake or dragging him behind me, but I'd be back.

"I don't want you to leave me too," she said, panic creeping into her voice as she clung to me.

It took me a few seconds to process what this was, because Baylee was normally an independent, strong woman who was perfectly okay being by herself. Then I remembered how I'd flinched when she mentioned being alone with other men, how that triggered me because of my cheating ex-wife.

"Baylee, I will come back." Her breath hitched. "I'm not leaving you. Memphis isn't leaving you. I can only imagine how his sudden departure and now me leaving, too, triggers you. But this isn't like with Dean." Her body trembled against mine. "We will come back, okay, Little Bit?"

After a few seconds of holding her wide-eyed, hopeful stare, she nodded and slowly loosened her hold on my shirt.

"Yeah, yeah, I know. It's just... it hurts here." She pressed a fist to her sternum. "And my mind is spinning through a thousand thoughts a second, each worse than the last, and—"

"It's called panic, baby. And it's totally normal after what you've been through. I'm sure whatever made Memphis leave so quickly made him forget that it would trigger you, make you think you were being left all over again."

She released a slow breath and nodded. "How are you so calm?"

I huffed and ran a hand down my face. "I'm so far from calm, Little Bit, that I'm legitimately afraid for Memphis's face when I see him." Her eyes widened in horror. "Just kidding. Kind of." I winked and slowly stood from the bed. "Close your eyes and think about all the dirty-ass shit we did last night instead of those other negative scenarios running through your head. We can discuss your favorite when I get back."

Saying those last words had that lingering bit of fear and worry slipping from her face. The second I turned to exit the bedroom, though, my reassuring smile slipped away. My boots slammed to the floorboards with every heavy step, the anger mounting while visions of beating Memphis bloody played on repeat.

The first place to look was her cabin. If he planned to bolt out of town, which I still didn't truly believe, he would head there to grab his gear.

As I jogged down the main road, my eyes locked on a figure holding a duffel bag exiting Baylee's place.

"That motherfucker," I snarled, picking up the pace.

Memphis didn't see me until it was too late, and I

crashed into him. With a shout, his duffel smacked to the ground when we both collided with the wooden railing around Baylee's porch. Blood pounded in my ears while anger heated my veins, making sweat drip down my temples and soak the back of my shirt.

His voice went in one ear and out the other as I yanked him to stand and pulled my fist back, seconds from demolishing his too-pretty face. But the fucker did something I didn't expect and struck first, ramming his knee into my balls.

I grunted, the pain shooting up my spine and down both legs, making my knees weak enough for my hold on his leather jacket to loosen. He spun away but didn't go far. Gripping the now-broken railing, he bent over, other hand pressed on top of a knee as he sucked down lungfuls of air.

As the pain receded, his words slowly filtered through.

"...for her," he spat. When he looked up, I almost stopped breathing at the devastation on his face. It was similar to Baylee's earlier. "You have to understand. I have to go now. Right the fuck now."

I held up a hand, making him pause when he reached for his bag. Standing to full height, grimacing through the lingering ache that spread from my balls to every damn cell in my body, I leveled an emotionless glare his way.

"Tell me why, and then you can go, because you didn't see her crying just now."

Some of the color drained from his face, and his gaze slid toward my cabin.

"Why? I just need to do something, but she can't know. I—"

"I will not stand here and explain triggers and what hers are. Fuck, think about it, kid."

Understanding dawned in his eyes, and he cursed, but

when he met my gaze, there was determination there. "She can't know."

"Why not?" I demanded.

"Because." He blew out a breath and checked his watch. "It will kill her, and I won't let anything hurt her like I know this will. I'll tell you, but please, save her from this. You can't tell her."

My brows rose. "I'm listening."

---

## 30

## MEMPHIS

The cigarette shook between my fingers as I inhaled a long drag, hoping it would calm my racing heart and tremors. Blinking at the sun hiding behind low gray clouds, I tried to think of anything other than the look of utter confusion on Baylee's face when I left her on Liam's bed. It had only been half a day, but it felt similar to withdrawal symptoms being away from her, knowing she was upset.

I didn't feel this way when Liam and I were in Caper, but that was a totally different situation. One, he was with me, two, she wasn't upset with me for leaving unexpectedly, and three, I wasn't planning a murder. Well, hopefully it wouldn't come to that, but I would do it as a last resort if it meant protecting my girl.

I checked my phone, ignoring the messages unread from Baylee, knowing they would rip me in two and make me run back to her before I took care of what I needed to here in Anchorage. Tapping on the thread with Mom, I read through her texts again, double-checking that I hadn't misread anything in my utter debilitating panic, even though I'd read and reread them a hundred times on the boat ride here.

> Mom: I need you to call me now!
>
> Mom: Memphis Tennessee Thomas, you call me right now!

My grip tightened around my phone, knowing if Mom wasn't so fucking exclamation point happy, I would've called her immediately when those two texts came through last night. But no, I thought she just wanted to talk since we hadn't in days while I was busy in Caper. I pushed off responding because at the time, my focus was on feeding Baylee, and then Liam went and did his little show.

I blew out a breath and closed my eyes, pushing that erotic moment to the back of my mind, needing to focus on the issue at hand. Relaxing my fingers to keep from snapping the phone in two, I scrolled to the messages I'd flipped out about earlier.

> Mom: Memphis, this is serious. You and Baylee are in danger.

Movement out of the corner of my eye drew my attention from the screen to someone leaving the hotel. I carefully watched and frowned at the three businessmen disappearing into a rideshare. Fuck, not who I was waiting for. Disappointment and worry filled my gut, wondering if maybe I was too late.

Shaking my head, I took another hit and tossed the spent butt onto the ground, grinding it into the sidewalk with the toe of my boot.

> Mom: Well, not danger danger, but danger.

That text, despite the confusion and fear racing through my veins, had my lips quirking upward. Mom was just so Mom sometimes.

Mom: Jerry, Dean's dad, came by the house to tell me that Bethany heard about you going to Alaska to find Baylee.

Mom: I'm so sorry, I didn't realize she'd react this way or I wouldn't have told my Bible study group about you finally getting your chance with Baylee.

Mom: You know Bethany has been… unwell since Dean's death. Grief twists people up sometimes.

Mom: And boy is she twisted up about you and Baylee.

Mom: Jerry even found a burner phone. All the calls were to Baylee's number. He found texts too, horrible texts that she sent to that sweet girl.

Mom: She told Jerry that Baylee didn't deserve to be happy because she killed her son.

Mom: So she's on her way to Alaska.

Mom: You have to intervene before she can get to Baylee. The things she's saying are… it will kill Baylee. She has such a kind heart. Hearing the hate and lies Bethany will infect her with will destroy that sweet girl.

Mom: She took a flight to Seattle yesterday afternoon and will land in Anchorage sometime tomorrow.

> Mom: Call me. I'll tell you what I know. Jerry is helping. He knows Bethany needs help and doesn't want her to hurt Baylee emotionally or physically. And his concern about both are valid in his mind. He doesn't know what she'll do if she actually gets to Baylee.

I called Mom while I waited for the boat Liam arranged to take me to Anchorage. Every word she repeated that Bethany had said to others in town or vented to her husband made me both sick to my stomach and raging mad. How dare she think she could pull Baylee into the twisted, toxic mess she'd fallen into after Dean's death.

Yes, she lost her only son, but that was not Baylee's fault. How she came to that conclusion in her warped thoughts was not for the sane mind to comprehend.

Based on the credit card charge Jerry noticed on their online statement, Bethany had checked into the hotel I was currently staking out. I'd wait for her to emerge and then...

Tackle her?

Talk to her?

Hell, I didn't have a clue what I would do, but there was no limit to how far I would go to keep Baylee safe. Which was how I'd ended up hurting her feelings by leaving Anchor Bay like my ass was on fire. I didn't want her to know what Mom said. If Baylee knew Bethany was here, she'd want to talk to her, see if she could reason with her. I couldn't take the chance that the verbal barbs Bethany might spew would take hold of my sweet, sweet Kitten.

Someone stepped out the side door, drawing my focus, only to make eye contact with someone I did not expect to see on this unexpected rogue mission. Langston pushed up the sleeves of his shirt, exposing the colorful ink decorating both forearms, and started my way.

"Don't look at me like that," he said when he stopped beside me and leaned back against the brick.

"You mean like how you looked at me when I first arrived, suspicious and cautious?"

He barked a laugh and shook his head. "Touché, Memphis."

"What are you doing here?" *And why the hell does he not seem surprised to see me loitering outside a hotel in Anchorage?*

"I'm staying at the hotel while West recovers in the hospital."

"Why aren't you there with him?" I asked, reaching for another cigarette.

He cut a hard look my way. "Apparently, I'm a pain in the ass and question everything they're doing and react... badly when he's in pain, so they asked me to leave."

I arched a brow while lighting the end and sucking in a lungful of smoke. "You mean they kicked you out. Of a hospital. Not sure I've ever heard of that actually happening to someone."

His eyes narrowed on the cigarette between my lips. "That shit will kill you."

"So I've heard."

"Being a medic, haven't you seen enough people with major issues that all stemmed from smoking to make you not want to touch that shit?"

"Not yet." I looked at him out of the corner of my eye. "Why haven't you asked why I'm here instead of back in Anchor Bay?"

"Liam called me." I grumbled under my breath about the intrusive asshole. "Said you might need some... help to convince this crazy person to head back home instead of coming to mess with one of ours." He shrugged and leaned his head against the brick, closing his eyes. It was then that I noticed how exhausted he looked. "You helped West, so whatever you need, man, I'm here for it."

"How is West?" I asked, monitoring the way he stiffened.

"He's okay. The surgery went well, and hopefully, if he follows the doctor's instructions, the recovery won't be too bad. But he's a stubborn asshole, so he'll probably ignore all their rules and start working again the second we get back to Anchor Bay. Who is this woman anyway? Liam didn't have much time to explain the whole fucking backstory."

I inhaled and held it for a second, allowing the burn in my lungs to ease some of the rising nerves. "It's Baylee's late fiancé's mom. Apparently, after Dean's death, she had some kind of psychotic break. She wasn't always this way. Back in high school, she was the best mom. We all wanted to hang out at Dean's place because she was so cool and always had a stocked fridge. But ever since Dean's death, it's like she's been poisoned from the inside out by her grief."

We stood in silence for a few seconds, both watching the door without being obvious.

"I think if anything happened to someone I loved, it would twist me into someone I didn't recognize or even want to be too. But that doesn't justify the actions she's taking now, coming here to spread that toxic shit. Baylee is innocence personified—"

"Not anymore," I said, tongue in cheek, hoping to lighten the mood. "Liam and I are doing a good job of corrupting her."

"Fuck, I do not want to hear that," he groaned, shaking his head. I huffed and took another drag. "She's nice to everyone, that's what I meant. And we were all there watching in the background as she fought her way through the grief that almost drowned her. There is no way in hell I could sit back and let someone drag her back into that again."

I studied the massive man for a few seconds before nodding. "Thanks. I'm glad Liam told you to come find me. I don't have a plan outside of stopping her from getting on a boat to Anchor Bay. Even with that, I don't know *how* to stop her."

"We try talking to her. Then, if that doesn't work, we escalate."

"Escalate to what?" I asked, not horrified or intimidated by the glee in his voice.

"To whatever it takes to protect your girl."

I nodded in agreement and shifted to angle myself toward the hotel's entrance. With every minute that passed, my nerves and anxiety rose, making me a twitchy, amped-up mess. I was about to tell Langston that I needed to take a walk around the hotel's perimeter to calm down when a tall, thin woman stepped out the glass doors, turning our way for just a moment before storming down the sidewalk in the opposite direction of us.

Pushing off the side of the building, I followed her, Langston keeping up despite me not saying a word. That brief glimpse of the woman's face was all I needed. It was one I recognized yet didn't. Bethany used to be full of life and joy. It showed on her round, cheerful face that always wore a smile. The woman who'd just stepped out of the hotel exuded bitterness, her too-thin face marked with deep wrinkles and thin lips that were tugged into what looked to be a permanent frown. But there was enough resemblance that I knew she was my high school best friend's mom.

"Where is she going?" Langston asked beside me, his voice low. "The docks are in the opposite direction."

"I don't know," I murmured.

We didn't have to wait long. After rounding the corner of a restaurant, Bethany ducked into a shady-looking liquor store, coming out a few minutes later with a brown bag tucked under her arm. Stepping into an alley between buildings, she twisted off the cap of whatever was inside and tipped it back. Wiping her lips with the sleeve of her coat, she screwed the lid back on and turned.

I knew the moment she recognized me. It took a few seconds, brows pulled in tight as she studied my face as if trying to piece together how she knew me. But when it all came together, a sneer pulled at her thin lips and pure hate overtook her face as a single finger came out, pointing at me.

"You," she hissed, taking a step toward me. It was only then that I noticed her staggering.

"She's drunk," I said under my breath to Langston. "We need to call the cops, or this will escalate, and we'll be the ones going to jail."

He nodded, pulling out his cell without taking his eyes off the approaching woman. "Not sure what I expected, but not this. She just looks... destroyed. Keep her occupied while I get the cops here."

Right. Occupied. Like I fucking knew how to do that.

"Hey, Bethany," I said, shoving both hands into the front pockets of my jeans, hoping that would make her feel less threatened.

"Don't you fucking speak to me," she screamed, drawing the attention of others hustling along the dirty downtown streets. "You don't get to talk to me. I know what you and that whore are doing behind Dean's back."

I swallowed hard, hoping that would help me keep my cool, but hearing her say that about Baylee made it difficult to not lash out. Only reminding myself that she was just sick and needed help kept me from screaming in her face.

"Look at you," she seethed, giving me a slow once-over in disgust. "You look like the fucking addict you are. Why are you here? Such a pathetic excuse for a son, who made your parents spend their whole life savings to pull you out of the gutter, fucking another man's—a good man's—future bitch of a wife."

Her frail hand came up, and I knew what would happen, but I still didn't block the hit. Her palm connected with the side of my face, the sound echoing along the street and in my head. I slowly turned my face back to her, gritting my teeth and keeping both fisted hands tucked into my pockets.

"You two don't deserve to live. He did. He was good, and all you are is a fucking pathetic addict who will end up right back on the streets. Where you belong." Spit speckled my hot cheek, but I still didn't move, barely even breathed. The stench of alcohol wafted over my face, up my nose, with every harsh breath she took. "And your whore—"

"Stop," I hissed, barely able to restrain my growing rage. "Say what you want about me, but not her."

"She killed him. He never would've enlisted if she hadn't been a selfish bitch and gone to school. She played him, used him for someone to come home to, and probably fucked half that damn college while he was missing her."

"You need to stop now," I demanded.

"Or what?" she screamed in my face, the toes of her shoes stepping on mine.

"Ma'am." Langston's deep voice filtered through the blood pounding in my ears.

"Fuck off," she said over her shoulder. Her glassy gaze bored into mine, and a sinister grin overtook her lips. Like with the slap, I knew what she planned to do but didn't do anything to stop it. As the brown bag rose, clearly intending to smash whatever was inside over my head, I held her glare. If this was what she needed to get it all out, then I'd let her.

Maybe then she could let go.

Maybe then she'd go away and never think of Baylee again.

Maybe then I'd finally be rid of the last bit of guilt and sadness over Dean's death.

But the smashing bottle never came. A shrill screech escaped her wide-open mouth as she thrashed in Langston's hold, his hand wrapped around her wrist, keeping it in the air, while the other arm was snaked around her waist, gently hauling her away from me.

It was like watching someone try to wrestle a wild animal. Bethany screamed profanities and all kinds of horrible, disgusting things about me and Baylee, wishing we were dead instead of her perfect son, as Langston fought to restrain her.

Well, *fought* wasn't the right word. Langston was twice her size, so it was more him trying to keep her contained without hurting her, or her hurting herself, than worrying that she'd do something to him.

At the sounds of sirens, I turned, putting my back to them to see a cop car hauling down the street.

A barked curse at my back and a shouted warning was all I had before something hard connected with the side of my head and everything went dark.

MUFFLED voices were the first thing to register as I slowly woke from a deep sleep. Mouth bone-dry, head throbbing, and zero memory of what happened had icy panic shooting through my veins. It was exactly how I felt after a multiday bender, which meant I'd fallen off the wagon. Sorrow and guilt and pain all mixed together, making my already nauseous stomach revolt.

Leaning to the side, I puked up whatever was in my stomach, my eyes squeezed shut, too afraid to see where I was and what I'd done. Fuck, I hadn't slipped since leaving rehab. Tremors shook my whole body, making me jostle whatever soft cushion I lay on.

"What the hell is wrong with him?" a familiar voice raged. "You said it was probably just a concussion."

"Fuck, Lang, you brought the guy into my hospital room demanding the attending doctor see to him. Give the doctor a break. He's about to piss his fucking scrubs," a voice I didn't know said, sounding both entertained and exasperated at the same time.

"Fix him," Langston ordered.

My lids snapped open as the memories flooded in. Vision fuzzy, I scanned the room, finding Langston standing beside the couch I lay on, arms crossed over his chest, and a much, much smaller man standing beside him wearing a white lab coat.

"Fuck," I rasped, throat and mouth so dry it felt like my tongue would crack.

The stiff cushion dipped beneath my hand as I pushed to sit up, but the room spun, keeping me in place.

"I'll get someone to clean that up," the doctor said and rushed out of the room.

"Lang, give him some space, for fuck's sake." I eyed the man in the hospital bed, who waved his good hand at me. "Not sure if you remember saving my life, but I'm West.

Langston brought you in here after you got smacked over the head with a vodka bottle."

"She was slippery as fuck," Langston snapped, then looked at the ceiling. "She wormed her way out of my hold and cracked that bottle against your skull. Thank fuck it didn't break."

"Yeah, stitches are a bitch. I'd know."

I nodded at West, agreeing with his statement.

"I thought I'd slipped, fallen back into my addiction," I murmured, my voice sounding too loud in my pounding head. "I'd take a concussion or stitches over that failure." With a groan, I finished sitting up and leaned back against the couch. "Did you call Liam, let him know?"

"I did," Langston murmured.

"Is Baylee okay?" At his silence, I peeked one eye open, not realizing they had fallen shut to block out the blinding sun cutting through the blinds right into my brain. "Is she okay?"

"She doesn't understand what's going on. Liam respected you not wanting her to know about the crazy woman. So yeah, she's okay, but he said she's worried and freaked out."

"I need to get back." I started to push off the couch to stand, but my arms gave out at the agony that sliced through my head.

"You're staying here overnight," Langston commanded, "where that good-for-nothing doctor can keep an eye on you, and then we'll get you home."

"He's a big softy," West said, sending Langston a look that spoke to their relationship being way more intimate than just friends. "But he will kick your ass to keep you where he thinks you're safe."

"Damn straight," Langston said with a curt nod.

Allowing my lids to close, I inhaled deeply and relaxed my tense muscles.

Tomorrow I'd go home, to the woman who made living and fighting my demons worth it all. And to a community that took me in without question and offered me hope of a better future, with a new family I never expected to want or need.

Home.

Yep, that was the exact word for what Anchor Bay had become for me.

## 31

## BAYLEE

My socked feet slapped the hardwood floors with every step as I paced the length of my living room. Both dogs and BamBam watched me cautiously, as if they knew I was on the verge of tipping over into a hysterical crying fit.

Again.

"I just don't understand why you can't tell me," I pleaded. "What if he doesn't come back from wherever he went?" I paused and turned to where Liam sat on the edge of the chair, gray eyes locked on me like they had been all morning. "What if he realized I'm not enough to keep him here and—"

"Okay, that's enough of that." He stood and strode to me, scooping me up in his thick arms and squeezing me tight against his chest. "You're not thinking straight right now, so I'm going to allow that remark about you not being enough to slide without punishment, but you only get that one." Cupping my face, he tipped it up to his. "You just have to trust me and Memphis both that what he had to do was to protect us—you, me, and himself. Can you do that, Little

Bit? Can you trust me when I tell you everything will be fine, and he'll come home to you?"

I chewed on my lower lip. "I do trust you," I whispered. "But all these worst-case scenarios pop into my head, and the idea of yesterday morning being the last time I ever see him breaks me. I know what it feels like to be the one left behind, Liam. I've done it once and barely made it through, and that was with someone who I...." I trailed off, not wanting to admit that last part out loud since it had only been recently that I actually realized it myself.

"Someone who you loved at one time, but you've now realized that it had faded, while what we have here is the real deal?"

I gaped at Liam. "How did you know?"

"Multiple lives, remember, Little Bit. I know because I feel the same way. I thought I knew love before all this, thought I'd loved with my whole heart, but I had no idea there was a depth of love where I felt it with my whole body and soul. It doesn't diminish the relationships any of us had in the past; it just makes us very aware of the amazing thing we have between us three now."

"Us three," I murmured. "I want that so bad it hurts, Liam."

"Same, which is why you being worried that Memphis wouldn't go through hell and back just to get back to you is crazy talk. He'll be home soon, but I will warn you." He grimaced and looked at the door. "There was an incident."

"What?" I said, voice so deep and dark that Liam looked shocked for a split second at my reaction.

"All I know is that he has a concussion, so—"

"And you're just now telling me!" I shrieked and shoved out of his arms. "We need to go to him right now." I pointed to the door and stomped my foot, which did not get the reaction I wanted. Instead of looking scared, he looked like he was about to burst out laughing. "Now, Liam. I don't know where he is, or I'd already be out the door going to him."

When he didn't move, I tossed both hands in the air and stormed past him. "Fine, I'll go alone."

"Like hell you will," he chuckled. "You don't even know where you're going."

"I'll figure it out," I hissed.

But as I reached the front door, the sound of the deadbolt clicking had me pausing. The door swung open. Elvis yipped and bolted past me, almost slamming against the door and closing it in Memphis's and Langston's faces.

"Hey, buddy," Memphis said, a wide smile splitting his face.

His bruised face.

He had a black eye, a purple and swollen cheek, and a huge goose egg that poked out of the side of his head where his blond hair was shaved close to the scalp.

I froze, almost forgetting how to breathe as I inspected every injury, committing them to memory. My anger and worry fought against each other for dominance, anger winning out when he winced as he bent down to scratch behind Elvis's ears.

"Who the fuck did that to you?"

Both men stilled, their gazes locked on me with a hint of fear in their expressions.

Memphis straightened and hobbled toward me.

"And you can't walk?" I screeched.

"Just from the fall. My hip looks worse than my face." He reached out, brushing his knuckles down my cheek. "Hey, Kitten. I missed you more than you can ever imagine."

Tears welled and leaked down my cheeks, but I held in

the desperate sob that wanted to escape. But despite all the relief at seeing him, that anger and need for vengeance continued to flare.

"Tell me, Memphis," I said, stomping my foot. "Tell me who did this so I can hurt them back." My hands curled into tight fists at my sides. "They don't get to do that to you and get away with it."

His responding smile was soft and shy. "The person didn't, Bay. The cops came and took care of the situation. The person responsible will get the help they need. Someone from their family is coming to get them."

"But I want to hurt them," I whispered, almost horrified by my words, yet I meant them.

Really, really meant them.

"And I love that you want to hurt them to defend me, but there's no need, sweet girl." He pulled me in for a hug, and my arms immediately went around his waist. "Fuck, it's good to feel you in my arms, hear your voice. I'm sorry I left like I did, but I had to go. To protect us, our family that we're starting here. I had to protect us the only way I knew how."

I let those words sink in.

Our family.

That sounded almost too good to be true.

Liam and Langston whispered about something, their voices too low for me to make out their words, but I didn't care. Memphis was back in my arms, and Liam was close by. Our family was back together—just the way it should be.

Memphis swayed in my arms, making my heart stop. Shifting positions, I draped his arm over my shoulders and pressed against his side to help support his weight.

"Come on, let's get you into bed. I'll get you some pain meds, unless you've already had some. Oh, and juice. I think I have some. That will help with your energy and hydration.

You have a concussion, should stay by your side to monitor your vitals."

Memphis's smile was wide when I finally stopped rambling to look up.

"What?"

"Nothing, Kitten. Just... happy. And I'll let you take care of me any way you see fit."

"Lucky," Liam grumbled, making me hide my smile against Memphis's ribs. "Never had the urge to purposefully fall off a horse before, but if that's what needs to happen, I'll do it."

I barked a laugh and shook my head. Pausing just outside my bedroom door, I frowned at the small queen-size bed. Looking over my shoulder, I took in Liam's massive frame and then scanned Memphis's.

"We need a bigger bed," I mused.

"And a bigger cabin so we can all have our own space for when we need it," Liam added.

"I'll go get Memphis settled, and then we can text Carl to see which of the bigger cabins are open," I said.

"Or we could take one of the empty lots and build our own, one that fits all our needs." Liam paused beside me and placed a gentle kiss on the top of my head. "How does that sound, Little Bit? A place of our own." He pressed a palm to my lower stomach. "For our family now, and maybe more one day?"

"I'd love that," I rasped. "Really, really love that."

"Then consider it done."

I watched him walk away, not realizing I was staring at Liam's ass until Memphis's weight pressed harder against me as he swayed on his feet.

*Right. Take care of this boyfriend first, then start designing the home of my dreams.*

"We'll need an ermine door," I murmured as we shuffled into the bedroom.

"Fuck, you're adorable, Baylee Smith." I tipped my face up to Memphis and smiled, finding him doing the same. "And all mine."

"Ours," Liam shouted from the other room.

"Ours," Memphis corrected.

I shook my head, rising onto my tiptoes to press a gentle kiss to the corner of his lips.

"Mine. All mine."

---

"I LOVE THIS KITCHEN," Memphis said as he lounged beside me on the couch. He looked at Liam and pointed at the iPad screen. "What are the odds we can get all that here in Anchor Bay?"

Liam squinted at the screen to see the Pinterest picture I had pulled up.

"It might take a while, and not everything will be exactly that. It'll depend on who will deliver here, but we can make something like that work for the new place."

Memphis and I shared a wide smile and high-fived.

"This is going to be epic," I murmured, swiping the screen. "Anchorage will have a lot of what we'll need, so we won't have to wait too long." Memphis shifted, his face scrunching in pain. "Medicine time?"

"Fuck, how long does it take to recover from a concussion?" he grumbled.

"Longer than two days," I joked as I slid off the couch and stood to get the Tylenol. "And your hip looked nasty. Did they do X-rays to make sure nothing was fractured?"

Before he could respond, there was a loud knock at the

door, the force making it rattle on its hinges. Liam looked at me and I shrugged, letting him know I wasn't expecting anyone. He was out of the chair between blinks and striding to the door with determined purpose.

His wide frame blocked me from seeing who was on the other side of the now-open door, but as soon as the voice hit my ears, the hair on my arms stood on end. As if sensing my nervousness, Elvis stood up from where he lounged in front of the fireplace and came to sit at my feet, Hank doing the same.

"Yeah, come on in," Liam said, tension clear in his tone. "What is this all about?"

My heart hammered as the sheriff, Oliver, Brandon, and Carl filed into the cabin. Their expressions ranged from resigned to suspicious, the latter on the sheriff's tight features.

Brandon and Carl moved to flank Liam. I looked at Memphis, who grabbed my hand and jerked me back down onto the couch, tucking me against his side.

"Where were you yesterday afternoon?" Sheriff Johnson demanded, looking at Liam, puffing up his chest.

Liam, to his credit, didn't react to the accusing tone or fake bravado from the sheriff. Instead, he looked at Oliver and arched a brow.

Oliver sighed and placed a hand on his father's shoulder, giving it a firm squeeze. "Let me handle this, Dad," he offered.

"It's Sheriff Johnson," he snapped, flabby cheeks going red. "We need to know exactly where he was yesterday afternoon to rule him out."

"Rule him out?" I whispered to Memphis, not taking my eyes off the five men. "For what?"

"I was here yesterday with Baylee," Liam said, rubbing

his jaw as if attempting to ease the tension. "And Memphis. Langston was here for a little while too." He crossed his thick arms over his chest and glared down at the short, overweight man. "Why do you want to know?"

Oliver and his dad exchanged a look before the sheriff waved at Oliver to explain.

"Jasper Cain didn't show up for last night's shift at Sips, which was normal for him, but Paul still called us to do a wellness check like he always does. I figured I'd find Jasper passed out on his floor like I have many times before, but last night was different."

"How so?" Brandon asked, clearly not knowing what this was all about either.

"I found him at his cabin—you know, the one about thirty minutes outside town. But he wasn't passed out or even drinking or playing those fucking video games he loves." Oliver looked at Brandon, Liam, and Carl before sliding his concerned gaze to where Memphis and I sat on the couch. A small smile curled his lips when he saw Hank at my side, but then it slipped as he sighed. "I found Jasper Cain dead in the middle of his living room."

"What?" we all exclaimed in unison. I jumped from the couch, but Memphis tugged me back down. I landed next to him with a huff.

"What happened to him?" Carl questioned.

"At first it looked like a suicide, and the note we found beside him supported that. It said he was sorry, that he took the blame for all the missing women over the last few months, and that they were all dead."

"What the fuck?" Liam said, disbelief in his voice.

"But you don't believe it," I cut in, loud enough for everyone to hear.

Oliver shook his head and locked his intense gaze on

me. "No. Based on the evidence I recovered and the scene itself, I think it was staged."

"So, you're saying...." Brandon trailed off, unable to finish the sentence.

Oliver nodded, agreeing with Brandon's suspicions.

"Jasper Cain was murdered."

Keep reading for the conclusion to Baylee, Memphis and Liam's story!

Want to know what happens next in Anchor Bay? Find out more in Book 3, Only Theirs, coming this winter! Throuple reveal this fall!

# EPILOGUE
## BAYLEE

My fingertips brushed along the smooth, stainless steel appliance as I padded around the kitchen of our new cabin. A slight ache burned in my cheeks from how long I'd held my wide smile. The guys had told me to meet them here after work and ended up being done early because of a cancelled appointment. Both would be here soon, but I intended to savor the few moments alone to revel in the beauty and hard work we had all put in over the last several months.

A content sigh passed my lips as I leaned against the granite countertop facing the empty space. Soon it would be filled with a large, leather couch, side tables, rugs, lamps, and Liam's favorite chair. My cheeks heated, remembering all the fun we'd had in that chair. Of course it would make the move, we had too many more memories to make in it.

Along the row of windows that looked out over the back part of the property was where we'd put the dining table—it was big enough for just us three or could grow to fit as many of our friends who wanted to savor Memphis's cooking. Our dining room and kitchen now were filled nightly with several of our friends eager to try whatever Memphis created.

He loved cooking for everyone, seeing them enjoy it. Even I loved it, which made Liam happy since I was finally putting some weight back on. Pushing off the edge, I moved to the windows to stare out over the gorgeous view of the mountains. It was hard to look at them in the same way after everything, but I refused to let that evil taint the beauty before me.

Voices out front had me moving to the main room and out on to the wraparound porch. Langston stormed down the street barking orders to someone on his cell, no doubt West because there was no way he'd use that tone with his other partner. We all knew that tone sounded rude and demanding, but the big guy used it to mask the worry and fear riding him.

"Everything okay?" I called out, making him pause.

He nodded and dropped the phone from his ear. "GG got out again, that fucker."

Smiling, I shook my head. "Well, if you need any help finding him or if you need me after you do, let me know. The guys will be here shortly."

With a nod and "Thanks," Langston hurried down the road. Going back into the house, I gave in to the urge to take another peek at our bedroom. The room was massive; a huge empty bedframe sat in the middle of the room and a comfortable looking chair already sat in the corner by the bay window.

My gaze slid to the unframed door that led to the nearly finished bathroom. It took longer than expected because of all the tile needed for the extra-large shower, and it took forever for the massive, four-person bathtub to be delivered.

We had to go with a four-person one since one of my guys was the size of two men.

Shaking my head, I turned, sucking in a breath at finding Liam standing in the doorway watching me. His serene smile grew as he marched over and pulled me into his strong arms. A content sigh escaped as I melted against him, loving the wash of safety and love that flowed through me when I was in his arms.

"You didn't sneak a peek yet, did you?" he asked into my hair as he kissed the crown.

Pulling back, I rested my chin on his chest and gazed up at him. "Nope, been checking out all the work you all have done in the parts of the house I'm allowed to see."

"Good girl," he said, placing a kiss on the tip of my nose. Releasing his hold, he stepped back but grabbed my hand, interlacing our fingers. "Come on. I'll show you my secret project."

"Should we wait for Memphis?" I asked, following him. Excitement sang through me, making my breathing choppy. I'd waited weeks to find out what was hidden behind door number four.

"I'm here." I turned away from Liam leading me down the hall as Memphis stepped into the cabin. He brushed a few rogue hairs out of his eyes while toeing off his boots. "I wouldn't miss this."

"Should I be worried?" I asked with a nervous laugh.

Memphis only winked and grabbed my free hand, giving it a slight squeeze.

Nerves had my stomach rolling. Liam shot me an anxious expression as he twisted the doorknob and slowly opened the door. Dropping my hand, he placed his against my lower back urging me to go in first.

The moment he flicked on the lights, I sucked in a sharp

breath and my fingers came up to cover my parted lips. I turned in a slow circle taking in the various pet beds, climbing trees, and was that a ball pit? A small door cut into the wall grabbed my attention, pulling me closer to see if my assumption was correct.

Yep. It was a tiny door that led outside. Big enough for an ermine.

One particular ermine.

I spun around, eyes wide and leaking happy tears.

"You made a room especially for BamBam?" I rasped, wiping at my wet cheeks.

Liam nodded. "BamBam and future woodland creatures you rescue—"

"Kidnap," Memphis said around a fake cough.

"Or others that you don't want to leave at the clinic overnight or need to foster back to health to get them ready to be adopted. We can adjust the door if needed. I didn't want to make it too big or—"

I cleared the short distance between us and leapt. Thankfully with his quick reflexes, he caught me midair and held me tight. Legs wrapped around his waist and arms looped around his neck, I gazed up at his handsome face.

"Thank you," I rasped around the unshed tears clogging my throat.

"Memphis helped too," he said, scanning my face. "Do you like it?"

"Like it?" I scoffed. "I love it, I love you." I flicked my gaze to where Memphis leaned against the doorframe with a content smile on his face. "And I love you. I cannot believe you did this."

"Don't you know by now, Little Bit? We'd do anything for you."

Fresh tears trailed down my face and fell to Liam's

flannel shirt. Not because of the room but of the moment and the many, many more moments the three of us would have in the future. I was happy, truly happy. After months and months of grief eating me alive, I was finally free.

Free to love.

And most importantly....

Free to live a life worth living.

"I can't wait," I said to them both.

"Can't wait for what?" Liam asked.

"For tomorrow, and the next day, and the next day, and the day after that. I can't wait for all the days I know that are coming with you two."

Nothing was guaranteed in this life, but that made me relish every moment even more.

Forever.

Want to know what happens next in Anchor Bay?
Find out more in Book 3, Only Theirs.

# ALSO BY KENNEDY L. MITCHELL

Anchor Bay: An Alaskan small town suspense, MFM, interconnected standalone series.

Our Chance - Anchor Bay prequel

Forever Theirs - Aiden, Miles, & Aspen

Claiming Ours - Liam, Baylee, Memphis

Only Theirs -

Book 4

Book 5

In Clear Sight: A Small Town, WITSEC Interconnected Standalone Series

Safe Haven - FREE Prequel

Guarded by the Marshal*

Cherished by the Agent*

Saved by the Officers *

Hidden by the Doctor *

*Now available in Audio!

Protection Series: A Dark Romantic Thriller Interconnected Standalone Series

Mine to Protect *

Mine to Save *

Mine to Guard *

Mine to Keep *

Mine to Hold *

Mine to Love *

Mine to Share

Mine to Shelter

Mine to Shield

*Now available in audio!


SEALs and CIA Series: A Navy SEAL Interconnected Standalone Series

Covert Affair

Covert Vengeance


More Than a Threat Series: A Connected Bodyguard Romantic Suspense Series

More Than a Threat

More Than a Risk

More Than a Hope

More Than a Threat Series Boxset: Complete Series


Power Play Series: A Protector Romantic Suspense Connected Series

Power Games

Power Twist

Power Switch

Power Surge

Power Term


Standalones:

Finding Fate - Dark, Captive Romantic Suspense

Memories of Us - Contemporary, Small Town Romance

# ABOUT THE AUTHOR

Kennedy L. Mitchell lives outside Dallas with her son and very large goldendoodle. She began writing in 2016 and has no plans of stopping.

She would love to hear from you via any of the platforms below or her website www.kennedylmitchell.com You can also stay up to date on future releases through her newsletter or by joining her Facebook readers group - Kennedy's Book Boyfriend Support Group.

Thank you for reading.

facebook.com/KennedyLMitchellBooks

instagram.com/kennedylmitchellbooks

bookbub.com/profile/kennedy-l-mitchell

# ACKNOWLEDGMENTS

This series was a labor of love and heartache for sure. I can't say thank you enough to everyone who has helped me along the way in my healing journey. If you can't tell I'm in a bit of a mess in my personal life but writing through it is super healing. Darlene, Kristin, Chris and Em, thank you so much for always reading and providing the best feedback as I wrote this second book in the new series. Your feedback and support not only for the book but personally is invaluable and I'm so very thankful for you.

And thank you to my amazing ARC and promo team for all the posts, shares and reviews. All your effort is greatly appreciated. I couldn't do this without your help or want to! Engaging with you and hearing that excitement for my words keeps me going when I don't know if I can do this anymore.

And of course thank you to my amazing editors Kristin and Mandy and proofreader Sarah who make my words make sense - lol.

To you the reader, thank you for giving this series a chance. I've always loved the idea of a series based in Alaska and I hope you enjoyed the first book in this new series.

And I also have to give a shout out to my attorney who advised me to not list a certain someone by name and kill them off in a very painful way. It was sound advice even though there is one version of these books where she dies a lot that are just for me. Sleeping with a married man, knowing he was married, is super shitty. I hope you get incurable crabs and the day you deserve.